Dewey Lambdin is an American nautical historical novelist. He is best known for his Alan Lewrie Naval Adventures series, spanning the American Revolution and the Napoleonic Wars. A member of the U.S. Naval Institute and a Friend of the National Maritime Museum in Greenwich, England, he spends his free time working and sailing. Besides the Alan Lewrie series, he is also the author of *What Lies Buried: a novel of Old Cape Fear.*

An Alan Lewrie Naval Adventure

JESTER'S FORTUNE

DEWEY LAMBDIN

1⍉ CANELO

First published in the the United States in 1999 by Dutton, New York

This edition published in the United Kingdom in 2021 by

Canelo
31 Helen Road
Oxford OX2 0DF
United Kingdom

A CIP catalogue record for this book is available from the British Library.

Print ISBN 978 1 80032 019 2
Ebook ISBN 978 1 78863 327 7

Look for more great books at www.canelo.co

Printed and bound in Great Britain by Clays Ltd, Elcograf S.p.A.

This one is for those long-suffering folks who were deluded enough to take me on as one of their authors long ago; George and Olga Wieser at Wieser & Wieser, and Jake Elwell, who not only has to "baby" me, but a newborn of his own, who just *might* be a tad less of a bother than I.

And, for Foozle 1985–1997

One of the sweetest, most affectionate and loving "lap" cats it's ever been my privilege to amuse and cater to, whenever she wished – for the regal little gold eyed minx she was.

Bye, li'l grey girl. Sleep tight, "Foozey."

Heu, quibus ingreditor fatis! Qui gentibus horror pergit!

Alas, to what destinies doth he move forward! His coming
is the terror of nations!

Gaius Valerius Flaccus, *Argonautica*, Book I, 744–745

Prologue

It was a chilly, blustery March morning, only just a little warmer than the winter days that had preceded it. Here, even near the ocean at Nice, springtime was only beginning to make its mark, and that – like the temperatures – was only a matter of degree. Icy mountain streams that the coaches had crossed on their madcap dash from Paris, roaring down the steep slopes of Provence days before, had begun to swell and churn with meltwater from the towering crags of the forbidding Maritime Alps.

Yet, it was a clear, cerulean blue morning, and the winds off the Mediterranean were now and then stronger than those that slumped off the snow-covered slopes far inland. Each sea-gust was as tantalisingly warm as the easy, unguarded waft of a sleeping lover's breath. By the end of the month – no later than the middle of the next, certainly – the rugged mountain roads, now nigh-impassable, would melt clear, then begin to dry. The passes that led east and south would be usable. And, God willing, the young general in the lead coach thought, there would be good campaign weather.

His army could finally begin to march.

He almost scoffed at the condition of *his* army! He'd seen them, here around Nice in their winter quarters, in conquered, compromised, and complaisant Savoy; ragged, hungry troops with the pinched faces of starving foxes. Some in blue tunics and Republican trousers, as required in Regulations; some still in Bourbon white of pre-Revolutionary Royalist regiments. Patched and raveled, all of them, by now, their shoes and boots worn out, wearing wooden sabot clogs, feet wrapped in tattered remnants of blankets or Italian peasant straw sandals. Hats as varied as civilian or military fashions, they wore whatever they could trade for, mend or steal. Wool peasants' berets, long-tasseled Jacobin caps – even their sleeping caps.

He had 36,570 infantry, the young, newly promoted general pondered – for he was a man in love with numbers – 3,300 cavalry,

1,700 artillerists, engineers and field police, stable-men, farriers, armourers, aides or commissionaires – 41,570 officers and men, all told.

He frowned. An uninspiring infantry, though, a cavalry arm on the worst collection of spavined nags he'd ever beheld. Too few guns to suit him, since he'd come up from the Artillery. But these men had secured Marseilles in '93, had besieged, then retaken Toulon in the same year, skirmished and fought little wastrel battles in those hills against the Piedmontese and Austrians, even routed their General de Vins and secured the Riviera from Savona to Voltri the previous autumn. They'd spent a winter's penury, grumbling and pinch-gutted, their pay so far in arrears, their precious news from home so long delayed, it would be a miracle if he could wield them in battle more than once without breaking possibly the only real army of any sort he'd get.

The young general leaned out of the coach windows to study those men who lined the approaches to the parade ground, as the staff carriages rattled into camp.

Pinched they might be, surly and starving, feeling abandoned by their own country, and their leaders, the Directory of Five, in distant Paris. But they were for the most part rugged men, an army made of men of the South; Provençals, Gascons, mountaineers from Dauphin and Savoy. And some of his Corsicans, of course.

He'd come south as quick as lightning, eager for the challenge no matter how daunting, fired by the charge in his orders from Barras and the rest of the Directory, from the Army:

Take this raggedy-arsed army into Piedmont and conquer all of the rich upper Po Valley; defeat the Piedmontese, then the Austrians. Conquer the Austrian duchy of Milan; cow the rest of Italy; secure a quiet border so troops could be turned against the last rebellious holdouts inside France; by his actions, divert the Austrians from an invasion across the Rhine. And loot. For God's sake, loot to fill the empty coffers before the great ideal of their Cause went down to abject defeat and the sneers of the world for a lack of money. Before it became an historical footnote for the want of a few *sous*! It was his plan, to the tee – accepted, at last.

"A reminder, Junot," he said to the harried aide-de-camp at his side, "M'sieur Saliceti is to go to those whimpering hounds at Genoa. Now we hold the whip-hand over them, *hein*? He is to arrange a loan on their treasury, at the most favourable terms he may obtain for France. We let them pay, or be conquered, as well. And Saliceti is to *demand* free passage for our troops through Genoese territory. Or else."

"Demand, sir?" Junot murmured in puzzlement, scribbling on a pad with a pencil – a French invention, the lead pencil. "But I thought—"

"*Oui*, demand." The general snickered. "For a reason, Junot. If nothing else, he must get grain for both men and horses. And boots. I insist on boots. With bread and boots, I can manage."

There was the staff to welcome his coach; the young cavalryman, Murat – the fearless. Mad as a hatter, as the English might say, like all cavalrymen. Like his senior, the mad Irish general Kilmaine, at his side. At the head of the pack stood General Louis Alexandre Berthier, the oldest at forty-three, and a former Royalist officer who'd fought with distinction in the American Revolution; Berthier, with a mind as quick as a musket's fire-lock, as calm and steely as the jaws of a bear-trap – his chief of staff, who forgot nothing.

Massena behind him, whip-thin and wiry, cursed with a nose like a down-turned sabre, and darting, shifty eyes. He was a former man of the ranks who'd spent fourteen years as a sergeant-major, since common men could not rise higher in the old Royal Army. A clever smuggler, it was said. Yet Massena was also known as a man whose shifty eyes were able to divine the least advantage of terrain, and that large nose of his could *smell* a way to do a foe a mortal hurt.

Massena he'd have to watch, though; it was well known he wished command of this army for himself. How best to use those eyes and nose to *his* advantage, yet keep Massena subservient, might prove to be a problem – as if the young general didn't have problems enough for three already. He would require Massena's loyalty to implement his complete plans for this army.

Even more of a puzzle was his last general of division, Charles Augereau. Incredibly loud, foulmouthed and uncouth, with the quick, scathing and glib *patois* of the Paris gutters; a slangy ex-sergeant himself, now risen to glory – and still as unbelievably lewd as any drillmaster, as chattery as a pirate's parrot. A fighter, though.

With these I'm to conquer Italy, the young general thought in chagrin, ready to shiver in despair. A gust of mountain wind made him almost do so, but he conquered the impulse by dint of will; he'd show no sign of timidity, dread or doubt before these ambitious officers

– not even the slightest pinch of second thoughts could he afford to display before his new-awarded army.

Salutes were exchanged, to-one's-face politenesses said before the troop review began. A horse was led up, a magnificent dapple-grey gelding, bedecked with all the martial trappings due a commanding general. The young man flung off his overcoat to expose his blue tunic, heavy with gold-lace oak wreathing, the sword at his side, the red-white-blue sash about his waist. By sheer perseverance – his thighs would never be strong enough to make him an excellent horseman – he'd become comfortable in the saddle at the old military school at Brienne.

No matter the egalitarian or fraternal ideals of the Revolution, the young general knew that the men in the ranks still stood in awe of the mounted, of those who could master a horse. A short fellow, as the general was, could loom over even the tallest of his hoary grenadiers. First impressions were important.

-

Instead of forcing the troops to churn the mud of the camp in order to pass his reviewing stand, their new general went to them, clattering from unit to unit, sabre-chains and bitt-chains jingling. And in most of the demi-brigades and battalions he saw, those that had served at Toulon – in his batteries on the south side of the harbour, or in the midnight charge in the rain upon L'Eguillettes Fort, where his 2,000 reserves had rallied old General Dugommier's 5,000 after they'd broken, and had conquered – he found familiar faces. And with his encyclopaedic memory, he came up with names and ranks to match those faces, and old japes to dredge up in comradely *bonhomie*.

He left a sea of smiles behind in every unit, those veterans he'd called to by name standing prouder among their fellows.

-

"Soldiers of France!" he called, once he'd completed the review and taken a stance atop a pile of boulders near the edge of the parade ground. "Soldiers of the Army of Italy... hear me! You are hungry. You are shoeless, ragged and tired. You have not the price of bread, meat or wine, and your pay is in arrears. And that is in *assignats*, not coin. Soon the Piedmontese, the Austrians, maybe even the 'Bloodies,' the English, will come against you. They intend to beat you. They still mean to defeat you, and with you... *la belle* France, and our Revolution! Then grind our nation into the dirt, and impose their kings and princes over us once again! Our foes are implacable. Therefore, so must you be. So must we *all* be!

"With me from Paris, I have brought General Chauvet, our paymaster. With gold! With coin!" the young general added quickly, before his soldiers could jeer and whistle at the mention of "Paymaster."

"Funds with which to buy rations, boots and blankets, at last."

He lied well, did the young, diminutive general; there were but 8,000 *livres* in gold coin, nearly all the bankrupt Treasury could give him, and 100,000 *livres* in bills of exchange – unfortunately drawn on the Bank of Cadiz, from a doubtful "friend," royalist Bourbon Spain – which no one might honour, not even the Savoians.

"France assigns this to you, soldiers, knowing even then they are still deeply in your debt for your past service," he continued, not even daring to turn and look at the commissioners, those civilian watchdogs and spies from the Directory, who could ruin a man, ranker or general, with a single letter – as damning as any *lettre de cachet* had imprisoned or murdered people before the Terror, when aristocratic back-stabbing was at its height in the days before the Revolution. A mention of "debt" owed could be construed as defeatist talk, spreading gloom and bitterness among his own troops!

"On all sides we are beset, soldiers," the general went on in a surprisingly powerful voice from such a wee frame; for he was deep-chested, if nothing else. "For now that is all that France has, and they send it to you, to ready you for another season's campaigning... to sustain you for a time, so we may defeat our foes, and protect all we cherish! All they have, to *you*, most of all!

"Soldiers of France, I have seen you... proud veterans of four years of fighting!" He bellowed. "We know each other, from earlier battles, *hein*? And I am most satisfied with your bearing... ragged though you are... because I see your pride! Your unflinching devotion to our Republic... and the steadiness of your eyes! Such men as you can *never* be beaten! With troops such as you, France will never be beaten! With hearts as stout as yours...!"

"Cheap theatrics," General Augereau grunted softly. "Jesus fucking Christ! General Schérer was an ass with ears, but a modest ass. Now, who pops up to replace him but—"

5

"He's good, Charles," General Andre Massena whispered back from the side of his mouth. "Have to give him that. Brilliant."

"Brilliant doesn't pay the whore," Augereau grumbled. "He marries Paul Barras's former mistress, this new bride of his… a favour for Barras, now he's one of the Five. And he gets us as his reward for taking the blowsy cunt… *pardon à moi*, the 'incomparable Josephine,' to wife. And if he shows me that miniature portrait of the bitch one more time, I'll rip his tiny leg off and beat his tiny skull in with it! *That'll* shit on his puppet show!"

General Andre Massena feigned a cough, partly in warning for the incorrigible Augereau to stop murmuring and carping; and partly so he could hide his helpless snickering fit behind a gloved hand.

Hello, what was this he heard, though…?

"Soldiers, to the east and south lies our duty!" Their elegant little general was roaring, pointing like a bronze statue for a far horizon, which prompted some of his troops to turn their heads to look.

"There lies Piedmont, ruled by that bloody-handed tyrant, their Victor Amadeus II… father-in-law to the beast who would come to rule us again, *Comte* de Provence… who would be *King* Louis XVIII! There lies aristocratic Austria, who would trample our beloved France beneath the boots of their enslaved peasants, yet deny *them* the rights you as free, Republican Frenchmen enjoy!

"Piedmont, soldiers!" The general shouted. "The Po Valleys, the great cities, teeming with untold wealth! Austrian provinces in thrall to despots! There! *There* is where I will lead you this year! *There* is where we will be victorious. *I* will lead you into the most fertile plains in the world! Rich cities and great provinces will be in your power! There, in Italy, soldiers… is where we are going to take the fight to our foes. *There* you will find honour, glory… and wealth! In Piedmont, in Lombardy… there we will gain *victory*!"

Loot and plunder, clean linen, purses bulging with gold, or things as simple as a belly or knapsack full of bread, meat, cheese and brandy, with a ration-waggon to follow along behind with more. Their little replacement general had lit a fire under them, Massena had to admit. He'd taken them by the throat and made them stand taller, of a sudden. The raucous cheers, the screams of avarice and pride, with the promise of glory-to-come now aflame in them, were deafening.

Even with the organised might of *Royal* France at their backs, armies larger and better trained than this one, Massena recalled, had come to grief twice in the last hundred years. Maillebois and Villars had both failed to invade Italy. So what did the summer hold for *this* tag-rag-and-bobtail army? he wondered. And wondered, too, had the Directory given him the command he'd lusted for so eagerly, would he have attempted anything this damn-fool daring?

"*Mon générals*," their new commanding officer said, once he'd quit his crag. "Junot, the list. See to it that these five generals of brigade are dismissed at once. I see no fire in their bellies or wits in their skulls. We begin tightening discipline and drill now. This instant. Berthier has the details for you. But I want this army of ours to be drilled, shod, clad and ready to march by the end of the month! There will be no half-measures. Discipline is the nerve of the army, and I will see it taut as a bowstring – or else!"

The general had removed his huge cocked hat with its wide gilt bands and Tricolour rosette to address the troops man-to-man, letting his rich chestnut hair fall free to either side of his face, like any good Republican, as common as any man in the ranks. Now he clapped it back on, called for his horse and sprang into the saddle with haste, as if not an idle minute could be wasted. He suddenly seemed two feet taller, even without the horse. Impatient with his spurs, he galloped away, with his aides scurrying to catch him up.

"Goddamn," Augereau breathed, now that it was safe to speak aloud. "Chilly fucking blue eyes he has. Did you notice?"

"Alert as an eagle, Charles. Rapt, I think the 'aristos' once called it." Massena agreed. "Impatient. Restless."

"You know, Andre, I can't understand it," Augereau grunted almost in awe. "Been a soldier all my life…"

That wasn't strictly the truth; he'd flogged stolen watches on the streets of Turkish Istanbul, taught dancing in the provinces for a time, soldiered in the French and Russian Armies – eloped with a Greek woman to Lisbon, too.

"…but damned if that little bugger doesn't half scare the piss out of me all of a sudden!"

–

Their general dictated, arms folded close about his chest, each hand clutching the opposite elbow, head down and pacing slowly. Rarely did he sit for long, Andoche Junot thought with a sigh as he scribbled.

Their general was possessed of a rather bad hand. When excited, or wrought by cautious care, his penmanship was almost illegible, and his French still littered with Italian-Corsican misspellings. His speech was laced with mispronunciations of even common words or place-names he'd heard over a hundred times. Perhaps he was cautious now, so as not to appear the stupid, dirty Corsican yokel he'd first been when he began school in France. Andoche Junot shrugged.

"...have been received by the army with signs of pleasure and the confidence owed to one who was known to have merited *your* trust," the general concluded the letter to the Directory. "The usual close, Junot. And the blah-blah-blah."

"*Oui, mon général.*" Junot smirked.

"I have a letter of my own to write now," his general hinted, shooing his aide to a desk in the other room. He took the chair where Junot had sat, drew out a sheet of paper and dipped a fresh quill in the inkwell. With a fond sigh, he drew from his waistcoat pocket a miniature portrait of his bride. They'd had only two days in Paris, in that splendid little house of hers at 6 Rue Chanterine, aswim in a pleasant grove of lime trees. Married on the ninth, into a coach on the eleventh, and in Nice by the twenty-seventh. How he ached for her, every waking moment! His incomparable Josephine! Though her real name was Rose Beauharnais, he'd always awarded his loves with made-up names. Earlier, there'd been Eugenie, in Marseilles – he'd called her his Desirée! He sighed. The curse of a man who'd once wished to be a great writer, one who'd create fantasies, epic tales of love so grand, of glory and martial conquest – grander than anything reality offered? He scoffed at that.

He tested the quill's nib by forming a string of vowels, then his name on a scrap. Too *Corsican*, Josephine had teased him during their courtship. "Your name smacks too much of Paoli and rebels, my dear, and that's not safe these days," that font of all marital joy had cautioned him. "Even though *mon cher* Paul is one of the Directors, and admires you, he cannot deflect all criticism of you, no matter how successful you've been 'til now. And Corsica... what happened there, *n'est-ce pas?* Before the British took it from us? Please them, *mon cher!* Be more 'Franchioullard,'" she'd coyly insisted.

He gritted his teeth, thinking of Barras, a good friend... one he owed so much. Had he *ever*, the handsome swine...? Had she... had they, *before*...? And with him away... *no!* It was impossible to contemplate!

And Corsica! He'd failed, there, on his native soil. Unable to subdue the few misguided fools who still followed that old rebel Paoli into another rebellion, this time against France. Before the "Bloodies," the British, had landed. And all the Royalists who'd fled there…! Not for much longer would they swagger over his ancestors' very gardens, he swore. Not if he could do anything about it, this fine summer of 1796!

One more deep, calming breath, a fond, doting smile at her portrait again – "an artichoke-heart's" smile? He stiffened. No, Josephine was his grand, his one, his only epic love!

Another essay at a round, sure hand, in the proper mood of the absent, ardent – trusting! – lover. He wrote his name. This time it came out round, firm, simpler.

Napoleon Bonaparte.

Book I

Felices, mediis que sedare fluctibus ausi
nec tantas timuere vias talemque secuti
huc qui deinde verum; sed sic quoque talis abito.

Happy, they who braved the intervening seas,
nor feared so long a voyage, but straightaway
followed so valiant a hero to this land; for
all that, valiant though he be, let him begone.

Gaius Valerius Flaccus, *Argonautica*, Book VII, 18–20

Chapter 1

Admiral Sir John Jervis was a stocky man, just turned a spry and still energetic sixty years of age. Still quite handsome, too, for he had been a lovely youth, and had sat to Frances Cotes for a remarkable portrait once in his teens. Duty, though, and awesome responsibilities, had hunched his shoulders like some Atlas doomed to carry the Earth on his rounded back. Keeping a British fleet in the Mediterranean, such was the task that wore him down now, countering the ever-growing strength of the French Navy. Suffering the foolish decisions – or total lack of decisions – of his predecessor, the hapless Admiral Hotham, who had dithered and dallied while the French grew stronger, frittering away priceless advantages in his nail-biting fogs, merely reacting to French move and countermove, or diluting his own strength in pointless patrols or flag-visits.

Now France was in the ascendant, and he was in the unen-viable position of being outnumbered at sea, should the French ever concentrate and come out. There were no allies left in the First Coalition possessed of anything even approaching a navy; the Neapolitans' feet had gone quite stone-cold after Toulon had fallen in '93, and sat on the sidelines. British troops were still committed to the colonial wars, dying by the regiments of tropical diseases on East and West Indies islands where Jervis himself had held the upper hand.

To guard the Gibraltar approaches, he had to send a part of his fleet west, yet French line-of-battle ships still slipped into the Mediterranean from Rochefort, L'Orient and Brest, on the Bay of Biscay, fresh from the refit yards, some fresh from the launch-ramps. Over twenty-three sail of the line were at Toulon, that he *knew* of. French grain convoys from North Africa and the piratical Barbary States had to be hunted down and intercepted. He had to hold a part of his fleet in San Fiorenzo Bay, near the northern tip of Corsica, Cape Corse, just in case the French sallied forth from Toulon.

The Barbary States, encouraged by general war, had to be kept under observation, before his supply ships and transports proved to be too great a temptation for their corsairs in their swift *xebecs*.

Then there were the Austrians – goddamn them.

They were the only ally left that had a huge army. Even that very moment, they were skirmishing along the Rhine for an invasion of France, and still had enough troops to threaten a second invasion in Savoy, then into the approaches of Toulon. With Toulon his again, he might breathe easier; that French fleet would be burned, properly this time, or scattered to fishing villages in penny-packets.

But the Austrians were not happy with His Majesty's Government, nor with the Royal Navy, at present. Late the previous year, General de Vins had lost his army – they'd run like terrorised kittens – at the very sight of French soldiers, losing him the use of Genoa and the Genoese Riviera as a base. And, of course, they'd blamed being run inland and eastward on lack of *naval* support.

Captain Horatio Nelson's small squadron, now much reduced by wear-and-tear, now blockaded harbours where they had funneled supplies and pay to the Austrians the previous year, plodding off-and-on that coast, which was now French-occupied, and hostile. A valuable duty, aye, Sir John mused most sourly; but not much use in supporting a new Austrian spring offensive.

Hands clasped in the small of his back, he stomped the stern-gallery of his flagship, the 1st Rate HMS *Victory*, taking a welcome few moments of fresh air from his stuffy great-cabins, away from the mounds of paperwork, away from the warnings and cautions from London, which charged him to coddle the Austrians no matter what, and keep them in the war, and to maintain sea-contact with them so the gold and silver could flow to purchase their allegiance.

He heaved a great round-shouldered sigh and scrubbed at his massy chin in thought, trying to conjure a way in which to remain concentrated for a sea-fight, which he was pretty sure he would win should it come. British Tars were unequaled, and his own ships, even at bad odds, he was certain, could still outsail, outmanoeuvre and outfight the poorly practiced French. He must remain strong, yet fulfill *every* area that demanded the presence of Royal Navy ships.

"Excuse me, Sir John," his harassed flag-captain interrupted, "but Captain Charlton has come aboard as you bid, and is without."

"Hah!" Sir John harrumphed, with very little evidence of pleasure. But then, "Old Jarvy" had never been very big on Pleasure. "Very good, sir, send him in."

—

Another of Hotham's. "Old Jarvy" frowned from behind his desk in his day-cabin as Captain Thomas Charlton entered. He'd never met this fellow, even in peacetime service when the Royal Navy was reduced to quarter-strength. Good enough record, he'd found, but nothing particularly distinguished since the American War. Good patrons, Charlton had, though; even if Hotham *was* his principal "sea-daddy," there were enough recommendations from others *he* trusted more who had vouched for him.

"Thomas Charlton, come aboard as directed, sir," the man piped up, with just more than a touch of cool wariness to his voice. "Old Jarvy" was one of the sternest disciplinarians in the Fleet, known for a volcanic temper when aroused. Known for using a hatchet when a penknife would suit others, too, when it came to dealing with those who'd irked him. Charlton reviewed his recent past; *had* he done something wrong?

"Captain Charlton, well met, sir. Take a seat. And I will have a glass with you," Sir John Jervis offered, almost sounding affable.

With a well-concealed sigh of relief, Captain Charlton sat, his gold-laced hat in his lap, happy that it wouldn't be *his* arse that was reamed out – not this time.

A few minutes of social prosing, enquiries about acquaintances, even a politic question as to his predecessor Admiral Hotham's newest posting; then Sir John put the situation before Charlton, liking what first impression he'd drawn of the man.

Not that he had that much choice; those senior post-captains he knew well enough to trust, some of whom he'd stood "sea-daddy" to, or those he'd learned he could trust with responsibility once he'd taken command, were already busy about his, and their King's, business. He counted himself fortunate that he'd found another he could trust; much like turning over a mossy rock and *not* finding the usual slug!

Charlton was nearly six feet tall, a little above middle height; a slim and wiry sort, most-like possessed of a spare appetite and a spartan constitution. Most captains in their late forties went all suety, to "tripes and trullibubs" from too many grand suppers and the arrival of modest wealth and good pay, at last.

A lean, intelligent face, well weathered by wind, sea and sun. He wore his own hair instead of a side-curl wig, which was wiry, going to grey the slightest bit, though like most well-to-do Englishmen who could boast membership in the Squirearchy, that class which led regiments, captained the King's ships, or sat in Parliament (as Jervis had) Charlton still owned a full head of it. A very regular, sturdy sort was Charlton; salt of the earth. Or salt of the sea. His brown eyes sparkled with clear-headed wit, and his brow hinted at a cleverness, an ability to extemporise, should duty call for it. Well, not *too* clever, Sir John hoped. Like young Nelson off Genoa at the moment, there were only so many and no more in every generation who had experience enough to temper their cleverness with caution. For better or worse, Charlton would just possibly do, Sir John decided.

"I expect Admiral Man's arrival weekly, d'ye see, sir," Sir John told him. "Eight more sail of the line, and several more frigates. Relying on the promise of his reinforcement by Our Lords Commissioners of the Admiralty, I may now make such dispositions which I've had planned for some time. Such as keeping a squadron far west, to keep an eye on the Straits of Gibraltar. And the Dons. I cannot imagine a *least* likely alliance – Levelling, Jacobin France, and the Spanish Bourbon Crown. 'Twas Bourbons the Frogs chopped when the Terror *began*, hmm? Their fleet at Cadiz, Cartagena, and Barcelona, d'ye see. Spanish banks honouring French notes… signing a nonaggression treaty with 'em. Should *they* come in against us… well!"

"Perhaps Spain's long-term hatred for us outweighs their hatred for the Revolution, Sir John?" Captain Charlton posed. "There's our possession of Spanish soil at Gibraltar."

"Aye," Sir John said with an appreciative smile – his first that was not merely polite – thinking that his choice for an onerous and fraught-with-danger mission would turn out to be a sensible captain, after all. Even if his voice was a little too nasal, and Oxonian "plumby" in local accent. He sounded more House of Lords than House of Commons, where *he'd* sat. Still, the Italians and the Austrians might expect a British officer, sole representative of his nation's navy, to sound more like the ambassadors they were used to. Or, being foreigners, might not notice the difference.

"Have you any Italian, sir?" Sir John pressed. "Or German?"

"A smattering of both, Sir John." Charlton frowned in puzzlement.

"Capital!" Jervis actually beamed. "Simply capital! As for the necessity, now sir… with Genoa gone, and the Austrian army far inland, we cannot cooperate with them, nor communicate. There is the matter of Vado Bay, where…"

"They ran like rabbits, Sir John?" Charlton dared interpose.

Jervis nodded. "Hence, no way to ship them the cash subsidies to fund their armies on the Rhine or in Italy. The Austrian Netherlands are lost, the Dutch and their navy are now French allies, and block the route down the Rhine, or overland through the Germanies. The only port left open to Austria is Trieste, on the Adriatic."

"I *see*, sir!" Charlton tensed, though filled with a well-hidden exuberance. This smacked of an independent command, of responsibility far from the everyday control of the flagship. Thirty years Charlton had served, in war or peace, from Gentleman Volunteer at age twelve, to Midshipman, then a commission, and *years* as a Lieutenant. Patrons had eased his climb up the ladder, had gotten him a brig o' war during the American Revolution, promotion to Commander, then at last a ship of his own and his captaincy. Where he'd languished since, even if he did have good patrons and was well connected. He'd not gotten a ship of the line when he'd been called back to the Colours in '93. He was just senior enough for a 5th Rate frigate, HMS *Lionheart*, one of the new 18-pounders of 36 heavy guns, plus chase-guns and carronades.

But what Sir John Jervis was offering him was a *squadron*, he speculated. Might it also include a promotion to commodore of the second class? Fly his own broad-pendant at long last, with a flag-captain under him to supervise the day-to-day functioning of his new ship? Perhaps exchange for a 3rd Rate 74, even an older 64, or one of the few ancient 50-gunned 4th Rates?

"You're to have a squadron, Captain Charlton," Sir John said, as if in answer to his every dream, that instant! "A thin 'un, given the paucity of bottoms we have at present, but a squadron nonetheless. It cannot come with a proper broad-pendant, I fear. That's the leap in rank reserved for Our Lords Commissioners to decide."

Of course, Charlton realised, deflating a little, though hiding his disappointment as well as he'd concealed his enthusiasm. An English gentleman was *raised* to be serene and stoic, no matter what! Admirals on foreign stations couldn't promote at will. But a good performance during a brief spell of detached duty *could* incline the Admiralty to reward him. *If* he made good, *if* he could safely steer a wary course 'tween diplomatic niceties, neutrals' rights and the zealous performance...

"There's your *Lionheart*," Admiral Jervis was saying. "Then I may spare *Pylades*. She's new-come from Chatham, a 5th Rate, thirty-two guns. A 'twelve-pounder,' being a tad older, of course. Benjamin Rodgers is her captain. A bit 'fly,' but a fighter. About as active as a hungry terrier in the rat-pit, I'm told. Only two others, d'ye see, ship-sloops, I'm sorry to say. But their shallower draught is certain to prove handy in the Adriatic 'midst all those islands. I may spare *Myrmidon*. An eighteen-gun, below the Rates. Six-pounders."

"A most felicitous choice, Sir John; thankee," Charlton said with a broad grin.

"Aye, her captain's known to you," Jervis stated, very flatly.

An admiral departing a foreign station was allowed several few promotions without Admiralty approval; one Midshipman to Lieutenant, without having to face an Examining Board of post-captains; one Lieutenant to Commander, and one Commander to Post-Captain. When Hotham left, he'd anointed Lt. William Fillebrowne from his own flagship's wardroom (the surest route to quick advancement, that) to Commander, and put him into *Myrmidon*, to replace another favourite who'd gotten the Departure Blessing to Post-Captain into a 6th Rate Frigate whose own captain had gone sick.

Charlton and Fillebrowne, both protégés of the same patron, were surely known to each other already, Jervis thought. Perhaps were from that same mould that Hotham thought most valuable to the Fleet. He had no wish to curry favour with Hotham in this regard – damn his blood! – but they might work together the better for being "dipped" in the same ha'porth of tar. Charlton he thought he might be able to trust. Fillebrowne, well...

Come to think on't, he mused as his cabin-steward poured them a top-up of claret, the one time he'd met Fillebrowne, he'd struck Jervis as a bit too suave, too cultured – too quick to smarm and try to "piss down his back." With the same Oxonian mumble as Hotham or Charlton. A very smooth customer, entirely. Tarry-handed, Jervis grudgingly allowed, but with cat-quick wits, and the amusedly observant air of the practiced rakehell, who went about with his tongue forever stuck in his cheek.

Jervis thought he could trust Charlton to handle this mission – *and* keep a wary weather eye on Fillebrowne, for Fillebrowne wasn't the sort Sir John wished to have round him.

"The last vessel I may spare is a tad more potent, sir," Sir John said with a smack of his lips after a sip of wine. "HMS *Jester.* Another ship-sloop of eighteen guns. But French eight-pounders, which is to say, English nines, in our measurement. Just came in to water from the Genoa blockade. Hate to deprive Captain Nelson, but, needs must. Commander Alan Lewrie."

"Ah," Charlton commented, frowning a bit. "Took her late in '93, didn't he, sir? Quite a feat, I heard tell. Being chased by a frigate and a brace of corvettes after Toulon? Took one for his own, dismasted the other and the rescue force took the frigate?"

"That he did, sir," Sir John agreed, with a matching frown.

"Spot of bother, though, something 'bout cannonading civilians in a Genoese port he raided?" Charlton squirmed diplomatically.

"Completely disproved, sir," Admiral Jervis countered, though he continued to frown. "A gasconading lie put out by French spies and agents provocateurs. The matter was looked into and he was found entirely blameless."

"Didn't he, uhmm… oh, some months ago, sir." Charlton dared to quibble further. "Took a prize near Vado, then sailed her straight onto the beach and *wrecked* her, just so he could chase some Frenchman? Mean t'say, Sir John… a perfectly good prize?"

"Rode inland and shot the fellow," Jervis related, nodding slowly in agreement. "Two-hundred-yard shot, with a Ferguson rifle. And spared us no end of bother from this Frog Navy captain. Chief of all their coastal convoys, raiders and escorts, so I've been informed. A rather nasty customer. But he stopped his business most perfectly."

"A bit unconventional, though. Don't ye think, sir?" Charlton essayed. He was not *yet* a Commodore, not *yet* one of the anointed, so well regarded by his commanding Admiral or London that he could veto a ship or captain. To be allowed to pick and choose, that was a favour granted only a remarkable few. And this was about as far as he could go, or ought to go, to suggest to Admiral Jervis that he would *much* prefer someone else; some other small ship. Taking a Frog corvette, being all dashing and brave – well, anyone could be brave, even the daft and foolhardy. Wrecking a valuable prize, going ashore and leaving one's command, just to pot a Frog, well, that made this Lewrie sound as mad as a March hare!

"Unconventional, hmm." Sir John pondered over his claret. He rubbed his chin once more and then broke into an icy grin. "To say the *least*, sir! And, it doesn't signify. After all, beggars can't be choosers, hmm? But he's all I have to spare. It may occur, sir, that Lewrie and *Jester* will prove useful to you. Above all, he *knows* how to fight! And he's experienced in blockading with Captain Nelson's squadron. And you'll be hip-deep in supposedly 'neutral' merchantmen where you're going."

"Of course, sir," Charlton replied, aware that he'd just been taken down a peg by the Admiral's "beggars can't be choosers" remark.

"You must first of all sweep that sea clean of French traders, warships and such, should they be there in force," Jervis directed, back to business. "You are to completely estop the traffic in naval stores — Adriatic oak and Balkan pine — which supports the French fleet in the Mediterranean. You will stop and inspect every ship you meet, determining their bonafides, and whether they are laden with a contraband cargo or sailing to a French-held port."

"Aye aye, sir," Charlton replied firmly.

"Further, you will liaise with our allies the Austrians and perform for them any task which a Royal Navy squadron may do to keep their friendship," Jervis hammered out, though not without a slight sneer about Austrian "friendship." "Have an eye toward strengthening or expanding what poor excuse they deem their Adriatic Squadron. As for Venice, well, make a port-call or two. Put a flea in her ear 'bout throwing in with us. Venice *may* be on her last legs, but she still is possessed of a substantial fleet of ships and useful bases in the Ionian Islands. The Foreign Office is working on that aspect now, and the presence of your squadron might *just* tip the scales in our favour, d'ye see. Escort and protect any and all British trade, as well. Goes without sayin', hmm? And the merchant vessels of the Neapolitans, Papal States, Venice… and other… how do they put it? 'Ships of those nations in amity with His Majesty's Government'?"

"I see, sir." Charlton nodded soberly.

"B'lieve 'twas Pitt the Elder," Sir John mused, "but you must not quote me, sir, said that 'trade follows the flag'? Well, this time round, perhaps the flag must follow trade, hmm?"

"Of course, sir." Charlton nodded again.

"*Pylades* and *Jester* are here, at San Fiorenzo Bay, sir," Sir John grumbled. It was rare that he made a jest, and he'd thought it a rare good'un; though Charlton hadn't risen to it. "*Myrmidon* is down in Portoferrajo, on Elba. She escorted a troop-ship, so we could begin fortifying Elba and the isle of Capraia. At least protect the sea-lanes to Leghorn. And Corsica's flanks. Close the Tyrrhennian Sea to French ships, at least, should they have a plan to seize those isles first, d'ye see."

With Genoa gone, her port city and capital now regarded as hostile, Tuscany was wavering, too, much like the Neapolitans. Admiral Jervis all but winced as he considered it. The Tuscans were leery of allowing Great Britain to base its fleet out of Porto Especia, or Leghorn, any longer. Garrisoning Capraia and Elba was a safeguard so that Tuscany did not think to put troops on them first!

"You will sail as soon as the wind allows you, Captain Charlton," he said. "And gather up *Myrmidon* on your way. Written orders and such will be aboard *Lionheart* no later than the end of the Second Dog-watch this evening. Along with copies of Admiralty and Foreign Office directives to me, too. To enlighten you. As much as Foreign Office despatches may enlighten anyone, hmm?"

"Very good, Sir John," Charlton said, rising. "And thankee for the opportunity, sir. For your faith in me. You shan't regret it, I swear to you."

"I'd best *not*, sir," Admiral Jervis cooed in reply, with that bleak and wintry smile of sardonic humour of his. "Good fortune, sir. And good huntin', Captain Charlton."

"Aye aye, sir!" Charlton nodded, wilting, in spite of the honour just done him. And vowing to himself that he *would* prove worthy of his awesome new trust – if he died in the attempt. Or had to kill somebody else to do it!

-

In the great-cabins he'd just left, Admiral Sir John Jervis allowed himself a brief moment of leisure to savour the satisfaction he felt in having done himself, and Captain Nelson, a favour.

This Lewrie fellow was a bit too much the "fly" character to suit him. A stallion more suited to the rare oval racecourse, or the neck-or-nothing dash cross winter fields in a steeple-chase. And the source of his information was the Foreign Office, their own spies, those who'd used Lewrie before. He was too headstrong to suit them as well. Too prone to take the bit in his teeth and gallop to suit the gallant Nelson.

But perhaps Lewrie would be the perfect addition to Charlton's ad hoc, understrength and isolated squadron. "Old Jarvy" might have just done the Captain a huge favour. Or the greatest harm. Only time, and events, might tell.

And either way, *he* was shot of him!

Chapter 2

He was making good practice, well into a bawdy little tune of an earlier century: "Watkins' Ale." He sat on the aftermost taffrail flag-lockers, feet atop the edge of the coach-top built into the quarterdeck to give his great-cabins light and air. The skylights were open to air out those cabins, and his cox'n Andrews was supervising a working-party in repainting and touching up the ravages of two years' active commission.

Damme, but I've got rather good at this, he exulted, fingering a sprightly elaboration onto the basic melody, like grace-notes on a bagpipe. *Should* be good at it, he further pondered, as Mister Midshipman Hyde turned the pages of the songbook for them; after all, 'tis been ten bloody years I've been tootlin' on this thing!

A flageolet, some might call it, were they speaking classical. But really it was a tin whistle. He had no lip for a proper flute, fife or recorder, such as his wife Caroline played so well. To most of his ship's people – his Irishmen, Welsh, his Lowland Scots and the West Country folk – it was called the lowly penny-whistle.

But it felt like a penny-whistle day to Alan Lewrie, Commander, Royal Navy, and captain of HMS *Jester*.

Caroline had bought the first one in the Bahamas, back in '86, as a Christmas gift. That one he'd lost in '93, when his mortar-boat went down in Toulon Harbour during the siege. And good riddance to bad rubbish had been most people's opinion, for he'd been horrid at it. This new one Caroline had waiting for him when *Jester* returned to Portsmouth to refit and re-arm, spring of '94, before her voyage back to the Mediterranean.

The last year or so, the isolation enforced upon a captain – a *proper* captain – had turned him to playing, more and more. Until he'd come to a *semblance* of mastering one musical instrument, no matter how humble. Quite unlike a gentleman's flute, it had few holes, and a limited, very Celtic scale. Hornpipes, Scottish ballads, Irish jigs and reels, old English country airs… he leaned more to those, anyway, of late.

And if Mister Edward Buchanon, the Sailing Master, was right, Lewrie mused as he played – *if* the ancient Irish Celtic sea-god Lir had taken *Jester* and her captain into his watchful care, even down here in the Mediterranean, *Jester* and her captain paired as a "lucky" ship and lucky leader – then the Celtic scale of notes would be more than apt. And pleasing, should such thoughts *not* turn out to be a crock of moonshine!

"Oh, here's one, sir!" Mr. Hyde chuckled, once they were done with the curious old maid, done in at last and seduced by draughts of "Watkins' Ale." "A little slower, perhaps, but… 'Barbara Allen'?"

Mr. Hyde had bought himself a guitar the last time he'd gone ashore at Genoa and was getting decent at it; he had even dared to sit in with *Jester*'s amateur musicians among the hands, with their fifes and fiddles, and pluck or strum along as they played tunes for Morris dances or evening horn-pipes. Lewrie envied him: a captain had no chance to do anything more than clap along in time and watch such antics, taking pleasure in being a mere listener. A midshipman, as a petty officer, and aloft barefooted with the hands most of the time, *could* mingle without suffering a loss of dignity.

"Aye, let's give that 'un a go," Lewrie said, chuckling. "Bit of an odd choice to include, though. The book is called *Pills to Purge Melancholy*!"

"We could make a reel of it, sir." Hyde grinned. "And I do know the words."

"Right, then."

A *splendid* penny-whistle day! A day without care. For the hands, it was "Make And Mend," now that *Jester* was victualed proper.

Except for the few hands and warrants in the harbour-watch and anchor-watch, most were free for once to "caulk or yarn" however they wished; to nap and catch up on lost sleep, gab and tell tall tales under the awnings spread below the course-yards. Carve wood or salt beef so old it could be made into snuff boxes, rings or combs! Or, simply whittle, chew tobacco, smoke a pipe or two on the upper decks, write letters home, or dictate letters to those who could write; read letters over again, or have them read to them by the literate. Some amused themselves playing with a pet bird, a cat or a puppy.

The crew was free of what now seemed like a pointless, and disheartening, blockade of the Genoese Republic, free of escorting merchant convoys cross the Ligurian Sea, or patrolling for raiding French privateers or warships. HMS *Jester* lay serene at anchor, for once, and, for officers and hands alike, seemed to be at peace. Or was this a calm before a storm?

Her yards were crossed and squared to geometric precision, her braces, halliards and lift-lines as taut as bowstrings, all her running rigging showpiece-perfect. Her boats were alongside, soaking seawater into planking too long kept dry on the boat-tier beams which spanned the waist. They nuzzled at both larboard and starboard entry-ports like contented piglets, lifted to thump softly like hungry barrows now and again by the slight wind and wavelets of San Fiorenzo Bay.

Belying her "Bristol-Fashion" perfection, though, were laundry and loose-hung sails. Fresh water for washing clothing was a luxury rarely allowed; the ration was a gallon per man per day, and most of that went into the steep-tubs to boil rations. In port, they could use as much fresh water as they liked, for a water-hoy came alongside almost every morning to replenish *Jester*'s ready-use casks on the weather deck. So, during a "Make And Mend" day, sailors scrubbed the irritating, thread-grating salt from their clothing and hung it up to dry, so it wouldn't sandpaper their hides or wear out, for a time.

So, too, the suits of sails. Salt crystals, mildew, damp-rot or dry-rot could ruin her sails: the set she wore, or the set stored below as replacements, *or* the heavier storm-canvas suit. A spell in harbour was a priceless opportunity to change over completely, sluice them down with fresh water and scrub them with stiff brushes, go over each seam and patch, sew and mend, to avoid having them weaken, split or blow out during a gale. Then the men hoisted the sails aloft, bent them onto the yards and let them hang slack, to air-dry them properly before being stored away on the orlop again; or clewed up, brailed up and harbour-gasketed.

Three days *Jester* had lain at her moorings, to her best bower and a stern kedge-anchor, and been cleaned "from keel to trucks," and all the thousands of petty, frustrating things that could go amiss on a ship put right. Her huge water-casks were rowed ashore, scrubbed clean and refilled; cords of fire-wood and kindling were fetched aboard; bosun's stores, spare gun-tools, new striker flints, powder and shot were fetched from the stores ship, old HMS *Inflexible*. Rice and pasta by the case, which now had almost totally replaced weevily ships' biscuit, was piled on her stores-deck, along with pipes, kegs and barricoes of wine and rum for her beverage needs, and thousands of onions, scallions, leeks, garlic cloves and such for anti-scorbutics, which also made the poor rations palatable. Small orchards' worth of lemons, oranges and other local acid-fruits, dried raisins, currants and plums were loaded; they were anti-scorbutic, too, so *Jester*'s people didn't perish of scurvy. There were open-topped bins of fruit, including some rare apples, scattered round the main mast's trunk, so the hands could eat as much as they liked, for once – even if dour, sardonic (and lately even *more* irritating) Ship's Surgeon Mr. Howse denounced the whole idea of acid-fruits being allowed in a tropical climate. Brought on biliousness, and bilious fevers, so please you, he'd insisted! As if those could kill, instead of being quickly eased by a belch or a good fart, Lewrie thought sourly.

"No, let's start over," Lewrie insisted after one verse. "It don't sound right that fast, Mister Hyde. Let's do the proper measure."

He tilted his head back, eyes closed; he knew "Barbara Allen" well enough by ear, anyway. His head was bare of his gold-laced cocked hat, his medium brown hair was bleached at the sides almost a taffy-blond by cruel sun, his neck-stock was cast aside and his shirt opened to mid-waist, and his sleeves were rolled up above his elbows. The sun was nowhere near the torrid murderer of a high-summer day, when Corsica stewed under her infamous "Lion Sun," felling ships' companies and regiments down by dozens.

There was just enough warmth to make it blessedly pleasant, and just enough of a light breeze from the Sou'east, up from Egypt or Cyrenaica, to hint at the heat to come as spring blossomed anew.

An idle day of rest. He smiled round the mouthpiece of his tin whistle. A day to celebrate, too: mail from home, fresh livestock in the manger, and a rare Corsican yearling bullock already slaughtered, with a large joint saved out for his own supper. Fresh salad greens as well, and loaf-bread, for a change. Only local cheeses, but succulent and moist, not desiccated, worm-ridden Navy Issue, four months in-stores before they were even opened.

And money!

Say what you would 'bout "Old Jarvy," Alan pondered rather happily, but he's put the fear o' God into the Prize-Court! After a full year or more of wrangling over dotted *i*'s and crossed *t*'s, or a comma

26

misplaced, they'd honoured *Jester*'s captures at last. He was moderately wealthy – on paper, at least. A tenth paid in specie to officers and men, the rest in certificates of exchange. Over £10,000 sterling, and his share two-eighths' of that, or £2,500! With any good luck at all, the Prize-Court would cut loose of the rest, almost doubling his profits!

Swaying a little, improvising on the third verse, he was feeling just over-the-moon with himself…

"Oof!" He grunted, as Toulon landed in his lap. "Neglected, are we, puss? My playing *that* bad?"

The black-and-white ram-cat's tail was bottled up and lashing. He was here for commiseration, not a regular petting.

"Chivvied out of your napping place, hey? Bad smells below, in your kingdom?" Lewrie chuckled, stroking his pet into a gentler mood. "Well, won't be for long."

"Boat ahoy!" Mr. Midshipman Spendlove could be heard to shout over the side at an approaching rowboat. He was the unlucky one in the rotation for harbour watch on such a fine day.

Couldn't be, Lewrie puzzled to himself; though with half a hope, perhaps. More likely orders, an idle visitor off another warship. Or a letter from shore? He stood and tucked the penny-whistle in the waistband of his slop-trousers, giving the arid little port town of San Fiorenzo a wistful glance. There he and his mistress, Phoebe Aretino, had enjoyed such a blissful little house for so short a time. Hell, he could see it from the quarterdeck, plain as the nose on his face!

She'd become known as La Contessa Phoebe, no matter she'd been a soapmaker's and washerwoman's daughter. And a naive courtesan in Toulon.

No, he thought with a shake of his head; that was ended. She'd told him off proper, once and for all, after her unlookedfor visit at Leghorn, when they'd been on the outs already. After catching him with the leg over another woman.

Surprise, surprise, he thought, a touch sarcastic; all for King And Country, that… to bed a Frog spy, under orders, mind! But he'd not been able to *tell* Phoebe that. Again, under strictest orders.

He imagined it'd turned out best; he sometimes consoled himself that losing the bewitching little minx was in the cards from the beginning. But *had* she come back to San Fiorenzo, to her native Corsica, to see to her many and varied small-business enterprises? Had she seen his ship at anchor and thought of him, as he still thought of her, now and again? God, it was bloody madness, *but…*!

"*Lionheart!*" was the returning hail from the longboat. And, as Alan went to the starboard quarterdeck bulwarks to watch, he could see the bow-man raising four fingers, to indicate the grade of honour due their visitor. Four fingers – a bloody Post-Captain! And Alan couldn't recognise the fellow in the stern-sheets, the lean man wearing a *pair* of epaulets; a Post-Captain of more than three-years' seniority! Perhaps one of "Old Jarvy's" minions, from the flagship?

"Bloody, bloody Hell!" he spat, feeling as if he'd just been caught on the "jakes," with his clothing round his ankles! Middle of a "Make And Mend" day, though it wasn't the customary Sunday; the men were scattered and idle, and *Jester* was about as presentable as a Thames turd-barge at Dung Wharf! And himself with no time to go below and change, or way to delay a senior officer until he could!

And, like an omen, a bank of clouds scudded cross the sun, throwing sweeping shadows over the harbour. The fickle spring Sou'east breeze died away, replaced by a gust that swung about from the Nor'east, making the slight chop shiver into a million tiny wavelets, making *Jester's* shrouds keen, ghost-like.

A gusty land-breeze, off the Alps, down from the Nor'east. From Italy. Cool enough, for a moment, to make him shiver as well. Half his mind – the logical, experienced mariner half – told him it was sign of a change in weather. But the other half, which was almost beginning to *believe* the Sailing Master's superstitions, told tales of elder sea-gods and portents.

A peace 'tween storms, Lewrie decided grimly; indeed! And he had the odd fey feeling it was ended. Gone and done it again, he chid himself; I should know by now, whenever Life gets soft there's the Devil to pay in the offing!

"Side-party!" Lewrie bellowed. "Sergeant Bootheby, turn out!"

"'Tention on th' weather decks! Ship's comp'ny, fall in, face starboard an' off-hats!" Will Cony, the Bosun, was shouting.

"An ill wind, Mister Hyde?" Lewrie sighed, going forrud to meet their strange arrival, as the side-party mustered quickly, with even the Marines in their small-clothes, and no chance to toss on tunics.

"Ill winds never blow anyone any good, sir." The eighteen-year-old frowned.

"My, my, sir! Such pessimism in one so young!" Lewrie teased.

Though he wasn't smiling when he did.

Nor when the Nor'east gust faded, the harbour waters calmed to a brief, glassy-stillness and the sun and the insistent, warmer Sou'east breeze returned.

Chapter 3

Palms slapped on Brown Bess muskets, and the Bosun and his new mate, Sadler, trilled their calls as the makeshift side-party assembled to greet the officer who'd clambered up the man-ropes and battens, ascending at last to the starboard gangway. Lt. Ralph Knolles was there, in the proper fig (and thank God for that! Lewrie thought) to present his sword in salute. On-watch crew members doffed their hats, while the off-watch "Make and Menders" stood bareheaded, at *some* form of attention, anyway, amid all their flopping laundry.

Lewrie scampered forward, stuffing his voluminous shirt-tails into his casual slop-trousers, scuffing his old shoes as he all but hopped to roll down the trouser legs to his ankles.

"Captain Thomas Charlton, come aboard, sir!" he heard the man in the perfect uniform announce to Knolles. "Your captain?"

"Sir!" Knolles almost barked, distracting Charlton's eye from Lewrie, until he'd gotten *somewhat* presentable. "Welcome aboard, sir. Allow me to name myself to you – Lieutenant Ralph Knolles, sir, First Officer."

"Captain Charlton, sir?" Lewrie said at last.

"Yer hat, sir!" his cabin-servant/valet Aspinall whispered at his side, proffering his abandoned headgear at the last instant. Alan clapped it on his head quickly, leaving a rebellious rogue's lock of slightly curly hair under the front brim over his forehead. "Commander Lewrie, sir, your servant. Welcome aboard."

"Ah," Charlton replied primly, giving him a head-to-foot once-over, cocking a single sardonic eyebrow at what he beheld, as Lewrie doffed his hat in salute. *Slop-* trousers! Charlton sniffed to himself. No stockings on his ankles! Man's lucky to shew himself shod! Post-Captain Charlton's gaze went to the penny-whistle that Lewrie held in his left hand, along his side like a truncated small-sword. "Ah," he reiterated. "So *you're* Lewrie."

"Aye, sir," Lewrie answered. "Beg pardon, Captain Charlton, but we're having 'Make And Mend,' after a quick refit, and I wasn't expecting—"

"Quite." Charlton nodded, seeming to relent a bit. "Pardons to you, sir, for not prefacing my intention to visit with a note before I did so. Or simply sending you a summons aboard *Lionheart*. My ship, yonder." Charlton pointed to the fine 5th Rate that lay farther out in the harbour. There was a note of pride in his voice. "*Well?*"

Oh, Christ. Lewrie groaned to himself, feeling the urge to fidget. Bastard wants a glass o' something in my bloody cabins!

"You'll have to excuse the mess, Captain Charlton, but may I offer you a sip of something refreshing?" Lewrie beamed.

"Quite," Charlton answered, as inscrutable as the Sphinx.

"This way, sir," Lewrie offered, glaring at Knolles, trying to mouth "Full kit!" at him without Charlton being aware. "Aspinall?"

"Aye, sir?" his lank young servant piped up.

"Dash on ahead and get us chairs, glasses and such."

"Aye aye, sir," Aspinall grunted.

Lewrie cursed himself again. He'd gestured with the damned penny-whistle! This was *not* making a good first impression at all!

–

The odour of fresh paint predominated; fresh paint, linseed oil and varnish. All the deal-and-canvas partitions had been struck below, as if the cabins had been stripped for battle. Dining furniture, the sideboard, wine cabinet, desk, sofa and chairs had been shunted over to the larboard side and covered with scrap tarpaulins. The sleeping coach and that damnable big-enough-for-two hanging bed-cot were in plain view. Captain Charlton took in the clutter, the sight of a Free Black tricked out as Cox'n, chivvying the working-party out, up the narrow companionway ladder to the after quarterdeck, so he and this… this Lewrie could speak in private. A weedy young valet, too weak-looking to draw breath, was trotting out two good armchairs in the middle of the deck, a collapsible tea-tray between them, and a pair of glasses. As far as possible from any still-wet surface.

"Will you take claret, sir? Brandy? Hock?" Lewrie offered, crossing to his desk to throw up a paint-splotched tarpaulin cover, open a drawer and hide that silly penny-whistle from further view. "Or we have most of a pitcher of lemon and orange water, sir. Sweet and tangy. With a *weak* admixture of Italian spumante, o' course."

"Like a cold gin punch without the gin, sir?" Captain Charlton enquired, with what to Lewrie felt like *immense* forbearance and patience. "Aye, that sounds refreshing."

Aspinall poured from a pewter pitcher so cool, compared to the heat trapped belowdecks, that it almost frosted. "Bit o' winter ice from shore, sir," he explained shyly to their visitor. He topped up those glasses with an opened bottle of sparkling white wine.

"Remarkably refreshing," Charlton allowed after a sip or two. "Now, sir. Reason for my unannounced call 'pon you."

"Oof," Lewrie grunted again, as Toulon the two-year-old ram-cat leaped into his lap. He'd grown considerably and had filled out to be quite a lapful, all sinew and sleek fur. He stretched out upon Lewrie's thigh, head out towards Charlton, paws hanging atop Lewrie's knee, tail slightly bottled and the tip thrashing below his master's chin. His yellow eyes were half slit, coolly regarding this possibly hostile newcomer, unblinking, with his ears half flat and his whiskers forward on guard. "Toulon, sir. Where I got him, so it seemed…"

No, this ain't goin' well at *all*! Lewrie thought with a sigh.

"Uhm, yahyss… quite," Charlton rejoined, with a sigh of his own; that sort of sigh Lewrie had heard often in his school-days, the sort associated with tutors or instructors he'd let down badly.

"'Bout the same sort of disaster, Toulon is, too, sir," Alan said, for want of something cleverer, and then instantly regretting it.

Charlton fixed him with a dead-level glare for a moment, nigh the same sort he'd been getting from the ram-cat, as if he couldn't quite believe his eyes. A Commission Sea Officer, a full Commander of the Royal Navy, sitting cross-legged with a twelve-pound feline in his lap – half-empty glass in hand – amid a barking shambles of a great-cabin, dressed as out-at-the-heels as a dockyard drunk and stroking the damn beast as if nothing much were amiss!

"Just came from *Victory*, Lewrie," Charlton said at last. "Had a word with Admiral Jervis. I am charged with command of a new squadron. And you, and *Jester*, are to be a part of it."

"Good, sir." Lewrie brightened.

"Good?" Charlton queried sharply. "Why 'good'?"

"Because there's little value in blockading the Genoese Riviera any longer, sir. We've lost it," Lewrie replied straightaway. "The French now have the good coastal roads – Marseilles to Genoa – open year-round. Less coastal shipping to intercept, d'ye see, sir."

There, that sounds sensible, Alan thought; so he won't think he's dealing with a hen-head, after all. He wouldn't have to be the one to admit that to Captain Horatio Nelson, his present squadron commander, or to his favourite, that toplofty earnest prig Captain Cockburn, he and *Jester*'s presence were about as welcome as wasps at an outdoor wedding.

"With the Austrians and Piedmontese cut off from us inland, we serve no useful purpose on the Ligurian coast," Lewrie went on, since Charlton made no move to cut him off. "Had we sent the entire fleet against Toulon west of Cape Antibes to draw them out to battle last year, it might have been a different story, but—"

"So you think Admiral Hotham was in error, sir?"

Uh-oh. Alan all but cringed; a tiny voice told him to get off that subject quickly, since he didn't know Charlton's patrons.

"Outnumbered, hence cautious, sir," was all he'd say, so he wouldn't have to rise to the bait.

"I see," Charlton replied, noncommittal.

"This summer, sir," Lewrie dared opine, "the French will most-like force the matter. *Try* and retake Corsica. That'll take transports. Spread the war farther east, perhaps. Deprive our Navy of Porto Especia and Leghorn, too. Outflank us on land and force the issue with the Austrians. And I'd imagine that your squadron will be in the thick of it. That's why I said 'good.'"

He squirmed a bit in his chair, though Toulon wasn't moving.

"First impressions aside, Captain Charlton, *Jester* is more than ready, at an hour's notice. We're nearly two years in commission, with pretty much the same crew, sir. Shaken down and sorted out main-well. Experienced, battle-proven and ready."

Charlton lifted an eyebrow at that, took a temporising sip of his drink and used the time to think – and to look about the cabins. What he'd seen on deck, beneath the temporary mess, had not been unpleasing; *Jester* was set up as Bristol-Fashion as anyone could ask, and her people had appeared clean and fairly sober, a fit and healthy lot. And, with that chin-high open curiosity and ineffable sense of "how dare he come aboard to judge us" – that inner pride of men who'd been tested and proven their mettle. Much like, he wished to believe, the spirit of his own ship's company.

It struck Charlton that Lewrie's great-cabins were not *quite* the sybaritic sort he'd expect of someone so casually unconventional. The colours were muted. A proper deep red Navy paint upon the bulwarks and the gun-carriages. A glossy-varnished oak wainscoting above the gun-ports, as were the overhead deck beams. Vertical hull timbers were the same dark forest-green of the ship's gunwales, whilst the rest of the planked interior wood was, well, half painted, at present, a deep, mellow, beach-sand tan, picked out here and there round the transom sash-windows with gilt; the overhead 'tween the glossy deck beams was a light, neutral grey.

Half painted, and only half cleaned. There were still stains and smudges of gunpowder visible. The black-and-white chequer of the painted canvas deck covering was worn through round the cannon, though, where the carriages had recoiled in battle or been run in and out in countless drills.

And those great-guns, those long-barreled 9-pounders he saw; barrels not only free of rust, but gleaming under glossy black paint. Gun-tools immaculate, though worn. Carriage trucks as scuffed as an old pair of shoes – a sign they'd never sat idle for long.

"You're quite right, Commander Lewrie," Charlton said, after a long, disarming moment of silence and adjudication. "This summer will see a *lot* of action, more than like. God willing, it will see French anarchy and revolution conquered. And our cause, and right, upheld. Formal orders from the flag will, no doubt, come aboard to you shortly. I will send a draught of my initial strictures aboard, as well. Or better yet" – Charlton smiled for the first time in what seemed to Lewrie an aeon of frowning – "do you dine with me, at seven bells of the Second Dog, this evening, aboard my ship. There I will explain our mission more fully. To you and to my own officers. And to Captain Rodgers, of *Pylades*. For the nonce, I will call 'pon him after I leave you and make the same invitation. So we may get to know each other the better – our strengths – and our weaknesses."

"Captain Rodgers, sir?" Lewrie brightened with hope anew. "That wouldn't be a *Benjamin* Rodgers, would it?"

"In point of fact, it is, sir," Charlton told him. "Do you know of him, Commander Lewrie?"

"'Deed I do, sir!" Alan said with a pleased-as-punch laugh. "We served in the Bahamas, 'tween the wars. And a merry… and busy old time of it did we have, sir. It'd be a pure delight to serve with him again. Much less renew our acquaintance."

"*Good* friends, were you?" Charlton enquired calmly, feeling help-less at the thought that he was saddled with *two* subordinates cast from the same slapdash mould!

"Aye, sir," Lewrie admitted. "He even stood godfather to my eldest son in '87. Though we haven't been in touch lately."

Charlton took another fortifying sip, whilst he pondered that latest revelation. Lewrie had an *eldest* son, born in '87. Born in the Bahamas, hey? Pray God, to a white, *English* lady? Logic dictated that there was at least one more male offspring in the woodpile.

He studied Lewrie once more, trying to balance what little he knew of his reputation, what he'd seen as a first impression in these last few minutes, with what was slowly being revealed. Paradox, he shrugged to himself.

Lewrie was about three inches shy of his own six-foot height; almost courtier-slim, about eleven or twelve stone. Perhaps early thir-ties, he guessed. That meant he'd married damn young, when still a lieutenant. Quite unlike himself, who had waited until his captaincy to wed. Good cabin furnishings, from what little he could see peeking from beneath the painters' tarpaulins. Coin-silver lanthorns stacked atop the sideboard; rather exquisite Turkey or Chinee carpets, now rolled up, but their tag-end coloured patterns showing. Married for *love*, most like, in infantile "cream-pot" love; and perhaps not well at all – yet, with all signs of moderate wealth. *Her* money? Captain Charlton speculated. Is he that sort? Or is this recent, a result of *Jester's* many prizes? Dash it all, but this Lewrie was turning out to be a most perplexing devil! Captain Charlton rather preferred his conundrums a bit more… solvable.

"Well, I shall leave you to the rest of your refit, Lewrie," Charlton announced, finishing his glass.

"Will we be sailing soon, sir?" Lewrie asked as they rose.

"Soon as the wind obliges, sir." Charlton smiled at the man's eager-ness to be off, to be up and doing. "Perhaps in the morning, after a good meal and a good night's rest."

"I can have this finished and under way then, sir." Alan chuckled.

"When you come aboard this evening, sir…?" Charlton posed in midstride for the forrud doors.

"Aye, sir?" Scrub the filth off – put on *real* clothing, he mused.

"Bring a copy of the receipt for this marvelous cold punch, sir. I must admit, it's *quite* zestful."

35

"But of course, sir!" Lewrie said, breathing a sigh of relief. "You have Tuscan *asti spumante* in your lazarette, sir? Or should you allow me to bring that as well? Or… 'tis really so much better if one uses a *proper* champagne, sir."

"I possess neither, at present. Send to shore for *spumante*, I s'pose?" Charlton shrugged, almost in a good mood by then. "As for a *Frog* wine, no harm in drinking it, d'ye think?"

"Ask of Captain Rodgers, do you go aboard his ship, sir. He's sure to have some. His very favourite in the whole world. Politics or war aside, he's bound to have a case squirreled away for special occasions. And a chance for action is just that, sir."

"Aye, I'll enquire of him, Lewrie."

Good God, Charlton thought, once more betwixt being reconciled to Lewrie and Rodgers. He was being put on warning that they were a proper pair of blackguards. Does Rodgers tipple a *lot* of wine? More than is good for a man beyond a gentlemanly brace of bottles a day?

The door that led to the gun-deck, at the forward end of the great-cabins, had been left covertly ajar, Lewrie noted. Some quick-witted sod with an ear to the ground, he thought. As he walked with Charlton to see him off, he caught a flash of scarlet and white; a Marine in proper kit, at last. There was a subtle thud of a musket butt on the deck beyond. Knolles had most-like cleared the rigging of laundry, sent the Marines below for tunics, hats, belts and gaiters and had *Jester* and her full complement ready to give their new senior officer the right sort of sendoff.

"Oh, bloody… 'ware that…!" Lewrie burst out, as Charlton clapped his large cocked hat on his head.

Captain Thomas Charlton walked on a pace or two, though his hat didn't. It remained, plastered to the still-wet varnish of one of the overhead deck-beams by its "dog's vane" and riband bow, tied beneath the gold-laced loop and gilt button of rank on the left-hand side. He reached up for it… *back* for it.

"Uhmm, yer hat, sir?" Lewrie blushed scarlet.

"Uhmm, yayhss," Charlton fumed, just as red-faced. "Quite."

Chapter 4

"Lewrie, you gay old dog!" Captain Benjamin Rodgers boomed in glee as he pumped Alan's hand vigourously. "Yer a sight for sore eyes, damme 'f ya ain't. How do ya keep, sir?"

"Main-well, sir," Lewrie replied, just as gladly. "You've come up in the world, I see. And well deserved, too."

He noted, though, that Ben Rodgers only wore a single bullion epaulet on his right shoulder; a Post-Captain of less than three years' seniority. Back in the Bahamas, he'd been an eyelash away from gaining his due promotion, been jumped into a "post ship" as soon as his old sloop of war, *Whippet*, had paid off in England, perhaps by late '88! It seemed that the same spiteful patrons and well-connected allies of their venal former commodore on that station, who'd blighted Lewrie's career from '89 'til the start of the war, had vented their spite on Rodgers's as well. It was said, Lewrie remembered, that "you can't keep a good man down." But there was a lot that the haughty, and criminal, could do to hide a friend's crimes, and make a good man's rise extremely slow. Lewrie feared that Rodgers might bear him a grudge, but his exuberant greeting put paid to that worry. If he'd suffered, he showed no sign of grief over it. He would let "the dirty" slide off his back like water off a duck's.

"When, uhm… *did* you make post?" Lewrie had to ask, though.

"In '93." Rodgers shrugged, but with a triumphant gleam. "On half-pay 'til the Nootka Sound troubles in '91. Even sailed as far as Cape Town for the Pacific 'fore I broke passage and the mail packet caught up with me to call us off. Barely back home, wasn't I, when the Frogs went and made life int'restin' again, hah! And you, sir? On yer own bottom, wearin' an 'iron-bound' coat? When? Still married, are you? Caroline's well? D'ye have an even *larger* brood?"

Thank God Rodgers was still the same brisk and stout fellow Lewrie had known long before, as windy as a Cape Horn passage.

His hair and complexion were Welsh-dark. He'd been eating well, but hadn't turned *all* tripes-and-trullibubs; he'd always been stocky and square. His face was more lined with a captain's cares, his hair beginning to thin. A fuller face made him strangely more youthful-seeming. And, in spirit, he was the very image of his old slyly puckish, boisterous self.

"*Three* gits, my *God*, sir!" Rodgers roared, shying away in mock fear when Lewrie had answered most of his quick questions. "Oh, good! The bubbly. Aye, I'll take a refill. Damme, I *know* farm livin's boresome as the Devil, Lewrie, but... mean t'say!" He bellowed in mirth, as that properly spiked champagne punch made the rounds anew.

"And yourself, sir?" Lewrie japed in return. "Still a bachelor, I trust? Any new Betty Mustins? No by-blows round *your* ankles?"

"None I *know* of, mind." Rodgers laughed, touching the side of his nose. "Nor wife, either, I'm that proud to admit. Wondrous fine as yer Caroline is, sir, fetchin' as some of the doxies've crossed my hawse, the very *idea* of wedded bliss is enough to put me off me feed! Can't see how you've stood it all these years, bless me if I can!"

"Pretty much like the press-gang, sir," Lewrie rejoined with mirth of his own. "God made womenkind the bosun's mates of our world. They slip you the king's shilling 'fore you've noticed, and you're in, with no way out. Once aboard, they *train* you, same as we turn lubbers into sailors. Lay into you often enough with their tongues, 'stead of starters. Only problem being, they're the only ones who know the lore, and only tell you what you need know, *when* they think you need to know it. Damn-all more to learn, of course, but they're not telling 'til—"

"Speakin' o' rope-end starters," Rodgers muttered, almost nudging Lewrie off his feet, "remind me t'tell you 'bout the one I met in London 'fore we sailed. Touch o' the ol' hair-brush t'her, and you'd think she was entered in the Derby!"

And why do I think I *know* her? Lewrie silently shuddered. An old "bareback ride"? My half-sister, Belinda? Sounds familiar...

"Gentlemen," Captain Charlton announced at last, playing the genial host, "I am informed supper is ready. Captain Rodgers, do you sit yonder, to my starboard side. And Commander Lewrie, here to larboard? Apologies, Charles..." he said to his First Officer, one Lieutenant Nicholson, a grave and studious-looking young man with dirty-blond hair. "Fear you must take seat below the salt, and perform the role of Vice. Toasts and all."

"With pleasure, of course, sir," Nicholson assured him.

It was, surprisingly, very much unlike a typical English supper. Oh, the conversation was strictly limited, of course; nothing which amounted to shop talk was allowed. Religion, Politics and Women were right-out for subject matter, as well.

It was all books, plays, music and such, amusing trivia gleaned from the latest London papers; hunting, harvests, Fashion, all about which Captain Charlton was very well informed, displaying an impressive range of interests and a fair amount of knowledge.

But the soup course was a tangy, creamed-shrimp bisque instead of the mundane, and expected, oxtail, turtle, or pea soup. The fish that followed was a local snapper, but dredged in flour and crumbled biscuit and served crunchingly hot, aswim in lemon juice and clarified butter. Corsican doves appeared, breasts grilled separately, wrapped in fatty bacon; a mid-meal salad to cleanse the palate, but still piquant with a vinegar and mustard dressing. There was, at last, a roast. Not the hearty (and leather-tough) local beef, but a brown sugar-cured Italian shoulder of pork, sauced with a subtle mix of Worcestershire and currant jam. The removes had been baby carrots, tiny pigeon peas and small stewed onions, along with potatoes. Each, though, had come with its own enhancing spicing – the potatoes especially, surely the last shriveled, desiccated survivors from *Lionheart's* orlop deck, from home. But they were diced small, then pan-fried with minced onion, some melted Cheddar, a dab of treacle and a Jamaican pepper sauce.

Books, well, Lewrie could converse on some, at least. Gossip, plays, and music? He was near hopeless. But, *food*, now! He and their host were at it like magpies, comparing Cantonese, Bengali, Bahamian, Mediterranean and Carolina Low Country cooking, all but bawling "you must give me that receipt!" to each other.

"Books, dear Lord, sir!" Rodgers dismissed airily, somewhere in red-faced mid-feed. "I'll admit t'only readin' the one. And that a damn thin'un. 'Twas a book set us on the right trail in the Bahamas, though, wasn't it, Lewrie? To hunt a pirate chief?"

The wines were rather good, too, though Charlton apologised for each as they appeared with each course; they'd only come from Vigo, he said with a shrug, where *Lionheart* had broken her passage the past spring.

There's more to this'un than most people'd suspect, Alan told himself, after a grand couple of hours at table with Charlton. He's not yer typical English sea-dog. There's a brain abaft that phyz o' his. And Lewrie cautioned himself to wait awhile longer before forming too quick a judgement of his new superior. And took a care to not imbibe too deep in his wines, either. It was a cruel ruse, but a useful one, to observe one's junior officers when they were deep in their cups, *in vino veritas*. Fortunately, even Rodgers, ever fond of spirits, knew that one, too, and while hearty, stayed upright.

The tablecloth was finally whisked away, the water glasses removed and the port, nuts, cheese and sweet biscuits were placed within easy reach. Lieutenant Nicholson, once they'd charged their glasses, did a midshipman's duty from the foot of the table as Vice, proposing the King's Toast, and they drank to their sovereign. Even if King George III *had* been talking to trees in Hyde Park lately, thinking them to be Frederick the Great of Prussia, as rumour had it.

"Sweethearts and wives, sirs," Charlton offered next, with a cocked eyebrow, giving them a searching, amused glance before finishing the traditional Saturday mess toast. "May they never meet!"

And why'd he look so long at *me* for? Lewrie wondered as he was forced to echo that platitude. Has the bastard *heard* something?

"Now, sirs," Charlton said more seriously, "I would suppose you've received your formal orders from the flag by now? Good. That makes you mine, officially. I also trust you've seen to victualling, and stores, 'pon the receipt of a transfer to a new command? Again, good. Nothing to delay a dawn departure but thick heads, should the winds suit. I can tell you now, we're off to the Adriatic. What was known as the 'Mare,' or the Gulf of Venice."

Charlton took pains to outline the political situation, using many of the same terms as Admiral Jervis had that morning: the strengths, or lack of them, of the maritime nations that fronted that sea, and just how much help, or friendship, they might expect to find.

"Damn' shoal, I've heard, sir." Rodgers grimaced. "*Pylades* draws 'bout two-fathom-four, proper laden. Your *Lionheart* must draw nigh three. Be like glidin' 'cross the Bahama Banks on tippy-toes, anywhere close inshore. Like Lewrie and I did once, sir."

"Well, like *I* did, sir," Alan began to rejoin. "You went north-about the Banks, while *Alacrity* did the—"

"I would hope that we could avoid, sirs, the rockier eastern shore on the Ottoman Turk and Austrian side," Charlton interrupted, knowing the sound of a long-winded heroic reverie when he heard one. "Let those sleeping dogs lie, hey? I believe our greatest concern will be in the Straits of Otranto, the mouth of the Adriatic, and the nearby Ionian Sea. Those Venetian Ionian Islands, to the east'rd, have deepwater harbours for watering and victualing. By the by, you *are* aware of a new diplomatic nicety? Since the largest 42-pounder coastal artillery piece may throw solid shot three miles, many nations are now claiming sovereign jurisdiction up to three miles off their coasts, guns or no. A safe enough offing, even for *Lion-heart* and *Pylades*, Captain Rodgers, d'ye see. And she does draw nigh seventeen feet aft, as you surmised."

Four little ships, Lewrie pondered as he chewed on a chocolate biscuit and waited for the port decanter to make its larboardly way. Only four ships, far from aid, unless the Austrian Navy was a whole lot better than he'd seen off Vado Bay last year. A week's voyage, too, should the winds be contrary, for orders or information. There were too many Republican plotters, too many spies and their agents to trust a message sent overland ever arriving. Or being true.

"You frown, Commander Lewrie," Charlton noted.

"Sorry, sir. Wishing there were more of us."

"A wish every senior British officer shares of late, Lewrie," Charlton agreed with a faint smile. "Had I my way, there'd be a good dozen ships. Half dozen of the line, *and* a half dozen sloops of war and frigates to scout. But then a more senior man would have charge of 'em, not me. And we'd miss this grand opportunity of ours."

He shook his head with a sheepish chuckle. "Had I my way," Charlton went on jovially, "I'd wish for it all! Be a full Admiral of the White, richer'n the Walpoles, maybe next-butone in line for King! But we must play the hands we're dealt, and there it is."

"Growl we may, sir," Nicholson chimed in, "but go we must?"

"Aye, there's that saying, too, Charles, my lad."

"Venice, hmm…" Rodgers mused aloud. "D'ye think we would be puttin' in at Venice sooner or later, sir?"

"Of a certainty, Captain Rodgers," Charlton assured him.

Rodgers all but rubbed his horny palms together in glee. "I've heard good things 'bout Venice. Carnival and, well, hmm! That it's a paradise for sailormen. Fiddler's Green and Drury Lane together!"

"Show the flag, of course, sir," Charlton assured them. "Do a short port-call now and again. See if Venice, and her navy, which I am assured is still quite substantial, might be available, should a further French offensive on land threaten her interests, certainly."

"Well, *right*, then!" Rodgers boomed, beaming like a lands-man being offered his first off-ship leave in a year.

Lewrie thought of Venice as well, his mood brightening; to actually see *Venice*! Rough or no, you can't beat a sailor's life when it comes to seein' the sights! Even if I still don't know if I half care for this transfer, 'course, everyone knows how leery I am. Chary of free victuals, half the time, damme if I ain't! Still…

"What *is* that old saying, sirs?" Nicholson posed, looking for all the world as if Charlton's *in vino veritas* ruse had succeeded only with his very own First Lieutenant, who was (since he was so full of platitudes) in-the-barrel, took with barrel-fever, in his cups, three sheets to the wind, in-irons, most cherry-merry – that is to say, nigh half drunk.

Too bad, old son; should've warned you first, Lewrie thought with a smirk.

"Which old saying is that, sir?" Charlton enquired.

"'Bout Venice, sir. Something… 'see Venice and die'?"

"Bloody—" Rodgers gawped.

"Naples," Lewrie corrected him quickly. "That's 'see *Naples* and die,' Mister Nicholson."

"Never could keep those straight, sir, thankee," the Lieutenant replied.

"*I've* seen Naples," Lewrie added. "And it hasn't killed me yet, I assure you. Left me a tad flea-ridden, mind, but—"

"I do believe it refers to the city's beauty, Mr. Nicholson," Charlton grunted, sternly glaring at his First Officer. "And not to a curse for any who lay eyes on it. That Naples is so lovely, a man who goes there has seen all that life could offer, so—"

"Fleas, my God!" Rodgers hooted. "Alan, you still have that tatty old yellow ram-cat, what the Devil was his name?"

"William Pitt?" Lewrie replied. Damme if I care for all this talk o' dyin', either! he thought.

"Aye, that was his name. Never took to me, I can tell you."

"He passed on, I'm sorry to say, sir," he had to admit.

"He has a new'un," Charlton told Rodgers. "And I doubt he'll take to me, either, hey, Lewrie? Protective damn puss, he was!" he added, trying to cajole the sudden morbid turn in conversation away.

Lewrie grinned back. "His glare is worse than his nip, sir. He's a scaredy-cat at heart. I doubt he could take a bread-room rat two rounds out of three. But he'd win the race by a furlong should the rat take after him!"

Charlton almost nodded approval at Lewrie's light touch. He opened his pocket-watch. "Speaking of platitudes, gentlemen, and of playing the hand one is dealt… it lacks a quarter hour 'til ten. Time enough for a rousing round of whist before we adjourn?"

Whist? Lewrie all but gagged. Bloody… rousing… *whist*? It was a damn' slow game, to his lights, and one had to actually pay attention! Nothing like Loo. His in-laws, damn 'em, and Caroline were all mad for it, of late; he'd be happier down at the Old Ploughman, staking the next pint on Shove, Ha'penny, if there was nothing else to do on a slow afternoon.

"Do we have a slant of wind in the morning, sir, I think I'd best return to *Jester* and alert my people. Have a last look-round, while *Inflexible* is within reach," he lied most plausibly.

"Ah, what a pity, then. Rodgers? No? Oh, well." Charlton shrugged. "Speaking of, Lewrie, our fourth ship, *Myrmidon*, is at Portoferrajo, on Elba. Should the wind come fair, I'll require you to sail first and dash on ahead, carrying my orders to her and her captain, Commander Fillebrowne. Expect us off Elba's western cape. Stand off-and-on, should we be delayed. Then it's off on our great new adventure!"

"Certainly, sir," Lewrie replied, rising as Charlton did. "At first light, without fail."

Odd, he called it "our grand adventure," Lewrie thought as they gathered up hats and swords; but damme if the old cock ain't rubbin' his *own* hands in glee, like Ben, at the notion. Free of the Fleet and an independent squadron to command; only four of us, even together, "In Sight" when a prize was taken, and there must be hundreds of contraband vessels to take, too! Might be a duke's ransom in prize-money out of this, after all! And seein' Venice into the bargain! 'Less Charlton is lookin' forward to puttin' the leg over half the Venetian whores in all Christendom, too?

"My thanks for a most enjoyable evening, sir," Alan told his host. "And for such a splendid meal. I can't recall when I've ever dined so well 'board ship. Even in a well-stocked harbour."

"'Twas nothing, really, sir," Charlton purred, all modest. "Perhaps our next *rencontre* will allow us time for cards, hey? Keeps the mind sharp, does whist. Once we're established—"

"But of course, sir," Lewrie lied most flawlessly.

Only on a *very* cold day in Hell, he promised himself, though. Whist? Mine arse on a band-box!

Chapter 5

Portoferrajo was a military engineer's dream, a small city at the tip of a long, rugged and narrowing peninsula, east of Cape D'Enola, with its harbour held on its southwest side, well sheltered and surmounted by more headlands, separate from the wider bay, as if held between a lobster's tough pincers. It bristled with forts.

Fortunately, *Jester* didn't have to enter the port proper, but sail up near the harbour moles near the Torre del Martello, where she discovered an old two-decker 74, and HMS *Myrmidon*, at anchor.

The old two-decker was *en flûte*, most of her guns removed, so she could carry a full battalion of British troops. Which troops were still aboard her, Lewrie could see, crammed shouder-to-shoulder upon her upper decks; with all her boats alongside but idle.

"Damned odd," Lewrie said aloud, once Lieutenant Knolles informed him that their ship was firmly anchored. "I'd think they'd be ready to go *shooting* their way ashore by now."

"Anything to get off that old scow, sir," Knolles replied with an agreeing grin. Troopers were more sanitary, less crowded than slave ships – but not by much – and a good officer wouldn't let his men be penned aboard one a second longer than necessary.

"Cutter's alongside, sir," Bosun Will Cony announced, knuckling his brow. "An' Mister Spendlove's mustered wi' yer Cox'n an' th' boat crew. Well-kep' li'l ship-sloop, she is, sir."

Lewrie turned his gaze upon *Myrmidon*.

"Not half as handsome as our *Jester*, though, hey, Will – Mister Cony?" He corrected quickly. Cony had begun as his hammockman when he was a midshipman during the American War, then his manservant, Cox'n, and senior hand during a whole host of adventures. And misadventures.

"Not 'alf, sir, but…" The thatch-haired fellow smiled back.

"But sleepy, damn 'em," Mister Buchanon, the laconic Sailing Master, observed in his West Country lilt. Sure enough, *Myrmidon* hadn't shown much interest in their arrival.

Lewrie felt an urge to get some of his own back, to make up for how badly he'd been caught wrong-footed the other day by Captain Charlton. He briefly considered having Mr. Midshipman Hyde hoist "Captain Repair On Board." This Fillebrowne, Lewrie had learned, was one of Hotham's Departure Promotions, hence about the least senior on Admiralty List, barely dry from being "wetted down." He'd *have* to take a preemptory summons from another warship, even one almost a sister to his own, as Holy Writ! Come aboard half shaved and half dressed?

I say "Leap!" you ask "How high?" on yer way up, Alan thought. Something to be said for a single *shred* of seniority, when I'm feelin' spiteful an' roguish, he mused most happily over the prospects. Or, better yet, oh dear Lord, yes!

"Bosun," he barked, giving Mr. Cony his due this time. "Trot out the jolly-boat and a crew for Mr. Spendlove. He's to go over to the transport and enquire what the delay in landing is. Respectfully, mind. I'll go aboard *Myrmidon* myself."

"Oh, aye aye, sir!" Cony grinned, knowing his captain's moods from a long, and entertaining, association. "Side-party! Muster on th' starb'd gangway fer th' cap'um!"

–

"Welcome aboard, sir," a harassed-looking young Lieutenant said after he'd taken *Myrmidon*'s welcoming salute; a most impressive turnout, that, Lewrie noted. "I am Stroud, sir. First Officer."

"And your captain, Mister Stroud?" Lewrie posed, with an eyebrow cocked in what he felt was a most Charlton-esque demand.

"Uhm, sir, uh… Captain Fillebrowne is ashore, sir," Stroud stammered, having trouble sheathing his sword in fumbling nervousness. He was one of those frank, open, pudding-faced young fellows, a typical naval nonentity who had, most likely, clawed his way up the Navy's career ladder by sheer perseverance, not wit.

It was barely gone seven bells of the Morning Watch, about half past seven a.m. *Jester* had had a lucky slant of wind round the tip of the town and into the anchorage, making landfall at "first-sparrow-fart."

Lewrie made a production of extracting his watch from a waistcoat pocket, opening it with a flick of his thumb and peering at its face, as if to confirm the time, his eyebrow even higher.

"Portoferrajo in the business of *early*-rising, Mister Stroud?" he asked, masking the cruel glee he felt. This was even better than catching this Fillebrowne with his hair mussed or with shaving soap round his ears! The fellow'd slept ashore the previous evening, Alan was dead certain. "Or is your captain?" he asked in a lazy drawl.

"I sent a boat, sir," Stroud replied, sounding about as miserable as he looked under Lewrie's withering, knowing glare. "Soon'z we saw you rounding the point, er, Commander…?"

"Lewrie, sir. Alan Lewrie. HMS *Jester*," he informed him as archly as he might. From long and embarrassing remembrance of being the butt of such doings in the past, his "arch" was worthy of a round of applause from the theatregoers in Drury Lane. "It really is too bad, Mister Stroud. I bear despatches from Admiral Jervis and Captain Thomas Charlton, who is, I am given to believe, standing off-and-on the western shore this very instant, ordering *Myrmidon* to put out to sea and join him instanter."

Stroud, a much-put-upon junior officer, winced as if someone had just trod on his feet. "I sent a *boat*, sir," he insisted for a second time. "Captain should be returning…"

Stroud's face lit up like sunshine after a quick peek shoreward, turning Lewrie's attention to a gig that was rowing so quick, on a beeline to *Myrmidon*, that it looked as if all the Hounds of Hell were at her heels. "That'll be our captain, sir," Stroud said, and slunk off out of throwing range, should the confrontation come to it; safely behind the fully accoutred Marines of the side-party. Marines who, Lewrie noted, were so bemused by the impending disaster as to go red in the face and sneak cutty-eyed looks at each other. Whether for a martinet's comeuppance or in commiseration for a good captain who was about to be caught with his breeches down, Lewrie didn't know.

"Ahoy, the boat!" *Myrmidon*'s Bosun shouted the obligatory challenge. "*Myrmidon!*" the bow-man shouted back with leather-lunged demand, thrusting a hand aloft to show four fingers, no matter how often this ritual would be performed or how familiar her own gig and captain were to them.

There came the thud of the gig against the hull planking, then a soft curse as the bow-man missed the main-chains with his first try with his boat-hook. The rasp of steps on well-sanded boarding-batten timbers, a faint squeak as the pristine white man-ropes, most neatly served with decorative Turk's Heads, took a load, and twisted in the entry-port dead-end holes.

As Commander Fillebrowne's hat came level with the top batten of the entry-port, bosun's calls trilled, muskets were presented and the Marines stamped their booted feet in unison. Swords flashed with damascened dawn light on glittering silver fittings, and *Myrmidon's* people came to attention, bare-headed, facing starboard.

The officer who appeared on the gangway, doffing his hat to the crew, was not quite what Alan had expected. That he would be younger, in point of fact even younger than himself, didn't come as *too* much of a surprise. Service aboard a flagship, under the fond care of his doting "sea-daddy" and commander of the fleet, was an achingly envied shortcut to the usual years of plodding that most captains-to-be suffered; the sinecure of the very well connected – or immensely talented and promising, Lewrie reminded himself – was allowed to barely an hundredth of the Navy's junior officers.

No, the fact that Fillebrowne was so disarmingly *not* abashed by a career-ender for most others, was in fact all but *smirking*, was the shocker!

Fillebrowne was about Lewrie's height, though leaner, and a touch more elegant, even as hurried and disheveled as he looked. He sported rich, chestnut hair and dark blue eyes. Hair most unseamanlike, that; he'd lopped off the usual plaited long queue at the nape of his collar to wear it blocked over the gold lace, and had shorn it short enough to brush forward over his ears and temples, to lie upon his brow, like the style featured on the busts of Apollo-like Roman youths. It was a modern affectation of the youngbloods, the bucks-ofthe-first-head back home, he'd learned from Charlton. Who'd been just about as leery over this new fad as Lewrie was. Fille-browne was a *damned* handsome beast, too!

"Welcome back aboard, sir!" Stroud gushed, interposing between them before Lewrie could even raise a hand. "Sir, this is Commander Lewrie, HMS *Jester.* With immediate orders, sir."

"Commander Lewrie, sir, how *do* you do? Commander Fille-browne. But then, you already know that, I must assume. Your servant, sir. Orders, did you say, Mister Stroud? Then I must also assume it means an immediate departure. Pipe 'Stations for Getting Under Way,' Mister Stroud, then report to me aft, once we are ready in all respects."

Damn' smooth, Lewrie thought; a languid tone, a hint of deviltry behind his smile, with his eyes twinkling like the cat that lapped the cream pot! And that bloody "Ox-mumble," like some-one'd sewed his bloody jaws shut! Lewrie was more than ready to take a great dislike to this idle fop, who sounded as if his papa owned half a shire, with more titles to choose from than a dog had fleas!

"My abject apologies, Commander Lewrie, for not being aboard to receive you properly," Fillebrowne smarmed on, "but I had a pressing engagement ashore. Will you take a quick cup of coffee with me, sir? Tea? Whilst you discover to me the nature of these mystifying orders?"

With a graceful wave of one hand, a faint touch near Lewrie's arm that invaded his personal space without actually *touching* – which was an absolute taboo for proper English gentlemen, to actually *touch* each other unless it was a handshake or they'd known each other for years – Fillebrowne tried to propel Lewrie aft, towards the portal to his great-cabins. As if *ordering* him to join him aft, as if Lewrie were *his* junior!

"There'll be no time for that, sir," Lewrie snapped, turning mulish and stubborn, almost ready to plant his feet before allowing himself to be moved. "Your ship has been detached from the Fleet to a new squadron, under Captain Thomas Charlton. He's on his way here right now, and we're to meet with him off to the west, soon as—"

"Old Thomas?" Fillebrowne smiled. "How wonderful!"

Damme, I should have *known*, Lewrie chid himself; junior or no, I'll have to watch this bastard. He's more lines out than a raveled fothering-patch! Wonder who he *doesn't* know?

"—as soon as you can scrub her rouge off yer ears, Commander Fillebrowne," Lewrie concluded, putting a telling shot 'twixt his wind and water. "Costly piece, was she?"

Oh, God, that was a good'un, Lewrie exulted to himself; reproof, *and* a caution 'bout "costly." As in, costly to one's career. His own eyes twinkled, in spite of his best efforts to appear stern.

"Not tuppence, Commander Lewrie," Fillebrowne confessed, quite proudly. "I *never* pay. Not when there's so many obligin' sorts for free. Must confess I'm much obliged to you for arriving with new orders. Now I may escape this witch's cauldron, without a political scalding."

"*Well* connected, was she?" Lewrie enquired, thinking that some aristocratic papa would come looking for Fillebrowne with sword in his hand, and family honour and Mediterranean *vendetta* in his heart.

"God, no, sir, nothing like that." Fillebrowne chuckled. "A vintner's 'grass widow.' Quite tasty morsel, with him off to prune a vine or two on Mount Orello. Nossir, I refer to the lashes Old Jarvy would put on me once he learned the locals don't *want* us here."

"That's why our troops are still aboard the transport, then?" Lewrie asked, arching a brow again at how nonchalant Fillebrowne was.

"Damme, will you look at that!" Fillebrowne snapped, leaning back with his hands on his hips to peer aloft at the commissioning pendant, which had gone fretful and all but slack. "It's happened just about every bloody morning since we came to anchor here. Winds off the sea die, and these hills block the land breeze 'til two bells of the Forenoon, or so. It appears I can offer you that coffee, after all, sir." Fillebrowne sighed exasperatedly. "I'll scrub off her rouge, aye, and her perfume, and have time for a shave, into the bargain. Better yet, have you eat your breakfast yet, sir?"

"A moment," Lewrie decided. Oxonian fop or not – a shameless rakehell rogue – Fillebrowne at least *sounded* like a sailor, not some Whip-Jack sham. He crossed to the entry-port to look down on his boat crew. "Andrews?"

"Aye, sah," the onetime Jamaican house servant, who'd traded actual slavery by running away from his masters and accepted informal servitude in the Royal Navy, replied, looking up with a sunny smile.

"Row back to *Jester* and instruct the First Lieutenant to stand ready to hoist anchor and set sail as soon as the wind returns. Then come back here and wait for me."

"Aye aye, sah. Up, me bucks. Unship ya oahs…"

"B'lieve I will take that coffee, Commander Fillebrowne," Lewrie agreed, sharing a smile with his host. A smile of discovery, Lewrie realized ruefully.

The bastard's *me* – he all but gasped to himself – if you took off five years and kept me a bachelor! Or *not*, he further qualified.

–

"Bloody awful place, Elba," Fillebrowne drawled as he grimaced so his cabin servant could shave a spot under his jaws. "The Dons hold Porto Longone, on the sou'east coast. Governor-general and all, since the oared galley days. Matter of fact, the Frogs took it once, but Don Juan of Austria – won Lepanto, you'll recall? – got it back for Spain.

The Medicis held Portoferrajo till the War of Austrian Succession, when the last'un died, and Austria got this port. Easy, there, Gwinn! I'm too young and pretty to die of a cut throat. And what'd the ladies do without me, I ask you?"

"Pardon, sir." His manservant chuckled. "I wouldna wish to *deprive* nobody."

"Rest of the island's supposedly Tuscan, under the Princes of Piombino. But they'll dance to any strong party's tune. They've a government here, too. Of a sort," Fillebrowne rattled on. Fearful of a cut throat or marred handsomeness or not, he was cheerfully at a thick slice of toast and jam between razor swipes.

"Didn't we almost buy the damn place, back in '86?" Alan asked between bites of his own and swigs of piping-hot strong coffee – the sort he really liked, and which few Englishmen seemed to brew, if one didn't clout them alongside their skulls to remind them every so often. "Same as we almost got Minorca and Corsica?"

"There was talk of it, sir," Fillebrowne agreed, with a more cautious nod as Gwinn laid on with his razor afresh. "But, again, the French – Louis the Umpteenth… the one got guillotined? – scotched it. They've always had their eyes on this place. *Why*, I can't—"

"So, in spite of their jealousies, all three parties have banded together to reject a British garrison?" Lewrie surmised.

"Well, sir… as for the Spanish, I doubt anyone's bothered to tell them yet," Fillebrowne hooted in derision, flinging off Gwinn's towel and rubbing his fresh-shaved chin. He came to the sideboard to pour himself more coffee. "Poor old buggers haven't a clue which *day* it is, 'less it's a festival on their church calendar! And nobody is telling the Boncampagni family, either. They're the Tuscan royalty on the island – whelp out the new Prince of Piombino every generation. Long as the peasants aren't revolting and the iron mines make money for them, they couldn't give a tinker's damn. No, it's the Austrians. Baron Knesevich, the stubborn old bastard, he's their governor-general. He's the one holds the whip-hand round here. And he doesn't *want* a British garrison, 'less there's certain 'guarantees.'"

"And we must be *so* very kind to the Austrians, mustn't we, Commander Fillebrowne?" Lewrie singsonged a sneer. "Wouldn't do for them to be upset with us, God forbid."

"Might take their toys and go home," Fillebrowne grunted, digging into his half-completed breakfast dishes with almost a carnal abandon.

"And we'd have no one left to play with. Mean t'say, sir, are we actually allies, or not?"

"There's Spain, like to come in against us… and why they were ever *with* us, I still can't fathom," Lewrie wondered aloud. "This Baron Knesevich could use the help, should a Spanish squadron show up with reinforcements for *their* garrison. Or the Tuscans send one before we do, to enforce what passes for their neutrality."

"Like I said, sir" – Fillebrowne shrugged, with knife and fork at poise position over a chop – "if he'd stood us off another day, I'd have to be the one to sail back to San Fiorenzo and tell Old Jarvy. And you can imagine the filleting I'd get as the result of that. Senior Navy officer on the scene? Pity you even came to anchor, too, sir. That makes *you* senior man, temporarily."

"When in trouble, when in doubt—" Lewrie began to quote the old lower-deck adage.

"—hoist your main, and fuck-off out." Fillebrowne ended it for him with a wicked grin. "Aye, sir, exactly."

"Leaving the colonel of that infantry battalion, and the captain of the transport—" Lewrie again began.

"—holding the most honourable bag, so to speak, Commander Lewrie," Fillebrowne interrupted again, with a devilish grin and wink.

"And that, as soon as 'dammit,'" Lewrie concluded.

"Now you've delivered these orders to me, sir," Fillebrowne asked as he wiped his lips and chin, "would it be telling, were you to let me know where it is we're going, under old Thomas?"

"The Adriatic, sir," Lewrie informed him. "Trieste, the Ionian Islands. Maybe even Venice."

"Venice, my *word*, sir!" Fillebrowne gasped in sudden delight, his face lighting up a like a child's at a country fair. "The architecture! The music, sculptures and paintings!"

"The what?" Lewrie asked, rather surprised by Fillebrowne's odd first choices for enthusiasm.

"Tintoretto, Canova, Titian… that whole talented Dago lot, sir."

"And *Casanova*, sir?" Lewrie smirked, thinking that he had formed an accurate first impression of his man.

"Well, that, too, o' course, Commander Lewrie," Fille-browne told him with a man-of-the-world shrug. "Once you get the Carnival costume, or her seed-pearled gown off, though, Venetian mutton is sure to be the same as Portsmouth mutton. God only made so many types, didn't He, sir? Your pardons for saying so, sir, but you've gained your name in the Fleet – the 'Ram-Cat' – for your fondness for the fair sex, not so?"

"I will own to my share of youthful… uhm," Lewrie replied with a worldly shrug of his own, quite at ease with Fillebrowne – and more than a bit pleased to note how far his repute had spread.

"So you surely do agree, Commander Lewrie," Fillebrowne said with a teasing note in his voice, "that, as an experienced 'fancier,' as it were, you've found that *all* cats are grey in the dark?"

"Hah!" Lewrie laughed with a bark. "Mind now, sir, a touch o' scent and a thorough wash helps. Her own teeth… or the lack."

"Mhmmm," Fillebrowne cooed appreciatively. "I look forward to Venice's wives and daughters as much as any of my lower-deck people. Though it may go against my grain, perhaps even the hired courtesans. The art, though… the opportunities *do* intrigue, however."

"A collector, are you, Commander Fillebrowne?" Lewrie asked.

"Runs in the family, so to speak, sir." Fillebrowne chuckled as he poured them more coffee, not waiting for his manservant Gwinn to do the honours. "Done the Grand Tour nigh like a religious rite, time out of mind, as it were. Victims of the usual shammed masterpieces the mountebanks fob off on unwitting English visitors. Shame of it was so great, my grandfather actually studied up before he did his Tour, so he wouldn't be cheated or embarrassed to shew his acquisitions off back home to his friends. My father and his uncles, and hence my elder brothers and I, have become rather astute collectors. Missed *my* shot at a Grand Tour… Navy career and all. This war, now! Limited as I was board the flagship, even so I've been able to glean a few small but precious, and *genuine*, articles to ship home. From the French émigrés. Going for a song. Damned rare things they came away with, I can tell you, sir! Then it was sell up or starve, thankee!"

"Aye, I've seen some of that," Lewrie agreed casually.

"*Lovely* thing about a war, Commander Lewrie," Fille-browne said breezily, stirring sugar into his coffee; a rather fine set of ornate French cups, and baroquely overelaborate coin-silver spoons, Lewrie observed, seeing them with a fresh eye. "Prize-money, loot and plunder – illiterate soldiery coming away with jewelry fit for a duchess, bartering it away for a tuppence, or drink. A necklace, do you imagine, sir, ancient beyond belief, made by Benvenuto Cellini, famous for its craftsmanship, not merely its weight in emeralds, and I got it for three hundred pounds, sir? And bedded its owner, to boot?"

"Well, hmm…" Alan began to say, suddenly put off a tad by Fillebrowne's boast. And by the venal look in his eyes.

"Venice, now, sir!" Fillebrowne schemed on, oblivious. "The French, I'm certain, will try for Corsica again this year. March on Piedmont, perhaps? Lots of wealthy and titled refugees forced to run because of it. The French Royalists will head as far as their legs, and their hoarded 'pretties,' will carry 'em. Florence, I'd expect. *And* Venice. Far as possible from danger. Before the Austrians beat the Frogs silly, I anticipate Venice will be flooded with valuables. All up for sale at penny to the pound. A buyer's market, and *mine*, I hope," Fillebrowne concluded with a raptorial smile of avarice. "That'll set my brothers back on their ears, when they see what they missed! With cargo space unlimited now, think of the sculptures."

Lewrie cocked a wary brow over that, and could not keep a frown of faint distaste from his features. Here he'd been, almost coming within a hair of *liking* Fillebrowne for his brazen and open "damme-boy" air of the practiced rakehell since it in many ways reflected his own rather casual outlook on Life. But then had come the piggish eyes and the crafty, calculating look of a "Captain Sharp," who would profit on others' sufferings. And do it as cold as charity.

Lord knows I'll never be promoted to saint, Lewrie thought in disgust; no one'll bury *me* a bishop. But practiced sinner such'z I am, I don't think I'd be *that* glad to cheat people. *Hope* I wouldn't, at least!

There was, too, his long, though admittedly never looked-for, service in the Navy. He'd been beaten, and he'd learned, since being all but press-ganged as a midshipman sixteen years before. The Navy, the ship and beating the foe came first, last and always – even to a poor example of seaman such as himself. Fillebrowne was pleased to have command of a warship so he could buy bigger articles and store them on the orlop? Amass untold, but heavy, wealth to carry home, because it was impossible to ship such things, let them out of his sight, to be broken or lost, until *Myrmidon* paid off?

Mean t'say, he told himself with a deeper scowl, every man has to have a hobby! I've my penny-whistle and the occasional quim, but not this. Swagger, cajole, toady and smarm as manly and "bully-buck" as Fillebrowne might, he wasn't Lewrie's type, after all. Underneath all that "hail fellow, well met" *bonhomie* was a scheming, heartless swine, no matter his patrons, his rapid rise, his possible talents as a Navy officer, or his ancestors. An egotistical, self-absorbed bastard! A one even bigger than I, Lewrie had to admit, weighing his own faults (and they were legion) in the balance, and happily finding himself to be damned near blameless in comparison.

"Well," Lewrie said with a cough, gazing up toward the coachtop skylights for any sign of a breeze, so he would have a good excuse to depart.

Fillebrowne had run down like a cheap pocket-watch, real-ising that his enthusiastic rant about collecting, and his schemes, had come too close to a home-truth; that he'd said too much, revealing all those wrong things he'd usually squirrel away from proper gentlemen. Lewrie saw a quick glint of anger on his phyz.

"Found some rather good bargains at Corsica, too," Fille-browne told him more coolly, his plumby "Ox" or Etonian sounding sneer-lofty, from clenched jaws. "Quite a trade in secondhand, at San Fiorenzo or over at Leghorn. I'm certain you've seen some of them, sir. Even fetched them off from Toulon yourself, sir? After Admiral Hood's evacuation? Some rather rare, precious and *darling* pieces 'mongst the first wave of émigrés? Quite delightful finds, they were."

Lewrie felt the fist in his lap, out of sight, tighten suddenly, and his ears went red with anger.

Who on Corsica had turned into the biggest broker of furniture, statuary, art, dresses and jewelry, who might Fillebrowne have dealt with, but Phoebe Aretino? Where *else* 'd a body go to hunt up bargains?

By God, did he… did she…? During? 'Course not, she wasn't *that* huge a whore, ever! After, sure. After she caught me at Leghorn, and came back to San Fiorenzo. For spite. And you'd throw that in my face, you smirkin' shit? That you've bedded my ex-mistress? *In* that house I rented for her? *On* that duke's bed I paid for?

Much as he'd like to smash the man's face in, he took a sip of coffee to temporise. Win a mistress, lose a mistress, he thought; and then she's somebody else's, 'cause she's not the sort to go without a man. Needs a man in her life, that's her way. He warned himself not to be jealous over her. But he couldn't help it. Knowing there'd be others after him, intellectually, was one thing; but to have it all but said to his face by the fellow who'd done it, to gloat and to row him beyond all temperance, well, that was quite another story!

"Ahem," Lewrie said as calmly as he could. "Thankee for a fine second breakfast, Commander Fillebrowne. But I fear I must be returning aboard *Jester*. Should that land breeze come, I'd regret any delay in using it, or keeping Captain Charlton waiting too long."

"Of course, I quite understand, sir," Fillebrowne replied, as they both rose, "one captain to another, hmm? A moment, and I'll get my coat and hat to see you off, properly."

All but simperin' at me, Alan fumed silently; smug hound!

"Venice, I'm told, isn't noted for its cuisine, surprisingly," Fillebrowne prated on as they left the great-cabins, to the thuds of musket butts and the scurry to reassemble the side-party on the gangway, "but do we get our run ashore, I'd be honoured to sport you and your first officer a shore-supper, with me and mine. Become more familiar with each other and our ways, should our two vessels come to be paired? Bags of shallow water in the Adriatic, where our two frigates could not dare, hmm?"

"An excellent suggestion, Commander Fillebrowne," Alan agreed unwillingly, forced to be pleasant in public.

Quite the practice I'm gettin', he thought sourly, that recent breakfast turning to ashes in his innards; lies to Charlton over his bloody whist, and now to this!

"It will be a red-letter day for Mister Stroud, d'ye see, sir." Fillebrowne chuckled. "After all, he has so few chances to meet men such as yourself. Such a famous officer. The 'Ram-Cat,' hey, sir?"

Damn yer blood, you… Lewrie thought.

"I must own to being a bit in awe of you, myself, sir," Commander Fillebrowne told him further, seemingly all earnest. Betrayed, though, by the tiniest hint of drollity at the corners of his eyes; all but taunting. The sort of insubordinate air that could get a common seaman triced up and lashed!

"Now you do me *too* much honour," Lewrie replied, doffing his hat to the salutes, the long, warbling calls of bosun's pipes, with his teeth on edge in a humourless smile. "Sir," he spat in warning. "Too, too much, *indeed*," he drawled, his eyes gone from merry blue to Arctic grey, as cold and menacing as a drawn sword blade.

Fillebrowne doffed his own hat, caught that subtle sea-change as he lifted his head from a departing nod and paused for a second, as if suddenly wary that he'd bitten off a tad more than he could chew. He scrubbed that smirk from his face and turned sombre.

Eat a hatful of shit and *die*, ya bastard! Alan devoutly wished as he scampered down the boarding-battens to his cutter.

"Shove off, Andrews," he hissed.

"Aye, sah," his Cox'n replied crisply, knowing the signs of a man contemplating mayhem. This was quite unlike the usual easygoing way of his captain. He smelled trouble in the offing.

May take more time to make up my mind 'bout Charlton, Lewrie fretted stonily, till we've served together a watch or two. But *you*, me lad, I can read you like a book already. That's the last time you ever *dare* sneer at me, no matter how clever an' subtle you think yerself! What was it Choundas threatened at Balabac? "I'll rip off your head an' shit in yer skull"? Cross me, Commander Fillebrowne. Cross me, I *dare* you!

"Smahtly!" Andrews bawled at his oarsmen. "Put ya backs inta it!"

Lewrie looked up at him, met his eyes. Andrews cocked his head and raised a questioning brow, and Lewrie rolled his eyes in a silent reply, made a sour grimace as he pursed his lips as if he wished to spit something over the side.

"Wind's comin, sah," Andrews offered hopefully. "'Bout tahm."

"A-bloody-men, Andrews," Lewrie grunted. "A-bloody-men!"

Book II

Inde omnem innumeri reges per litoris oram,
hospitii quis nulla fides; sed limite recto
puppis et aequali transcurrat carbasus aura.

Then along all the line of coast come kings
innumerable, whose welcome none may trust;
but let thy canvas speed past with
straight course and level breeze.

Gaius Valerius Flaccus, *Argonautica*, Book IV, 613–615

Chapter 1

Two days of sailing South, past the Egadi Islands and Cape Boeo, west of Sicily, into the Straits of Sicily. Then another day beating East-Sou'east, South-about Malta, on the open sea. Then a fourth day, butting against an Easterly Levanter, heading Nor'east for the Ionian Sea. The squadron barely logged 150 sea-miles a day, in fretful winds that never quite seemed to make up their minds as to which point of the compass they cared to blow from one hour to the next. A slow passage, certainly – but a sure one, at least.

There'd been very little merchant traffick to be seen, beyond a few anonymous slivers of t'gallants on the hazy horizon every now and then, for most vessels preferred to stand closer inshore, north of Malta, or in the dubious safety of Neapolitan waters. As far as they could from the hostile Barbary Coasts to the far south, naturally, if they were legitimate. Some flotillas and fleets of scruffy fishermen had made their appearances when they were within sight of Sicilian or Maltese shores. But for them the sea seemed swept clean of the bigger game they were sent to seek.

The pair of frigates, *Lionheart* and *Pylades*, sailed in-company, a short column in line-ahead, about two miles apart. *Jester* and *Myrmidon* Charlton had flung out far ahead, another twelve miles or more; *Myrmidon* to the landward side, and *Jester* up to windward, to the Sou'east. Still within good signalling distance, however.

Four days, and a bit, at sea.

And, like the winds, Lewrie was still fretful. Going over his encounter with Fillebrowne, cringing with embarrassment or surging hot with a sullen rage, betimes, as a man will when reliving the chagrin of a hasty retort or stinging comment twenty years in the past. Or like running his tongue over an aching tooth. They both could still evoke the same quick hurt.

"And... time!" Mr. Buchanon rasped as the half hour and the hour glasses were turned, and the very last of the eight bells marking the end of the Forenoon, and the beginning of the Day Watch, chimed at the forrud belfry. The Sailing Master, Mr. Wheelock the Master's Mate, a pair of midshipmen, and Lieutenant Knolles all lowered their sextants to make their observations on slates or scrap paper. This was the daily ritual of the Noon Sights, when by chronometer, sextant and the height of the noon sun *Jester* reckoned her midday position to determine where she was and how far she'd run since the past noon reckoning. Noon Sights was also the dividing line, that last chime of the ship's bell 'twixt the previous day and the beginning of a new one, no matter what a calendar, or a landsman's arising, said ashore.

"Thirty-eight degrees... twenty minutes north latitude, I make it, sir?" Midshipman Spendlove opined hesitantly.

"'Tis or 'tisn't, sir," Buchanon grumbled. "Own up t'it or hold yer peace."

"Thirty-eight degrees, twenty minutes North, sir," Spend-love declared more firmly, though Lewrie noted that he held one hand behind his back with a pair of fingers crossed.

"Thirty-eight degrees, uhm... nine minutes North, *I* make it," Knolles puzzled, holding his scrap of paper at arm's length, as if he had misread it. He gave his sextant an experimental shake, a tilt to either side, to chase the gremlins from it.

"Ten minutes, sir," Wheelock commented.

"Closer t'ten minute," Buchanon sighed. "Mister Hyde?"

"Oh, thirty-eight, ten, Mister Buchanon, sir," Hyde chirped in quick agreement.

"Toadyin' wretch," Buchanon groaned. "But, aye... ten's more like it. Now, longitude, sirs..."

"Eighteen degrees, ten minutes East," Lewrie snapped. "Which places us about a day's run South of the Straits of Otranto. Or one hundred twenty miles Sou'west of Corfu, the nearest Venetian-owned island. Do you concur, Mister Buchanon?"

"A moment, sir... a moment." Buchanon grinned, bending over the binnacle cabinet and the jury-rigged chart table. "Aye, sir. Or there-'bouts. Slates, gentlemen. Let me see yer... conjurin' tricks," he said to the midshipmen. "You, 'specially, Mister Hyde."

Lewrie stowed his sextant in its velvet-lined teakwood case, careful with the latch. He gathered up his own cased chronometer as the others completed their reckonings, after a long glance to see if his was running even close to the Sailing Master's, the First Lieutenant's or the larger master, which was Admiralty-issue.

"Done, sir," Buchanon said at last, handing him the reckoning, scribbled on a slip of margin – paper scissored off a completed sheet of foolscap. "Thirty-eight, ten North; eighteen, eleven East." The Sailing Master whispered the last, with an apologetic shrug.

Lewrie shrugged, too, thankful that Buchanon covered his error. It wasn't a great one, that. But he'd been too distracted to reckon properly, had gotten sloppy with his sums. And was still too fretful to keep his guesstimate to himself.

"Sights completed, sir," Lieutenant Knolles reported officially.

"Very well, Mister Knolles. Dismiss the starboard watch, and set the larboard. Then pipe the hands to dinner."

"Aye aye, sir."

"I'll go below, sir," Lewrie told him, heading for the after companionway ladder by the taffrails. Andrews was there to take the sextant case, while Lewrie carried the chronometer box, handling them both as if they were eggshell-delicate, and not quite trusting to the brass carrying-handles.

–

He wrote in his personal log, noting the weather, the sea state, their position at Noon; that decks had been swept, washed and stoned in the pre-dawn, that the hands had exercised at gun-drill for an hour and a half in the Forenoon, followed by Secure, an inspection, then an hour of small-arms and cutlass drill before Clear-Decks-And-Up-Spirits. Two men on bread-and-water, no rum or tobacco, for malingering; two down ill and one ruptured, trussed and on light duties after trying to shift a wine keg for the Master-At-Arms, by himself.

Damn fool! he thought.

He threw down his pen and leaned back in his chair, restless and irritable as *Jester* bowled along, thrashing into the winds, and taking a quarter-sea on her starboard bows, which made her thrum and creak.

Did I read more into what Fillebrowne said than what was there? he asked himself for the hundredth time. *He can't be* that *large a fool, to think he'd serve me sauce with impunity, can he? I have to work with him, dammit. Surely he knows better. He has to work with* me! *Does he think Captain Charlton will protect him? Greedy pig or no,* he's competent. Runs a taut, trig ship. Patronage only goes so far; it can't make a complete fool of a commander, or a captain. Damme, his First Officer, Stroud, was so protective of him. Those Marines of his thought it was funny, but they seemed worried about him, too. Only been in charge of *Myrmidon* a dog-watch and has that sort of loyalty already, so…

'Less he's too idle, he let's 'em get away with murder, that's why they cosset him. A stern captain'd ruin their lives! No…

"A sip o' somethin', sir?" Aspinall intruded on his thoughts from the doorway of his pantry across from the dining-coach.

"What?" Lewrie snapped irritably.

"Afore yer dinner, sir." Aspinall cringed. "Would ya wish a glass o' somethin' wet, 'fore yer dinner, sir?"

"Uhm, no." Lewrie sighed, sure that spirits – before the sun was well below the main-course yardarm – and his foul mood, would be a bad combination. "Don't think so, Aspinall. But thankee." Alan softened.

"Aye, sir," Aspinall replied, ducking back into his pantry.

Toulon padded to the desk after a good yawn and stretch, and a thorough tongue-wash on his favourite sofa cushion, to starboard. A prefacing *Grr-murr!* of effort to announce his arrival, and he was up on the desktop, to sniff at the quill pen and bat at it hopefully. Lewrie smiled for the first time that morning and teased him with it, holding it over his head. Toulon half reared on his hind legs to bat at it, turned excited pirouettes as Lewrie circled the quill, slashing with both paws at his "birdie."

"Deck, there!" came a faint, thin cry from high aloft. "Deck, there! Sign'l fum *Myrmidon!*"

Toulon caught his "birdie," crumpling the spine of the quill in his paws, and bore it to his mouth as Lewrie cocked his head to hear.

"Two… strange… sail!" The lookout slowly read off the distant bunting. And Lewrie was out of his chair, shrugging into his coat and hat, halfway to the after ladder to the quarterdeck, before the man finished shrilling "…up… t'windward!" Toulon remained on the top of the desk, flop-ping onto his side to gnaw and claw his prey with his back feet, oblivious.

"Masthead!" Knolles was bellowing aloft through a brass deck-officer's trumpet. "Anything in sight?"

"Nossir!" the lookout bawled back, after a long moment to scan the weather horizon with his hands shading his eyes like a dray-horse's blinders. "Nothin' in sight!"

"Up to windward of *Myrmidon*," Lewrie grunted, joining Knolles by the wheel drum. "Due East, or up to her Nor'east, perhaps?"

"Aye, sir, I should think so." Knolles grinned, removing his cocked hat to run his fingers through his blond hair; a sign of joy or agitation, Lewrie had learned by then.

"Mister Spendlove?" Lewrie called over his shoulder.

"Aye, sir?"

"Bend on 'Acknowledge' to *Myrmidon*, then repeat the hoist for *Lionheart*, astern," Lewrie instructed.

"Aye aye, sir."

"Mister Spendlove?"

"Aye, sir?" The lad checked in mid-turn.

"Make sure you preface the hoist to the squadron commander with 'From *Myrmidon*,' so he doesn't think the two strange sail lie windward in sight of *us*, sir."

"Aye aye, sir!" Spendlove heartily agreed. It wouldn't be the first time that signals had been misread or missent between ships since he'd come aboard *Jester*.

"Two ships or more, sir!" Knolles enthused, almost clapping his hands together as he swung his arms at the prospect of action or easy prize-money. "Fine weather for a pair of ships to come running off-wind through the Straits of Otranto. French, perhaps, sir?"

"For Taranto or Calabria, if they're inshore of *Myrmidon*; for Malta, too, perhaps," Lewrie speculated. "Neapolitans, Maltese or God knows what, so far. Come on, Fillebrowne. Tell us a bit *more*!"

"*Lionheart* acknowledges our hoist, sir," Spendlove told him a moment later. "Nothing more, sir."

"Mister Knolles, I'd admire you eased us a point free." Alan frowned, fighting the urge to chew on a thumbnail. "That will let us sidle more northerly, towards *Myrmidon*. Within sight of whoever or whatever these strange sail are."

"Aye, sir. Quartermaster, ease your helm a'weather, a point free, no more," Knolles told the helmsman. He opened his mouth to call down to Bosun Cony in the waist, to alert the watch for a sail trim, but thought better of it, for the moment.

"Aye aye, sir!" Mr. Spenser parroted. "Helm a'weather, one point. Her head's now Nor'east by North, half East!"

"Deck, there!" the main mast lookout shrilled. "Sign'l fum *Myrmidon*! *Three* strange sail, t'th' East'rd!"

"Repeat again, Mister Spendlove." Lewrie fretted, pacing the deck plankings, head down and scuffing his shoes on the pounded oakum between the joins. "Aloft, there! Where, away... *Lionheart?*"

"Lar'b'd quarter, sir! Crackin' on royals!"

"Sail *ho!*" the foremast lookout added. "Three sail, d'ye hear, there! *One* point off t' *larboard* bows!"

The day wasn't too hazy, Lewrie noted, laying hands on the top of the windward bulwark and gazing down at the creaming quarter-wave of *Jester*'s wake; a lookout can see twelve, thirteen miles. Wind's just strong enough to tempt a body sailin' large, or broad-reachin', to hoist t'gallants, at the very least. Maybe royals, too. Put 'em hull-down... maybe another six miles off, he calculated deliberately. Seven miles, should we be seein' royals only? Twenty miles, say, up to windward of us and *Myrmidon*?

"Three strange sail, d'ye hear, there!" the foremast lookout added. "*Turnin'!* Hard'nin' up t'weather! T'gallants an' tops'ls!"

Lewrie smiled to himself, leaning back, gripping the cap-rail, and peering up to the Nor'east, where he imagined *Myrmidon* might be, though he couldn't see her from the deck. Three sail, who had just espied a strange ship – *Myrmidon*, thrashing full-and-by to windward, almost dead on their bows – and swinging further out to sea, turning more Sutherly, to give her a wide berth. Or to avoid being spotted? That didn't sound much like innocent merchantmen out on their "lawful occasions." There wasn't any fighting in the Ionian Sea, not yet. Why would three ships be sailing together, unless for mutual aid and defence? And bearing up to the wind, to slip round the seaward flank of a single strange sail?

"Mister Knolles?" Lewrie called, turning to face his second-in-command.

"Aye, sir."

"Pipe 'All Hands,' sir. 'Stations for Stays,'" Lewrie ordered. "Do they try to reach south on us, we might be able to cut them off. Put the ship about, on the larboard tack."

"Aye aye, sir! Mister Cony? Pipe 'All Hands on Deck'!"

As the bosuns' calls, the "Spithead Nightingales," sang their urgent song, Lewrie turned to gaze out to sea a little more Easterly of *Jester's* thrashing bows, riding spring-kneed to her motion, feeling the power in her, the thrum and dance of her – vibrant, alive and onrushing. And closing the distance with each loping, hobbyhorsing bound over the brine.

"Hungry 'is mornin', she is, sir," Mr. Buchanon said from his side, a little inboard in deference to a captain's sole right to the windward side of the quarterdeck. "He be, too, sir. Yer permission, sir?" At Lewrie's nod, Buchanon stepped up to the bulwarks, put his own hands on the cap-rail, and stared down into the rushing, creaming wake close-aboard – a wake that was already becoming a sibilant, impatient hissing roar, tumbling in snowfall whiteness. His lips moved, and he smiled.

Lewrie cocked a wary eye at Buchanon; the Sailing Master was becoming even more superstitious lately. He put it down to *Jester* being ordered into an alien sea, one Buchanon had never sailed, never studied.

Surgeon Mr. Howse, saturnine and laconic as ever, came on deck by the larboard ladder from the waist, his terrierlike Surgeon's Assistant, Mr. LeGoff, in tow, again as ever.

"Some bustle this morning, sir?" Howse enquired gloomily, as if fearing a justification for his presence aboard. "Should we lay out the surgery? In expectation of battle, Captain?"

How could a reasonable question rankle him so? Lewrie wondered. Howse always had a way of shading or inflecting even "please pass the port" to sound like a retort, a challenge – a sneer!

"There'll be no need, 'til we beat to Quarters, Mister Howse," Lewrie told him. "We haven't identified our three strange sail yet."

"Sharp scalpels, sir," Buchanon interjected, frowning, pursing his lips in sadness. "As a caution. 'Ey's blood-hunger on th' wind."

"Smell it, did you, Mister Buchanon?" Howse puzzled, cocking his head and all but nudging LeGoff in the ribs to clue him to a jape. "Or did your sea-god Lir speak to you directly?"

"Hands at stations, sir… ready to come about," Lieutenant Knolles reported.

"Very well, Mister Knolles. Helm alee, at your discretion."

"Aye aye, sir. Quartermasters…?"

"A man'd go through Life so cocksure, sir…" Mr. Buchanon was sputtering in frustration, not so educated as to be able to spar with

Howse's droll disdain of what was, to him, a matter of fact and deadly-dangerous bit of sea-lore, "wi' eyes t' see, an' ears t' hear, but—"

"I put my faith in Science, sir," Howse declared. "And, do I put stock in a god, He'd be the Great Jehovah... *not* some creaky old peasants' legend."

"Enough, sir," Lewrie snapped. "This quarterdeck is not... *my* quarterdeck is not the proper place for philosophical disagreement. The both of you," he was forced to add. "Attention to duty, sirs."

"But sir," Howse deigned to protest, though with much humour, "to render equal by comparison, in the guise of philosophy, a myth of pagan arising and—"

"Hard of hearing, Mr. Howse?" Lewrie boomed, feeling happy to have a valid reason to vent his spleen on the obstreperous, trimming bastard, who was never happy but when *made* unhappy, martyred once more by a witless world, an unappreciative Navy. "Damn my eyes, Mr. Howse, get yourself below, if you can't take a hint and shut up!"

"Very good, sir," Howse purred, bowing his way backwards, his hand on his heart, his dark eyes burning with righteous indignation. Lewrie was afraid he'd made the bloody man's day for him, given him a noble new scar, at which he would most happily pick for weeks!

"Bloody-minded man, sir," Buchanon sighed. "Thankee."

"Didn't do it for *you*, Mr. Buchanon," Lewrie told him.

"He's with us still, Cap'um, sir. Have no fear on 'at score. But, like I said, sir... he be hungry," Buchanon stated slowly. "A fight we'll have, 'is mornin'... do 'ey have th' stomach f'r it."

"Thankee for telling me, Mr. Buchanon," Lewrie replied in slow gravity, not quite knowing what to think. Though he'd heard and seen stranger, this commission, aboard this ship.

This Fate-chosen ship, Lewrie added to himself, to hear old Buchanon tell it! What sign'z he seen, what portent did he...?

It could have been the quartermasters on the helm, Spenser, and his fellow, the Hamburg-German, Mr. Brauer, easing *Jester* a half-point free, off the wind a touch, to gather speed to carry her through that difficult thoroughbred-leap of tacking 'cross the power of the winds.

It could have been a rising of the winds, too, that caused such an eerie keening in the rigging as she increased her pace, as Knolles waited for the perfect moment, the perfect combination of a wave from the quarter-sea under her bows, along with a tiny backing of the wind, to put her about. The deck thrust upward as she set her stiff shoulder to the sea, heeled a bit more and clove it with a dragonlike roar as she neared what felt like eleven knots.

"Helm alee!" Knolles bellowed at last, and her bows swung up toward the eye of the wind, and Lewrie knew it would be a clean'un. He eyed his hands on the deck below; well drilled – over-drilled – by now, as they leaned to take a strain on weather braces and sheets to cup that power until the very last moment, while others tailed on flaccid lee-side rigging to catch her, meet her, once she'd thundered through stays.

Fully roused, her upthrust jib-boom and bowsprit speared the horizon as *Jester* swept round, rising to another lifting wave, canted to the wind's new direction as she tacked, barely losing a yard leeward or a single beat of her swift pace.

If there's to be a feast, he thought, half accepting the superstition as a talisman, she's ready for it! A good sign, that tack. A good sign, indeed… for starters.

Chapter 2

"Deck, there!" The foremast lookout shouted. "Two Chases... go close-hauled! Larb'd tack!"

They'd seen *Myrmidon* and *Jester* first, back when they'd still been "Strange Sail," and had continued running South, perhaps bearing a bit more to windward as *Jester* had loomed up over the horizon. The sight, though, of two frigates looming up had settled the matter. A hoist of flags, answered by the strange ships, had shown them to be French. Now they were officially enemy vessels, "Enemies Then Flying," or Chases. Two of them, at least. The third, which looked to Lewrie like a large frigate, had maintained her Sutherly course, interposing herself between the squadron and the pair on the wing.

"Might even be one of their big forty-fours," Lewrie commented after scrambling down the ratlines from the windward mizzen mast. He'd gone at least as high as the cat-harpings for a better view, *without* playing spider on the futtock-shrouds to gain the mizzen top platform.

"And that makes whoever she's escorting damn valuable, sir!" Mr. Knolles chortled with glee. "They wouldn't waste one of their best for nothing." Valuable, as in costly for the French to lose in battle. But also valuable as in worth a pretty penny at the Prize-Court, enriching the meagre purse of a lieutenant with large dreams for the future.

"Deck, there! *Myrmidon!* Tackin', sir!"

Hull-down by now, only five or six miles off, Lewrie could see her from the deck as she altered from a quarter-view to broadside-on.

"Now let's see what Monsieur Frog will do, Mister Knolles. A tack to deal with Fillebrowne? Or stand on, to deal with us? Mister Hyde? Mister Spendlove?" Lewrie speculated, prompting his midshipmen to do some tactical thinking.

"I'd tack, sir," Spendlove declared quickly. "Force him to go about, to show us his stern and deal with *Myrmidon*."

"Before our frigates come up, sir, aye," Hyde stuck on, put out that he hadn't been the first to speak.

"Before those prizes get too far up to windward, sirs?" Lewrie japed, looking astern. *Pylades* was leading the two-ship column, closing to within nine miles. Beating to weather always took *such* a long time that a ship too far upwind was usually as safe as houses, with a hopelessly long lead against any pursuit. It was a mere five miles, perhaps, to those escorted vessels beyond, which had just gone hard on the wind; and it might take *Jester* the rest of the daylight to catch them up. The French frigate was boxed, and if she didn't shift herself and run in the wake of her two charges, soon she'd have *Jester* off her starboard bows, with *Myrmidon* off her larboard quarter.

Might have twenty-eight 18-pounders on her gun-deck, Lewrie told himself; another ten 8-pounders on the quarter-deck, and chase-guns at bow and stern – might even have some carronades to match ours. But she can't run the risk of fighting us too long. Her rigging gets cut up, and the frigates'll finish her, sure as Fate!

Much as he disliked the notion of facing 18-pounder broadsides with *Jester*'s frailer flanks, it might come to it. Mr. Buchanon might get his "bloody" morning, after all. And Mr. Howse, one more reason to despair at the futility of war. As if death and dying were Lewrie's willful doing!

"Deck, there! Frigate's tackin'!"

"Stations for Stays, Mr. Knolles, quick as you can!" Alan snapped. "So we don't lose a single yard on her!"

–

Once more, *Jester* came about, heading a touch east of Nor'East. Pointed almost dagger-like at *Myrmidon*, which was on the opposing tack and crossing her bows. Lewrie went aloft once more with his telescope.

Shammin' it, are you? he asked the distant French captain. Do a sloppy tack, just then, to reel us into gun-range? Make us cocky?

The big frigate hadn't been well handled, had luffed about as she'd come up to Stays, and had slowed to a crawl. They'd gained a full half mile on her before she was back up to speed bound Nor'east.

Myrmidon would still pass astern of her, though, slant-wise; and *Pylades* and *Lionheart* were still too far alee to matter much for the time being. Close enough to worry her, though?

"Mister Knolles!" he shouted down. "Hoist the main and mizzen t'gallant stays'ls! Get every stitch of canvas on her she'll bear!"

And the winds… still out of the Sou'east, a backing Levanter. A sign of a weather-change, perhaps, he thought, lowering the telescope for a moment. He turned to look a'weather, over the arm threaded into the mizzen shrouds to maintain his perch. It was a clear horizon with no high-piled clouds to become thunder-heads, no haze of a squall line. But there were cat's-paws and seahorses out there, faint wispy white irregularities that presaged a stronger breeze, winking at him from a slowly rolling sea.

"More wind coming, Mister Knolles!" he called down, then swung about to descend, to end up jumping from the bulwarks to the deck, and go to the wheel to peer into the compass binnacle. "Might back on us, half a point, pray Jesus. We might be able to carry those t'gallant stays'ls. And half-reefed royals, too!"

"Aye, pray God, sir," Knolles echoed.

Half an hour more, and *Myrmidon* had crossed the French frigate's stern, still two tantalising miles shy, even as *Jester* had gained one. The frigate was slowly slipping to larboard of *Jester*'s bows, becoming hidden from the quarterdeck by the heads'ls and forecourse. *Jester* was weathering her, pointing a precious half or quarter point closer to the wind, even *with* all that sail aloft.

"She's heeled too much, sir," Buchanon noted. "'Ey all three are, you'll note. Sailin' too much on th' shoulder, not th' keel. A long chase, but 'less she does somethin'…"

"Deck, there! *Myrmidon*'s firin'!"

The pristine outline of the other ship-rigged sloop was smudged by a ragged haze of powder smoke, which ragged astern in a spreading, thinning pall, ragged alee and almost hid her from sight before they heard the faint, dull *foomph* of firing over the keen and roar of the wind and sea. It was a hopeless, impatient gesture at two miles or more distance. Even with the quoins full out from beneath the gun-barrels, they could never elevate high enough, not even with all the heel of *Myrmidon* going close-hauled.

Then, as *Myrmidon* sailed clear of her gun-smoke, she turned to show *Jester* her stern, turning up onto the wind to tack. And all that smoke, which was now reaching them, was flying 'cross *Jester*'s bows at a faster rate.

"Here's that wind, Mister Knolles," Lewrie warned. "Backing!"

"Helm alee, meet it, Quartermaster!" Knolles cried. "Nothing to loo'rd, and mind your luff!"

Just as the shrill wind in the rigging could begin to rise in pitch, *Jester* wheeled slightly to meet it, to conform to it without a falter… and rise on a wave of that quartering sea under her cut-water to aim herself a bit to starboard of the French ship.

"'At wind-shift didn't reach her first?" Buchanon puzzled to the quarterdeck staff. "Ah, 'ere she comes!"

The frigate heeled, as the change in direction and strength got to her at last. *Really* heeled, as if she'd been overcanvased, with a bit of her starboard side showing, trying to round up into it, nigh a broach! *Myrmidon* had completed her tack successfully, and now lay off her starboard quarter, with *Jester* just about dead astern. Close, too, Lewrie noted with a grin; well, closer. Her falter had cost her a quarter mile of her lead.

And those two beyond she was protecting – they were heavily laden or poorly managed. Merchantmen, without a doubt, both of whom were rapidly being overtaken by their own escort and her pursuers. After a long glance, Lewrie didn't reckon that they were more than two miles to wind-ward of the frigate – and *she* was now within two miles' range of *Myrmidon*, with *Jester* a mere two miles astern of that.

"We'll allow Commander Fillebrowne the windward side, Mister Knolles," Lewrie said. "Stand on as we are. Long as this breeze holds, that is."

–

Another half hour passed, every ship thrashing and panting for the far horizon, but with the British warships closing the range, and the French frigate getting close enough to run down her charges. On her present course, she'd pass between them, risking being "winded" by the massive spread of sail on the right-hand of the pair, slowing her even more. Every now and then, the impatient Commander Fillebrowne lit off his larboard bow-chaser, whenever *Myrmidon*'s bows were on the rise. The shot still fell far short in the frigate's wake; a poor old four-pounder, Lewrie supposed, one that wouldn't even smudge her paint, *should* it score a hit.

Still too far apart to beat to Quarters, Lewrie had the rations fetched up, with one man from every six-man mess dashing below to the berthing deck to bring up what had been abandoned. Today, like every Friday, it was a "Banyan Day," so the hands weren't missing much. A portion of cheese, some ship's biscuit, what remained of their mushy peas and their beer. More hop-flavoured water, that, than a genuine beer, a mere gnat's piss; but it kept longer in-cask than unhopped water did, and was never reduced in amount, like real water was. A sailor, ship's boy or bosun got a gallon a day of it.

"Yer Shrewsbury, sir," Aspinall offered, fetching his plate to the taffrail flag-lockers, where Lewrie could dine in a semblance of privacy.

"Sandwich," Lewrie countered.

"Not th' way I heard tell it, sir," Aspinall countered, getting his little laugh again; his former master in London had told him that it had been Lord Shrewsbury who'd first ordered cold meat on a split half-loaf, creating the first "sandwich" at the gaming-tables, too avid on a winning streak to break it, and not Lord Sandwich.

"Cold pork, sir, sorry. Mustard, a slice o' mozzarella, with sweet gherkin… Shrewsbury, sir," Aspinall tittered, after turning "mozzarella" into a short aria.

"Oh, do bugger off, Aspinall," Lewrie growled in good fettle.

"*Very* good, sir!" His manservant crisply replied, as if he'd never left a great-house's employ. "Uhm, sir…? Do we catch these ships, d'ya think there'd be a payout *soon*, sir?"

"Knowing the lethargy of our Prize-Courts, Aspinall, I'd not hold my breath waiting." Lewrie sighed between wolfish bites and blissful chewing. "Why? You're not 'skint,' are you? In debt?"

"Nossir, nothin' like that. Just like t'have somethin' t'hand, like… t'send home now an' again," Aspinall was quick to assure him. "Never told my ma I was signin' 'board a warship, 'til it was done."

"She poorly?" Lewrie enquired.

"A tad creaky, sir. Had a good place, when I left, but… never know when her people's position might change, or they take on someone younger t'do fer 'em."

"Better this than go for a soldier, if you couldn't find some house yourself, to do for," Lewrie told him. "Aye, I'll see what the Prize-Court's up to, if you're worried."

Aspinall was such a quiet fellow, always sidling about below on his chores, that he'd never given him much thought. "Creaky"… that could mean rheumatic and feeble, all but unemployable when he signed aboard, and that was two years ago and more! His old clerk, Mr. Mountjoy, had written the lad's letters for him, read the one or two he'd gotten in reply, which were surely penned for his mother by a literate neigh-bour, shopkeeper or fellow house-servant.

Just *like* a ship, Lewrie thought with a sigh, washing down a bite of... by God, it's a sandwich, damme'f it ain't, and no matter *what* Aspinall heard it called! with a swig of small-beer; right on the verge of a fight, and there's an hundred niggling things a captain has to give an ear to!

"Yea!" Midshipman Hyde exulted. "Think he hit her that time!"

Lewrie gnawed off a larger bite and set the plate down, to get to his feet and go forward for a better look. The frigate was lashing along, but still overpressed, within a half mile of her merchantmen. *Myrmidon* was up to Range-To-Random-Shot with her bow-chaser. And his own ship would be, in another ten minutes, should she stand on as she was. Time enough for a well-practiced ship to get herself ready.

"Ahem, Mister Knolles," he said, swallowing. "Kindly beat us to Quarters. I think we're close enough, at last."

"Aye aye, sir! Bosun, Sergeant Bootheby, turn out your drummers! Beat to Quarters!"

–

Gun crews closed up, starboard ports open and great-guns run out, *Jester* was up to within two miles of her foe, off her lar-board quarters, after weathering her all day. *Myrmidon* was up to windward, pelting away upon her starboard quarters. The French frigate *must* turn and fight, Lewrie thought. Which of us, though? He sketched a tack to head Sou'east, should she turn on *Myrmidon*. But she'd have to tack herself to do that.

Might haul her wind, and let fly with her larboard batteries 'gainst Fillebrowne, he speculated. Point herself straight at us if he does, and...

"Haulin'!" Half a dozen throats spoke at once. She *was* hauling her wind, falling away from the wind to take it abeam, trying for almost due North! And the taut fullness of her main-course over the middle of her gun-decks was bagging, gone flaccid as it was brailed, buntlined and clewed up. So it wouldn't catch fire when she fought!

"Mister Knolles, haul us two points free, and ease the braces," Alan ordered. "But be ready to come back on the wind when I say so. Mister Crewe?" he called to the Master Gunner below.

"Aye, sir?"

"Ready with starboard broadsides. Load with chain, bar and star shot. Quoins out, and aim for his rigging!" Lewrie chortled. Being alee of their foe had one advantage: His windward guns would be elevated higher than the frigate's, which would be firing her larboard battery, the lee side... the canted-over, low side. Even with *her* quoins fully out from beneath the guns' breeches, they could not reach quite so far.

He looked astern. *Pylades* and *Lionheart* were only three miles back now and close-hauled as dammit, coursing along on the razor's edge of the wind with frothy moustaches of foam under their bows, intent on closing to pistol-shot range. He'd have help soon if they got into trouble. Though he didn't plan on letting this Frenchman best him.

"A point higher, sir. Sidle up and close the range." Lewrie fretted, pacing the starboard bulwarks, from the gangway ladder near the trunk of the main mast, to abeam the wheel-drum. "Wait for it, Mister Crewe! Pick your moment when we round up!"

The frigate was on *Jester*'s starboard quarter now, as if *she* had become the pursuer, not the pursued. But she had *Myrmidon* alee on her larboard, abaft of abeam. Lewrie thought Fillebrowne a knacky fellow – he could have pressed on, crossed her stern, got off a quick raking broadside and rushed on to deal with the helpless merchantmen.

'Least he's stayin' to fight, Alan breathed in relief.

"Haulin'!" those half dozen commentators shouted once more. A change in aspect, as the frigate fell away even more off the wind, her gun-ports open and filled with black muzzles. She'd turn on *Myrmidon* first!

"For what they're 'bout to receive..." Spenser breathed from the helm, with Brauer and two mates now manning it.

"Better them than us'n," Mr. Tucker the Quartermaster's Mate completed.

Savage bellows, far deeper than the barks of a chase-gun, those Frog 18-pounders roared out, her whole side lit up and befogged by a well-timed broadside! Huge pillars and feathers of spray rose round *Myrmidon*, and her masts swayed drunk-enly as she was struck, recoiling from the shock. Canted over, the frigate couldn't hope to dismast her with guns aimed high enough, except the 8-pounders on her quarterdeck; but the brutal shock might suit their purpose just as well.

"Close-haul, Mister Knolles! Get ready, Mister Crewe!" Alan screeched. "As she comes back on the wind!

"Ready... wait'll she steadies, lads! On the up–roll... *fire*!"

Jester's side turned orange for a moment, as nine 9–pounders went off as one, and a blinding torrent of spent sparks and powder–fumes burst into life, the gun–trucks growling like wounded swine as they lurched inboard 'cross the oak deck planking, to snub and groan at the full extent of the breeching–ropes spliced to the heavy iron ring-bolts in her sides.

"Stop yer vents! Swab out! Charge yer guns...!" Mr. Crewe was howling, at men who'd suddenly gone half deaf to the fierce but higher barking of the 9–pounders.

"Off the wind, Mr. Knolles. Two points free, again."

"Aye, sir." Knolles coughed, turning his attention inboard after trying to see what damage they'd done.

As the smoke thinned and drifted off alee, Lewrie could espy some damage aloft aboard the frigate, which was rounding back up to lay closer to the wind. They'd caught her at a bad angle – for her, at any rate; almost forward larboard bows-on, their iron–mongery all aimed close together. She was missing her main and fore royal masts, high above the deck, and her fore t'gallant, and fore t'gallant stays'l were holed and flapping, ready to tear apart from the bolt–ropes! They'd crippled her!

More firing, as *Myrmidon* let loose with a broadside, at last. Terri-erlike yips of anger, from those punier 6–pounders of hers on her gun–deck. Splashes and feathers of spray, close–aboard the enemy waterline, along her gunwales and chainwales.

"Ready, sir!" Crewe reported from the foot of the starboard ladder. "Disablin' shot, still, Cap'um."

"Very good, Mr. Crewe, we'll be rounding up shortly." He beamed back. Closer still, too; they were now well within Range-To-Random-Shot – less than a nautical mile! He watched the frigate go hard on the wind, to serve *Jester* a crushing broadside.

"Helm a'weather, Mr. Knolles! Haul our wind, and show them our stern!" Lewrie called. "Can't stern–rake us bad at that range!"

"Aye aye, sir!"

Jester sagged down off the wind, showing the frigate her stern, making a slimmer target of herself, as a duelist would to expose less of himself to his opponent's pistol. The frigate's side lit up again, smothering her in a shoal of smoke.

"Steady, thus!" Knolles shouted, chopping his forearm to show the course, after a glance aft.

Spray, close-aboard, the fatal moaning and screeching of heavy shot as it missed the ship by inches, caroming off the wavetops near the starboard side. More feathers of spray to starboard and larboard, first tall and impressive at First-Graze, then ricocheting past in a series of bounds. And a quick, hard shudder, and the deadly *thonk!* of a ball striking *Jester*'s sides. And another, a twisting yaw, as if the stern had been struck so hard it had been shoved alee by main force – with the *thonk!* of a hit followed by the parroty squawking *Rrwwarkk!* of shattering timbers and punctured planks.

"Helm alee, Mister Knolles. Lay us full-and-by. Mr. Crewe? Stand ready!" Lewrie barked, angry that his beautiful ship had been hit, and suddenly filled with a need for vengeance.

Up to the wind's edge they swept again, the deck canting over hard before she steadied. Mister Crewe paced aft behind his gunners, judging the best moment, kneeling to peer out a gun-port. "Ready... on the up-roll! *Fire!*"

A monstrous jarring bellow of noise, the decks blotted out by an opaque, reeking fog. The deck shuddered in sudden recoil as she heeled once more.

The smoke cleared quickly as Mr. Crewe fisted and shoved his men to hasten their work, kept them hopping to stop their vents and swab out, to align the run-out tackle and recoil tackle, then begin to reload.

"Splendid, Mister Crewe! Serve 'em another!" Knolles cried, slamming his right fist into his left palm over and over.

They'd decapitated the French frigate! Now she was missing both fore and main royals entirely, and both fore and main t'gallant sails were flagging bits of shredded laundry. Lewrie eyed her with a telescope and saw ant-figures scurrying from her main top along the main-course yardarm to free the gaskets of that large sail, to restore the power she'd just lost. The frigate rode more upright on her keel, now they'd shorn her of that overpress of sail. Slower, unable now to scamper off to weather, she'd have to stand and fight. But, like a wounded bear, she'd be a more dangerous foe, with her guns at last firing level, not heeled over and limited in range.

"Avast, Mister Crewe!" Lewrie exulted. "Load with solid shot! We'll pass ahead of her and bow-rake her. Mister Knolles! Haul our wind again! Two points free, for a smaller target, while we reload."

"Aye aye, sir!"

And there was *Myrmidon*, off the frigate's larboard stern, with a broadside of her own that peppered the sea round her transom of a sudden, worrying at her flanks like a terrier.

And astern...! Lewrie turned to look aft. *Lionheart* and *Pylades* had almost *leapt* windward, as if conjuring themselves within one mile or so of *Jester*. They'd be in the thick of it soon!

Gunfire! Bags of it, as the frigate lit off a broadside, very ragged and irregular, still cocked up as close-hauled as her damaged sails would let her. Still aiming for *Jester*, to give as good as she got, and die game!

Shot-splashes towered from the sea, and Alan could *see* one dark darting ball come bowling up from First-Graze over the quarterdeck in a shrieking bound! Black and fearsome as it sizzled past almost within arm's length, leaving a hot gust of wind that fluttered his coat.

The *Thonk!* and *Rrvwarkk!* of a hit that struck *Jester*'s weak stern! Another squawking cry as another grazed her starboard side, but didn't penetrate, flinging a hen-coop's worth of fractured hull-planking over the quarterdeck bulwarks. The forward gangway bulwark seemed to burst to yet *another* hit, bulging inward but not breaking, yet flinging foot-long splinters about in a flurry of engrained dust and smoke. A waister from the starboard fore-braces was hurled off the gangway to the gun-deck, quilled like a porcupine!

And a last, shuddering *Thonk-Rrvwarkk!* as an 18-pounder shot smashed into her starboard side, down low, up forward, screaming in at over twelve hundred feet per second, and nothing could withstand that – no sloop of war ever built was made to take such a pounding.

"Bloody...!" Lewrie breathed, once he knew the last of that French broadside was done. The waister was clawing at his stomach, screaming high and rabbity as Mr. LeGoff the Surgeon's Mate and his loblolly boys came up from the fore hatchway with a carrying board. The waister's belly was pierced by almost a baulk of oak, groin pierced as well by less of a splinter, more like a two-by-four. LeGoff looked aft and shook his head to Lewrie's brow-cocked question; there was nothing to be done with a set of wounds like that. The Surgeon's Mate turned his attention to those three other people – a Marine private and two seamen – who'd been splintered, but stood a chance.

"Mister Knolles, put her on the wind," Lewrie growled in rage. "Serve her the same... in bloody *spades*!"

"Helm alee, Quartermasters. Full-and-by!" Knolles obeyed.

"Wait for it, Mister Crewe!" Lewrie called, eying the range. They would almost be close enough to use the 18-pounder carronades on the forecastle and quarterdeck. His cox'n, Andrews, was gun-captain on one of them. He shared a look with him, and Andrews nodded, grim and ready. "Double-shotted... a bow-rake!"

Far faster than the frigate now, which was hauling her wind to aim for *Myrmidon*, which had gotten up almost abeam, *Jester* would pass ahead of her at last. Faced with the danger of a bow-rake into her frailer curved bow-timbers, the frigate must turn up almost "in-irons" to the wind, or haul her wind alee even more, to avoid it.

"Ready, sir!" Crewe reported eagerly.

Only two cables off, Alan speculated; a toucher under five hundred yards. "Fire as you bear, Mister Crewe!"

"Right, lads! As you bear, hear me? As you *bear*!" Crewe scampered forward to the Number One starboard-side nine-pounder. "*Fire!*"

Bowstring-taut flintlock lanyards were pulled as each cannon came level with the frigate's bows, even as she tried to wheel up to wind once more to avoid the fire, trying to take what was coming at an angle, so the balls wouldn't punch through but would carom off, sparing her bare gun-deck from sudden slaughter. Carronades bellowed with deep, coughing roars, the 9-pounder artillery barking, then more carronades went off from the quarterdeck as they sailed past. There were keener gun-slams somewhere off to starboard, unseen in the clouds of powder residue. It was *Myrmidon*, spared by *Jester*'s actions from a close-range broadside that she would have had to tack to avoid. She fired her own broadside first, on a parallel course with the French frigate, adding to the carnage Lewrie most devoutly wished for.

And then the smoke thinned and blew alee, and *Jester* was out in the clear, to windward of the frigate at last. Lewrie turned to give her a scathing search, pleased by what he saw. Her beak-head rails and her figurehead were gone, the petty-officers' roundhouse by the foc's'le bulkhead was starred with shot, and no one living stirred by her chase-guns or fore-sail sheets. Her fore-mast was canted over as if shot from its keel step.

"Damn knacky," he whispered. *Myrmidon* had put about in her gun-smoke, was swinging up 'cross the wind and rapidly falling astern of the frigate, to avoid that delayed broadside. She'd cross their stern and boot her up the arse with a stern-rake, into the bargain! Fille-browne was a shrewd tactician, he had to confess.

"Sandwiched her, by God," Lewrie laughed.

"Or is that 'shrewsburied,' sir," Knolles drawled, even if he was a tad pinch-mouthed and pale from their hammering.

"Not you, *too*, Mister Knolles," Lewrie groaned.

"Stand on after the merchantmen, sir?" Knolles enquired.

"Aye, we'll take the left-hand'un, fine on our starboard bows, Mister Knolles," Lewrie decided, lifting his telescope to eye her and estimate how long it would take to catch her up. "We'll leave t'other on the right hand for *Myrmidon*. Assuming *Lionheart* doesn't recall us?"

"Signal, sir!" Midshipman Spendlove shouted from the taffrail.

Lewrie frowned, wondering if Captain Charlton *would* need their presence to finish off the frigate. Was he the overly cautious sort?

"Our number, sir!" Spendlove read off, stepping up onto the signal-flag lockers and balancing with one hand about the larboard lanthorn post. "'Pursue Chase More Closely,' sir!"

"Well, right, then." Lewrie sighed in relief. They'd begin the cruise with prizes. Another good omen, he thought.

"More, sir!" Spendlove shouted. "She sends… 'Well Done,' sir! Our number, and 'Well Done'!" he concluded proudly.

"Mister Crewe, secure the guns," Lewrie instructed the Master Gunner from the forrud quarterdeck nettings overlooking the waist and the still-smoking barrels. "And pass the word. The flag sends us a 'Well Done.' Pass the word for the Purser, too," he called down to the grinning, smoke-fouled sailors of his crew. "Small-beer to be served up, a mug a man. 'Tis thirsty work, beatin' the French, hey lads?"

That raised a cheer from them. There'd be prize money from a big French frigate. Hull and fittings, stores and guns might earn a total of £20,000, with them receiving an eighth – plus "head and gun money" for every seaman aboard, and each artillery piece. For battle, it had been relatively bloodless, too, barely a whit of what a real slaughter it might have been.

Mister Rees, their ship's carpenter, came up from the mid-ships ladderway, brushing past the happy and relieved sailors, a look of some worry on his face, and Lewrie steeled himself for bad news.

"Hulled, sir," Mr. Reese reported at the top of the starboard quarterdeck ladder, doffing his knit cap. He was fairly young for his warrant, hawk-faced and eagle-beaked, but baked into premature middle age by a lifetime at sea, his dark Welsh complexion permanently bronze. "One int' yer great-cabins, sir, an' yer stern-lights all smash. One, a'low that'un, Cap'um. Fish-room an' bread-room stores're scattered Hell t'breakfast... can't breathe down t'ere fer all t'biscuit-dust. Starb'd quarter scantlin's all smash, but nought below t'waterline. Forrud bulwark... but ye seen that'un, I guess, sir. A day's labour, in harbour, t'replank, starb'd. Last'un, sir..." Rees said with a gleam in his eyes. "Clean puncture... t' rough t'surgery, sir."

"Good God, was anyone...?" Lewrie gawked. That was a shot in the orlop, *below* the waterline, even if...!

"T'surgeon, Mister Howse, sir..." Rees marveled. "Wearin' a clean set o' breeches, I'm told, Cap'um. Clean t'rough scant-lin's, an' t'second futtock, caromed off t'berth-deck wale, int' t'orlop, an' jammed int' a knee-timber. B'lieve t'gent'man collected himself a wee splinter'r two, sir, but all's well."

Lewrie found it very hard to hide a spiteful smile. He coughed to clear his throat and turned his gaze outboard. But he saw Rees in much the same predicament.

"Aye, Mister Rees, thankee for your report," Lewrie said. "Do you sound the well, though, just in case one lodged below."

"I'm on it, sir," Rees said, knuckling his brow and turning to go. Then here came Cony in his wake to make his report.

"Sir, we come through right fair," he related. "No riggin' in danger, no damage below th' waterline, no guns dismounted. I run into Mr. LeGoff, an' 'e tol' me t'tell ya... three wounded. Marine Private Dykes... Landsmen Orick and Siler. 'T ain't too bad, consid'rin'. Be a few weeks o' light-duty, God willin', an' they'll be right as rain. Ord'nary Seaman Butturini, though, sir... well, 'e ain't got long."

"One of our Maltese seamen, aye." Lewrie sighed. It was such a short "butcher's bill"; but any one was much too long. "Didn't see much hope for him right off. I s'pose you've a bottle of rum handy?"

"Well, o' course, sir," Cony said with a sad grin. "I'm th' Bosun, ain't I?"

"Him and his mates... see he goes comfortable, if you would," Lewrie told him. "I'd be obliged."

"Aye, sir. An' I'll tell th' sailmaker."

"Right." Lewrie nodded abruptly. It would be Mr. Paschal's duty to sew up a canvas shroud for Ordinary Seaman Butturini and be ready to stitch him into it, once he passed over; with a final stitch through the nose, so everyone would rest easy that he was really gone.

"Pity 'bout Mr. Howse, though, ain't it, sir?" Cony chuckled. "'Eard-tell Mr. Buchanon swore they wuz blood on th' wind. Didn't think h'it'd be *his*, though. Why, 'tis enough t'put th' fear o' God in a man, Cap'um Lewrie, sir! *Which* god, now…"

"Get along with you, Mister Cony," Lewrie said with a smirk.

"Aye aye, sir." Cony grinned, doffing his plain cocked hat.

There was muffled gunfire astern. Lewrie turned to see that French frigate, now being engaged by *Lionheart* and *Pylades*, two miles or more alee. *That* wouldn't last long, he thought. Nor would those two merchantmen, which were clawing their way eastward, into the teeth of the wind, but too heavily laden to escape. It had barely gone two bells of the First Dog-watch – half past four P.M. They'd be up with the merchantmen they were chasing a little after sunset, he reckoned; and *Myrmidon* level with hers a bit before. Prize-money, and a handsome letter to Jervis – then the Admiralty – from Charlton for a plucky afternoon's work. So promising a beginning, aye… yet…

A man had died. One of their Jesters had died. And what sort of foreboding omen was *that*? Alan wondered.

Chapter 3

They were two big, fine three-masted ships, almost large enough to be mistaken for 4th Rate 50-gunners or very large but older two-deck frigates, and their arrival in the Austrian port of Trieste, with the British ensign atop their mizzen masts, might have led an observer on shore to think them part of a powerful squadron at first glance. A closer inspection, though, would have shown the French Tricolour flag flown lower, from their stern gaffs. Led by a pair of sloops of war, followed by two unmistakably British frigates, the six vessels swept into harbour about midday, their eighth on-passage, after calling for pilots beyond the bar, then standing off-and-on until someone in authority woke up and took notice of their arrival.

"Sleepy damn' place," Lewrie observed dryly, giving Trieste a good look-over once *Jester* had made-up to a permanent Austrian naval mooring, and had rowed out a single kedge to keep her from swinging afoul of the other ships in port.

British ships, mostly, he noted. Trieste was Austria's one and only naval base, home of their own small East Indies Trading Company to the Far East. But it was remarkably empty and inactive. Buoys dotted the glass-calm waters, but very few were taken, and the network of quays and warehouses were bare of bustle. He'd expected a busy seaport, just as full of commercial doings as Plymouth... damn, even a faded Bristol! Nowhere near a Liverpool, or the Pool of London, of course, *but...*!

There were damned few warships flying the horizontal red-white-red crowned flag of Austria, either. There was a trim little gun-brig sporting a commissioning pendant, a pair of *feluccas*, such as he'd come to know from his Mediterranean experience. There were even a brace of what looked to be *xebecs*, long, lean and low to the water, like Barbary Corsair raiders. What looked to be a 6th Rate frigate now careened on a mud flat, mastless and abandoned, half rotted to pieces.

And there were galleys! Small galleys with only one short lateen mast, lateener-rigged, with spars as long as they were; with row-boxes built out like "camels" on either beam, and pierced for dozens of oars or sweeps on either side. There were even more ashore, run up on launch ramps, and partially sheltered from the weather by open-sided sheds, such as he'd read in Homer's *Iliad* was the Greek fashion, back in the ancient days of Athens' glory two thousand years or more before!

Scabrous, too, that half dozen afloat, as if ships' timbers were prone to leprosy; and like the *xebecs*, they were armed only at the bows with what he took for heavy artillery, and only empty swivel-gun brackets lining their sides. Except for small harbour-watch or anchor-watch parties, they were as abandoned as ships laid up in-ordinary, though their guns hadn't been landed.

To top it off, completing Lewrie's disappointment with his first sight of fabled Trieste, it was a grey and gloomy day, with low clouds clinging to the grim-looking surrounding hills, and barely a breath of wind once inside the breakwaters and moles.

Lionheart was last to come to anchor, to make-up to a red nun-buoy. She was doing it handsomely, reducing sail, brailing up, turning up, with "buoy-jumpers" under her figurehead as she ghosted to a stop within feet of the buoy – and firing a Royal, 21-gun salute to Austria and her Emperor, Franz II, as she did it! Even as a boat was got down off the falls and rowed her kedge anchor-out astern.

Then they waited for a reply. Then waited some more. Every sailor in the squadron began to titter, speculate aloud and roll his eyes as they waited a long piece more.

Finally, some activity could be espied along the ramparts of a harbour fort. Half-dressed soldiers shrugging into coats and clayed belting, tossing shakoes to each other as if they'd picked up someone else's in their rush, or simply forgotten them. Muzzles emerged from a row of embrasures, and the first shot in reply bellowed out.

"An' here I always thought 'twas th' *Spanish* who were slip-shod," Mr. Buchanon snickered. "'Ese fellers put *siesta* t' shame, sir!"

"Delivered twenty-one... was received of..." Knolles chuckled, rocking on the balls of his feet as they counted them. "Was that five and six, *together*? My *word*! There's seven... well, come on, eight..."

"Of eleven," Lewrie said after it appeared that the last shot had been fired. Or the gunners had fallen asleep from sheer boredom, he thought sarcastically. Since Captain Charlton did not fly a broad pendant of the blue from his masthead as even a Commodore of the Second Class, the fort had saluted with the number due a mere Captain… though a captain with four warships should have gotten thirteen, with or without broad pendant. That was simple logic. And good manners!

A rather ornate oared barge, fit for a full admiral, or Lord Commissioner of the Admiralty back home, at last appeared, stroking a leisurely way out from a stone quay to *Lionheart*. There was an officer in the stern-sheets, almost awash in gold-lace fripperies, wearing a dark blue coat, with pale blue cuffs and turn-backs, pale blue waistcoat and breeches. Lewrie snorted with derision at the bouquet-sized egret plume arrangement on his cocked hat. 'Bout fifty birds perished for *that*, he thought with a dismissive shrug.

"Right, then, gentlemen," Lewrie snapped. "Bosun over-side to square the yards, break out the brooms and give 'er a last sweep-down should anyone come callin'. Mr. Knolles, I'll have the quarterdeck awnings rigged. It looks very much like rain 'fore sunset. Mr. Cony, do you get *all* the boats down. The Austrians will be taking charge of our prizes, and I want our prize-crews back aboard as soon as they do. Pipe a late rum issue, then hands to dinner, Mr. Knolles."

"Excuse me, sir?" Mr. Giles, the Purser, harrumphed to gain his attention. Their rather "fly" bespectacled young "Pusser," along with his newest "Jack-in-the-Breadroom," Lawless, were almost wringing their hands in anticipation of a run ashore in search of fresh victuals and such. "Could we have a boat, sir? Once the Bosun's done?"

"Of course, Mister Giles," Lewrie agreed. "Boat crew will *not* await you ashore, though. Remember last time, hmm?"

Giles wasn't a naval officer, exactly; not in the chain of command. He was a civilian hireling, bonded and warranted. The last time, at Leghorn, he'd taken most of a boat's crew inland to help fetch and tote. Half had snuck off from him and had gotten stupendously drunk in a raucous quarter hour before the cox'n could collar them!

"No grappa in Trieste, sir." Giles winced into his coat collar. "Nor rum, neither, pray Jesus."

"Indeed, sir," Lewrie intoned. "By the way, I've a taste for turkey. Should you run afoul of one…"

"Turkey, sir, aye," Giles replied, making a note on a shopping list. "So close to the *Turkish* Empire, one'd think, hah? Thankee, sir. Come on, Lawless. Perhaps Mister Cony may row us ashore, once he's done squaring the yards and all."

"Aye aye, sir," his lack-witted new clerk mumbled.

"Shoulda flown th' French flag, all o' us, Cap'um," Buchanon said with a sigh, looking at the fort, which had gone back to its well-deserved rest and now looked as forlorn as a fallen church. "'*At'd* lit a fire under 'em. Or fetched in 'at frigate."

"Well, we didn't, so there it is, Mister Buchanon," Alan spat.

Bad luck, all-round; inexplicably, instead of a last broadside fired for the honour of the flag and a quick surrender, the French hadn't struck, as they seemed most wont to do these days in the face of superior force. They'd gone game to the last, losing more masts and spars, shot through and riddled, but still firing back, until a lazy-fuming spiral of whitish smoke had risen from her amidships. A fire had broken out below-decks, and then it was *sauve qui peut*, as the Frogs said – "save what you can." They left her like rats diving off a sinking grain-coaster. Far astern, round sunset, Lewrie could see a tiny, kindling-like spark of flames, then a sullen bloom of red and amber as the fire, accidentally or intentionally set, reached her magazines and blew her to atoms.

"Signal from the flag, sir," Spendlove called, intruding upon his broodings over all that lost prize-money. "'Send Boats,' sir. For the French prisoners, I'd expect." *Lionheart* had taken aboard most of the frigate's survivors, after plucking them from the sea, and a gaol ashore in a port now at war with France was the best place for them.

"Very well, Mister Spendlove. Mister Cony? Belay your squaring the yards. Or Mr. Giles's trip ashore. Lower every boat and row to *Lionheart* to transport prisoners ashore. Sergeant Bootheby, your Marines to form an escort-party... pistols and hangers'd be better in the boats, I'd presume."

"Aye aye, sir... pistols and hangers," that stalwart baulk of ramrod-stiff oak replied crisply; though Lewrie was sure by the glum expression on his face that Bootheby would much prefer muskets tipped with gleaming spike-bayonets, to show the sluggard Austrian garrison what *real* soldiers were supposed to look like... all "pipe-clay, piss an' gaiters."

"You'll see to the rum issue, once the boat crews have returned aboard, Mister Knolles, then their dinner," Lewrie prompted.

"Aye, sir. And the awnings are ready for rigging."

"Very well, I'll be below, sir. Out of the way."

Which was where he stomped for, irked that a sensible routine of a single ship would forever be altered and amended by the presence of a squadron commander, and a day-long flurry of signal flags. And feeling just glum enough to resent the constant intrusions a bit!

–

There'd been no turkeys available, no decent geese, either. Mr. Giles had returned with some fresh-slaughtered and skinned rabbits, and Aspinall had jugged them in ship's-issue red wine. It may have been a Tuscan or Corsican, but it was commonly reviled as the Pusser's Bane – "Blackstrap" – thinned with vinegar, and about as tasty as paint.

Fortunately, a boat had come from *Lionheart* about four bells of the Day Watch, bearing an invitation – more like an order, since it was from Captain Charlton – to dine ashore that evening, as guests of the Austrians. Number One full-dress uniform, clean breeches, waistcoat and linen, well-blacked shoes with silver buckles (gilt if they owned a pair), presentation swords (were they so fortunate, etc.). Hair to be powdered and dressed, and blah-blah-blah... Captain Charlton was determined to impress their allies if it killed him.

"Aspinall, heat me up a bucket of fresh water," Lewrie told him. "And hunt up that bar o' soap. We're to shine tonight. Or else!"

–

Boats crews in neat, clean, matching slop-clothing took them to the quays, landing them in strict order of precedence. Carriages waited to bear them townward to what Lewrie took for a medieval guild-hall of a place, a towering, half-timbered Germanic cuckoo-clock horror of a building, simply dripping with baroque touches, right down to the leering gargoyles at the eaves and carved stags and hunting scenes round the doorway, with sputtering torches in lieu of lanthorns to light the street and antechambers. He expected one of those bands he'd seen in London, so loved by his Hanoverian monarchy, whose every tune sounded very much like "Oomp-pah-pah-Crash/bang." That or drunken Vikings!

A very stiff reception line awaited them, made up of civilian, military, and naval members. The men glittered in satins or heavy velvets or gilded wool, no matter how stuffy it was, with sweat running freely to presage the expected rain. The women... Lord, he'd never seen such a *fearsome* pack of chick-a-biddies, all teeth and teats, all bound up pouty-pigeon-chested in lace-trimmed gowns as heavy as drapery fabrics, with double or even triple chins declining over scintillating brilliants, diamonds or pearl necklaces. Everyone's hair was powdered to a tee, pale blue or starkest white, and how he kept from sneezing his head off during all the bowing and curtseying, he couldn't fathom.

"*Permittez-moi, m'sieur le capitaine Charlton, j'ai l'honneure... presentez-vous, le burgomeister, uhm... le maire...*" An equerry said with a simper, a suppressed titter and a languid wave of his hand.

"Thought they were Germans," Rodgers muttered from the side of his mouth. "What's all this Frog they're spoutin'?"

"Court-language, sir," Lewrie whispered back. "Prussians and Russians, looks like the Austrians, too. Can't bloody stand their own tongue. Not elegant enough, I s'pose. Ah! Madame Baroness... *oui,* baroness? Von Kreutznacht, *enchanté. Simply enchanté!*" He bowed to a particularly porcine old biddy who sported a rather impressive set of whiskers and moustache under all her powders, paints, rouges and beauty marks. She resembled a hog in a tiara.

"*M'sieur le Capitaine, uhmm...!*" She tittered, or tried one, at any rate. She had a husky voice as forbidding as a bosun's mate, and was about five stone too heavy to be *seen* tittering. She offered her hand, and Lewrie pecked dry lips on the back of it, looking for a spot free of jewelry or liver-spots. He heard the clash of heels in the line, the double-snap of bootheels thrummed together, combined with a short bow from the waist. He didn't think he'd try that, no matter what they thought of his manners.

"Swear to God," Fillebrowne grated between bared teeth in a rictus of a grin. "But that last 'un, sirs... she *oinked* at me."

"Which 'un?" Rodgers asked him, now they were down among those lesser lights of the receiving line. "Oh, the baroness, Fillebrowne?"

"Aye, sir. Her. A *definite* oink."

"That sound lascivious, Lewrie." Rodgers smirked. "D'ye think?"

"Oh, quite, sir!" Lewrie replied gayly. "Were she merely being polite, 'twould have been more a husky grunt. But, an oink, now...!"

"You lucky young dog, sir!" Rodgers wheezed softly. "Not a dog-watch ashore, an' a baroness throwin' herself at ya. Oinkin', an' all! Damme'f I ain't envious, sir. Mind, ya might strain somethin', puttin' th' leg that *far* over. But think what a tale ya'll have t'tell, sir."

"Handsome and *dashing* sort, such as yourself, Commander," Lewrie could not resist cruelly jibing, "must surely *expect* to be oinked at."

"Uhm," Fillebrowne commented, his eyes slitted in well-hidden anger over Lewrie's barb, "hah, sir!"

—

Supper was an ordeal. The four British captains were seated in a sea of Trieste's finest, far apart from each other, and pent in with people who could not, or would not, speak a word of English. The linen, china, centrepieces and silverware were gorgeous enough, and there were nigh a whole platoon of servants in livery, one for every two diners, *à la Russe*. It was a heavy feed, though: potato soup, very greasy goose, a bland fish course that resembled mullet, the salad wilted, dry and fleshed out with what Lewrie took to be grass clippings. Roast venison, jugged hares, a whole roast hog, all made the rounds before it was done, topped with gargantuan, toothachy piles of sweets. And with Trieste's finest tucking in like they'd just come off forty days aboard the Ark!

Finally, after circulating amid the coffee, chocolate and tea drinkers, after listening politely to some untalented musicians and a male soloist doing some incomprehensible (and stultifyingly boring) *lieder* in German, they were allowed to ascend a wooden staircase for the first floor and were ushered into a smaller chamber, where they were delighted to find cheese, biscuit, shelled nuts and port waiting on a bare-topped mahoghany table.

"Welcome to the gun-room, gentlemen," their host said with an anxious smile of welcome. "Or as close as you'll find, this side of Portsmouth." And he said it in English, with a Kentish accent!

"Major Simpson, my thanks, sir," Captain Charlton said with some pleasure as he was shown to a seat near the head of the table and was presented with the port decanter and a goodly-sized glass. "The major, had you not already gathered from the receiving line introductions," he said to the others, "is the senior naval officer here in Trieste. One of the most senior navy officers of the Austrian Empire, rather."

"That's true, sir," Major Simpson replied. "Oh, there's a man over the Danube flotilla senior to me, but…" He was nigh preening. "Do allow me to name to you, sirs, my officers…"

It was von Something-umlautish-von-Glottal-Stop something other. Half the officers wore the same pale blue breeches, waistcoat and cuffs that Simpson sported; the rest were from the Liccaner or Ottochaner regiments of Border Infantry, who formed the Austrian Marine Corps, dressed in tobacco-brown coats with sky-blue cuffs, breeches and waistcoats.

Major George Simpson, Lewrie soon learned, was the genuine article, an authentic Royal Navy officer, one of those thirtyish lieutenants of ill-starred fortune when it came to patronage, prize-money or promotion. The Russians, Turks, every foreign power with hopes to build a navy had hired them on to smarten up their own landlubberly officers and crews. Christ, the Russians had even taken the Rebel John Paul Jones to lead their Black Sea fleet at one time!

"Can't tell you what a joy it was, to see a proper squadron of British ships come to anchor, sir," Simpson told them. "You'll be in the Mare long… or is this simply a port-call?"

"We'll be operating out of the Straits of Otranto, mostly, sir," Charlton told him. "With the odd patrol to sweep up French or French-sponsored mercantile traffick. And to cooperate with your Emperor… Franz II's squadron 'gainst the French. Lend you every assistance to ready your ships for any future action which may occur this season? Urge Admiral Sir John Jervis, our new commander-in-chief in the Mediterranean, to write to London on your behalf, anent supplies, arms and such. Ships and crews, hmm?"

"Now, that would be wondrous fine, sir!" Simpson exclaimed, and translated that news in German for his compatriots. "The annual naval budget, d'ye see, is rather limited of late. Austria's a land power, mostly. Keep control of the Danube River, and protect Trieste. A lion's share of the military budget goes to the army up on the Rhine, or over in Piedmont and Lombardy. Every little bit is welcome."

"Now, sir…" Charlton purred after a sip of port, "tell me how you stand. What's your strength? Besides the vessels in port at this moment."

"Uhm, d'ye see, sir…" Simpson blushed, "this *is* the Austrian Navy, sir. All of it."

"Aha," Charlton said, raising an expressive brow in surprise.

Thought so, Lewrie told himself, sharing a weary frown over the table with Captain Ben Rodgers, who was all but rolling his eyes.

"We've *Le Ferme*, sir, the brigantine, and two feluccas… armed merchant ships, really," Major Simpson confessed, wriggling about in his chair like a hound might circle on a fireplace mat. "We've those two schebecks… brace of twenty-four-pounders in the bows, and some light side guns, and the Empire *has* authorised me to increase the number of gunboats from seven to sixteen. The same sort as was so useful during the siege of Gibraltar."

"Nothing else, uhm… cruising the coasts, or…?" Charlton asked with a hopeful, but leery, tone to his voice.

"Sorry, sir, that's the lot." Simpson grimaced. "And it's been the very Devil to get the city of Trieste to see their way clear to giving me funds enough to start the new gunboats. The governor of the port, and the mayor… the burgomeister, sir? You see, uhm…"

Here comes another, Lewrie warned himself; that "you see, uhm" sounds like a bloody dirge already! You see, uhm… I'm poxed?

"The naval budget is very small, sir," Simpson went on, wearing a sheepish smile, which he bestowed on the British captains, hoping for a single shred of sympathy. "And a fair portion of it… sixty thousand *guilden* a year… comes from the port of Trieste itself. And they'll not pay for more navy than *they* think is necessary for their *own* defence, sir."

"These *sea* going gunboats, Major Simpson?" Ben Rodgers prodded, stumbling over the unfamiliar, and most unnautical, rank.

"Uhm, d'ye see, sir…" Major Simpson began to say.

Bloody Hell, *another'un*. Lewrie groaned to himself, pouring his glass brimming with port when his turn came.

"Harbour defence, mostly, sirs," Simpson admitted, palms up and out like a Levant rug-merchant. "Point of fact, save for *La Ferme*, our brigantine, the vessels here at Trieste are almost useless unless there is a calm sea and a light breeze. I've written again and again to the Naval Ministry in Vienna, sketching what vessels'd prove more useful… mean t'say, sirs, that's why they hired me on, hey? For my deepwater experience? But…" He tossed them another palm-up shrug. "The Hungarians have a better flotilla."

"Aren't the Hungarians part of the Empire, though, sir?" Lewrie just had to ask.

"Oh, aye, they are, sir! An important part," Simpson assured him. "Hundreds of years ago, the Hungarians advanced to the coast, the Croat lands, and the Croats were most eager to make alliance with them, then with Austria. Then Austria became dominant over the Hungarians, though they keep a certain measure of semi-autonomy. Most of the coast, that is the Hungarian Littoral. Fiume, Zara, Spalato, Ragusa… it extends quite far. Well, *sort* of Spalato and Ragusa, d'ye see. They're still either Venetian ports or independent. There's the independent *Republic* of Ragusa, quite old. Genoese or Spanish enclaves on the Dalmatian coast – hated Venice since Hector was a pup, so they've played everyone off against the other. Though Turkey still claims them, they're mostly Catholic, Venetian or at least Italian."

"Ah, hmm!" Captain Charlton purred, wriggling in his own chair, as thoroughly puzzled as the rest by then. "Perhaps, sir, you might fill us in on the eastern shore's doings? Its nature?"

"Well, sir," Simpson replied slowly, "it's rather complicated, d'ye see, uhm…"

First had come the Roman Empire, so Simpson carefully related to them; then the Eastern Byzantine Empire had held sway, punctuated by a series of local princedoms or kingdoms that had aspired to be empires – Macedonians, Albanians, Serbs, then Bulgars or Hungarians, what had been the Dark Ages. All had been swept away quite bloodily by another, finally by the all-conquering Turks; back when they *had* been all-conquering, of course. Venice, Genoa, Spain, the Italian city-states all had nosed about, warring with each other until Venice had become great and had carved out a province that had run the entire length of the eastern shore. Only to be lost, except for a few remaining bits of coasts round harbours, to the Turks, at last, in the 1400s.

Below the Hungarian Littoral was the Independent Republic of Ragusa, which Turkey still claimed but was too weak to conquer any longer, and let it go in semi-autonomous bliss, long as tribute was paid to the Sultan, while all inland was Muslim-Slavic, termed Bosnia or Herze-govinia. South of there was Montenegro, another semi-autonomous province of the Turkish Empire, but which still held a small Venetian enclave with a fine harbour, called Venetian Cattaro. Montenegro was almost totally Muslim, too. The Turks still ruled Albania, even more mountainous and forbidding than Montenegro; but that too was pretty much in name only, and Venice still clung like weary leeches to the harbours of Durazzo and Volona, with shallow, narrow coastal lands, as *Venetian* Albania.

Venice still held the Ionian islands, down at the mouth of the Straits of Otranto, off the Albanian coast: Corfu, Cephalonia, Zante and

Cerigo, plus some appendages only goats could love. Off the lower Ionians, the Turks owned the Morea, which was their name for the Greek Peloponnesus, famed in Homer's works, part of the long-ago exterminated Byzantine Empire.

"The coast is mostly Catholic… Hungarian, Croat and Venetian," Simpson related over a second decanter of port. "Inland, though, they are Muslim, all down through Albania and the Morea. Forcibly converted long ago, though you couldn't tell a Balkan Slav Muslim from a European. Now, you still have some Greeks, Eastern Orthodox Church, down in the islands, the far southern lands… sheltered by the Venetians. Betwixt Venetian ports and such, the coast is Muslim, so it's rather tricky, depending on where you go ashore. Far inland, there are many Eastern Orthodox Serbs, still clinging to their mountaintops. Turks never could get at 'em easily. Toppled their empire in a night and a day, Lord… four hundred years past. They've a *Serbian* Orthodox Church of their own, 'stead o' looking to Roosia or wherever other Slavs look to as the seat o' their religion. Oh, lowermost Montenegro, there's the port of Dulcigno. Muslim, independent, home of the Dulcigno Corsairs. Just behind them, by the Albanian border, is the Rebel Pasha of Scutari. Not quite as bad as the Barbary Corsairs, but they're *aspiring* people. Split off, like the Mamelukes who rule old Egypt? 'Tis a hellish stew, the Balkans and Dalmatia."

"It sounds very much like it, sir," Charlton grunted.

"Well, worse than that, sir. D'ye see, uhm…"

Don't tell me, they're cannibals! Lewrie scoffed in quiet derision; and *they* ate Captain Cook! He needed more port. Badly!

"So much trampling back and forth, Captain Charlton," Simpson grimly mused. "All of 'em were great, one time or another. Even with the Turks ruling most of it, the people're so intermixed. Every little valley… all those peoples, religions, languages in some places. Any slightest thing sets 'em off, and then it's holy war, neighbour 'gainst neighbour. They take their tribal backgrounds and their religions *damn'* serious in the Balkans, they do, sir. Red-Indian, massacreing serious. Give 'em a wide berth, that's my best advice to you."

"Yet where does the best Adriatic oak come from, sir?" Rodgers enquired. "From the eastern shore? Or from higher up, round Trieste, or Fiume?"

"Bit o' both, but mostly from the north, Captain Rodgers," the good major allowed. "From Venice and Trieste. What the Hungarians do, in spite of orders from Vienna…" He gave them a hopeless shrug.

94

"So we must investigate that shore, I take it, sir? In spite of the problems?" Lewrie asked, not liking the sound of it. "The Venetian ports, too?"

"Aye, the Venetians." Charlton perked up like a spaniel at the sight of a fowling-piece. "I'm told their fleet is still a factor in this region. What's their strength, and where do they base?"

"Well, sir... officially that is," Simpson told him, "they have twenty ships of the line, still. Two-decker 68's, what we'd take for an under-gunned 3rd Rate 74. Some 60's, same as an *over* gunned 4th Rate 50? Smallish. Ten real frigates, again smaller'n we're used to, most of them like our 6th Rates, and shallow-draught. Fixty or sixty sloops, brigs o' war, *xebecs* or oared galleys, all told. Laid up, in the Lido at Venice, the various ports... most of 'em in-ordinary with their guns landed. Haven't seen much of them at sea since their last war with the Tunisian Corsairs back in '92, just before their Admiral Angelo Emo died."

"And the Turks, sir?" Charlton wondered.

"Lord, sir! The Turks?" Simpson laughed, as did the rest of the Austrian officers. "In the Black Sea, to keep an eye on the Roosians, mostly. What else is left, and that ain't worth much, mind... is anchored inside the Golden Horn below the Sultan's shore-guns, should they turn mutinous on him. At best they patrol the Dardanelles, to keep out tricky folk like we infidels, so the world may leave 'em be, sir."

"So we wouldn't encounter any off the Balkans, sir?" Fille-browne enquired. "Not even a revenue cutter or two?"

"Not in a month of Sundays, sir." Simpson chuckled. "Balkans are so poor to start with, there's little revenue to protect! And the local pashas, however they style themselves, too weak to collect or enforce it. Should there be *some* money scraped up, it never goes beyond a pasha's purse, you may be certain... the Sultan bedamned."

"*Seeraübers*," one of the Austrians sneered. "Der pirates, *Ja? Sehr viele*... zo mahny ist, *meinen herren kollegin?*"

"The *kapitan* refers to you as his colleagues, sirs," Simpson translated. To Lewrie's ears, even hearing the man's name for a second time, it *still* sounded hellish like "Von Glottal-Stop/ Atchoo"!

"He warns there are many pirates on the coast," Simpson added, "like the Corsairs of Dulcigno. With the Turks sunk so low they can't, or no longer have the will to guard their coasts, some local buccaneers have gotten into the game. Albanian, Montenegran, Bosnian, some Greeks from the Morea…"

"Die *Uscocchi*," Kapitan Von Glottal-Stop growled, as morose as a drunken badger; the *fourth* bottle of port was making the rounds, with some local stuff, too – a gin-clear paint remover.

"*Ja, danke herr kapitan.*"

Simpson squirmed, turning a furious eye on the fellow for a second. "Croatian pirates, d'ye see, sirs. Their rulers, the Hungarians, try to keep 'em in line, but…"

"*Ungarischen, pah!*" Herr Kapitan Von Gargle-Umlaut-Argey-Bargey spat in anger from the other side of the table. "*Arschlochen! Die Ungarischen Kriegsmarine, die Godtverdammte Uscocchi, ist!*"

"He says the Hungarians don't try too hard to rein 'em in, sir," Simpson unraveled for them, blushing. "Being so new to the sea, Croats make up a fair number of their sailors so far."

"Like good English smugglers, Major?" Lewrie japed. "The best seamen in time of war? Worth your time to snare 'em… 'pressed, or as volunteers?"

"May one catch them first, Commander Lewrie," Simpson agreed, a touch bleary. He wasn't feeling any pain himself by then. "I must confess our compatriots the Hungarians have recruited many for their flotilla. Or turn a blind eye to their doings, at times. For their continuing goodwill. After all, the Uscocchi are stronger than most of the freebooter bands. Damn near own the myriad of islands along the coast, d'ye see. And their presence keeps the other raider bands out of Hungarian waters. I told you, 'twas a hellish stew in the Balkans. There's hardly a coastal community safe from piracy or slaughter. Not much to *loot*, d'ye see, though… 'tis mostly tribal or religious grudges being worked off. Greeks 'gainst Turks, Turks 'gainst anyone Christian, Croats 'gainst Bosnians or Serbs, and vice versa. And 'gainst Muslims, which is pretty much everybody *else* down the coast. Your best hope, Captain Charlton, is to see that British merchantmen keep well out to sea, over towards the Italian shores. Venetian waters are safe enough, and down 'round the Straits, Naples keeps a lid on things. The Papal States, though… in the middle of the western shore… not much of a navy, these days. Nor army, either! So you'll see raids over there now and again. Though even the Uscocchi don't stray far from their home waters in the islands. Too easy to hide 'mongst 'em, sir."

"Uhmm, yahyss…" Charlton drawled, suppressing a yawn. "Now, as to those prizes we fetched in, Major Simpson… or any others we may take, once we hit our stride, hmm? Does Trieste support a Prize-Court, since Austria is a belligerent 'gainst France?"

"But of course, sir!" Simpson beamed. "Survey, inspect and valuate any prize you fetch in. Imprison or parole any passengers or crews who are French, allied with them or shipping contraband. We've already discussed it, the governor, the burgomeister, and I. All are most enthused at the opportunity. Once condemned and purchased, those ships and their cargoes will be most welcome on Trieste's markets."

"Supplies, sir," Charlton pressed gently, "victuals, firewood and water. Perhaps the odd cask of gunpowder, stand of shot... naval stores and your famed Adriatic oak for repairs... now and again?"

"Well, uhm, sir, d'ye see..." Simpson shrugged helplessly. "At present, uhm..."

Useless bastards, Lewrie groaned silently; some allies!

"Well, perhaps we could meet again, sir," Charlton suggested, hiding his disappointment rather well. "We must spend at least a day more at anchor, making repairs from onboard stores. Your people to take charge of the prizes, freeing our prize-crews aboard at present? Oh, excellent, sir, thankee. Would tomorrow be convenient? There's so much for us to discuss, before we sail for Venice, to announce our presence... Splendid! Well, sir. It's quite late, I see. And this has been a most enjoyable evening, but..."

—

"Shoddy sorts, Lewrie," Rodgers growled as they stood apart, waiting for the carriages to bear them back to the quay. That rain had finally come, sullen, chill and depressingly steady. "Not worth a tinker's damn, they are. 'Less there's more to 'em than we've seen today. Or tonight." Rodgers yawned, too, digging out his watch to peer at the time. "By Jesus, half past midnight!"

"Well, sir," Lewrie agreed softly as a coach clattered up at last. "I'd suspect, long as we're about the Adriatic, they'll not be sticking *their* noses out to sea. Didn't sound as if they'd seen the sea-side of the breakwater in a dog's age."

"All they're good for is swillin' an' drinkin', it seems." Ben Rodgers chuckled. "Lord!"

"Well, sir... a man's got to be good at something!" Lewrie smirked.

"Least Charlton sounds as if he knows what he's about. Smooth as silk, did ya mark him? A perfect diplomat. *And* a fine hand when

it comes to fightin', thank God. At pistol-shot range. By the way...
thankee for cripplin' that bastard frigate, you an' *Myrmidon*. Might've
been a *real* scrap if you hadn't."

"Well, *I've* got to be good at something, don't I, sir?" Lewrie
laughed as a liveried catch-fart opened the door and lowered the step
for them so they could hop into the coach.

"Aye, ya always were a scrapper, Lewrie," Captain Rodgers said as
he settled in the rear seat, forcing Lewrie to take the forward one.
They were both relieved to be free of the estimable Captain Charlton,
though; he and Fillebrowne would ride in the second. "Prize-money
to start with, bags of honour with Old Jarvy, right off. Well, four of
us 'In-Sight'... may not be *that* grand a share-out, but it's a start. I'd
hope we could cruise together, *Pylades* and *Jester*. Like the old days...
me a bit offshore, you further in. We made a hellish pair o'shit-stirrers,
'deed we did, sir."

"I'd admire that, too, sir," Alan truthfully said. "Aye, like the high
old times."

"Here, this Fillebrowne," Rodgers puzzled, after another giant
yawn. "Know much of him? One o' Hotham's 'newlies,' ain't he?"

"Well, sir..." Lewrie said, suddenly guarded. And feeling that flush
of embarrassed irritation all over again! "But so is Charlton in a way."
And, as the coach rattled and swayed over the poorly cobblestoned
road, he related his first meeting with Fillebrowne at Elba, and what a
first impression he'd formed. Without being *too* spiteful-sounding, he
hoped!

"They come up so fast these days, Lewrie," Rodgers sighed, a fist
over his mouth to cover another yawn. "So did we, come to think
on't. Nicest, gentle-mannered Lieutenant in th' world, jumped out
of th' gun-room or wardroom, onto his own bottom, well... there's
always a few turn into th' world's biggest bastards. Never know what
a command'll do to a fellow. And the newest, Lord... did ya ever note
it? Get such big heads, 'tis a wonder there's a hat'd *fit* 'em! Scared o'
makin' an error at th' same time, too. I'd expect Fillebrowne needs half
a year o' command t'gain his confidence. *That'll* take all th' toplofty
starch out o' th' lad. New shoes pinch sorest, 'til ya break 'em in. An'
captain's shoes th' snuggest."

"I'd s'pose there's something in what you say, sir," Lewrie had
to admit. Hadn't he been half terrified, his first day aboard *Alacrity*?
Whole- terrified 'board *Shrike*, when he'd been jumped to First Officer,

fresh from an Examining Board in '82, and knew just enough to be dangerous… but nothing near what a Lieutenant should?

Even if Fillebrowne had schemed, even *murdered*, to gain his promotion and his command, the sudden strain, the sense of isolation aft in the great-cabins and the immense, unpredictable and everlasting burden of total responsibility would turn a *saint* grumbly!

"Perhaps I should find him a kitten, sir," Lewrie chuckled in the dark interior of the coach. But Ben Rodgers wasn't listening to him any longer. He was awkwardly draped across the opposite leather seat, legs asprawl to either corner and his head tucked over sidewise like a pigeon would, to tuck his head under a wing to roost. Hat on sidewise, too, almost over his nose, and beginning to snore about as loud as an ungreased bilge-pump chain.

"Oh, Christ!" Alan sighed, tweaking his nostrils shut as Ben Rodgers relieved his heavy Teutonic supper at last. A belch or two of stentorian loudness, that put a throaty gargle to his snores for a moment; then the sort of fart that'd make most producers sigh aloud with delight and pride. And make the rest envious.

"Dignity of command," Lewrie reminded himself in a soft voice, as Rodgers produced another that quite turned the air blue. The coach-horses couldn't do a finer! he thought. This'un now, was ripe and pungent beyond all imagining, making Lewrie grope for the sash-window's release strap to let it down so he could stick his head out!

His own supper sat heavy, his breeches as tight as a glutted tick, so… well, two can play this game, he thought. And Rodgers, lost in a creamy, greasy, alcoholic stupour, had the *gall* to wriggle his nose at the result. But, he snored on, most thoroughly oblivious.

Well, damme, Lewrie thought; the nerve!

Chapter 4

"Let 'em go?" Lewrie ranted upon his quarterdeck, once he'd read the letter that Charlton had sent aboard. "Mine arse on a band-box, sir, but… let 'em *go*? Well, damme!"

The older midshipman from *Lionheart*, a fellow in his mid-twenties named Birtwistle, cringed and took half a step back from Lewrie's sudden fit of pique at that unwelcome news from the Venetians.

"Well, sir…" Birtwistle said with a shrug, when he could get a word in. "Since the captain only *requested* a ruling from the Doge and the authorities ashore, it isn't as if we're *bound* by it. We never turned the ships over to them, so they're ours to deal with as we like, the captain said to tell you, sir. B'lieve the letter goes on to say—"

"And what did the Doge and his senators say to that, Mr. Birtwistle?" Lewrie fumed.

"Didn't ask 'em, sir," Birtwistle grunted. "The captain said he thought they'd most-like be wringing their hands over it. But it'd be *all* they'd do. Captain Rodgers is to take charge of them, and sail them back under escort to Trieste and a real Prize-Court."

"Well, that's more like it," Lewrie sighed, at least a trifle mollified. "Thankee, Mister Birt-wistle, for deliverin' this."

"Captain Charlton also sent this, sir…" Birtwistle said, as he reached into his uniform coat's breast-pocket to produce another of those letters. "I'm to wait for a verbal reply, sir."

Lewrie wrenched the letter open, expecting more bad news, but was delighted to find that Captain Charlton wished the pleasure of his company, along with one of his officers or midshipmen, to accompany him ashore that evening for another of those diplomatic suppers.

"Ah," Lewrie said, eyes crinkling in delight. "Very good, sir. Pray, do you render to Captain Charlton my utmost respects and thanks for the invitation, and I will fetch along my First Officer, Lieutenant Knolles. We'll be aboard *Lionheart* by the start of the First Dog."

"I'll tell him, sir," Birtwistle assured him, doffing his hat and making an escape before something *else* set Commander Lewrie off.

-

Let 'em go, mine arse! Lewrie groaned.

After a day of repair work, the squadron had sailed for Venice, on a beautiful morning with a brisk little Easterly gushing down off the Balkan mountains. Twenty miles out to sea, they'd stood, outside anyone's territorial claims. It wasn't much of a voyage; seventy or so sea-miles to the west. But they'd come across several merchant-ships and had been forced to overhaul them and speak them, anyway. Two had been British, one a Maltese. But the last two had made sail and run as soon as they'd spotted them, and it had taken half a day for the swifter *Jester* and *Myrmidon* to come up to musket-shot of them and fire a warning under their bows.

Fetched-to, and all else aluff, they'd boarded them, to discover that they were both "neutrals," one a Dane, the other Dutch. But once a good search had turned up *more* ship's papers, they'd found that both were French-chartered. And the Dutch ship was not a refugee, but one of those still working from a *Batavian* Republic port, which meant that she was from a French ally.

And she was crammed with tons of compass-timber, naval stores, masts and spars! The pitch, turpentine, tar and such was crammed below by the tun and cask, the spars atop that, the masts slung to either beam of her gangways and weather deck. The compass-timber, though, in the rough, was piled any-old-how, atop sawn oak plankings and baulks.

And rare, and valuable beyond belief to the French Navy! Just about to anyone's navy!

One could steam or bend straight-cut oak to some sort of shape, though it was costly. But to find the boughs, the butts of oak that were curved by nature, which could be adzed into the thick, stout oak beams that arced upward from the keel of a warship, which made first, lowermost futtocks, upper-deck tumble-homes, re-inforcing bow or stern knees, well… it took over fifty acres of oak-trees to make a ship of the line, and not one tree in a thousand yielded proper compass-timber for all the sweet curves of a well-built ship.

They'd fetched them into Venice, hoping to have them condemned, thence subject to prize-regulations, but they'd waited two days for a judgement. Two days of rocking, pitching and yawing, with anchors set four-each, as a Sutherly blew up the Adriatic – foreign warships were not allowed inside the Lagoon of Venice, especially behind the shelter of the Lido, where the Venetian ships and their many small island fortifications were located. Two days of heaving and snubbing, watching a wind-driven tide-race run in through the entrance channels, and wishing a biblical flood on all quavering, cowardly Venetians!

Well, if they were too sniveling a lot, too proud of their own neutrality to risk getting embroiled in this war, Lewrie thought... fuming again for a moment at what Charlton had mentioned in his first letter – that the two prizes had cleared from a Venetian port, after all, and should be allowed to complete their voyages, since *they* had found no fault in their papers...!

"Damn 'em," Lewrie muttered. "Damn 'em all. Root and branch."

Two whole days they'd lain at anchor, watching the lights, the constant coming-and-going ashore. Watching Venice light herself up in a misty swirl of faery-light each evening, and glitter like a precious, unattainable pearl... so near and yet so far, the other side of a sandbar and barrier island. It almost made him feel empathy with some of those ancient, hairy and flea-ridden barbarian Huns or Teutons who'd come down from their primeval Germanic forest hovels to the gates of a civilised old Rome; there to sit in awe and wonder (scratching away, of course) and realise what complete *hogs* they were in comparison!

Spires, soaring belltowers and cathedrals, great palaces and mansions, all shimmering in rosey-hued dawn or a liquid, lambent gold of sunset, shrouded in morning mists and fogs... verily, the Shining City, just out of reach, like a cup of water for Tantalus.

But, like one of those old barbarian sword-swingers, Alan ached for a shot at revenge, too; at taking Venice by storm, if they played it so aloof and grand. So he looked forward to their trip ashore with a feral, wolfish hunger. And vowed he'd not be overawed, no matter what!

–

"Ooh!" though.

"My word!" Lieutenant Knolles breathed.

"Umphf!" Captain Charlton was heard to sniff in appreciation.

"Ahhh…!" A moment later, from even the sardonic and mostly silent Fillebrowne, as their gondolier pointed out another magnificent *scuola* or *palazzio* even finer than the last, along the Grand Canal.

"Christ, shit on a biscuit," Lewrie muttered under his breath.

Venice was ten times grander, more impressive (dammit all, more awe-inspiring!) than London, even on a good day! Its every mansion, its every fine public building, palace or cathedral, was taller, more ornate, more colourful, or simply bigger, than anything Sir Christopher Wren had wrought, even Saint Paul's! The Duke of Marlborough's Blenheim Palace might be a match… but Lewrie thought it'd be a near thing were he to compare Blenheim against Venice's best.

And old! Ancient beyond any Italian city he'd seen, areek with the smell of ancient glory, of conquest, power and wealth. Shit-arsed English Crusaders had ridden these canals on their way to the wars in the Holy Land! Had begged or pawned their wealth for Venetian ships to take them there. He'd thought Naples a very classically Roman city, to be adored and studied, but this…! Why, some of these palaces had been old when the Crusaders had come, when the Turks had come, still inhabited by the same princely families!

It was getting on for dusk, and the Grand Canal was ambered with sundown, the walls of the houses, palaces, mansions, cathedrals, towers… even the plebeian warehouses and such, were glowing with the fading light, as if they soaked it up during the day to radiate back like pig-iron, which stayed red-hot for a time after pouring. Lanthorns lit up the faces of the tall buildings, round the steps that ran down into the Canal, round the magnificent entryways… atop the pilings that led along the Grand Canal, and winked down every byway or turning as they passed them; the waterfront streets – the *fondamenti* – were as lit up as the Strand along the Thames, and every side-street ashore winding round enticing, intriguing corners was prelit with firefly glows in a grey-blue dusk.

And even at dusk, the Grand Canal teemed with a thousand boats of all sorts, though most were the artfully curved, fragile-seeming gondolas. They breezed past each other with bare inches to spare, in an unending stream, crossed each others' bows from side-canals from inshore *campi*, as effortlessly, as majestically, as languidly as swans on a lake or pond. All were painted not a funereal black, but a shiny, a glossily sleek ebon, each sporting a tiny lanthorn of its own, dressed with gilt, silver or polished brass tokens as big as firedogs. Many held canopied midship shelters, like open coaches, those shelters filled with men and women in the height of fashion...

"Ooh!" Lewrie gulped in awe once more, in spite of himself.

Beyond the height of fashion, some of them, as if Fashion had risen to a high art form.

"Aah!" Fillebrowne all but groaned, as a lady in a passing gondola deigned to reward them with a regal, and imperiously lazy, nod of her head as she wafted past. Her hair was done up bigger than a watermelon on a form, powdered, dressed, crimped and curled, and sprigged with miniature portraits, bows, ribands and what Alan took for *jewels*! Streaked, though... a bit of powdery white, some blonde, some natural Italian coffee-brown? That'd take her hours, he thought. Her gown had been dripping with flounces, furbelows, laces, ribands, tiny seed-pearls sewn into intricate patterns. And, like a faery queen, there she'd gone, as if she'd never been, an unutterably lovely but forever unattainable paragon of feminine beauty! But wait, here comes another just as fine, attended by some simpering, ribboned fop!

These were masquers... from the six-month Carnival season, he suspected; draped in light cloaks, bibbed fronts of black, though all embroidered with pearls, sequins and gold-lace thread. The man wore a dark veil over his tricorne hat, which slumped over his shoulders and cloak, a black-and-white mask with a prominent bird's beak. So did his consort! Her veil over her high, cabbage-shaped hat and gigantic hair fell below her mask, pinned up over one ear as if she were a Moor or Turk! Even more gondolas presented idle revelers, out taking a cool boat in the refreshing night air, dressed much the same – though Alan didn't think he ever saw two masks exactly the same. And those that didn't wear masks might as well have; there was a stiff, frozen air to their features, as if bored beyond life, as they chatted in sweet whispers so wearily.

Liquid, languid and lazy was the soft Venetian Italian he heard as their boats neared others; above the almost constant sound of song or music from shore or from a larger gondola. There was a full bloody concert band, in one instance; six gondolas in-line-ahead, trailing a larger boat filled with young revelers and with violinists, flautists, harpists and oboe players sawing or huffing away like anything! And gondoliers sang... perhaps only for each other? he wondered... with the one same tune springing from one boat to another, until the whole Grand Canal seemed to pick up at the right point and sing along in harmony!

It was magic, it was bewitching, it was beguiling, this Venice! It...

Stank, he noted, of a sudden.

They'd come in through the Porto Lido, one of the sea-channels nearest the city, threading between its long, south-jutting breakwater barriers, in Navy boats. They'd landed at one of the *lazaretti*, the customs and quarantine stations, and transferred to a local sailboat, a very odd-looking craft, indeed, called a *sanpierota*, which mounted a single, trapezoidal gaff-sail far *aft* of amidships. It was beamy in the extreme, so shoal-draught Lewrie thought it incapable of sailing over a heavy dew – but the Venetian authorities at the Lazaretto insisted they take it. A heavy British rowing-boat would surely come to grief in the Grand Canal, much less the narrower *Rios;* there was no way to employ both sides of oars in all that heavy traffic. And, should they allow their Navy hands two hours of idleness once they were ashore, it was very possible they'd never *see* them again – run off to taste an indolent Lotus-Eaters' paradise!

The *sanpierota* proved to be a most stable and swift sailboat, though, and bore them the several miles from the *lazaretto* to the Canale di San Marco in moments, on a pleasant little breeze; over to the Isola di San Giorgio Maggiore, and its imposing cathedral; thence to the Dogana di Mare – Customs Point – roughly across from the Doge's palace, on the far side of the Bacino di San Marco. And there had yet been a pleasant sea-wind.

They'd changed to a gondola from there, and a gondolier who had *some* English, at least. Into the Grand Canal for a sunset tour, past the Cathedral of Santa Maria della Salute, past all those regal, faery-like palaces and such. Under the soaring Ponte dell'Accademia, following the arc of the canal...

Until they'd been... "winded," so to speak. Just about level with the Palazzio Balbi, and the Palazzio Contarini della Figure, where the canal took an abrupt starboard turn, where no breeze could reach.

'Tis no wonder they're heading out, Lewrie realised, wrinkling his nose and fanning his face with his hat, of a sudden, as the garbage-midden reek overpowered him; I'd go sailin' out where the air's clean of an evenin', too! Shut in a bit from a spectacular Adriatic sunset, the prospect to either hand suddenly didn't look *quite* so faery-like, so otherworldly. It was just a row of bricks and such, set along a slackwater ditch the colour of the Thames... which bore the cast-offs of London down to the sea.

Must toss *everything* out the windows, and hope they don't hit a passer-by, he thought sourly. Into the canals... out of sight, out of mind... if not the nostrils.

There were dead fish, he noted, bloated and belly-up, just below the murky surface. Carrot-tops, browned lettuce leaves, more fish-guts lay waving like indolent ribands, at which the surviving fish nibbled with desperate hunger. It suddenly resembled the Hooghly River, which ran past Calcutta, the most inaptly-named Pearl River, just off Jack-Ass Point at Canton, Dung Wharf along the Thames...

Some rather ripe turds went wafting by, close-aboard – while a gay song trilled from shore, taken up by their gondolier. The corpse of a tiny calico kitten... Lewrie felt an outraged sulk coming 'pon him. Why, it was all a fabulist sham! he thought. A trick of smoke or mirrors! He expected bodies in the water, too – human ones. After all, hadn't Machiavelli grown up here in Venice? Didn't the Venetians murder people left, right and center... officially *and* unofficially? Then let the tides do their work, unlike the rest of the Mediterranean, which mostly had none. No, he thought, casting a chary eye upon the latest wonders round the bend in the Canal... it ain't so grand, at that!

–

They took a hard turn to starboard into the Rio di San Luca, just short of the Palazzio Grimani. A hard larboard swing, into the Rio Fuseri, then a landing on the Fondamenta Orseolo and a stroll to St. Mark's Square, as night came down for certain. It must have been some saint's day or Carnival event, for there was a continual popping of fireworks, bands of revelers dancing through the streets in gaudy costumes and more of those masks, the din of bands competing with each other from balconies or side streets, and their way lit by a multitude of torches or street-lanthorns. Mountebanks clad as harlequins, atop impossibly tall stilts, who leaned on upper-floor balconies to share a glass of wine with hosts in masks, or play *gallant* to some young lady. Jugglers, acrobats and mimes were two-a-penny, dancing dogs, begging bears...

"Ah, here's the place I was told of," Captain Charlton said, leading them into a restaurant. Lewrie noted he had a slim notebook in a side-pocket, to which he referred now and again. "This comes well recommended."

"As long as *they* aren't on the *carte de menu*, sir," Fille-browne commented, pointing out the two dozen cats that sat, lay or gamboled just without the doorway.

"Known for its seafood, I was told, sir," Charlton rejoined. "And 'tis hard to disguise cat-meat as cat-fish, d'ye see, haw haw? The aromas fetched 'em, I shouldn't wonder. Fetched me, at any rate."

Charlton put a hand to that pocket, that slim notebook once more creasing his brow in remembrance, as if to dredge up some fact he'd read from it, like a mentalist performing a parlour-trick, or a raree-show.

He's never been here, either, Lewrie told himself. Yet he's determined to play the knowing host; the experienced guide!

"...city's nigh awash in cats. A thousand-thousand of 'em, I wouldn't doubt. Living along a canal, at water-level," Charlton went on genially, "they must be worth their weight in gold, in holding down the rat population. Your sort of town, I expect, hey, Commander Lewrie?"

"It could grow on one, sir," Lewrie allowed, as a half dozen of the more active beasts came to twine about his ankles, scenting a mark of his Toulon on his stockings, shoes and breeches.

–

An adequate supper – more than adequate, really. There'd been huge shrimps, cuttlefish stew, stuffed green crab, stuffed sole, with a gigantic mullet big enough for all. And oceans of wine to slosh it all down with. Then, it was off they went for a *ridotto*. Charlton explained that their diplomatic gestures would be made with Venetian authorities there, instead of being invited to dine.

"Too busy celebrating, sir?" Lewrie asked, cocking an eyebrow at that news. "They won't sup with us, but they'll have us in for an hour or so at a *casino*?"

"Just so, Commander Lewrie," Charlton sighed. "Just so."

"An infuriating damn people," Fillebrowne sneered in sympathy.

–

They were just about the only people in the palatial *ridotto* not in costume or masks. Those Venetians who hadn't tricked themselves out as Moors, fanciful beasts or clowns, and wore normal clothing, might as well have been in costume, for their dresses and suitings were as overly ornate as Court-dress at Versailles before the French Revolution. They might dress more soberly during the daytime, but at night, in a casino, they went all-out, as colourful and fanciful as an entire flock of peacocks. About half not in full costume still clung to a black-and-white mask, no two alike, from what Lewrie could see – or posed and preened with filigreed, lacy butterfly-like eye-masks on sticks, which could be purchased or rented, holding them to their faces like quizzing glasses.

Cloth-of-gold, cloth-of-silver, lacework so intricate, so laden with tiny seed-pearls or German glass they appeared to shimmer as they strolled, and almost reflect whatever they passed! Men's suitings so snugly tailored, so embroidered, so flounced with lace, they resembled the parody of a proper suit that had delighted Lewrie back in his teens in London – before his father had press-ganged him into the Navy, o' course! – the old "Macaroni" style. And those men… piss-proud, as toplofty as lords, the few unmasked faces frozen into masklike coolness, just at the instant before a sneer. Foppish, weak, limp, languid… or overpadded, full-cheeked and looking so smugly satisfied with their lots. Or, Lewrie speculated, so magnificently *bored*, rather!

"Uhm… a bit *gaudy*, would you say, sir?" Ralph Knolles said in a quiet whisper from his larboard side. "My *oath*!"

That last comment came at the sight of a pair of harlequins pawing each other as fond as lovers, tilting their infernal beaked masks out of the way to exchange a playful kiss. Under the voluminous costumes, it was impossible to see were they man and woman – or *another* sort of combination.

"Never catch *English* folk capering like this, sir," Lieutenant Knolles declared firmly.

"Be surprised, Mister Knolles." Lewrie smirked. "Not at home, at any rate. Overseas, now… in a flock o' foreigners… with no one they know watchin'…"

"Have to be drunk as badgers, sir, e'en' so," Knolles countered.

"That, too, sir." Lewrie chuckled wryly. "Or that *first*! And then… out comes the bed-linen, and it's a Roman orgy!"

Sumptuary laws were being flouted on every hand, the strictures against ostentatious display of wealth broken by every hemline. Lewrie felt, even in his very best shore-going dress-uniform he was pretty much like a sopping-wet wharf-rat among these glittering, preening peacocks. A liveried servant's uniform was more ornate, more impressive! And he wondered when he or Captain Charlton might be instructed to go fetch a fresh tray of drinks... or clean up someone's mess!

The *ridotto* was another Trieste, though, when it came to bodily odours. As grand as a king's palace though it was, as high and baroque its ceiling, well... it was quite close, the air still, and filled with hundreds of revelers, strollers and gamblers, and the only breeze came from idly waving hands, the coquetry of ladies' fans or the uprush of wind from a full thousand flickering candles.

For a people supposedly "married" to the sea... and all the water that went with that, Lewrie smirked... the Venetian aristocracy didn't seem to *hold* much with water! No matter how layered in Hungary Waters or Colognes, they were a pretty stale bunch!

The landing-party strolled, glasses in hand, trying to be pleasant, searching for the officials Charlton had planned to meet. Knolles, free of his arduous, unending duties as First Officer for a rare evening, and the other lieutenants or midshipmen, who were rarely let off the leash of Duty, either, ogled the women. Alan saw that Commander Fillebrowne was nodding, raising an appreciative eyebrow, smiling a rogue's smile for every likely-looking lady – all but stroking a moustache he didn't have, in fact! All to no avail. "Ahem!" that worthy coughed finally, frustrated, his neck aflame below his fair hair.

Damme, the Venetians think we're *funny!* Lewrie gawped silently.

He took a diffident stance, their second tour of the gigantic salon, returning the cool, imperious, nose-high glances of the Venetians with a matching coolness, striving for Distant-But-Charming. But he saw amusement, a flicker of faint disgust – a subtle tilt of their heads, a tiny lift of expressive brows, or eyes that crinkled in mock horror to discover barbarian *foreigners* among the privileged. And it was the women most of all whose moist ruby lips cocked at one corner in faint revulsion. Worse, Lewrie could conjure... scant pity for the rude, crude, party-crashing English interlopers!

"Uhmm, this feels like a rum go, sir, why don't...?" Alan said from the corner of his mouth to Captain Charlton as he came level with his shoulder.

"Cuts a bit rough, I know, Lewrie, but..." Charlton said with a shrug, his own face frozen in a polite smile for one and all.

"Well, I've run dry, sir," Lewrie whispered, tilting his stem-glass. "You'll excuse me for a moment, so I may put in to 'water'?"

He broke formation and headed for a long buffet table where the wine was cooling, to snag a glass of something to soothe his bruised ego. It wasn't that he was trolling a line to hook a new doxy, after all, he told himself; that madness with Phoebe Aretino had been daft enough, thankee! Isn't as if I've been soundly *rejected* by Venetian ladies if I wasn't *tryin'* to put the leg over one of 'em, now, is it?

Still, he felt abashed and curtly dismissed. Like a stable man allowed in the parlour for the first time, 'stead of the kitchen garden. He wondered if he should pull a forelock of hair, or…

No, lads, you haven't a hope, he sneered, as he watched some of the junior officers craning their necks to look at a pair of approaching beauties. Neither have I, more's the pity. Oh, well… I s'pose that's best. Last thing I need is another dalliance, really. Another mistress, 'specially a rich Venetian one. The Venetians have covered their bets on amour round here.

He got a second glass of wine, savouring this one more slowly, as he began to observe the social doings of the Venetian elite; for his own edification, naturally… nothing more than that. How *would* the most beautiful women in Europe, in the most romantic city in the entire civilised world, carry off their affairs? he idly wondered.

After a few minutes, though, he cocked an eyebrow in wry amusement of his own. "Romantic, mine arse," he whispered softly. "Seen more enthusiasm from Greenwich pensioners!"

Lewrie had been raised in London, in Saint James's Square (not the *good* side, admittedly) under the indifferent care of his sire, Sir Hugo St. George Willoughby, in a house where a pretty chambermaid had two choices – getting "stuffed," or developing a fair turn of speed. In those times before Sir Hugo had gone smash, when they'd had "blunt" and *some* measure of social acceptance, he'd had entré to routs, drums, balls, salons and teas among the better sort. Well, perhaps not *quite* the better sort – rather the ones who'd admit the bastard son of the bastardly Sir Hugo.

When he wasn't being bounced from one public school to another, and that the result of his own actions, the result of drink, idleness and low companions (though he did post some rather good marks before the usual ouster!), he'd been under a rough sort of tutelage, when Sir Hugo could spare the time away from his usual pastimes – such as quim, money, gambling, quim, profit, pleasure, brandy and quim. Along with huntin', quim, shootin', fishin'… and quim. There were Belinda and Gerald, his half-sister and half-brother, as examples, too. One now a high-priced Drury Lane trollop, the other a sodomite, and, if God was just, *still* a press-ganged landsman in the Royal Navy – after Lewrie had discovered him in a London Docks buggery-hell, and pressed Gerald himself! Dead-drunk, conked on the noggin to begin with, and tattooed with fouled anchors before being delivered downriver to the Nore. It was the best three shillings, for that tattoo, that Alan had ever spent!

Anyway, with that family of his as tutors, Alan had come early to a prodigious knowledge of pleasure and romance, of the eternal verities of Love, such as… "Always get yer cundums from the Green Lantern in Half Moon Street. Sheep-gut's best. You get a maid 'ankled' – it's twenty pounds. You get a spinster girl of a good family pregnant, and I'll bloody kill you! Widows're best, 'grass' or real 'uns."

So he knew what flirtation looked like, what veiled passion or desire looked like. And this wasn't it.

Oh, there were men and women strolling together, heads close in simpering whispers. Fans, brows, mouths and lashes fluttered in what *seemed* the age-old game of Eros. Yet they looked so unutterably and listlessly *bored* by it all! As if just going through the motions of coyness, seduction, betrayal or flattery. To be polite, so please you!

No, the only thing that seemed to set their blood truly aflame were the gaming-tables. That was the only sport in the house that set bosoms heaving, lips atremble or breaths ashudder; made those painted, rouged, pasty-pale mannequins of men roar or whimper. Only a roll of the dice, a good card to take a trick, made women cry out in pleasure or distress. No, the gaming-tables were the only animated sign of natural life in the great-hall!

Romantic Venice! Lewrie sneered to himself. Awash in, and tolerant of, cats or not, the city was turning out to be…

"I say, there!" someone shouted. Actually shouted – and in an imperious, aristocratic En-glish drawl, too! "You there, sir! One in the sailor-suit!"

Lewrie swiveled about, trying to espy who was calling, and just who in a "sailor suit" he was jibing!

"Is that a man, wearin' king's coat?" A tallish fellow in the Venetian tricorne hat and hood – the *bauto* – disguised by a black-and-white bird–beaked mask, waved. A shorter, squarer version stood at his side, draped in a cape that seemed to hide a beef-cask figure. "Or is that king's coat wearin' the man, hah?"

"What the…!" Lewrie began to growl.

Until the taller figure first – then the shorter – ripped off their *bautos* and masks to come forward, hands extended.

"Alan Lewrie, you old rakehell, sir!" The taller one gushed. "What are you now, a bloody post-captain? Recall me, do ye?"

"Peter?" Lewrie exclaimed in shock, and stupefied to discover an "old school chum" in Venice, of all places. "Peter Rushton? And… damn my eyes, if that ain't Clotworthy Chute with you!"

Speakin' o' low companions, Lewrie cringed to be reunited with the idlest of the idle, the most Corinthian of Corinthians, boon companions of bottle, brothel or deviltry…! Was this a good idea? Or was Dame Fate slipping him another spoonful of "the dirty"?

"Give ye joy, Alan, me lad!" Peter Rushton shouted for all the world to hear, as he came up to embrace him like the Prodigal Son just come back from the swinery. "Give ye joy!"

Chapter 5

Peter Rushton and Clotworthy Chute, of all people! He hadn't seen or heard from them in years – for which he'd thanked a Merciful God more than once. At Harrow, Peter had been the Honourable, a second son not in line to inherit estates or peerage, dissolute and devilish, and out like most second or third sons to enjoy life to the dregs, instead of becoming boresome-but-proper firstborn heirs. The Navy, and the King's Regiments, were positively stiff with such young wastrels. Peter would have gotten the lesser title once his father had gone toes-up – Sir Peter Rushton, Bart., hereditary knight and baronet. Whilst his older brother – from what Alan could recall of a visit from that worthy to Harrow, in the *short* term Lewrie had spent there, a rather grim and forbidding hymn-singer – would rise from his current knighthood to be the next true baron, heir of all and a true peer of the realm. And Peter would remain on a short leash and a miserly annual remittance for the rest of his natural life – if his stern father and dour brother had any say in the matter! When flush, Peter tended to spread himself rather *wide* cross the world, beyond even his own rather thin-stretched bounds of sanity, in an orgy of Spending and Getting, ranti-poling and gambling, a true Buck Of The First Head who made even the most dissolute and depraved gawp in awe of his daring. Last Alan knew, Peter's short leash was £1,000 a year – a sum that could go in a single evening.

Clotworthy Chute, well... Clotworthy had always been the oily young swine, who could toady to his betters with the latest jest or the juiciest gossip, could badger and terrorise his inferiors, knew where and how to obtain drink, whores, copies of exams or alter test results, made small loans or steered fellow students who were "skint" or overextended to usurers of his own ilk. Tuppence here, sixpence there... then on to shillings, half-crowns and pounds. Last he'd seen of Clotworthy in London, winter of '84, he'd become a polished

"Captain Sharp" who lured newly inherited young "Chaw-Bacon" heirs, or "Country-Put" heiresses into both vice and poverty, posing as their smiling guide to what was Fashionable and Fast; finagling a hefty commission for his services, if not a loan he'd never repay. Chute knew to the pence just how much a body was worth, at first sight – and exactly how much he'd be able to "touch" them for.

Ain't the sort o' people I could *ever* introduce to Caroline, he told himself; nor the sort one wants down to the country for a week or two, either! Besides – they know too much about my younger days, and damme'f I want any o' *that* comin' out, now!

"So, what brings you to Venice, Peter?" Lewrie began charily.

"Kiss his ring, Alan, old son," Clotworthy wheezed. His fast life had included many good feeds indeed, Lewrie noted; Clotworthy Chute was quickly going to tripes-and-trullibubs. "Or his big toe, haw haw! I name to you, sir..." Here, Clotworthy had himself another good whinnying wheeze. "...the Right Honourable Lord Peter Rushton... Baron!"

"Mine arse on a band-box!" Lewrie recoiled in utter shock.

"That's 'mine arse on a band-box,' *milord*!" Peter whooped with glee. "Gawd, Alan... the look on yer face!"

"Well..."

"'*Turne, quod optanti Divum promittere nemo – auderet, volvenda Dies en attulit ultro*,' you old scoundrel," Lord Peter cited. "I b'lieve they *beat* that'un into us, hey? 'What none of the gods would have dared promise to your prayers, see what rolling Time has brought, unasked'? Pater passed over, round '86. Spent a *horrid* three years in the country... Desmond swore 'twas the Army for me or nothing; nor any money, either. Bought me a set of Colours with the 17th Dragoons. Not a captaincy, damn him, and told me to live on my Army pay. *Army* pay, I ask you! Why, the mess-bills took that the first week! But then, last year, Desmond had the good grace to pass over, as well—"

"Food poisoning, they said," Clotworthy interjected gaily. "A Frenchified, saucy somethin', wasn't it, milord?"

"A made-dish remove, *à la Mayonnaise*," Peter gushed. "Took him off by morning... fiancée, too, damn near. *And* her parents."

"The *last* time she tries to impress a suitor with her cookin', I warrant!" Clotworthy barked. "Avoid 'em, Alan, old dear. Avoid made-dishes like the very Plague!"

"…just *shy* of his wedding, d'ye see, Alan, so there wasn't an heir left standing," Peter breezed on, still sounding amazed by such a turn of fortune. "Acres, rents, title, seat in Lord's… Christ, can you feature it?"

"So, what brought you…" Lewrie insisted, not anywhere *near* being able to feature it. And wondering, with Clotworthy Chute along to help Peter spend his newfound fortune, if there'd be a farthing of that immense wealth left in six months!

"Grand Tour, old son." Peter chuckled. "Late to the game, but here we are, seein' the sights and all."

"Pete… uhm, milord," Lewrie amended, "I don't know you quite noticed, but… anyone tell you there's a war on?"

"Well, of course there is, Alan!" Peter hoorawed. "Spent time in the Light Dragoons, after all. But that's way over there. No, we came over to Copenhagen on a Swedish ship, neutral as anything. Spent some time there… *lovely* little city, *stap* me'f it ain't! By coach, into the Germanies. Dreadful bore-some, that…"

"Women like blacksmiths," Clotworthy shivered. "All arms an' moustachioes. Spit a lot, too. All that German, I expect."

"…Berlin, too." Peter laughed easily. "Lord, might as well be in Roosia. Flat as a tabletop, and cold as charity. Sullen brutes in the streets, worse than the London Mob. Bavaria, though…!" Peter said in awe. "Then, Vienna, too! *Splendid* place!" he brayed. "Then down to Venice for Carnival Season. *Leagues* away from the fighting… bloody *leaguès* away! Might even do Florence, Rome… there's talk of Constantinople 'fore we're done. See the splendours of the mysterious East, hmm? Or the Holy Land."

"Well, hmm, milord…" Clotworthy demurred. "That's Shockley's little side-trip, him and his new bride. And he can be a stodgy sort."

"Our traveling companions, Alan…" Peter told him. "Met them in Vienna. Sir Malcolm Shockley, baronet. Int'restin' fellow, do you enjoy investments, enterprises and such. *Beastly* rich, d'ye see…"

"More int'restin'z his *bride*, rather," Clotworthy snickered as he snagged a brace of champagnes from a newly arrived tray: one for his "patron" Lord Peter – and one for himself, of course.

"Well, yayss…" Peter drawled, lifting a brow significantly. "A little batter-puddin'… all peaches an' cream. A few years on her, but… still a 'goer.'"

"And, has she 'gone' yet for you… milord?" Alan drawled back, lifting his own brow.

"Hang it, Alan, 'twill always be Peter and Alan betwixt us!"

"Then…?" Lewrie prompted suggestively.

"No, damn her eyes." Peter sighed. "Not sayin' she don't have the rovin' eye, but… so far, she ain't rove in *my* direction. I just *may* be too poor. *Told* you Shockley was beastly rich. Iron, coal and *Lord*, I don't know what else!"

"Leather-goods, wool-spinnin' and cardin'," Clotworthy related with a sage tap on his noggin. And if anybody would know a rich man's business better than that man himself, trust Clotworthy Chute to know it, Alan told himself with a wry grin. "Five years ago, he was little more'n a Midlands farmer… bringin' in the sheaves, hey? Vast estate, but poor soil, so I heard. The sober, *hardworkin'* squirearchy sort."

Clotworthy seemed to shiver at that image he presented, as if it were an unnatural condition beyond the pale.

"But when the war began, he… bless me…! went into Trade! Or the next closest to it." Clotworthy posed with a faint sneer for an ungentlemanly nearness to *made* money. As if this Shockley were the cobbler or miner himself! Shrewd investments, crops and such, were one thing in English Society – but dealing with it directly, with no agent or solicitor as a buffer, was quite another!

"Now he makes uniforms, boots and knapsacks, saddles and all." Peter frowned in amused disdain. "That rocky estate of his turned out to be just *riddled* with oceans of coal and iron ore! So, he turned out his tenants and started grubbin'. Mines, smelters, foundries… *steam engine woolen mills*…? Makes just about everything now. And rakes in his guineas by the hogshead. By the *hogshead*, I tell you, Alan! Put some funds in with him soon as I get back home, I believe."

"Long as you don't spend 'em 'fore you get there, Peter," Alan chid him gently. "Still gamble deep?"

"Found religion," Peter quipped.

"You… bloody what?" Lewrie hooted. "*You?*"

"Income, and out-go, Alan," Peter joshed. "The ledgers. Long as Pater was payin' my bills… well, he couldn't let a son of his be known as a public debtor, now, could he? So, he covered me. Then it was Desmond's turn… such as it was. Inherit, though… know there's damn-all to fall back on if I squander it. Mean *t'say*…"

"Now it's *your* money, that is," Lewrie interpreted.

"Exactly!" Peter barked. "And it's nowhere *near* what I suspected… well. I'll take a hazard now and again, still. But…"

Lewrie looked at Clotworthy, who looked back at him and then tossed his gaze heavenward and rolled his eyes in failure, as if to complain that his free ride had gotten wary, and what he'd expected as his due wasn't to be forthcoming. Lewrie had to smile in commiseration. He remembered Peter as a charmingly amusing wastrel… but no one could ever have called him a *stupid* wastrel. And Peter had known Chute's wily ways, ever and anon. Amused by them, certainly, but never so much so as to be lured *that* far. No gullible cully, he; no calf-headed innocent!

"So, what brings *you* to Venice, Clotworthy?" Alan wondered.

"An heir." Clotworthy shrugged. "Series of young heirs, rather, who put their silly heads together and realised I'd gulled 'em. Before the Bow Street Runners and the magistrates could be sicced on me… and I still had all that lovely money!" He chuckled with bald-faced honesty. "Mean t'say, Alan…! I worked damn hard for it, if I do say so myself, and damme if they'd get a groat of it back before I'd had my joy of it! A long vacation in foreign climes seemed to be in order. And since Peter was off to soak up Culture…"

"Can you ever go back, though, Chute?" Lewrie asked him.

"Year'r two…" Clotworthy shrugged, appropriating an entire tray of champagne for the three of them from an irritated servant, who was clad in some livery that was grander than most full admirals back home. "Under another name, perhaps? The old fox never… ah!"

"Lord Peter!" some woman called out gaily. "Look at all I've *won*! Oh, aren't Venetian *casinos* simply heavenly?"

They turned to greet the newcomer, a short, petite blonde, who came forward with a spread lace handkerchief literally heaped with an entire pint of glittering Venetian sequins and ducats. Dribbling gold coins, which her maidservants scurried to retrieve before some Venetian loser found a way to retrieve his own fortune from her cast-offs. She was clad in a frothy but slimmer new-style gown, all shimmering silks and gauzy half-nothings which bared her arms and upper breast. A most impressive, milk-pale, sweetly cherubic breast, Lewrie noted, first of all. Infantlike, and only slightly pudgy arms, sure to be as soft and yielding as a baby's bottom, every toothsome morsel of her.

She was with a greyer older man, one who dressed neatly, soberly in bottle-green "ditto," though his watch-chain and fob, shoes and the gilt buckles upon them, the fineness of his linen, announced him as a man of great, though refined and subdued, wealth.

"Ah, Sir Malcolm… Lady Lucy," Peter began smoothly. "Allow me to name to you an old friend—"

"Oh, my *God!*" Lady Lucy Shockley shrilled aloud, causing a hitch to the orchestra. "It *is* you!" She declared, quite forgetting her new-won gold and strewing it over the marble floor in a tinkling shower.

"Is it… you?" Lewrie gasped in return, though thinking, Damme, one bloody surprise a night is *quite* enough!

And shivering in stupefaction to see her again, after so many years. Shivering, too, to see the furrow of irritation form on Sir Malcolm Shockley's brow. The man was the size of a Grenadier Guard, and people that big and brawny – and that bloody rich! – were best not nettled! *No* husband, in fact, with a face that wroth!

"Ma'am…" Lewrie tried to most-civilly purr, to begin a saluting "leg" of a bow. But she was up to him, upon him, before he could put one foot forward, and squealing with a most public delight. "S-so good to see you…" Lewrie stuttered. "Been years and *years*, what?" He added, for Sir Malcolm's benefit. And his own safety.

"Alan Lewrie!" she whooped. "Why, just *look* at you!"

"Lady Shockley… Lucy… *Lady* Lucy, uhmm…!" He gawped back.

Lady Lucy Shockley now… but long before, back in 1781, when he'd been a "newly" in the Caribbean – HMS *Ariadne* had been condemned, he'd served aboard the *Parrot* schooner, had come down with Yellow Jack, and had awakened to a vision from Heaven – Lucy Beauman, niece to his admiral, Sir Onsley Matthews, sent to Antigua to avoid the slave rebellions on Jamaica – and his unofficial "nurse" as he'd regained health. So fair-complected, so fair-haired, so petite and promisingly rounded! So blessed with eyes the colour of tropical shoal-waters! So unbelievably *rich*! And, at seventeen, so smitten with him.

Unfortunately, Lewrie recalled, about as ignorant as sheep! And pray God she's gotten wiser, since! he sighed.

Chapter 6

"Shockley," Lucy gushed to her new and suddenly testy husband, "Alan was my first love. Now, after all these *years*...! So dashing and brave a midshipman he was. Why, he fought a duel for my honour with that beastly soldier... *whatever* was his name?"

No, she hasn't learned a bloody thing. Lewrie sighed to himself again, determined to put a bold face on it anyway, and wishing there was a way to clap a gag in her mouth. Sir Malcolm gave him a look; one of *those* looks – the sort that promised swords or pistols.

"Lord, an age ago and more, Lady Lucy," Alan forced himself to chuckle. "Back in our *childhoods*, what?"

Well, let's not *trowel* innocence on, Lewrie warned himself. If he protested too loudly, it'd be a sure sign of guilt. Even if he had never even laid a finger on Lucy... not that he hadn't ached for a shot at her, God knows. Even if he'd "rattled" his way out of a union with her – and all her father's lovely money! – by having an affair with a Kingston town "grass widow," which had redounded to his bad repute when it had become public.

Sir Malcolm still wore a chary leer, one dubious brow up. What *did* the dedicated duellists call the situation? Lewrie wondered. "Grass Before Breakfast?" The grass one ate, face-down and dying... or those turfs of sod laid atop a fool's grave!

"And here you both are," Lord Peter blathered on happily, "and in Venice, of all places, for your *rencontre*. And both wed."

"Yes!" Lewrie enthused, ready to kiss Peter's ring, big toe or buss his blind cheeks for his statement. "Though I cannot recall you ever meeting Caroline, did you, Peter?"

"A brief glimpse, in '84... some chop-house on the Strand." Lord Peter frowned. "I think. Lovely girl, though. Wasn't she, Cloth-worthy?"

"We're in Surrey now... near Guildford," Lewrie rushed out. "We rent from her uncle, Phineas Chiswick. Three children now."

"You don't say!" Peter gawped.

"So what brings you to Venice, Sir Malcolm?" Lewrie enquired, turning to him.

"Ah, Captain Lewrie—"

"Commander," Lewrie corrected, tapping the single plain epaulet on his left shoulder.

"Commander Lewrie... as to why... we're on our honeymoon, as it were," Sir Malcolm related, unbending a little. "A Grand Tour I never had the chance for, as well, though Lucy did hers before, in company of her family. Surrey, hmm... rather a lot of sheep down there, now? You raise sheep, sir? Sell your wool to whom? A lot?"

"W-why..." Lewrie stuttered, unsure what happened to wool after it'd been shorn. That was Caroline's arranging, and as long as it gave them income, he wasn't particular. "Various agents, Sir Malcolm. Depending on the best offers. I've been away since '93, but for a brief refit at Portsmouth. Didn't even get home to Anglesgreen, so—"

"Oh, Shockley!" Lucy chid her husband. "Not business, now! Do give Alan a chance to get his breath before purchasing his output."

"Couple of hundred head, Sir Malcolm... sorry. Not much worth in comparison to others roundabout." Lewrie shrugged. "A glass with you, sir? To your good fortune and your happiness," he offered, snagging a brace of champagnes. "And many glad years of both, sir!"

"Commander Lewrie, we thought you'd gotten lost," Captain Charlton interposed, completing a third circuit of the salon, with the rest of his officers in tow. With a great sigh of relief, Lewrie did the honours for introductions, happy to trot out a Right Honourable Lord to his superior.

And Charlton, for all his stiffness, practically fawned upon Lord Peter, was aware of who Sir Malcolm Shockley was, and impressed by him as well! He gushed, as they all did, over Lucy's hand, offering slavering congratulations to the "happy new couple." After the cold shoulder they'd gotten from the haughty Venetians so far, to run into some fellow Britons was doubly welcome – and most especially that they were titled and rich... and, in Lucy's case, damned handsome! Commander Fillebrowne was almost ravishing her hand!

As for how they were all known to each other, Peter Rushton and Chute were glad to fill them in, relating those episodes of their days at Harrow together – including the Coach-House Incident, when they'd blown it to flinders and burnt it to the ground in revenge upon the school's new governor, who'd *dared* crack down on his riotous, rebellious students.

"And you the one with the port-fire, Lewrie... tsk-tsk," Captain Charlton mused. "The things one learns at public-school these days..."

"And a quick end to my days at Harrow, sir." Lewrie blushed.

"He was always forward and dashing, you know, Captain Charlton," Lucy supplied. "Burned a French privateer to the water-line, too, when he was a midshipman. And fought a duel for my good name at Antigua?"

"Cut the fellow, Lewrie?" Fillebrowne enquired archly. "Or did you blaze with pistols?"

"Cutlasses, sir," Lewrie told him smugly. "Killed him dead."

"Ah, hmm!" Lieutenant Knolles gasped, learning something new about his captain. Though with much more enthusiasm and appreciation than the "Ah, hmm!" that was forced from Fillebrowne.

"And have we made contact with our Venetian hosts yet, sir?" Lewrie asked.

Charlton sighed, cutting his chin toward a pair of men across the salon, who were being fawned upon by a whole herd of sycophants. One was garbed in a baggy, colourful harlequin's costume, jingling the bell-tasseled head of a Court Fool on a stick, and guffawing in a silly bray that sounded much like a drunken, demented donkey. The other of the pair was caparisoned in back-and-breast armour of the fifteenth century, such as one would see on ancient heroes who'd fought the Battle of Lepanto against the Turks, or sailed in Spain's Armada, with the long hose and puffy pantaloons, the leg-o'-mutton sleeves and stiff ruff collar, to boot. Though, on closer inspection, the man's plate-armour was very light papier-mâché, not steel. Nor was the enormous chopper of a harem-guarding eunuch's sword at his hip anything more than a silver-painted wooden caricature.

"One, would you believe, sirs, madam," Captain Charlton sighed, much put-upon, "is a member of the Three... the senior overcouncil of the Venetian Senate... more powerful than the figurehead Doge, it is said. T'other, well... I was *told* he was a senior general. I leave it to you as to which is which. There will be *no* business done this evening. They're having too good a time to be interrupted, don't you know! Tomorrow, perhaps... ten in the morning. An aide *said* ten, though our trade consul informs me that *may* mean noon or later. Before dinner... and siesta. The next morning, else."

"Ah, hmm…" from all, in one form or another, at that dismal news.

"Commander Lewrie, with Captain Rodgers off to Trieste, you're next-senior to me, sir," Charlton ordered. "Do you stand in my stead, tomorrow… a trip to their Arsenal, whilst I wait upon their Senate? I'm assured we may purchase Venetian charts of the Adriatic. Accurate and up-to-date charts. Something the Austrians at Trieste either will not share or were ignorant of, d'ye see?" Charlton pinched his nose at the bridge between his eyes, as if suffering a monumental headache.

"Of course, sir. Happy to oblige." Lewrie nodded. "A chance for a look-'round, at what their fleet—"

"You come ashore tomorrow?" Lucy interjected. "Oh, Shockley! We simply *must* have Alan to our lodgings for dinner! There's so much to catch up on. And I'm simply positive you both will get along like a house afire, why…"

Why don't I just slit my wrists now, Alan groaned, and avoid a bloodbath later? After making such an ass of himself over Phoebe Aretino, he was mortal-certain he didn't need another woman mucking up his life. Even were Lucy still single, still just as cow-eyed, just as… my word, *Dumb*…! as she'd been long before.

"I couldn't intrude 'pon your honeymoon, Sir Malcolm," Lewrie countered with a bluff and, he hoped, seemly modesty. "We're in port, and a neutral port, so briefly, with so many things to see to. Ships, d'ye see…" He shrugged. "You were married how long ago? Pardon my enquiring?"

"'Bout six months, sir," Sir Malcolm replied.

"Well, there you are, then… still in the first magic year of bliss!" Lewrie chuckled. "Ain't relatives and such to leave the new couple alone, sir? Besides…"

Something had gotten the Venetians excited at last, diverting his attention to the far end of the vast salon. Costumed people were shouting and waving their hands, the music was slithering to a halt and gamblers snatched up their wagers or winnings, left off their moans or sighs of pleasure to join one throng or another, swirling about like suddenly hostile mobs against each other, advancing up the great hall.

"Montagues and Capulets, ready to fight?" Lieutenant Knolles pondered.

"Must have run out of the *good* wine," Captain Charlton snickered.

"*I francisi!*" Someone wailed. "*I francisi!*"

The French! Lewrie didn't like the sound of that. Something with the Frogs involved was always rife with disappointment.

"The Austrians…" Captain Charlton translated, bit by bit, from the gist of a full hundred stammering commentators. "Bloody hell. Your pardons, Lady Shockley. The French have come east, it seems, sirs. And fought the Austrians… Montenotte… Millesimo… Dego. Wherever those places are. *Beat* them, by God!"

"Beat the French, sir?" Lieutenant Stroud of *Myrmidon* exulted in joy. "Why, that's marvelous news!"

"Ah, no." Charlton gloomed, of a sudden. "Seems the French have beaten the Austrians."

"Montenotte, that's inland from Savona, west of Genoa, Captain Charlton," Lewrie supplied. "The others are, too, I recall. We were there last year, working out of Vado."

"Marshal Beaulieu and his Austrians are in full retreat. Falling back on Alessandria." Charlton continued to interpret from snatches.

"Why, that's…" Fillebrowne blanched. "That's halfway between Genoa and Milan, sir! Fifty miles or better, from Savona or Genoa."

"Marshal Beaulieu, mean t'say!" Lord Peter Rushton barked. "I do believe… didn't we meet him in Vienna, Sir Malcolm?"

"We did, milord," Sir Malcolm averred, looking as irritated as he had with Lewrie's presence. "Damn impressive soldier, he seemed to me. Why, the man's reputed to be another Caesar, an Alexander! Off to join his troops for the spring campaign… military genius."

"Splendid party, that was, too. Lucky to be invited." Rushton chuckled. "Short introduction… their Emperor, too, why—"

"Fought the Piedmontese, too, it sounds like," Charlton grumped, interrupting. "Their General Colli. Is *he* reputed to be a military genius? Anybody? Well, then…" He clapped his mouth shut and went iron-spined, his face a natural mask as hard as any the Venetians wore. The eyes of the room were gradually shifting to them, their British guests: the only men in the room in real uniforms, the only men present wearing *real* steel at their hips. Allies of the Austrians, representatives of the government that sponsored the First Coalition against revolutionary, Republican France. People looked towards them to see how they handled this news, to read omens from their demeanour, for good or ill.

"My word," Charlton whispered to them. "*Routed* the Piedmontese, do we believe the tale. San Michele… Ceva. Hmm, it would appear this General Colli is *not* another Caesar or Alexander. Now, where are Ceva and San Michele? Fillebrowne? You're our Italian student."

"In Piedmont, sir," Fillebrowne muttered back. "I mean… they lie north and west of Genoa, sir."

"Anywhere *near* this Alessandria the Austrians are running for, though, Commander?" Charlton snapped.

"Uhm… I don't believe so, sir. Sorry."

"So, that means the Piedmontese are being pushed one direction… back into their own country," Captain Charlton summed up. "And the Austrians are being driven east, away from the Piedmontese. Don't like the sound of this. Rout, something… massacre, something. Venetians are either the most excitable people in Europe… starting at baseless rumours… or all four wheels have come off the coach!"

"Damme, sir, how could the Frogs…" Sir Malcolm Shockley said, shaking his head in disbelief. "Never was in the Army, d'ye see, but… they're led by corporals and sergeants, I heard. Poor-equipped as they are, as poorly led… peasant hordes, not real *soldiers*! How can they defeat the best army in Europe? Add up the pluses and minuses, do your sums… why, it's unheard-of!"

He made it sound like a solid business transaction, done between two honest tradesmen, which had inexplicably gone sour; as if the "art" of war were a hard, immutable science.

"New French general…" Charlton gleaned further from the swift, liquid Venetian Italian that swirled around them. And noting that even the gaily begarbed senator of the Three and that Venetian general were chewing their thumbnails and looking pasty-faced. "French columns just about everywhere they turn… foot, horse, artillery… like a *flood* of Frogs. Avalanche. Some fellow… Buony… no, Buonaparte. Bonaparte."

"Bonaparte?" Lewrie croaked aloud. "Or Buonaparte? Why, I've *met* the bastard, sir!"

"You *what*?" Several gasped as one.

"Siege of Toulon, sir," Lewrie explained. "Knew him then as a colonel of artillery. Buonaparte, he called himself. A Corsican. My… someone I knew from Corsica, at San Fiorenzo Bay, told me… *he* had known the family, 'fore they moved to Marseilles and we took Corsica."

Close, Alan thought; almost blurted out "my mistress" and "she"!

"Buonaparte was the one arranged the fall of the forts on those Heights of de Grasse, 'twixt the Little and the Great Road, which made Admiral Hood withdraw. Couldn't hold the anchorages with guns against us from *there*, sir. Sank my ship, too. Off to the east, in the Great Road."

"Do tell, sir," Charlton urged, fascinated.

Aye, give me a willin' audience, Alan smirked to himself, preening a bit. Married or no, impressing Lucy, and Sir Malcolm!

"*Zélé* was a floating mortar-battery. Mixed crew, Spanish bombardiers, Royalist French Navy gunners, and 'bout twenty hands off my last ship, HMS *Cockerel*. This Colonel Buonaparte spotted fire for the Frog mortars at Fort Le Garde and sank us. We got ashore, he rode down and took us prisoner... those of us that lived. She blew up, sir. Took my sword. My old sword," he added, clasping the hilt of his new hanger. "Before Spanish cavalry showed up from Fort St. Margaret to save us."

"So you've met him... face-to-face, sir," Charlton pressed.

"Aye, sir. Young fellow, 'bout early twenties or so," Lewrie expanded further, as they urged him to divulge all. "A wee sprog, bit taller'n a hop-o'-my-thumb. Slim, handsome in a way... eyes as old as Moses, though, sirs. Very grave and wily-looking. A knacky sort."

"And he took your sword?" Lucy wailed. "The one your captain gave you for saving your ship from that French privateer, the one you burned when he was down with Yellow Fever? That *lovely* hanger, with all the silver seashells?"

Lewrie almost winced!

Fifteen *years* ago, you silly mort, and you have to remember it so damned *well*? He saw that wary frown and furrow come back to her new husband's brow.

"Aye, that's the one," he could only grunt, and stare off into the middle distance, looking stern and longing for that missing mark of his honour. It didn't help that Lucy Shockley, *née* Beauman, could just as well recall every detail of what she'd worn to church on Epiphany of the same year! Earbobs, swords, moire-silk... it was all Fashion, to her. What grand things people wore!

"Why, the cad!" Lucy fumed. "Surely, one who'd just up and take another gentleman's sword is... well, he's certainly no gentleman himself! Little better than a thievish Frog!"

"Took it, did he?" Charlton asked. "Just because he wanted—"

"Asked for my parole, sir," Lewrie replied gruffly. "I could not give it, not and abandon my crew... the Royalist Frenchmen most of all. They'd surely have guillotined *them*, sir! So I handed it over, sir."

Captain Charlton gave a satisfied little grunt, nodded his head in approval, as most of the other men did, with tight-lipped smiles of that man-to-man appreciation of "having done the right thing" in trying circumstances.

"Pen me an account of that, sir," Captain Charlton decided as he drew out his watch to peer at. "Admiral Jervis may find any impression you formed of this fellow Bonaparte, or Buonaparte, useful. Hmm... it really is getting late, and our boat-crews are festerin' over at the *castello di lazaretto.* Much to do tomorrow, before we curtail this port-call of ours and get about our proper business... at sea, where we belong. Call it an evening, shall we?"

"Aye, perhaps," Sir Malcolm agreed. "Now that Lucy's won most of the *ridotto's* money, after all. After this news, I very much doubt the Venetians will be gay company. Shall we go, my dear?"

"Us, too, most-like, hey, Clotworthy?" Lord Peter tittered. "I would appreciate you calling, though, Alan... mean t'say, don't we owe you for 'tatties' yet? Will a shore supper suffice, before you sail? And you can catch me up on all your doin's. Been too damn long."

"It has, milord, and aye, I'd be grateful," Lewrie agreed with a smirk. "'Twas only two-and-six, but that was in 1780! The interest due should cover a meal and a bottle or two by now, hey?"

"Perhaps we could all dine together, Alan? Commander Lewrie, I mean t'say," Lucy posed, quite fetchingly and coyly. "And I may hear all about your wife and family... and how you've fared these many years."

"Yes... do come by, Commander," Sir Malcolm relented. "We'll all sup at our lodgings. Compare family and children, hmm?"

"I'd be delighted, Sir Malcolm, and thankee," Lewrie said, smiling as if he meant it. But he was sure there was a catch somewhere.

"Uhm, shouldn't we send word to Admiral Jervis, though, sir?" Commander Fillebrowne queried. "In light of this new development..."

"No, sirs," Charlton countered stubbornly. "First of all, let us wait for the morning to see if these rumours of battle and defeat are true or pure fantasy. And, if true... *how* true they are. Italian imagination may have inflated them far beyond reality. It all may come to be patently false or based on mere skirmishes, not an all-out invasion. Milord… Sir Malcolm… Lady Shockley… good evening to you all, sirs, ma'am. You will excuse us. Until the morrow?"

–

So, out of the *ridotto* they went, to their separate gondolas at the water-steps. Surprisingly, the denizens of the *ridotto*, once they had absorbed the tidings of a whole series of improbable French victories, had settled down to their pleasures again, as if their gambling-palace had been crashed by a beggar who'd raved in madness but had been ejected, and all was once again well with their world. Simpers, sighs, laughter… some of the embarassed sort, from people who'd made too much ado over nothing – climbed a chair to escape a ravening rat, which had turned out to be a child's dormouse. Sweets strains of violins, harp and flutes – Domenico Scarlatti, a local boy – could be heard wafting from the interior to the boat landing. Patrons leaving the same time as the English were fanning themselves, swaying to the music in personal dazes of idle joy once more. Once more masked, cloaked anonymously in their *bautos*, and lost in the beautiful dream that was the city of Venice.

A little further on, Lewrie thought it changed to something airy and even sweeter from Vivaldi as they were stroked down the canals for the Bacino di San Marco, the dulcet notes almost shimmering as gossamer and light as the sparkling lamplight on the ebony waters as they went past another *ridotto* or *palazzio* filled with guests and languid merriment. As they stroked away from it, out to the beginnings of a night-breeze off the sea, the sound faded slowly, tantalisingly, like the calls of the Sirens.

Captain Charlton handed them some treats he had purchased some-where on his circuitous and frustrating rounds of the hall – *diavoloni*, he called them, passing the ornate box around, sweet chocolates filled with creamy liqueurs or bran-dies. It was a most indolent way to end an evening, Lewrie thought. In a city without cares.

Then, as the *concerto* band faded at last, astern their gondolier began to croon, picking up the song of another, far across the Bacino at the Fondamenta di San Marco; the other a single tiny light in the gloom:

Fummo un tempo felici

Io amante ed amato,
voi amata ed amante in dolce stato…

"Ees-uh Signore Tasso, signores," he told them. "Greatest of-ah them all. A true poet of-ah love! You come-ah to Venice… you find-ah love, *signores*!"

Christ, I bloody *hope* not! Lewrie yawned to the night.

Chapter 7

"Come!" the voice within HMS *Lionheart*'s great-cabins bade.

Lewrie entered, hat under one arm and his clumsy, rolled bundle of charts under the other. Captain Charlton was in his shirtsleeves with his waistcoat open, sleeves rolled to the elbows and scrubbing his face at a wash-hand stand. Though the winds had come up from the south that day, and quite fresh, they'd brought a stifling, palpable humidity to a city lying that far north. A first sign of true summer – along with another flood in Saint Mark's!

"Ah, Lewrie... back with yer charts, I see!" Charlton beamed as he took a towel from his steward to complete his ablutions. "Damn-all *close* ashore today. Winds or no. I'm fair parched... as I 'low you may be, also. A glass with me, sir?"

"Delighted, sir," Lewrie replied, more than happy to be given a glass of something cooling.

"No Frog champagne, I fear, sir." Charlton shrugged in apology as he rolled down his sleeves, redid his neck-stock and rebuttoned his waistcoat. "Though this Austrian *sekt* I discovered ashore is just as sprightly, if a tad too sweet. Ah, well... 'twill serve, I trust."

"Most nicely, sir," Lewrie allowed, plunking into a comfortable padded chair at Charlton's genial insistence and accepting a glass of Austrian almost-champagne from the steward. It was very cool, indeed.

"Metal bucket, sir," Charlton informed him with an amiable grin to Lewrie's raised brow in query. "Cool water to begin with, then salted heavily. Soak a bottle an hour or two, then... Now, sir. Did they have the charts we need?"

"I obtained a full set for every ship, sir," Lewrie replied as he unrolled one for example. "General chart of the Adriatic, and just as detailed as one could wish. Two more each, in smaller scale, dividing the Adriatic into upper and lower halves... one of the Ionian isles, and harbour charts for their principal ports. Not much on the Austrian or Hungarian littoral ports, though. And for the Turkish possessions they're rather sketchier. As though Venetian ships haven't gone close inshore in the last century, sir. The Balkan shores are by guess and by God, sir."

"Yayss…" Charlton drawled lazily. "Since the Treaty of Utrecht in 1714, they've written off any hopes of reclaiming lost territory over there. So why bother to correct one's charts concerning what one may not have, hmm? *Terra incognita*. 'Here be dragons,' that sort of thing. Out of sight, and out of mind. The Venetians are rather good at that, letting things slip their minds, if nothing can be done about them anyway. Or, rather, if they're too vexing to think *about*!"

"I take it things went well, ashore today, sir?" Lewrie asked.

"As much as could be expected, Commander Lewrie," Charlton said with a weary, frazzled air, running a hand over his greying hair. "We will be allowed to enter Venetian ports in the Ionians, their territory in Montenegro, Albania and such – for wood and water, only, d'ye see. And that for no more than twenty-four hours at a time, weather permitting. They've sent orders for their local governors and such to admit us as long as we pay *scrupulous* attention to their neutrality. Do we violate it, however, they'll deny us entry. With their full force of arms, was how they phrased it to me."

"I shiver in my boots, sir," Lewrie scoffed.

"How come you by that, sir?" Charlton snapped quickly.

"Beg pardon, sir, but… *what* force of arms?" Lewrie rejoined. "At the Arsenal this morning, Captain Charlton. Lord, what a pot-mess! They've ships laid up in-ordinary, two-a-penny, aye, sir. But they're rotting at their moorings! Harbour watch and anchor watches set, with warrants and their families living aboard. *Bearded* with weeds, sir! Forecastles and waists built-over with huts or shacks, like receiving-hulks back home, sir. No seamen to be seen, and damn few naval officers. No ships under construction, sir… no ships being fitted out or repaired. Place was full, but idle as Sunday in Scotland. Hundreds of idlers loafing about, *pretending* to do some chores."

"Like our own HM Dockyards, hmm?" Charlton posed.

"A thousand-fold worse, sir," Lewrie scoffed. "It's more like a series of palaces than a dockyard. Dependents of yard workers swarming like drone bees, but damn-all *work* being done. There are fountains in the Arsenal yards, sir. *Wine* fountains! Not temporary, for Carnival, but permanent stone fountains. Shift a couple of planks… go get yer cup o' wine. Tally salt-beef barrels… wet yer whistle again, sir. Then line up for dinner, sir… on the house, and take as much as you like. Then wash it down with more wine. All free, sir. Like a Roman dole. Bless me, Captain Charlton," Lewrie concluded his accounting, "they couldn't put a decent squadron together to overmatch ours were we to give 'em 'til Christmas!"

"Surely a seafaring nation, though, Commander…" Charlton said in puzzlement. "Mean t'say, Mistress of the Seas for nigh on a thousand years! The Arsenal must be *crammed* with stores, just waiting—"

"Bare-bones, sir," Lewrie interrupted. "Mast-ponds half-empty, very little timber seasoning… the rope-walks were idle, and I didn't see that much spare ropes or cable coiled up and ready. Mountains of shot piled up, hundreds of guns ashore… but more than a *little* rusty, from what I could see of 'em. I don't think the Venetians could sail out a force larger than the Austrians at Trieste could, sir."

"Yet, after the news this morning…?" Charlton puzzled some more. "Forgive me, sir… but I was able to confirm those rumours we heard at the *ridotto*. The French, under this new general Bonaparte, did beat the Austrians and the Piedmontese and split them apart. Even worse, so the Venetian authorities told me not two hours ago, they were *not* minor skirmishes, but all-out battles. The Austrians lost over six thousand men, sir, and were damn near routed! And there's been another battle with the Piedmontese… at Mondovi."

Charlton gloomed up, took a sip of *sekt*, and wriggled his lips as if in distress, to be the bearer of even worse tidings.

"At Mondovi, Commander Lewrie," Charlton intoned, "may we trust the account, the Pied-montese were also routed. And an entire corps of their army captured. Their General Colli has asked for an armistice… and that was several days ago. It may have been signed by now. So you see what that means, sir?"

"Piedmont's defeated." Lewrie gulped. "Out of the war. Out of the Coalition. And all Italy west of the Po River is now held by French troops?"

"Correct, sir. They may now march east into Lombardy at their leisure, using any route they fancy, from the Riviera to the Alps. I will give you and Fillebrowne more details soon as we are all together this evening. Did you see Commander Fillebrowne ashore during your travels, Lewrie?"

"Aye, sir," Lewrie grunted. "Dined with him. We were all together at the Shockleys' lodgings."

"So, he should be back aboard *Myrmidon* soon. Good." Charlton nodded. "And we may sketch out our operations, now we own such fine charts. Dine you both aboard, say... four bells of the First Dog?"

"Looking forward to it, sir," Lewrie told him with a pleasant grin, though inwardly less than enthusiastic from all he'd just heard. And what he'd seen and heard earlier.

–

In his own shirtsleeves, he pored over his new set of Venetian charts, in the privacy of his great-cabins aboard HMS *Jester*. Andrews was puttering about, polishing the fittings of his sword's scabbard to get rid of the smuts of a morning's handling. A glass of cool Rhenish sat near his hand on the desk. Toulon didn't care for the scent of any wine, so he left it alone after a tentative sniff. Though he *did* like the crinkly feel of those new charts! And those corners that didn't bear any tooth-marks yet...!

"Fine navigator you are," Lewrie cajoled, shifting the cat off the middle for a third time, exposing a maze of islands off the Balkan shores. In keeping with the times, he supposed, their original Venetian names were now in very small letters, and were mostly labeled with odd Slavic names, which mostly began with *otok* – followed by a string of consonants that only the *very* inebriated would even *try* to pronounce. Like someone had slapped the entire Bahamas or Windward Isles from the West Indies along the shore... it looked to be a Paradise for any ship bent on escape. Soundings showed fairly good deep water, right up to the steep coastlines, too, and very few shoals to bar a fleeing French vessel from taking any course she pleased, once inside the isles. He and the rest of the squadron would be haring after them like hounds in a game-park back home, dodging the mature oaks and bramble patches, and their prey – the hare – able to double back, then sit and laugh at it all, as they lost the scent where it had crisscrossed itself time and again.

Flop went Toulon, crushing the Balkans once more, on his side... tail lashing and legs outstretched for a tussle. "*Mrrr!*" he urged.

"Catlin', why..." Lewrie sighed, then gave up. He began to play pat-a-cake between Toulon's front paws, to touch him gently on the belly, before escaping his grasp. Toulon always started with claws sheathed... but that didn't last a minute, once he got excited.

The Italian shore (the one the cat wasn't smothering) looked to be more promising, though dangerously shoal and marshy. Lewrie thought that any French ships trading in the Adriatic – or any French warships – would stick to that side, to aid their cause in the north, if nothing else. Or distract Neapolitan, Venetian or Austrian troops to another threat, to further their army's successes against Piedmont. There was a slim hope that they wouldn't have to get tangled up in the snares of the Balkan shore and those islands. It was still a backwater to the real war.

He paused, took a sip of his wine and rose from the desk to go rummaging in the chart-space for other sources of information. Toulon padded after him, leapt to the top of the chart-table, and cried for their game to resume. Lewrie unfolded a map of northern Italy – not a sea-chart, but a true landsman's map – over Toulon, of course. And that was a special treat for him, to play Blind Man's Bluff from under cover.

It was frustrating; half the places Charlton had mentioned, such as Ceva and Montedotte, weren't shown. But Alessandria was, and Mondovi and that Cherasco, the Po River, Milan, Turin and Pavia.

"Damme," Lewrie breathed.

Cherasco wasn't a day's march from Turin, the capital of Piedmont. If the Austrian commander, Marshal Beaulieu, was falling back on Alessandria, then he'd left the line of the Po unguarded! If that little bastard Bonaparte, or Buonaparte, had marched that fast, over such a distance, from Piedmontese front to Austrian front and back... he had a clear shot at Pavia, Alessandria... even Milan, the capital of the Austrian archduchy of Milan! He'd struck Lewrie as a knacky little shit back in '93 – active as anything. Oh, but surely not!

There were fumblings and delighted little purrs from beneath the map as Toulon fought it. A tap or two, and he was whirling and clawing, creating an earthquake under Lombardy.

"Peek-a-boo, Toulon!" Lewrie whispered with a smile, peeling the map back to fold up. He was answered with a loud purr, and the cat laid out on his back, all four paws in the air and waving for sport.

Would they be going home, back to Admiral Jervis, after this? Lewrie wondered as he picked up Toulon and carried him back to the desk. With all the excitement for the summer happening far away, it didn't seem reasonable that their squadron could accomplish much for the good in the Adriatic.

Maybe send Fillebrowne for fresh orders, Lewrie speculated, and good riddance to bad rubbish! Before he…

Granted, Lewrie hadn't been in a charitable mood after leaving the Arsenal, after seeing how low the mighty Venetian Navy had fallen. He'd been a tad leery, too, of spending any more time with Lucy or her forbidding husband, Sir Malcolm. Or of having Peter Rushton get cherry-merry with drink and gush out things of the past that were best left in the past. Or dealing with that wily criminal, Clotworthy Chute! What could come out, what *more* social trouble could he tumble into, once they got to gossiping over old times? And his part in them?

Thankfully, Peter and Clotworthy had been away – off on their own low amusements, he suspected – but, to equal their pestiferous presence, Commander William Fillebrowne had turned up instead!

Of all gentlemen in the Royal Navy, Lewrie knew smarm when he heard it, having dished out more than his fair share in his time. And Commander Fillebrowne had been most definitely smarmy!

"Horrid foreign custom, sir," Fillebrowne had chortled, "the Venetian habit of *cicisbeo*. A proper Venetian lady must have one, d'ye see – with her family's approval, of course. Chosen with more care than her mate, I'm told, from only the finest select of Society. One never chooses from a lower ranking than oneself… that'd be a mortal shame, d'ye see."

"Why, whatever is it, Commander Fillebrowne?" Lucy had goggled, all coy and frippery as a minx.

"Her guide through life, her *amanuensis*," Fillebrowne had sworn in much good humour. Rather a *leering* humour, Lewrie'd thought. "This *cicisbeo* holds her muff, her cloak… trails along and steers her over her introduction into Society. Part dancing-master, diplomatic representative… tea-fetcher, hand-holder, father-confessor… some say her lover…!"

"Sir!" Sir Malcolm had barked, damned displeased by such talk.

"Her catch-fart, d'ye mean, sir?" Lewrie had interjected. "A simpering twit to stroke her ego?"

"Uhm… that too, Commander Lewrie," Fillebrowne had agreed. "It is said, I believe, that he is her lifelong teacher in all things. A male chaperone, admitted to her dressing chamber with her maids."

"Sure you're pronouncing it right?" Lewrie had scoffed, eager to both skewer Fillebrowne – simply because he'd taken a hot dislike to him – and to reassure Sir Malcolm that he was no danger himself. "We saw them, didn't we, Sir Malcolm, at the *ridotto*? Mincing about like so many 'Mollies' in men's clothing? It's certain to be said more like '*sissies*-bay-oh.' Sissy-boys."

"Hah!" Sir Malcolm had barked again; this time with amusement.

"A lifelong triangle… wife, husband and *cicisbeo*," William Fille-browne had insisted, sticking to his original pronunciation. "I have it on good authority. *Unspeakable* people, the Venetians. Every Italian society, for that matter." He shrugged off, as if he'd meant no more than to be entertaining, and informative. "Horrid custom!"

"Ah, dinner!" Sir Malcolm had enthused as the food arrived.

Witty, charming and amusing, had Fillebrowne been. Lewrie had let him have the stage, preferring to deal with Sir Malcolm over mills and weaponry, casting cannon, good swords and such. Yet, round the beef course, there'd come a sly, secretive stroking along the side of his boot beneath the table!

Better *not* be Fillebrowne! Alan had frowned to himself. Secret "Molly," is he? Oh, Christ, no!

Dining *en famille* on a spacious balcony overlooking the Grand Canal, seated at the opposite corners of a four-place table, there was no way Fillebrowne could reach him. And it surely wasn't Sir Malcolm! Lewrie warranted. He was all stocks, money and business talk.

No, directly across from him was Lucy, smiling so sweetly that butter wouldn't melt in her mouth, her huge aquamarine eyes so saintly-wide and cherub-innocent…! Yet, in one covert second, when conversation had lagged and the only sound was the scrape of knives and forks on fine Venetian glass plates – she'd cut her eyes to him, to see, had he noticed! And she had seemed almost amused when he'd drawn his feet away from her soft, slippered caress, or scooted his chair back a wary inch or so more!

Why, the brainless, pox-riddled trull! he'd snorted in affront. Not wed a year, and she's makin' sheep eyes at me again? Me, a man wed and… well, maybe what's in my soul shows, plain as day. But no! Not again. Not with her, certain!

They'd caught up on family doings. Her father and mother back in England, in the Midlands, along with her foppish brother Ledyard. Floss and her husband, her oldest brother and his wife Anne… and a rather sultry and seductive Anne, Lewrie had recalled in spite of his best intentions…! still in Jamaica running the plantations and the sugar, rum and molasses trade. There'd been a first husband, but he'd died in '89. There were children, now old enough to be left in care of governesses, or Eton school. Sir Malcolm's brood was grown, adult and away on their own pursuits.

"Heavens, Alan," Lucy had almost wailed in remembered grief. "After… I was disconsolate. Even after two years of mourning. But mother and father insisted I go to Bath to take the waters. And a bit of joy. And suddenly, one night in the Long Rooms…!"

She'd given Sir Malcolm a doting smile at that point, tou-sled a stray lock of his hair over his ear. And the old colt's-tooth had almost whinnied in shy delight to be so fawned over!

"Neighbours… not twenty miles betwixt us, all that time, but of different parishes…!" Lucy had gushed. "Father an investor, in the early days, though Shockley had never come to call upon us."

"How fortunate are life's turnings," Sir Malcolm had managed, blushing to the roots of his hair, but gazing upon his dazzling younger wife with nigh-on total adoration. "How surprising…"

"Serendipity, sir," Lewrie had recalled. "From Dr. Johnson's lexicography. I think. To seek one thing of value, and unexpectedly come upon another of even greater delight, totally unlooked for."

"How true, sir!" Sir Malcolm had sworn with heat. "How true!"

And God help the poor bastard, Lewrie thought, tossing off his Rhenish. She always *was* a brainless bit o' baggage. Spooning over the old toad… and running her toes over me at the same time! And over Fillebrowne, when I wouldn't serve, I think.

Round dessert, Lucy had turned to Fillebrowne for a time, and he'd gotten a strangled look, just after she'd shifted in her chair. Followed by lidded, half-hooded eyes, Alan remembered. And a damned smug air about him, too!

Damme, is she so bound and determined to put "horns" on Sir Malcolm Shockley, she ain't particular who tops her, 'long's it's done? She'd been just close enough to reach *him* with her tiny foot; he'd got that sleepy ram-cat look right after. A righteous man, Lewrie suspected, Sir Malcolm hadn't noticed. But then, the husband was always the last to suspect, in any event. And well Lewrie knew of that, and prospered from it in his wilder days among the "grass widows."

Should he suspect her himself? he wondered. An *innocent* man'd not. But then, he *wasn't* an innocent, was he? An innocent man would never have even caught that play between them. If that was what it was.

It wouldn't square up, dammit! What he'd known of Lucy Beauman in the West Indies, with her wide-eyed innocence, her blessed lack of worldly knowledge and weariness, well... perhaps people changed over a decade. But not by *that* much, surely.

And she'd been so fluttery and charming as she'd seen him out, as he'd departed before Fillebrowne. Just as if any flirtation between her and Fillebrowne had never occurred, and he was still her target! A ploy to let him know she was available? Alan speculated. A way to whet his interest, by using Fille-browne – to make him *jealous*?

–

"Pahh!" He spat softly.

"Sir?" His cabin-steward asked, leaving off his silent puttering.

"A top-up, Aspinall," he told him. "And before I forget again, tell my cook I'll dine aboard *Lionheart* this evening."

"Aye, sir," Aspinall replied, headed for the wine-cabinet.

Not that I *didn't* wish to top her long ago, Alan recalled, in his reckless, wild single days. Well, more reckless than he was *now*, he amended. In his teens, sure the Navy was a short wartime career, he'd been a penniless but handsome midshipman, 'bout the most fetchin' Mid there was in the entire West Indies, he reckoned smugly to himself. Dashing and rakehell, a born Corinthian, with that damme-boy glint to his eye that made prim maidens' hearts go all aflutter. The bad'uns *always* got the interest of the good'uns! And her family had been so rich, whilst he hadn't a hope of an inheritance, a living of any sort, beyond a poor remittance from his father – whenever Sir Hugo had remembered, or felt like, sending it. There had been hopes for a match, her family had been almost disposed to it, should he make something of himself, earn a commission. Well, he'd blown the gaff to the wide, now, hadn't he? He'd thought about her, even years after, had fantasies alone in his narrow bed-cot, and months at sea...

No, *stop* yourself, you damn fool! he chid himself sternly. She is married. So am I. And not a "grass widow," put out to pasture once the heirs were born, and a bored husband off with a mistress for sport.

And Sir Malcolm's so *perishin'* big! he reminded himself. Not of the "understanding" sort of fast-livers, or the City aristocrat circle, who'd stand aside or tolerate weekend "country house" games. Not the kind, Lewrie thought, who'd partake of a mistress on the side, either. One of those "all or nothing" gentlemen, in such *decent* love.

He'd have his fetchin' little wife *all* to himself, Lewrie realised, or put both of 'em in the cold, cold ground and be satisfied with the nothing. Made enough of a fool of myself, anyway, with Phoebe Aretino, and I'll not make *that* mistake again!

And certainly not with a married woman, not a married *English* lady. Mean t'say, damme... there are rules! 'Less both parties are amenable – that's the way it's always worked! But for a man to intrude into a reasonably happy marriage, well... *that*, he'd always held, was a caddish deceit.

Now, Zachariah Twigg trots Claudia Mastandrea 'cross my hawse again, he mused as Aspinall refilled his wineglass and he took a sip to cool his blood... or I cross *some* fetchin' mort's hawse... hmm. A night or two of "puttin' the leg over," four thousand miles and nigh on two years away from home, well... no harm in that. Long as it's foreign mutton... a mort I don't know. A decently amusin' courtesan... not a street whore... o' the commercial persuasion...?

But not Lucy. Definitely not! he swore to himself. And no matter how temptin' the bait she offers. Swear it, God. Swear it on a stack o' Bibles!

He put his left hand out as if to make that oath that instant. Unfortunately, his hand came down upon the desk, half upon a pile of notes from the Ship's Surgeon, Mr. Howse, and half upon Toulon's rear, quite near his "nutmegs." Lewrie glanced down. Howse's notes were on the number of seamen treated with the Mercury Cure for the Pox, after their last stay in port, out of Discipline.

He didn't think that boded too well as an omen for that stern "resolve" of his.

Chapter 8

One in the morning, and he'd been called from his bed, a regal and welcoming-soft real bed, in the *palazzio* of Count Salmatori, after a brief, bone-weary and dreamless sleep since eleven, when the Piedmontese legates had arrived in Cherasco. And still, they tried to quibble, these Royalists, these trimmers, who thought war a game, and victories and defeats temporary intrusions into their elegant lives of luxuries and privilege, serenely hair-splitting to maintain a shred of Divine Right for their odious king, Victor Amadeus.

Signores Salier de la Tour and Costa de Beauregard were both bland and vexingly obscure and sneaking. The general had had enough. Four days of marching almost without sleep, all across the foothills of the Appenines and the Alps, through narrow passes, along winding tracks in the mountains – horse, artillery and foot. And he'd fought battles so often, he'd lost count, though Berthier had it all written down. Won them all, routed them, stampeded them, slain them or took them prisoner. And still, Victor Amadeus the sleepy – called King of the Dormice for constantly nodding off in public – that vain bigot, champion of a new Bourbon monarch on the throne of France, that vicious old beast who'd revived the Inquisition against his own people, whinnied and shivered in dread of his folly, not a day's march away, and tried to negotiate favourable terms for himself! As if doing France the favour!

General Bonaparte yawned in their faces, then drew out his watch.

"…so you see, Your Excellency, the terms are so harsh," Signore Costa carped, pausing for a moment when he saw that this young Frenchman wasn't listening. "To take the fortress of Cuneo, the key to our whole Alpine frontier, as well… along with the monetary demands—"

"Since drawing the document of armistice up, Signore," Bonaparte snapped in good Italian, "I've also captured Cherasco, Fossano and

Alba. I've broken your army, broken your line at the River Tanaro and stand on the River Stura here at Cherasco. You ought to consider my demand moderate. It is now one in the morning, *signores*. I have ordered an attack across the Stura, to begin in one hour. At two, my armies," he lied most plausibly, looking red-eyed, haggard and remorseless, as unkempt and grumpy as a fiend from Satan denied blood, "march. And then, with no forces worth the name to oppose me, I will be in Turin tomorrow night. Where there will *be* no negotiating."

"Signore general, Your Excellency," Costa de Beauregard whined with his hands out in supplication. "Sacred honour was pledged, to the Austrians, the British… to stand by them—"

"Yet where are they, to stand by you, *hein*?" Bonaparte sneered. "Hard to stand, on your knees, under a heavier yoke than this I offer. Your answer. Accept my terms now – or nothing later."

Salier bowed his head, almost in tears. Costa looked at him and nodded his sad assent, as well. "Very well, Excellency. We will sign."

"*Bon!*" Napoleon Bonaparte nodded with them, grunting a tired but satisfied sound. Yet he then sprang from his elegant gilded chair at once, calling for coffee, as if his bone-weariness had been a sham. He went to a farther, smaller salon where his maps had been set up.

He allowed himself a wolfish smile, now his back was turned to those groveling Piedmontese envoys. Piedmont was his, just as he had schemed, their army and their will to fight crushed. The Austrian, Beaulieu, of the much-vaunted but slow-mincing "best army in Europe," had been gulled into taking his bait. His demand for free passage in the Genoese Riviera had, naturally, been told to the Austrians by the Genoese, and Beaulieu had come too far south, dividing that mightier combined army into eatable pieces. And Bonaparte had whirled between them, outflanking, out-marching, bloodying their noses in turn, destroying the corps each had sent to aid the other. Now Beaulieu was scrambling, faithlessly abandoning his allies, rushing for fortified Alessandria, taking the fastest roads to end up, Bonaparte was mortal certain, at the Austrian Archduchy of Milan's most powerful border fortress, that brooding monster at Pavia. Without having to enter Turin or force a crossing of the Stura, he could now wheel east and harry his rear and flanks before Beaulieu reached it. Send Massena, Augereau, or Serurier down to demonstrate before Pavia, and hoodwink him again!

General Bonaparte had always loved maps, along with mathematics. Precise maps, over which he could feel he soared like an omnipotent bird of prey, *feeling* every rise, every defile, every spot where troops could be hidden behind a fold, every possible place of ambush, like an eagle might ride an updraft. Pavia was far too strong, would result in weeks of siegework, and he didn't have the manpower or the time for such. A Royalist French Army had broken itself there long before, against an Austrian threat, and a French king, Francois I, had ended imprisoned. But there *was* a way across the Po River, at a place that would out-flank Beaulieu one more time, catch him wrong-footed, and let him threaten Milan itself. He ran his finger down the line of the Po to Piacenza. Maillebois's French Army had crossed that far downstream, just there at Piacenza, in 1746. A day's rest, a chance for his footsore army to loot more boots, grain and wine from the Piedmontese, and he would be off. Off on another lightning-quick march, and turn the Austrians' flanks, force them off the Ticino River, out of Pavia… or lose the garrison they left behind, after he'd beaten the field armies.

And the way was straight; the ground was good. Lovingly, his forefinger traced the topography, the turns in the roads, the rises of hills and the steep defiles of creeks that fed the Po. Few men had The Sight he knew he did. Very few commanders could form a vision of the ground from a map, as if they'd walked it from a common soldier's level. Not many knew how steep and demanding a hill without ever first seeing it; could spot, as if inspired, where guns should go to support attack; or sweep the *only* route a foe would have for a counterattack. It was, to General Napoleon Bonaparte, such a simple, instinctive thing, to have this Sight. And he was sure after only a few days' manoeuvring that neither his opponent Marshal Beaulieu, nor any of his lesser corps commanders had it.

"Excuse me, *mon général*," Junot yawned. "They've signed. Piedmont is ours. And a courier has come from Commissioner Saliceti. He's on his way and will arrive around dawn, the courier estimates."

"Hah," Bonaparte grunted, abandoning his map, letting it curl back up like a loose sausage. "Saliceti."

The army's chief representative from the Directory was a criminal, a vainglorious coxcomb. His uniform was grander than Bonaparte's, replete with red-and-white sash, bullion-trimmed, and he sported a hat so aswim in dyed feathers he could be seen from a newfangled kilometer away. Saliceti would come, like it was *he* who was the conqueror, with purse and saddlebags open to scoop up the loot that Bonaparte amassed for him. A part of it, the young general suspected, never made it to Paris's coffers, but stuck to Saliceti's grubby fingers, too! He'd not made things so harsh for the Piedmontese they'd keep their backs up, after all. He'd omitted to list specific paintings, statues and valuables from Victor Amadeus's palace that Paris had wished "for the enjoyment of the French people." Or so the Directory claimed. There was sure to be a row over those. Well, then, so be it. He had a war, *his* war, to fight – his way. Let the civilians squabble over the remains of his victories.

"Anything from Paris?" Bonaparte asked hopefully.

"Nothing, sir," Junot had to admit. Nothing from the Directory, *certainement;* but that meant nothing for the general from his wife, the incomparable Josephine, either. Junot almost scuffed the toes of his elegant high boots in chagrin. The general wrote her daily, yet there were entire weeks between her replies.

"Ah, well," Bonaparte sighed, not showing his disappointment. "The envoys have their coffee?"

"*Oui, mon général.*" Junot brightened. "Though they might have felt insulted. We only had the poor cups from your *portmanteau*, with the brass army spoons."

"A smaller equippage than when I was an artillery officer," the young general said, feeling full of energy once more. "A tale to tell them, I think. I've made rough notes for the army's movements in the morning. Flesh them out for Berthier to pass on. A requisition upon Cherasco for eight thousand rations, four thousand bottles of wine, and for every civilians' boots. You must have it copied and passed to the town council at once. Along with the usual warning about resistance from the populace, in any form. Reissue my caution to the troops about rape, pillage or indiscriminate looting, of course."

"*Oui, mon général,*" Junot sighed, knowing he would be robbed of even a tiny nap the rest of the night and would slave far into a new day.

"...clerks to copy the route-marches for the day after, with a map of the roads to Piacenza for each chief of division," Napoleon rattled on, striding back towards the larger salon. "And invent for me a proclamation... to the people of Italy. Of Italy, mind, not the principalities, *hein*? Mention respect of property, of their religion and customs, and blahblah-blah. To placate them. And stir up those who dream of unifying the whole peninsula. Even if it will be unified under French rule, Junot." Bonaparte snickered cynically. "Something about us, uhm… waging war with generous hearts, in there somewhere."

"Generous hearts, *oui, mon général*." Junot scribbled hastily, pacing alongside his shorter bantam-roosterish commander.

"…only against tyrants who seek to enslave us, not the common people… against all tyrants. *That* ought to stir up the shit-pot. Dash off something and show it to me before Saliceti arrives. I will be with these sheep-faced cowards 'til then. Sweetening their cup of gall we just forced them to drink, *hein*? And Junot?"

"*Oui, mon général?*"

"More coffee. A lot more coffee!" Bonaparte demanded, laughing out loud, for a rare change. "Ah, *signores*! A momentary delay, sirs. Now I may have some coffee with you, if you will permit? Sorry about the spoons and poor cups, but a soldier's *portmanteau*… I now get along with less than when I was in the Royal artillery…"

And he whirled away, instantly affable, as if he'd just had seven hours sleep, alert and filled with energy.

To placate the vanquished.

Book III

Fuga sub terras, fuga nulla per aurus.
Nec lacrime (ne ferte preces) superive vocati
pectora nostra movent; aliis rex Iuppiter oris.
Faxo Bebrycium nequeat transcendere puppis
ulla fretum et ponto volitet Symplegas inani.

No escape is there beneath the earth, none through the air
My heart is proof against tears (no groveling prayers!)
and appeals to heaven; 'tis elsewhere Jupiter counts for king.
I shall see that no vessel sails Bebrycian waters
and that the Clashers dance to and fro on an empty sea.

Gaius Valerius Flaccus, *Argonautica*, Book IV, 217–221

Chapter 1

It was Captain Charlton's thinking that they'd barely gotten on-station to perform the duties they'd been assigned, and it would be the act of timid poltroons to "leg" it back to the shelter of the Fleet at the first setback. He left a letter with the British consul, to go by the next departing merchantman, for Admiral Jervis. But he sent them out to sea. Fillebrowne's *Myrmidon* would accompany his *Lionheart*, to hunt off the Italian coast, near Brindisi, whilst *Pylades* and *Jester* would sail over to the Balkan side of the narrows and scout the seas nearer to Corfu and the other Ionian Isles, the coasts of Turk-ruled Greece – the Morea – and Venetian-held Albania, to scour the Straits of Otranto.

–

As soon as they fetched the Balkan coasts, off the Istrian Peninsula and the port of Pola, Lewrie was enchanted. It was so unlike any shore he'd ever beheld, like sailing into some fantasy world. The coasts and isles were steep-to, with hardly any beaches to be seen at the foot, but a thin bearding of gravel. Rough, craggy coasts soared upward, rising dramatically from the brilliant blue waters, which now mirrored azure late-spring skies. And they were timbered… so lushly wooded in pines or gnarled oaks, right down to the sea, except where they were too steep for trees' roots to cling, so steep that the hills were streaked here and there with vertical slashes of bare stone and skree-rock, as stark against the dark green forests as the striations of colour in a Venetian lady's hair.

There were coastal hillocks, folding and rolling like frozen waves, always upwards, always more impressive, until they merged in the misty distance with the true mountains, lightly shaded blue-grey and capped with snow and ice on the furthest, above grey granite and the immense forests.

And that archipelago of isles and islets, that transplanted Bahamas, resembled the erect, dolmenlike islets of the Chinese shore, round the mouth of the Pearl River that led to Canton, as if someone had jammed gargantuan pilings, or whole mountains, into the sea quite recently. Though they were inhabited, for the most part, the woods and crags of the coastal cliffs hid their peoples from view, so that Lewrie could imagine, at times, that they were the first explorers, the very first humans at all, to lay eyes on them.

And when they did stand close enough inshore to eye the coastal villages or towns that clung to the shoreline, they were mostly blank to the sea, walled right down to the water's edge, with windows three floors or more above, crammed so tight together they formed fortified enclaves against invasion.

Like his first sight of Naples a few years earlier, Lewrie's impression of those towns was of dusty, mildewy antiquity, like a Greco-Roman history come to life. There were true walled fortifications he suspected must have been built when the Romans, the Byzantines, ruled this Illyrian province of their respective empires. Grecian, exotic and alien, as otherworldly as an ancient painted frieze atop temples now tumbled in ruin, or the red-black pottery of the Classic periods, with their paintings of awkward, stylised warriors, gods and nymphs.

Some seemed very much like Venice – were Venice unwelcoming and unfriendly – as if a portion of the Grand Canal palaces had been transported, with church steeples and *campanile* soaring above an unbroken wall of balconies and windows and private boat-landings along the ocean; though poorer, shabbier, and so very much older.

The further they sailed south, though, the belltowers, the watch-towers, and the steeples of churches and cathedrals turned to slimmer, taller minarets, and the gilded onion domes of Eastern Orthodox churches, or Muslim mosques, dominated the towns' toppings, like illuminations from a Byzantine or Arabic atlas.

And the inhabitants of that coast…! They were alien to English eyes, the way they dressed themselves; some in turbans or fezzes, and loose-flowing robes over scruffy pull-over tunics, some in Hindooish, baggy *pyjammy* trousers, belted jerkins and skullcaps, in sandals or in poor, plebeian bare feet, like the poorest of the poor crofters of Ireland or the wild moors. What few women they could see with the aid of their telescopes at long-distance were hooded, veiled, head-covered or over-smocked like Venetians or Muslims, or cowled or kerchiefed in rusty black or goat-brown, like so many old Italian crones or widows. It was the rare merchant or visitor they espied in anything near to Western apparel. Hungarian, Austrian, Greek or Ottoman, it didn't signify – it was as if Europeans had flown by hot-air balloon to a distant planet to colonise it, but no matter how long or how hard they tried, a European hegemony would never take, not in a thousand more years! Even the cooking smells, the normal airborne effluents a tight-packed village or town produced, seemed otherworldly!

"Sorta reminds me o' Norway, sir," Mr. Buchanon said. "All th' fjords an' such. Wood-timber huts an' houses, where a body can see up the valleys 'at run inland. Poor as church-mice. Handsome, though."

"Aye, Mister Buchanon, it is handsome scenery. And impressive," Lewrie was forced to agree. "Though I still can't quite get the notion out of my head that we've been picked up and dropped on a new planet's seas. And all alone."

He left out the brooding notion he'd also formed; that once put there like Doctor Gulliver by a power unknown, they had no way back! And they would be doomed to Lilliput, Brobdingnag or Yahoo climes forever. Would there be a giant child to pluck them from the sea for playthings, would they tame flocks of Lilliputians to hunt their bread-room rats? Or would they converse with those damned talking horses, eventually?

–

"Sail ho!"

Just after dawn, the decks were still damp from the daily sluicing and holystoning, and everyone was shivering to a brisk little wind off the Balkan mountains, a Bora that put a touch of ice to a spring day.

Lewrie left off his pewter mug of tea to stand near the middle of the quarterdeck and gaze aloft expectantly, shading his eyes against the sunrise.

"Deck, there!" The lookout expanded on his first report. "Sail ho! *One* point orf t' *star*-b'd bows... due South! Full... rigged!"

"Hmm... not a local, then," Lewrie surmised. He turned to gaze at *Pylades*, a mile or more westward of *Jester*, and seaward. Both ships were trundling along under all plain sail – courses, tops'ls and top gallants – with the wind on their larboard quarters. Dead Reckoning of the hourly cast of the chip-log during the night placed them about level with the port of Spalato, in Venetian Dalmatia. Before the bows were the large islands of Hvar and Vis, barely visible above the sea. There was a good channel between those two isles, possibly one that this full-rigged ship, this obviously Western vessel, had used during the night, were she bows-on to them, and only one point to the right of their own bows. "Mister Knolles? Think we might have ourselves a bit of fun this morning, sir. Does she thread the islands…"

"Whereas an innocent trader would chart his course far west of them, sir?" Knolles smirked with sudden insight. "Out to sea of that cluster of islands… Bisevo? Or *however* one may pronounce them?"

"Very possibly, Mister Knolles." Lewrie grinned. "Pipe hands to breakfast, now, while—"

"Signal, sir!" Midshipman Hyde yelled from the starboard mizzen-mast stays. "*Pylades* makes… 'Pursue Chase More Closely.' 'Inshore' is her second hoist, sir!"

"Bend on and hoist an 'Affirmative,' Mister Hyde," Lewrie replied. "Quartermaster, down-helm. Lay us two points closer to the wind, on a soldier's wind. Mister Knolles, duty-watch to the braces."

"Aye aye, sir."

"Then we'll make sure everyone's had a solid meal before closing yon stranger," Lewrie decided. "Gruel, this morning, if I'm not mistaken, sirs? With a dollop of treacle? A princely dish for a hard morning's work."

"Oh, *aye*, sir!" the watch-keeping staff on the quarterdeck said with a droll roll of their eyes. "Princely!"

"I'll have a bowl, myself, sirs," Lewrie insisted with mock serious-ness. "Once I've gone aloft to 'smoak' our new arrival. Mr. Knolles, you have the deck. Keep my mush hot for me, now."

–

Once in the mizzen-top, he could see for miles, even with mists rising from a chill morning along the coast, shrouding the isles with a thin blanket of fog. The Chase was a full-rigged, three-masted ship; her tops'ls or t'gallants were already above the horizon, as she beat into the wind, laid over on starboard tack, and came roughly along a reciprocal course to *Jester* – North by West. Once she espied a brace of warships off her bows, Lewrie imagined, she'd turn and run back the way she came, through the Hvar-Vis channel. She could tack and swing eastward, and run into Venetian waters eventually; perhaps into Spalato itself to take shelter in a neutral port. She could haul off the wind and flee West – no, he groused, that'd lay her open to *Pylades* or getting entangled in that chain of isles round Bisevo.

And just how *did* you pronounce 'em? Lewrie wondered, grinning.

Cut between Hvar and Brac, thread the narrow gut between Brac and Solta, should the wind shift? They'd never catch her, then. But, from what he recalled of his last peek at those new Venetian charts, *Jester* had deep water anywhere she went in pursuit.

Another long minute went by, and still the merchantman stood on her course, as if her lookouts were blind as bats. He could determine that he was looking at t'gallant sails, now with a hint of her tops'ls showing below them – not twelve miles away, and she *still* didn't see them?

Finally! And it took ya long enough, ya simple bastard! Alan thought smugly. She was hauling her wind, swinging her masts in line with each other and pointing her jib-boom directly at *Jester*, as if to flee Westward, dodge round the lee of the Bisevo chain, brushing off pursuit. But *still* blind, Lewrie realized; she hadn't spotted Captain Rodgers's *Pylades* yet! And when she did…! There! Even close to twelve miles off, he could see her sway, as if startled by a mouse, as she realised the Westerly escape route was blocked by a second warship. And came back hard on the wind once more, putting her masts in line… was she? Yes, Lewrie decided, seeing the first rippling of her canvas… she was going to tack across the wind and flee Easterly!

"Mister Knolles?" Lewrie bellowed down. "A point more to windward. Hands aloft… shake out royals!"

-

Jester sailed the longer leg of an intersecting triangle between the wind, the Chase, and escape. But she had a long, clean waterline, and the winds pressed clear from the Nor'east, Leading winds or Fair at times, her best points of sail. The Chase was closer to the eye of the wind, Beating. While it felt faster, with a ship's speed combined with the wind's speed, they were fighting against it. The island of Brac lay before her bows, the narrow dogleg channel between Brac and Solta even closer to the wind's eye. She'd have to tack to stand into it, then do another tack to roughly her original course, to follow its winding into safety, all of which would slow her.

Cool, clear morning air, brisk and bracing, filled *Jester's* sails drumhead taut. The Adriatic was running seas of not over three or four feet, and *Jester* loped over them, pressed over less than ten degrees from upright, her forefoot and cut-water slicing through them as finely as the keenest butcher's blade, creating a rumbling, hissing, seething clash of foam, a slight yawing and lifting of her stern when the foresails, which lifted the bows, were now and then blanketed by those of the main and the mizzen. But she was gaining... relentlessly. And pointing *before* the Chase's bows, so that longer leg of intersection she sailed would meet with her long before she gained the islands' shelter.

"Haulin'!" the lookout shouted. "Chase'z haulin' 'er wind!"

Just shy of the isle of Brac, she was coming about, falling off the wind and showing them her stern. Lewrie stood at the lee bulwark on the starboard side, telescope to his eye, and another mug of tea in peril. He suspected the winds off the Balkan mountains had swung foul farther south, where the Chase lay – were come more Easterly with less Northing, or were altered by the headlands and hills of the islands from the Nor'easterly they enjoyed. She couldn't make the narrow channel without tacking at once, which would run her right back into gun-range! Lewrie turned to espy *Pylades*, now about three miles alee of *Jester*, and astern of her starboard quarter, blocking any attempt to turn and run back out the wider channel to the south between Hvar and Vis.

She was, however, well placed for a run through another channel, a little South of East, between Brac's southern shore and the north shore of Hvar! South of Venetian dominion, and safety!

"Half a point free, Mister Knolles. Pursue her more directly," Alan directed. "Mister Buchanon? The local chart, please, sir?"

"Here, sir," that cautious stalwart from the Blackpool fisheries all but chortled in glee. "Oh, 'ey've chose poor, sir. See here..." he said, happily spreading the chart on the traverse board near the binnacle cabinet, amidships by the wheel. "'Is Hav... Huvv... 'is 'break-teeth' island's long an' narrow, nigh on fifteen leagues, end t'end, an' less'n a mile'r two off th' mainland, at th' end of it, if she wishes t'turn the far point, and run back down its southern coast. With 'is wind t'day, I doubt she'd turn North, f'r Brac, or Spalato... same problem she had with 'at other channel. She's sailin' inta th' sack, sir. Her master must know ought o' 'ese waters."

"Or possess Austrian charts." Lewrie snickered as he turned one more time to look astern and alee for *Pylades*. The signal flags she'd first hoisted still flew; for *Jester* to pursue closely, and inshore. A flicker of canvas, a slight turn, and *Pylades* was slowing, well short of the entrance to that southerly channel. She cocked her bows up into the wind, some sails still trimmed to drive ahead, the rest backed or cross-sheeted to check forward motion, as if she'd failed to make it across on a tack – fetched-to, to wait for *Jester* to take that Chase, or to stay where she could dash off north of Solta, or below Hvar, to intercept if the strange merchantman emerged.

Here we go again, Alan Lewrie thought with a sigh, and recalled times in the Bahamas when Benjamin Rodgers had stood off safe, while he'd been forced to tiptoe through coral reefs with his little gun-ketch, *Alacrity*. There was no danger here of ripping *Pylades'* hull open. But someone must be the blocking force. And full post-captains got what they wanted, when compared to a lowly commander's wishes.

It wasn't navigational perils that worried Lewrie this time, no. Diplomatic, perhaps, should he run afoul of a Venetian patrol ship deep in their waters – what Charlton had warned him about. Or be separated from heavier guns in support, a full forty-five miles, should there be a French warship lurking at the far, unseen end of that channel. What other reason could this Chase's captain have to flee East into a sack, unless he expected some help at the far end of it? Lewrie pondered.

"Growl we may, but go we must," Lewrie whispered, lowering his telescope. "Quartermasters... make for mid-channel."

The merchant ship went out of sight for a few minutes, slipping into the narrow Brac-Hvar channel before them, before they cleared the point. Lewrie took another squint at the chart. The passage began as a narrows, with a low-lying finger of land and a mutton-shoulder point jutting north, once inside. For at least ten miles, the channel was a tight squeeze... perhaps only two miles or less wide. He frowned. Brac was blanketed on the north by tall hills and budding mountains, just the sort that could play "silly buggers" with even the steadiest breeze. About mid-length, the channel widened, turning into a rectangular bay, as Hvar narrowed and flattened like the outline of a cutlass blade.

He jerked his head up suddenly. Shared a worried look with Lieutenant Knolles and Mr. Buchanon in the second moment.

"Gunfire, sir!" Knolles grunted. "Upwind."

"Aloft, there!" Lewrie shouted to the lookouts. "See her?"

"Nossir! Not yet, sir!"

"Damn, damn, damn!" Lewrie spat, stomping round his quarter-deck, resisting the urge to dash forrud, scale the fore-mast, right to the truck-cap, for a look beyond or over that pestiferous damn point of land that blocked their view!

"Mister Crewe!" Lewrie called down to the waist. "Bosun Cony! Beat to Quarters."

He heard another stuttering, irregular series of distance-muffled, land-blanketed *bangs* came wafting on the wind.

Jester's crew thundered bare feet on oak planking as they dashed to the artillery, cast off the lashing and bowsings that held the guns secure and the gun-port lids shut. "Beau-Nasty" ship's boys came from belowdecks with leather cylinders cradled in their arms, which held the first serge powder cartridges. Gun-captains selected the best of the round-shot from the rope garlands, or the racks that circumferenced the hatch-ways, looking for shot without scales, rust or dents, to assure that they would fly straight and true. Flintlock strikers were affixed, their flints test-struck; tompions were removed from the muzzles; slow-match was lit and coiled around the water-tubs between the guns, in case the flintlock igniters failed. Water was sluiced from those tubs, where gunners would slave, and kegs of sand were opened to scatter about for sure traction. Aft and below, partitions for mates' cabins, the Marine quarters and the officers' and warrants' gun-room were stripped of furniture, the light deal hanging partitions and door-ways swung up out of the way to the deck-heads, or passed lower down to the orlop, so a shot that penetrated *Jester*'s side wouldn't create any more man-killing splinters than necessary.

Lewrie nodded to Aspinall on his way below to his post on the orlop as part of the carpenter's crew, knowing his own cabin was being reduced to an echoing bare oak chamber. Aspinall had Toulon under one arm. The cat had never liked the sound of gunfire, and had gotten the knowledge, at last, of what preparatory sounds for gunfire were. Were Aspinall not carrying him snugly and reassuringly, he'd have beaten everyone below, skittering with his belly an inch off the deck.

"Deck, there!" a foremast lookout howled. "Chase, there! Two point orf t'larboard bows! Orf t'wind! Runnin'... fine on 'er starb'd quarter!"

Jester at last had fallen level with the last stub of land that had blocked her view. And there was the Brac-Hvar channel, glittering and shimmering in the midmorning sun, spreading out before her. There was the Chase, that unidentified full-rigged merchant ship…

Coming straight for them! Flying her t'gallants and royals, and men aloft to rig out stuns'l booms for more speed! With a national ensign now flying from her mizzen…

"Dutch, sir. Batavian Republic," Midshipman Spendlove supplied.

"Mister Crewe, ready the larboard battery!" Lewrie snapped. "We will bow-rake her. Quartermaster, helm a'weather… one point…"

The French had taken the Netherlands, set up a puppet republic of "the people," captured the navy… and, to Lewrie's disgusted amazement, a rather popular Batavian Republic, too! One of their warships, now in the Adriatic, under French control? Even as a *grudging* ally, the Dutch had always been doughty sea-warriors. Why, one of their admirals back in the 1600s had sailed right up the Thames and gone home in triumph with a broom lashed to his masthead, in sign he'd swept the seas clean of the Royal Navy! *Jester* could be in for the scrap of her life, if it was a Dutch frigate they'd been chasing!

"Deck, there!" The lookout added. "Small boats t'weather!"

Lewrie looked astern again, hoping that Rodgers had spotted the sudden change in their situation. Sure enough, *Pylades* was back under way, with a bone in her teeth, coming up quickly and about two miles astern. She could be up to them in ten minutes, with her heavier guns run out and ready.

Local allies? Lewrie wondered, nibbling on a corner of his lips. Oh, horse-turds! Yet… who *are* those small boats, then?

He raised his telescope to eye them. *Xebecs*, he saw. Just like those Austrian *schebecks* at Trieste, or those light Venetian warships behind the Lido or the Arsenal. Low, fast, wickedly quick to weather, with heavy guns forrud, and light guns on the beams, swarming with men to work them with oars, if the winds didn't suit.

There! A puff of gunsmoke from the Chase!

From her *stern-* chasers? He goggled.

This was followed by shots in reply from the bow-chasers of the smaller vessels astern of the full-rigged ship. He could see three or four of them, spread out across the channel, lateen sails spread right-angled to their decks like curvey triangles, counter-cocked as they ran "wing and wing," so the after-lateen didn't blanket all of the forrud.

"Half-mile, I make it, sir," Lieutenant Knolles prompted, licking his lips. Lewrie shared a glance with him, stalked forrud to the edge of the quarterdeck, by the nettings overlooking the waist, to see his Master Gunner looking up in expectation. The gun-captains idled with the lanyards in their hands, ready to stand aside and draw them taut, to "fire as they bore."

"Mister Crewe... a *single* shot, sir!" Lewrie shouted. "One of the forecastle carronades. Put a shot 'cross the merchant-man's bows."

"Aye, sir!" Crewe replied. "Larboard carronade only... fire!"

"Well, I'm damned!" Lewrie crowed.

The heavy 18-pounder ball struck nowhere close; the "Smashers" were close-in weapons of great power, but they could only shoot half the required distance of half a mile, even with their elevation screws fully down. Yet the Batavian struck her colours!

In an eyeblink, men along the rails were flagging white cloths at them, were aloft and taking in stuns'ls; her taut royals, t'gallants and tops'ls and her courses were going flaccid and baggy in surrender!

"Quartermaster, steer a point more to loo'rd," Lewrie called to the helmsman. "We'll let her pass down our larboard side, to weather. Mister Crewe, if it's a scurvy trick, you'll serve her a broadside, no matter. Should her gun-ports open..."

"Aye, sir!" Crewe agreed, more than ready. After going to all the trouble of beating to Quarters and running out, to him it would be a shame to not let fly at *something*!

More off the wind now, *Jester* fell down toward Hvar, clearing her guns to deal with the *xebecs* as the merchantman held her course off the wind, running slowly Westward. She limped past them, less than two musket-shots up to windward, clewing up her courses to slow herself even more, with her few gun-ports firmly shut. Another minute more, and she was astern, off *Jester*'s larboard quarter and out of gun-arcs, showing them her vulnerable stern. She would be *Pylades*'s pigeon, then, Lewrie thought. The 5th Rate was close enough to deal with her alone.

The local ships came on, running up the channel, still spread out along the larboard side of *Jester*'s bows. They flew no flags, but still had their heavier bow-guns run out. Hesitantly, though... weaving just a bit, as if thinking about turning away, Lewrie imagined. He raised his telescope again. He could see raggedly dressed men aboard the one nearest, arguing and gesticulating like rug-merchants over a sour deal. The *xebec* had seen better days, he thought; her sails were patchwork quilts, her hull scabrous and filthy, patched, too, with newer wood in places, and her rigging as thin and worn, he could conjure, as a purser's charity. No one in uniform to be seen on her small, high quarterdeck aft, either. The crew wore smocks, jerkins, ragged-hemmed knee-length tunics that showed bare legs, or loose last-century style trousers.

"Definitely *not* a Venetian flotilla," he decided.

He lowered his telescope. The nearest *xebec* was standing on in pursuit, doggedly intent on catching up with the merchantman, in spite of the presence of two Western ships.

"Mister Crewe?" Lewrie called. "Give *that* 'un a broadside! Not a warning shot, mind."

"Aye, sir! Number one gun… as you bear… fire!"

Jester's 9-pounders began to bark, lurching inboard in recoil as they lit off one by one down her larboard side, billowing great stinking clouds of spent powder. Feathers of spray leaped from the sea, so close to the *xebec's* hull the pillars wetted her sails as they collapsed. At a quarter-mile range, they could hear the wrenching *thonks!* of timbers being ravaged by solid strikes.

As the gun-smoke trailed alee and they could see once more, it was a gratifying sight they beheld. The nearest *xebec* or light galley had whirled away, stern-on to *Jester*, her lateen yards hauled in taut and almost fore-and-aft, to beat out of range towards Brac, up north. The other three had turned tail and were beating up-channel for that mutton-shoulder point, all thought of pursuit or confrontation beaten – or shot – out of them.

"Secure, Mister Crewe. And good shooting!" Lewrie congratulated. "Mister Knolles, once the guns are bowsed up, we'll wear ship, end up running off-wind, on starboard tack. To close that merchantman."

"Aye, sir."

–

"Put th' wind up *you*, I'd wager!" Benjamin Rodgers wheezed with glee, once Lewrie was aboard *Pylades* and seated in the great-cabins, a glass of wine in his paws. "Not often a Chase comes about and *charges* ye, an' there's the biter, bit… by God! Think she was a frigate for a moment there, did ye, Lewrie?"

"Damn right I did, sir," Lewrie felt free to admit. In strictest privacy, with a good friend who wouldn't retell the story on him with a bit of spite. Well, of course, he'd retell it, Lewrie then realized. He'd dine out on it for bloody years, more-like! But at least it wouldn't be harmful to his reputation. "Though, sir…" he felt he had to quibble, "would you have signaled me, since *you* could see up that channel to what she was doing better from seaward, well…! That would o' been welcome."

"Batavian Dutch merchantman," Rodgers breezed on, top-ping up his own and Lewrie's glasses. "Cleared from a French port, Marseilles, to fetch timber. General cargo aboard, tasty Frog exports all. Care for a dozen-dozen o' champagne f'r yer lazarette, hey? Pipe'r two o' tasty claret? Almost into port at Spalato – Split, whatever – where they'd pick up oak, pine, naval stores and compass-wood for the Frog Navy. So close and yet so far, hey? Poor bastards."

"Damnation to Venice, I say, sir," Lewrie offered, proposing the toast with a raised glass. "To trade with a dangerous enemy."

"Aye, 'stead o' usin' their timber t'refit their own ships," Rodgers echoed a like sentiment. "Can't they see, the French win in Lombardy, and the damn war comes t'them, whether they like it or no? Been sittin' safe an' snug too long, with th' Austrians playin' constable for 'em. You can be sure, Lewrie… th' Frogs beat Austria this summer, there'll be French ships all over th' Adriatic, an' *then* where are the Venetians, if they're as unprepared as you told Charlton?"

"Up shit's-creek, sir." Lewrie shrugged. "Old Frog expression."

"By God, sir, but Captain Ten Bosch was glad t'see *you!*" Captain Rodgers hooted. "Thought he'd be knacky, an' duck north round Brac, an' then run up th' coast inside Venice's three-mile limit. Didn't think o' runnin' foul o' pirates, haw haw!"

"Those Croatian pirates we heard of in Trieste, sir? Those… Uscocchi?" Lewrie asked.

"No, this ain't their bailiwick," Rodgers countered. "Christ, though… just like the old days. Toss tuppence in the gutter, an' up pops all th' damn' pirates ya'd ever *wish* t'see. Serbs, Greeks, Turks workin' for some rebel Pasha… it don't signify. They've more bucca-neers in these waters than a soldier's got lice, anyway. 'Least we put the fear o' God in 'em this mornin'. Whichever god they wail to, at any rate. This might work t'our advantage, Lewrie."

"How so, sir?" Alan enquired dubiously. He'd had more than his fill of pirates in the Far East and the Bahamas.

"All our worries 'bout pursuit 'mong these islands." Rodgers winked. "Or goin' too close inshore. Did we see a Venetian warship, today, I ask you, sir? And I'll lay you any odds you want, we'll not see theirs, nor anyone else's, all th' way south t'th' Ionians, nor th' Straits of Otranto. We've a free rein, in th' first instance. And, were I a merchantman, I'd be more afraid of gettin' took by pirates'n I'd ever be o' bein' took by us. We don't cut their damn throats!"

"So they'd be afraid of getting close enough in to get taken," Lewrie realised, "that they'd be fair game for us, sir?"

"Exactly, Lewrie." Rodgers smirked. "Like that fellow Ten Bosch said this mornin'... we're the fryin' pan, the pirates're the fire. You stick your bowsprit inside the islands, go within spitting distance o' th' coastline, and you're sure t'get took. An' butchered like a steer 'cause yer th' wrong damn' religion, wrong damn' eye colour... by God, Lewrie! We're rescuin' angels in comparison!"

Chapter 2

For a backwater of the war, the Adriatic teemed with shipping. Farther on south, *Pylades* and *Jester* encountered another enemy merchantman, just west of Ragusa, and seaward of *Pylades*, in deep water. A fine two-masted brig became their prize, a prize that temporarily put up the French Tricolour flag before striking at the sight of *Pylades* and her open gun-ports.

By dusk of the same day, they'd met another, this one inshore of them, and beating hard to flee into the protection of Ragusa's fortress guns. *Jester* had begun the chase badly out of position, a bit too far Sou'west of her to cut the angle, this time, and had been forced to go right for her stern, only weathering her the slightest bit. It was the longest sort of chase, and they'd lost the race in the end. Once more, a French merchant ship had hoisted their blue-white-red Tricolour flag.

This time, however, it was in derision, as they sailed almost into spitting distance of Ragusa's well-armed fortifications before making the larboard dogleg turn that would take them into the harbour proper.

And, as Lewrie continued to close the coast to within a mile of the fortifications, with his gun-ports closed, all thoughts of fruitful pursuit gone... the French crew hoisted their bare arses over the rails and jeered their failure!

–

Dawn found *Jester* well south of Ragusan territory, and south of the tiny Venetian enclave of Cattaro, loafing along under all plain sail to a slight Easterly wind off the shore, a Levanter. Though a Levanter was usually a sign of bad weather – in this part of the world, *nothing* good ever came from the un-Christian East! – it seemed rather a benign beginning for a new day. And it was not as chilly as that Bora which had dominated on the previous day, from the North or Nor'west.

"Bar, sir," the Sailing Master intoned.

"Where away?" Lewrie frowned in sudden dread. Could those damn Venetian charts be trusted, or *not*?

"No, sir." Mr. Buchanon chuckled. "Bar, meanin' th' name o' th' town, sir. Off our larb'd beam, now, Captain."

"Ah." Lewrie reddened, irked that he'd taken fright of running his *Jester* onto an uncharted bar. "Just so. Now, Mister Buchanon… would that be a Montenegran Bar? Or is that the Albanian Bar? I mind the border's somewhere over yonder." He japed his way out of embarrassment.

"*Think* it's still Montenegran, sir," Lieutenant Knolles supplied, full of good cheer that morning. "Had a peek at the charts, just 'fore the change of watch. That rebel Pasha of Scutari the Austrians told us of? He's inland, somewhere just abaft of abeam. And the port of Dulcigno, sir? Where the Corsairs lurk? Allies, I'd suspect. Somewhere yonder, at any rate. Ah, coffee! Capital!"

Aspinall came up from the great-cabins with a set of mugs upon a hank of twine and a pot of coffee for them all. With him, unfortunately, came Lewrie's new clerk, Padgett, with a selection of ledgers under his arm. And up from the waist came the Purser Mr. Giles, grinning in a dangerous fashion, with his own new clerk, his "Jack in the Breadroom," Lawless. When a purser grinned, it could put the fear of God in even the greatest sinners, and Lewrie felt a sour shudder take him. It would be one of *those* mornings, then, all hen-scratches and receipts, all finger-cramp, eye-strain, and ink-smuts.

"Bloody…" Lewrie whispered, as he sipped his hot coffee black and unsweetened. Trying to make it last so long that perhaps Mr. Giles and his pettifogging ledgers might go away.

"Sail ho!" The main mast lookout halloed. "One point abaft th' larboard beam! Bilander! Sailin' large!"

"Ah, too bad, Mister Giles," Lewrie cooed, trying not to sound too gleeful at this most-welcome interruption. "Later in the day, sir? Or tomorrow? Same for you, Mr. Padgett, 'less there's something very urgent?" Lewrie more than strongly suggested.

"No, sir. 'Scuse me, sir." Padgett nodded and heading aft for the narrow, after-captain's companionway ladder. He wasn't half the man Lewrie's former clerk, Mr. Mountjoy, was; a taciturn, silent plodder of a fellow. Though he was *miles* more competent.

"Mister Knolles, once you've enjoyed your coffee, I'd admire you put us nearer the wind… say, Sou-Sou'east, to intercept. Plain sail will do, for now. No need to spook her too soon. And no colours."

"Aye aye, sir. Quartermaster…?" Knolles burbled, trying both to obey at once and finish a rather well-brewed cup of a very good Venetian coffee.

"Deck, there!" The lookout halloed, again. "Two sail! Bilanders both! One point abaft the larb'd beam, an' sailin' large!"

Lewrie set his cup down to rub greedy palms together. Two vessels to pursue, and both bilanders! They were hellish-ugly ships, bad as any hermaphrodite brig, with a large lateen mains'l aft and square sails on the foremast. From two years' service in the Mediterranean, he couldn't recall seeing that antique rig much, except on the French Provence coast, round Marseilles, Toulon and in convoys running the Riviera to supply the French army last year. Short, squat, round as Dutch butter-tubs… and not particularly fast or weatherly, either! Meat on the table?

He certainly hoped so.

So far *Pylades* had taken the honours, furnishing prize-crews for both their captures, and it was time *Jester* held up her end of the bargain. Both captures had been sizable vessels, requiring larger prize-crews to guard the sailors and mates they'd taken and to work their ships for them. It was quite likely that *Pylades* had given up over 30 hands from her crew already! Even a 5th Rate frigate had only so many hands to spare, before safeguarding prizes took so many people that she would be ill-served should they run across an enemy warship.

"Mister Spendlove?" Lewrie barked.

"Aye, sir?"

"Signal to *Pylades*. Inform her we've sighted two strange sail to the east'rd, and are closing the coast to stop and inspect them," Alan said quickly, even as *Jester* heeled as she took the Levanter more upon her larboard bows as she turned Sou-Sou'east.

He finished his coffee, begrudging his breakfast, which would be cooling and congealing below. But he didn't think, this time, to go to his cabins for it. No, he'd stay on deck to oversee every moment of their closure and possible pursuit. After Ragusa, and the sight of all those pale, round fundaments aimed at him, he'd be damned if he'd let a prize slip away again! Or let a Frenchman have reason to insult or jeer him!

It promised to be a clear, fine day. The sun rose a little higher over the forbidding inland mountain chains, casting its glow over the waters like the raising of a stage curtain. For a precious half hour it left *Jester* in murky shadows, alee of the dawn. And, for that precious half hour, *Jester* ranted and rolled, even under all plain sail, closing swiftly on a course almost at right angles to the unsuspecting merchantmen, with the knotlog's every cast showing over eight knots or better. The hands were spared the daily deck-sluicing and holystoning, sent down to their breakfasts early – so they could come back on deck, rig the guns for action and wait… completely ready for whatever came.

"Deck, there! Chases go close-hauled on larb'd tack!"

Turning upwind, Lewrie fretted, gnawing on a thumbnail corner. They're turning on the same course we're steering – Sou'-Sou'east. But close! Not four miles between us, now they've finally spotted us! Not like yesterday, Christ, no! Slow, wallowing… a scant wind…

Christ, pray not, he amended a moment later, still fretting, even though he could see that *Jester* was pinching up close-hauled a full half point, about six degrees higher to windward than the bilanders.

"Mister Knolles, Mister Cony!" he snapped. "Get t'gallants set!"

Bosuns' calls shrilled high and eerie and insistent, piping hands aloft, as Will Cony and his mate, Sadler, drove them by dint of call and the sight of their stiffened rope "starters" in their hands – an unspoken threat for the slow and clumsy.

Up the ratlines, out over the futtock shrouds and past the fighting tops to the upper masts they went. Spry young teenage topmen and wary top-captains scampered up, then out, along the arms of the t'gallant yards, even as the hands on the deck tailed on the jears and halliards to hoist those heavy yards up from their resting positions to far above the crosstrees. Men stood ready, freeing clew-lines and buntlines as gaskets were cast off. More wind-greedy canvas began to appear as the t'gallants were drawn down, bellying and flagging as crisp as gunfire. And *Jester* moaned as she heeled even more, masts groaning and hull-timbers resettling as she set her starboard shoulder to the sea and surged forward. T'gallant sails shivered into taut stillness, arced outward and alee by the force of the winds, set more fore-and-aft than the tops'ls, or the courses, in a proper spiral.

A rogue wave, a placid little three-footer, broke under her bows on her cutwater, and she drummed as she shattered it to foam. Another and then another, soggy crashes and hull-drummings, which turned to hisses and sibilance as *Jester* stretched her legs and began to lope, shrouds and rigging beginning a faint, atonal but eager hum.

"Nine and a quarter knots, sir!" One of the afterguard shouted after another cast of the log.

"Go, lady!" Buchanon muttered to their ship. "Go it, darlin'! Ah, th' joy o' it, sir! A fine mornin' f'r a neck-or-nothin' chase."

"It is, indeed, sir," Lewrie heartily agreed, springing at the knees, feet spread wide, to ride her as she galloped windward.

"Like she's hungry, sir," Buchanon extolled further. "Like ol' Lir's hungry with her. Not twelve mile more, an' 'ose bilanders'll be hard aground, do 'ey hold 'is course, sir."

Lewrie looked aft. Once more, there was Rodgers's *Pylades* back to leeward, a touch to starboard of *Jester*'s stern, should one of the Chases haul her wind and run Sou'west.

And that'd be about all they *could* do, Lewrie pondered; it made no tactical sense to try and tack this far offshore, to run northerly. Even the finest-handled warship – 5th or 6th Rate, or sloop – could not tack quickly enough without losing a horrendous amount of speed for a long minute or two, then a long minute or two more to accelerate back to her original speed. Should the bilanders turn, should one or both of them try and tack once they got closer ashore, *Jester* would be nose-deep in their transoms before they could say "*Merde alors!*"

Rising, swooping, her wake almost sizzling as it creamed along her quarters, *Jester* strode toward the two bilanders. Three miles, then two miles off. Then one mile and almost within Range-To-Random-Shot, with that ruggedly beautiful coast looming up higher and higher: stark, dramatic, green but seemingly desolate.

"Coasters!" A lookout called down. "Small ships t'wind'rd. A point off t'sta'b'd bows!"

"Damme, not again!" Lewrie growled, all but stomping his feet in anger. With a telescope to his eye, he could see a gaggle of sails off to their Sou'east, at least half a dozen. More damned pirates?

The bilanders weren't waiting round to find out. In the blink of an eye, the left-hand of the pair tried to begin a tack, whilst the right-hand bilander, which was leading by perhaps a half mile, hauled her wind suddenly, almost laying herself on her beam-ends as she swung abeam the wind, pivoting about to run off the wind to the Sou'west.

A quick glance astern told Lewrie that *Pylades* was well up by then and could deal with the one trying to run off the wind.

"Mister Knolles, we'll tack ship. Mister Crewe? Once we're on starboard tack and settled down, be ready with the starboard battery!"

"Aye, aye, sir!"

–

And, once settled down, after a breathless burst of energy from the hands to cross the eye of the wind, there the bilander was off the starboard side, just a bit forward of abeam, and within a quarter mile of *Jester's* guns!

"Ready, Mister Crewe!" Lewrie alerted him again. "We'll haul off a point, to let the entire battery bear. Helm up, quartermaster."

"Aye aye, sir. Helm up a point. Steerin' Nor-Nor'east."

"Starb'd batt'ry…!" Crewe bellowed over the rush of the wind in the sails and rigging. "Wait for it! Fire!"

Rolling slightly, rising slightly, atop the scend of the sea and stable for a moment – "on the up-roll" – the guns erupted. Great hot gouts of smoke and embers burst forth, to be quickly winged away alee; a full dozen long-guns or carronades flung solid shot at the struggling old bilander, and she disappeared in a furious froth of spray and pillars of foam, close-aboard her larboard side. That grotesque lateen mains'l, whose boom stretched from her amidships to far over her stern, shattered by the main mast trunk to come sagging alee like a broken goose's wing, as she shivered to the impact of 9-pounder and 18-pounder iron. She rolled hard to starboard in recoil, against the press of wind on her remaining sails, before rolling again, this time so far to larboard they could look down on her main deck. Without the balance of that lateen mains'l, and with square-sails and lateen jibs up forward close-hauled, she fell off fast, slowing in a welter of snuffled foam. Crippled.

Aha! Lewrie exulted to himself, seeing the Tricolour soar up her damaged main mast. She *was* a Frog, just as I thought! He then gave vent to a real, audible cheer as that flag was just as quickly hauled down, in sign she'd struck to them… to *Jester*.

"Mister Hyde," Lewrie called for his eldest midshipman, "do you take a party aboard her. With Mr. Sadler, the Bosun's Mate, as senior hand. My cox'n Andrews to assist. Mr. Knolles, fetch to! Mr. Cony, we'll fetch to! And hoist a boat off the beams for the boarding party!"

"Aye aye, sir!"

"Mister Crewe!" Lewrie crowed. "Damn' good shootin', sir, as you always do! Two guns to remain manned until the boarding party's aboard her. Secure the rest."

There were dozen things to do at once; take in sail, cock *Jester* up to the wind and rig out the falls and tackle to hoist a boat off the waist tier which spanned the amidships. And all the while he kept a wary eye on their supposedly helpless prize, which was now also cocked up into the wind, her yards nearly bare of canvas and her crew slumping hangdog and dejected at her rails.

It was a full quarter hour later that Lewrie had a moment to spare for what else was going on, and he was only called away from his own concerns by the sound of more gunfire down to the Sou'east.

Pylades had stood on, close-hauled on the larboard tack, chasing after the second bilander. She was three miles further inshore by then. Without her prize, it seemed, and venting her anger over it upon a host of local *feluccas* and small *xebecs.* The pirates had the bilander not only surrounded, but under way and heading inshore for Bar, snapping back with light artillery like a pack of starving wolves guarding their first kill in weeks from a rogue lion.

Lewrie raised his telescope to take a good gander, standing by the starboard quarterdeck ladder to the waist.

"Sir, it's Hyde!" Midshipman Spendlove intruded. Lewrie swung his ocular leftward, re-focusing on the figure of a grinning Midshipman Hyde on the captured bilander's larboard bulwarks, waving at them. The bilander had fallen down off-wind to *Jester* in the meantime and was now a bit less than a cable's distance – or 240 yards – off, and within hailing. He could see that the prize-crew had erected a spare fore-tops'l yard on her, aft, fitted with a longboat's lug-sail for a spanker, so she would have some drive and some leverage to counter her foresails for steerage.

"Speaking-trumpet, Mister Spendlove," Lewrie bade, trading telescope for the open-ended brass cone. "Mister Hyde!" He bellowed across the distance. "Follow in my wake! We'll head out to sea!" He gestured with one emphatic wave of his left arm westward.

"Aye aye, sir!" Came the answering wail, thin and reedy. "We'll follow you out!"

There was more gunfire from the Sou'east, thin and flat. A final fit of pique, it seemed, for *Pylades* was hauling her wind, turning away from the coast to make her own way out to deep water. Denied her prize.

Another quick exchange of telescope and speaking-trumpet with Mr. Spendlove and Lewrie could see even more boats had come out from shore – tiny fishing smacks, small coasters, *feluccas* or light galleys – just about anything that could bear sails or oarsmen. The second unfortunate French bilander was in the centre, within a mile of the shore, hemmed in closely between her original half dozen captors. Had *Pylades* contested them for her, Lewrie realised, she'd have been swamped on every hand by six dozen craft bearing hundreds, perhaps upwards of a thousand bloodthirsty pirates or half-starved villagers. They would look upon the coming of a European ship laden with rare goods like the inmates at Bedlam would the arrival of a drunken pieman in their midst, his trays heaped with piping-hot treats. *Neutral* Montenegran or Albanian villagers, he reminded himself with a snort of frustration, people they had no plaint against, nor any business fighting!

Were they as poverty-stricken as Major Simpson suggested back in Trieste, one scruffy bi-lander would represent a king's ransom, with all her nails, iron bolts, blocks, rope, furniture, guns and powder, as well as her canvas and cargo. And they'd fight to the last tooth and nail before they'd let her go, as fiercely as a she-bear defending her cubs. But it looked, from where he was standing, much like a horde of rats savaging a side of beef left unguarded!

"We'll not go inshore and cut her out, sir?" Spendlove asked.

"Doubt it, Mister Spendlove." Lewrie grimaced as he lowered his telescope. "Mister Knolles? Make sail, and shape a course Due West for now. We'll escort our prize out, and close *Pylades*."

"I mean, sir…" Spendlove gently insisted. "Mr. Buchanon says this stretch of coast is Muslim. Ottoman Turk. And she's French, so…"

"Want t'die, young, sir?" Buchanon sneered, having heard his name cited, as they plodded back toward the helm. "See some o' th' hands die t'save Frogs? Or a ship 'at'd be mostly looted 'fore dark anyways?"

"Well, no, sir, but… mean t'say, sirs… Frogs or no, they *are* fellow Christians. Even if they *are* Papists." Spendlove reddened. "I just wondered… what would happen to them, do we not…"

"Fetch a pretty penny." Mr. Buchanon sighed, rubbing the side of his nose. "Per'aps th' most value o' 'at prize, do 'ey sell 'em in a slave-market. Blue-eyed, white-skin Christians're valuable. Do 'ey not cut a few throats first, mind. Nor rough 'em up too vicious."

"As the old saying goes, Mister Spendlove," Lewrie said, as he slammed the tubes of his telescope shut and stored it in the binnacle-rack, "'God help the French,' sir. And it was their choice. Run in that close to a piratical shore to escape us? Well, on their heads be it, Mister Spendlove."

"An' 'ey *are* Frogs, after all, young sir," Buchanon reminded the midshipman. "Like you say, Cap'um… 'God help th' French.' For 'ere's ought we could do for 'em, now, 'thout gettin' dozens o' men o' our own killed t'save 'em. Poor motherless bastards."

Chapter 3

Captain Benjamin Rodgers, too, was of the opinion of "God help the French," and agreed with Lewrie that "on their own heads be it" if an enemy merchantman escaped their clutches only to stagger into even greater harm among the savages of the coasts.

"Look at it this way, Alan," he said, chortling, as they put their heads together just shy of Corfu. "It's a bit less prize-money for us, but do th' damn pirates get her, she's a dead loss for th' Frogs just th' same. One less bloody cargo t'help 'em build their navy 'gainst us!"

"Just so long as they only take outward-bound ships, sir," Lewrie reluctantly agreed with him, leaning forward to snag the neck of the claret bottle on the table between them as they celebrated aboard *Pylades* in shirtsleeves and unbuttoned waistcoats, their neck-stocks undone and comfortable. "Oh, I'd 'llow the locals as many of the timber or naval stores cargoes as they wish. Good huntin' to 'em, I say, but I'll—"

"Cargoes already bought an' paid for, mind, so 'tis double their loss," Rodgers interrupted, as had ever been his energetic wont. "May e'en be *triple* th' loss… do th' Frogs still have a maritime insurance fund, like Mr. Lloyd at his coffee-house in London. Or have a *sou* left in it? By God, sir… the grief! Their poor ships'-husbands an' owners… weepin' an' wailin' ev'rytime *their* little Lutine Bell rings! Haw!"

"But I'll fight tooth and nail for an inbound ship, sir," Lewrie persevered with a much-put-upon sigh well hidden from Rodgers. Falling back into old, forgotten habits, he consoled himself with a wry chuckle; it was difficult to get a word in edgewise when Benjamin Rodgers was full of himself and "chirping wordy"!

"Aye, poor wine 'board an outbound ship," Rodgers hooted, full of mirth, retrieving that bottle for his own enjoyment. "After they've drunk up all their 'bubbly.' *Mean* t'deprive me, th' surly bastards."

"*All* their export goods, sir," Lewrie rejoined in good humour. "They don't have that good an economy, that much silver or gold specie with which to pay for—"

"Amen and amen t'that, Alan old son!" Rodgers guffawed, banging the bottle on the table in his exuberance. "Aye, short as they are for solid coin, why... an' how many other nations' bankers'll honour any o' their Letters of Exchange, 'cause they're paper promises... not worth th' paper they're written on!"

"Bills of credit, but based on *what*, sir?" Lewrie said quick as he could, before Rodgers went on another tear. "Redeemed *when*, if ever—"

"An' ev'ry inbound vessel we take, then, is another nail in th' coffin for 'em," Rodgers exulted, getting to his feet to pace. "They have t'buy grain or starve, from th' Barbary States or their old chums th' Americans. Must be in bad debt with them already! Most o' their merchant fleet already swept clean off th' seas, blockaded."

"A huge drain, sir... on an already thin-stretched economy. Or treasury. Worst drain may be right here in the Adriatic. Can't win a war without a navy... can't build or maintain their navy without stores from the Adriatic. And can't purchase—"

"That'll be something t'tell Captain Charlton, next time we cross his hawse, wouldn't it, Alan?" Rodgers speculated. "That we're doin' a power more t'hurt th' Frogs than anyone else at th' moment. Makin' 'em bleed through th' nose for want o' timber. Might bankrupt 'em. By God, we could! Bankrupt 'em... d'ye think?"

"Very possibly, sir." Lewrie grinned. "And make a tidy profit in prize-money, in captured silver and gold for ourselves, with every inbound ship we take. As for the outbound, we might as well let the pirates have 'em. Or burn 'em, since—"

"Hellish waste, though." Rodgers sobered for a moment. "So far, we've seen some damn' handsome ships, for th' most part. Worth a lot to the Austrian Prize-Court. Not a third th' value of th' inbound, but..."

"Word might get round, sir," Lewrie suggested. "Might give pause to Frog shipmasters... those neutrals, too, who'd profit by smuggling for 'em. Word of Dalmatian pirates takin' their ships'd put the fear of God in 'em, too, sir. Wonder if there's a way to start a rumour..."

"We'll find that out tomorrow, Alan," Rodgers stated levelly, with a cunning leer on his phyz. "When we put into Corfu. Or rather, when *you* put into Corfu, in my stead."

"Once burned, twice shy, sir?" Alan snickered. "Still holding Charleston 'gainst me?"

"A bit, I must own." Rodgers chuckled. Years before, Rodgers had come aboard *Alacrity* in the pursuit of a murderous pirate and criminal who'd fled the Bahamas in a swift three-masted lugger after looting a private bank of all its assets. They'd followed almost right into harbour in the port of Charleston, South Carolina, where a Royal Navy ship wasn't exactly welcome so soon after the Revolution. They'd shot her to matchwood and taken her, right on the Charleston Bar, under the guns of the forts. And it had been Commander Rodgers who'd had to talk their way out and explain their doings, leaving Lieutenant Lewrie free to search their capture and arrest or kill the notorious John Finney. They'd gotten away by the skin of their teeth, without creating a diplomatic incident or starting a new war – but it had been a damn close affair.

"Just after dawn, Alan…" Rodgers decided. "We'll transfer all the foreign crews and prisoners to *Jester*. You take 'em into harbour an' land 'em. Into Venetian custody. They can't refuse you, bein' so bloody neutral an' all. Make it easier for us to safeguard th' prize ships, too. No sense in holdin' so-called 'neutral' Danes an' Dutch 'til we go back to Trieste. Nor reason t'hold French merchant sailors, either, who'd be set loose an' sent home sooner'r later, any-way."

"And should there be any smuggling vessels or French ships…"

"Aye, old son." Rodgers twinkled. "There's yer couriers f'r a damn' fine rumour o' piracy an' pillage. An' news o' Royal Navy ships sweepin' th' Adriatic clean as a tabletop. Make a sham o' waterin'… firewood an' water, th' usual sort o' port visit. No longer'n twenty-four hours, mind. Whilst I stay seaward t'guard th' prizes we have so far. Should there be a French warship in th' offin', my 5th Rate'd be more dauntin' than yer *Jester*. And with our prisoners gone, I reduce th' number o' hands needed to man th' prizes. Makin' *Pylades* almost up t'full complement again. An' my guns better served."

"Sure you don't relish a run ashore, sir?" Lewrie offered. "You didn't get your shot at Venice, and Trieste's a dead bore, so—"

"I'll get my quill dipped sooner'r later, no fear, Alan. Venice is still there for me," Rodgers countered, coming to pour them both up to brimming "bumpers." "From what you an' Charlton told me of it, it's not all it's reputed to be, though. Though th' sportin' ladies do sound fetchin'. Griggs?" he called to his manservant. "Trot out another o' this claret 'fore supper. You'll dine aboard, o' course, Alan?"

"Only if you swear you won't get me thunderin' drunk, Benjamin," Lewrie scoffed. "How could I start our rumour and do all you expect with a thick head tomorrow?"

"Seen you in action afore, sir. Thick head or no, you'll be up for it. Griggs, damn yer eyes? Smartly, now!"

Chapter 4

Corfu was another mountaintop risen from the sea, so close to the Albanian, Ottoman-ruled mainland that the eastern pass by the old fortress of Kassiópi, which guarded Corfu's northern strait, was within heavy gun-range of the Balkan shore. They went south, skirting along the western coast instead, all the way to Cape Asprókavos before sailing north again for Corfu Town.

The island was shaped like an irregular hammer; the northern end and Mount Pandokrátor formed the peen. It then tapered, trending southeast in an undulating series of wiggles, before the final eastward hump round Cape Asprókavos. In the middle of the island's eastern side was a cockspur, and upon that easterly-jutting cockspur's tip was Corfu Town, well sheltered from the fierce Boras of the Adriatic and those shrieking Levanters out of Turkey.

The harbour proper was on the north side of the cockspur peninsula, further protected by a massive breakwater and fortified seawall, under the towering battlements and gun apertures of the New Fort, which lay on the harbour's west. At the very tip of the peninsula was another fortress – the Citadel. The town lay between those two forts, crammed between the hills and the fortress walls. It was walled, itself, along the sea sides, and probably walled on the west and sou'west, too – quite sensibly – due to the island's importance to Venice for hundreds of years, and its proximity to their ancient foes just across the narrow straits.

Pylades, with her prizes, stood off-and-on in Garitsa Bay, south of the town and cockspur, slowly idling along under reduced sail as far south as the southern cape and back. She stayed well outside that newfangled three-mile limit of sovereignty that Venice claimed.

There were two small ships anchored in Garitsa Bay. And, did the colours they flew not lie, they were both Venetian traders – one a very shabby European-style brig, and the other a much older down-at-the-heels *felucca*. Neither seemed alarmed to see British warships on the offing.

–

Jester entered harbour under reduced tops'ls, jibs and spanker, ghosting along on a light zephyr of a morning wind that barely gave her steerageway. In port, along the ancient stone quays, lay more vessels: more *feluccas*, more *dhow* like coasters, a clutch of single-masted boats for inter-island travel to Ithaca and Paxos, called *caiques*. And there were fishing boats, of course. Another brace of Venetian merchant ships, too. And three foreign ships, one a Batavian Dutchman, a supposedly neutral Dane, and the last an outright French merchantman! These *did* show alarm as *Jester* came in between the harbour moles; even more alarm as she rounded up to the wind, which bared her starboard sides to the town and the ships as if she were about ready to open fire on them.

Lewrie smirked at the sight of them. And what was coming!

"Mister Crewe, open your starboard gun-ports!" He called down to the waist. "Ready, the salute! Eleven guns, no more."

"Aye aye, sir! 'Leven guns! Ready, number one starboard?" Mister Crewe shouted back. "*Fire!* If I weren't a gunner, I wouldn't be here… number two gun… *fire!* I've left my home, my wife an' all that's dear… number three gun… *fire!*"

The governor-general of the Ionians, what the Venetians termed the *provveditore di Isoli del Levant*, rated no more than an eleven-gun salute – the proper reply to what they *might* take as a 6th Rate would be a salute of eleven back. Noisy, stinky… but hardly dangerous.

"Christ, lookat 'em scamper!" Will Cony hooted, nudging Andrews in the ribs. "Like puttin' up a flock o' partridge, hey?"

"Fin' 'emselves a safe place ashoah, I'd wager, Will!" The cox'n grunted in like humour, to see the crewmen of the three merchant ships dash about like chickens with their heads cut off. And a fair number *were* discovering vital errands they suddenly had – in town!

"Mark that Dane, sir." Lieutenant Knolles snickered. "Her sailors are just as shy of us as the Frog sailors. A dead giveaway they're up to no good, too!"

"Aye, Mister Knolles." Lewrie chuckled. "We'll ask of her when we go ashore. Ready to let go, forrud! Hands aloft there! Brail up, all!"

"Hands on the braces... back the fore-tops'l, back the main tops'l!" Knolles contributed. "Lower away fores'ls... smartly, now!"

And *Jester* came to a stop, her sails disappearing quickly, just as the last gun of the salute barked forth, the tops'ls trying to wrap themselves round the masts as they braked her 'gainst the light winds.

"Let go!" Knolles added, followed by the roar and rumble of the best bower cable thundering through the larboard hawse-hole, the splash of the heaviest anchor as it plummeted into the harbour depths. Boats were being hauled to the entry-ports to larboard or starboard – to row out a kedge anchor from the stern, a slightly lighter cable mated to it. Deck-hands stood by the after capstan-head, the heavy pawls in place, to drum her round once the kedge was set. *Jester* then faced the town with her starboard side, aligned lengthwise in the long west-to-east harbour channel between shore and breakwater, instead of lying foul of other traffic.

Gun-port lids were lowered and secured, the guns swabbed out and bowsed secure to the starboard side once more with tompions in. The bower cable was wrapped round the fore bitts, frapped and stoppered to it with lighter line, and the messenger cable to the fore-capstan was put back below on the cable-tiers. Sails were by then completely furled and gasketed, bound neatly to the jib-boom and bowsprit, or the lower boom of the spanker, aft on the mizzen. Sail-tending lines were flaked or flemished, or hung in huge bights along the pin-rails and fife-rails. A quick glance aft showed their cutter returning, with Mr. Hyde waving to signal that it was clear of the sagging bight of the kedge-cable. The men at the after-capstan could begin to haul it in and swing about the stern, which had paid off sou'west and cater-cornered.

"Well, damme..." Mister Buchanon swore. "Again! Slower'n treacle! Where's our salute, I ask ye?"

Neither fort – the New Fort nor the Citadel – showed the slightest sign of activity. It was Trieste all over again. Worse. At least at Trieste they'd gotten a reply to their salute – late and clumsy as it had been performed. Corfu, it seemed, couldn't even be bothered with replying. The only things that stirred atop their walls were the flags!

"Ship's proper-anchored, Captain," Knolles reported about fifteen minutes later. "Your gig's below the starboard entry-port."

"Thankee, Mister Knolles." Lewrie nodded to him, doffing his hat in salute to Knolles's lifted hat. "I'll go ashore, then. Wish I had Mister Mountjoy aboard. At least he could speak some Italian."

"All that's wanting is to rig quarterdeck awnings, sir. And I'll see to that, soon as you've left the deck," Knolles promised.

"Very well, Mister Knolles. You are in charge until I return. Whenever that might be. I'll send word 'bout the prisoners soon as I get permission to land 'em," Alan told him, tugging his clothes neat. "Assuming there really are some Venetian authorities to talk with."

"Might be some saint's day, sir," Knolles opined as he walked with him to the entry-port. "Or they extend Carnival longer here."

"Might be they're blind and stupid into the bargain, Mr. Knolles," Lewrie hooted, doffing his hat to take the departure salute from his men.

"Oh… d'ye mean Venetian, sir?" Knolles japed back.

–

Corfu Town, though, was a most pleasant place, he had to admit: well-wooded, shaded, and park-like, with several wide, open squares and wide, collonaded main thoroughfares. A seeming maze of lanes and narrower streets, nicely stepped and flagstoned, climbed inland and towards either fort – some buildings rising to five or seven stories. They were rather plainly wrought, but well plastered and painted in pastels or natural shades. Perhaps the sea-wind swept most of the noisome stinks of town away before they registered, he thought, for Corfu had a pleasant aroma of countryside dust, olive and fig trees heavy with spring blooms in the hinterlands and jasmine, broom rose, wisteria and orange-trees in the bright little gardens. Pines, scrub oaks and even cypress trees sang a pleasant, continual rustling lullaby.

He'd gotten a tour of the place from the *provveditore*, a man who fortunately possessed *some* English, and an aide from Zante who was very fluent. Atop one of the defensive land-side walls, he'd seen greater bucolic splendours, as if some great lord of the realm had decreed long before that the entire island become a decorative park. The hills were bright green with budding olive groves, vineyards and orchards. Every holding he could see from atop the wall, whether a great-house or a more modest country farm villa, was as well landscaped as any estate back in England. The cypresses paraded alongside the dusty roads, while on the hills were silver fir, myrtle, holly-leaved kermes oaks, silver poplar and God only knew what else. And where the fields were not yet tilled or were left fallow for a season, they swayed fragrant with blue or white thistles or asphodels.

Now, standing on the stones of the harbour jetty, his clothing and hair ruffled by a scant but refreshing wind, he could admire every fine but plain aspect of Corfu Town: the wispy, cloud-laced sky against the ivory hues and faint weather-washed pastels of the houses and apartment blocks, the Venetian-style belltowers and church spires, or those forts made of Istrian limestone of a darker, rosier hue. Northward lay the rugged little island of Lazaretto, an ivory and green jumble. And all surrounded by a sea that was almost a peacock's wing blue. Even farther off on the Turk-held mainland were the Albanian mountains, shading off to a distant purple, capped here and there with stark white snow.

The *provveditore* had assured him that all the *Isoli del Levant* – or Ionians, to their Greek inhabitants – were almost as pretty, though none as fair as Corfu, and Lewrie wished he could stay longer than twenty-four hours to savour their beauty.

He almost wished, for a fond moment, that a man could settle there! The Navy and his wars had taken him to an hundred places that most Englishmen would never see except in black-and-white woodcuts or charcoal etchings, all grander, more exotic, more beguiling than a foggy, rainy and grimy England. He marveled to imagine that, were the world not besotted with hacking away at each other in this war, he'd still be captive upon 160 acres of Surrey smallholding – a *rented* smallholding! – in wee Anglesgreen, where nothing exciting would ever happen. Well…! There was a pang, to think how deprived was a sailor's lot, how seldom a man of the sea had a chance to savour such lush, well-ordered beauty. He felt another pang – this one of disloyalty not only to England, but to Caroline and the children – that he could contemplate escaping all that waited for him at home for this.

But, by God, he thought, we could all come here! Establish a decent school, o' course! Or fetch in a good tutor. A farm, well… much as he hated farming (or his lack of knowledge about farming!), an estate with a good overseer could work out. And the sea was so close… right at one's doorstep, really…

It should have been a happy thought. But Lewrie wore a distinct scowl, instead. And whispered for his own ears, "This is a place I'd fight to keep. Like that fellow Schulenburg they put up a statue for. By God, somebody should, 'fore the Frogs…"

"Excuse me, sir," Midshipman Hyde reported, with his companion Midshipman Clarence Spendlove with him. "That's the last of them, sir. All the prisoners ashore now, and Sergeant Bootheby's Marines ready to embark."

"Ah, thankee, Mister Hyde." Lewrie nodded, still staring out to sea, turning to inhale the gardens' sweetnesses before being forced back to *Jester's* stale and rancid reeks.

"Sir, do you think, since we're allowed 24 hours..."

"No shore-leave, Mister Hyde. Sorry," Lewrie moodily grunted.

"No sorrier than I, sir," Spendlove groaned. "It's a fine town, it appears. Very attractive, indeed."

Lewrie noted that Spendlove's gaze was riveted upon the bevy of local beauties who'd come down to see the excitement of a warship come to call, and the spectacle of the prisoners being landed. Girls whose angelic features stood out in stark contrast to the black or goat-brown gowns they wore.

Gowns, Lewrie took note, that were very low-cut in the bodice and promised a beguiling vista themselves, barely covered with stiff points of the headclothes that lanced down from their hair. As well, they wore white, embroidered aprons, overskirts turned back and tied behind and tiny waistcoats as vestigial as what Greek dancing girls had worn on those ancient jars, more colourful or more ornately embroidered. Some of the girls were clad in loose flax or linen peasant blouses and long satiny skirts, those blouses artfully tied to bare lissome olive-complexioned and inviting shoulders. Only the noblest of the Corfiots, recorded in their Venetian-inspired *Golden Book* of ancient aristocracy, wore the high hair, the huge hats or the *bauto*, or the lacier mainland fineries.

Lewrie couldn't help nodding and smiling at one or two, for they were exotically lovely. British sailors, British officers and redcoat Marines were a rare novelty, and these enticing girls seemed intrigued with them. Lewrie saw a half dozen open and approving glances, demure coquetries... or arrant, hip-rolling "come-hithers," within musket-shot.

"No, no shore-leave," Lewrie repeated himself. Partly for his own caution. Lord, lookee... I'm tryin' t'be decent, for a change, see? It was hard, though, to imagine not diving right in and making a swine of himself. "Not a good liberty port, young sirs," he explained. "It's hard enough to get the Venetian authorities to let us stay in port for 24 hours. Or land the noncombatant prisoners. And with that Frog merchantman here, too, well... there'd surely be a brawl, do you see? A knifing or a murder 'fore midnight, and we'd never be let in harbour again – *Jester* or any other ship of the squadron. And the authorities'd…"

He tailed off, sourly irritated, as Marine Sergeant Bootheby put on a short display of close-order drill to march his small Marine contingent down the quay from the town gaol, to the delight of the Corfiots and the sneers of the French sailors off that merchantman.

Whether the Venetian authorities on Corfu disapproved of brawls or not, there would be precious little they could actually *do* about them, he thought. During his tour of the town, and a rather good midday meal, he had learned several disturbing things about Corfu and the rest of the isles.

Such as the fact that the largest, oldest fort on the eastern point – the Citadel – was pretty much an empty shell after a powder magazine explosion a few years back in '89, which had leveled half the Old Town under its walls.

Such as the fact that the New Fort didn't have a garrison, either. There was a colonel and two captains, their manservants, cook and stable-hands. And that was the *entire* garrison of Corfu! The colonel and his officers still sent in musters to Venice, though, which showed a battalion, and were billing the Serene Republic for men who'd deserted, died or resigned at the end of their enlistments.

Such as the fact that the few ships of the Venetian Navy were laid up in harbour or drawn up on the strand for storage, and were as rotten as any he'd seen in the famed Arsenal at Venice itself. The sole officer of their navy couldn't put together a harbour-watch for a single galley or small *xebec*, though he still indented for their pay, ration allocations and funds for upkeep. And a fine living he had of that charade, too!

Even if there had been a military garrison worth the name, when he'd strolled on those land-side walls, Lewrie had found the artillery scattered at the embrasures almost "Will He, Nill He," many of them empty. The guns were so long unused that the carriages were half eaten by termites, as worm-holed as cheese; the guns themselves were gleaming under fresh black paint or soot blacking. But under the disguise they were almost rusted immovably to the stone ramparts!

And even the *provveditore's* residence had turned out to be quite small – most pointedly not the impressive *palazzio* down one of the main collonaded streets, which gaped empty and run-down. To save money, or to pocket the difference, Lewrie suspected, the *provveditore* rented a place just barely suitable. He hadn't even owned his own plates or glassware, but had had to send out to his landlord for extra to feed a foreign visitor!

How could anyone let himself slip so deep in sloth and graft, and become so corrupt he'd threaten the safety of such a blissful island? Lewrie asked himself with mounting anger. Such a lovely place, so strategic! And he actually spat upon the stones of the quay.

"Very well, then, young sirs," Lewrie decided, after taking one last, longing look to fix Corfu Town in his memory. "Let's get back aboard *Jester*. I wish to clear harbour by sundown."

Hyde and Spendlove lagged behind their captain on the way to the waiting boats, taking what brief joy they could of an idle quarter hour ashore after unending months at sea. Even the sight of the Frenchmen who cursed them – the recent captives or the ones off the anchored merchantman or the foreign sailors in France's pay – couldn't dissuade them from sighing with a longing of their own to be let free for a spell of idleness, shore-cooked foods, strange new wines and those alluring girls!

"'Tain't like him, by God, it ain't," Hyde muttered to his compatriot. "Deuced bloody odd, Clarence. I expected him to sleep ashore this evening. Do you get my *meaning*?" he drawled suggestively.

"Must be something which comes with middle age, Martin," Mister Spendlove whispered back with a sneaky grin. "After all, he's thirty-three and a bit, now. Past it, d'ye expect?"

"God save us if that's true," Hyde breathed softly, casting such an aching glance at another angelic Corfiot chit in the doorway of some dockside chandlery. "And here we are, with so few years left to us 'fore we suffer the same affliction."

"And so few opportunities," Spendlove agreed with a faint moan.

"Why, ever since he saw off that kept mutton o' his, that Aretino creature, he's lived the life of a bloody saint!" Hyde carped. "And so have we! Least, when he still had all his humours—"

"'Fore he spent 'em… spending with the ladies," the seventeen-year-old Spendlove japed.

"Were *he* off carousing, then there was a chance *we'd* be free to, aye." Hyde sighed in the very heat of an eighteen-year-old's frustration; that of a callow, brimful of "vital humours" cully. "Let me tell you, Clarence, 'tis been so long, I've… considered, mind… considered taking up 'Boxing the Jesuit.' Just to ease myself, d'ye see."

"Considered," Spendlove posed, tongue-in-cheek. He had ears… he'd heard Hyde's hammock-ropes squeak against the end-rings, late in the evening after Lights Out, as Hyde amused himself. Eased himself; though wasting one's limited and fixed allocation of humours led to lunacy and consumptionlike laxity of wit, body and spirit, too soon in life. Such as Captain Lewrie's new state. "With real girls…"

"Oh, you vile young seducer, you!" Hyde scoffed. "You scourge of a thousand chambermaids! As if *you* could advise me, 'bout women!"

"Not for want of experience, sir!" Spendlove shot back, louder. After all, had there not been a willing young tavern girl at San Fiorenzo Bay, at that little waterfront *osteria*, hard by the boat-landing? And had there not been both a boardinghouse chambermaid, *and* an actual whore at Leghorn, where even the dead could "put the leg over" a fetching mort for the price of a scone? No, Clarence Spendlove didn't think his few years on this mortal coil had been a *complete* waste of chances.

"You, Clarence? Little 'hop o' my thumb'?" Hyde went on, louder as well. "You've not a jot on the experiences I've had. Can't serve aboard *Jester* this long, without. Can't serve under the 'Ram-Cat'—"

"Sshh!" Spendlove cautioned.

"You wish to be just like him… when you grow up, that is," Hyde shot back, a bit more quietly.

"And who wouldn't, I ask you?" Spendlove shot back, ignoring his own warning. "Least, the early years, mind. 'Fore—"

"You gentlemen done skylarking?" their captain snapped from the edge of the dock, ready to enter his gig. "Shake a leg, then."

"Well, erm…" Hyde replied. "Don't we both, rather. Before we get too long in tooth for it."

Chapter 5

The squadron lay at rest, once more anchored in the millpond-quiet port of Trieste. On this visit, with the coming of summer, it was a much nicer-seeming place, no longer buried under gloomy skies, with all that drizzly, seeping rain and misty fogs. Securely anchored in an allied harbour, behind a breakwater fortified and armed against a raid, and with a walled town that was well patrolled by Austrian soldiers or city watchmen, Captain Charlton had allowed as how the crews could be let ashore, watch by watch, for some precious shore liberty. Those *steady* warrants and hands, of course. With not one man per ship able to speak German, it would be almost impossible for anyone to change his clothes and desert. And they had cause for celebration, after a month or more on patrol down south.

Pylades and *Jester* had managed to fetch in four prize-ships, and had been forced to burn three more, swept up farther south of the Ionian Isles; outbound carrying cargoes of timber and naval stores. *Lionheart* and *Myrmidon* had had a less productive patrol – they'd only brought in a pair of ships. Over on the Italian side of the straits, or the Adriatic Sea, it had been rare to run into a merchant vessel with improper, Colourable, papers and manifests. They'd encountered far more Neapolitans, Papal State, Venetian, or neutral traffick. They'd stopped thirty or more ships, and, while there had been some they'd suspected of being engaged in smuggling for France, their papers had either been legitimate and unimpeachable – or the very best forgeries they'd ever seen. More cautious than Rodgers and Lewrie, perhaps, they'd been forced to allow them to proceed on their voyages. Better that than being hauled into an Admiralty Court for unlawful seizure and sued to their eyebrows!

-

"Uhm…" Lewrie smiled with pleasure. "Sprightly, indeed, sir. And rather spicy, too. Hint of floral, to the nose? What did you say it was, again, sir?"

"A *gewürztraminer*, Commander Lewrie." Charlton beamed back at him, quite pleased that his officers liked his wine selection. "That is, I am told, German for 'spiced'… *gewürz*. Not too sweet on your palates, gentlemen?"

"Not at all, *sir*!" Commander Fillebrowne was quick to reassure his superior. "My word, sir, you must tell me the name of the shop you got it from. *Have* to have a case'r two of this aboard. Tastier than a proper port. Lighter, too," Fillebrowne toadied on.

"Right fine, sir," Rodgers told him. "Kinder on th' tongue than 'Miss Taylor,' nor half as raw. Doesn't pucker ya like a hock or Rhenish. Aye, I'd take a case'r two aboard, as well, sir."

Not all in one sitting, Lewrie thought with a secret grin. Rodgers was born with a hollow leg, holds his guzzle better'n any I ever did see, but Lord… what a packet he can stow away, and give no sign of!

"Perhaps the nicest bit come off from shore, sirs," Charlton said, turning moody and a touch fretful. "Sweeter by far than what I read in your report, Captain Rodgers, of what you and Lewrie learned of the poor state of Venetian defences, for certain. I would never have expected to see them let things get in such a shoddy fix."

"'Lo, how the mighty are fallen,' sir, aye. Something like that," Commander Fillebrowne cited with a commiserating shrug and head-shake.

"Something very much like that, sir." Captain Thomas Charlton grimaced. "S'pose it'd do no good to alert the Venetian senate to what venal situation obtains on Corfu, do you? Do no good to… tattle?"

"I doubt the Venetians would appreciate it, sir," Lewrie replied when it looked like no one else would rise to it. "There must be hundreds of their nobility profiting from some *other* corruption already. To alert 'em would cause just enough grief for them to resent us."

"And," Fillebrowne pointed out with a raised finger, "since the *provveditore* down yonder, and the others, are nobles recorded in their so-called *Golden* 'Stud' *Book*, they're untouchable."

"Don't know, sir," Rodgers countered with a sly look. "Venice is known f'r cleanin' up scandals quiet-like. Th' odd body dumped in a canal, anonymous stabbin's in the streets by hired *bravos*… stranglin' th' overgreedy with a silk noose in prison. Beats th' cost of a trial – an' th' public embarrassment – all hollow."

"Onliest thing is, Captain Rodgers" – Charlton brightened, wryly amused – "they've a tradition of killing the messenger who brings 'em the bad tidings, too!"

"Well, there is that, sir," Rodgers allowed with a wry grin.

Charlton set his glass on the dining table and smoothed down his unruly, wiry grey hair – hair, Lewrie noted, that had been more pepper than salt just scant months before they'd sailed for the Adriatic.

"I was ashore, gentlemen," Charlton announced, folding his hands in his lap and working his lips from side to side, as if trying to find a comfortable fit. "There are two items of note. One merely bad – and one utterly appalling. S'pose we should get the worst out of the way first. That old acquaintance of yours, Lewrie, this Bonaparte—"

"Oh, aye, did Latin verbs together, sir," Lewrie sniggered.

Charlton gave him a beetle-browed glare, which shushed him, and his too-quick wit, much like an irate tutor.

"Seems he's given the Austrians more woes, according to what the good Major Simpson told me," Charlton went on, after a last glare, for assurance that Lewrie was properly chastened and would make no more amusing comments. "Crossed the Po River into Lombardy round the beginning of May. Ignored their fortress-city of Pavia and found an unguarded stretch where no one ever would have thought to look for him – at Piacenza. Fillebrowne, you're still our expert on Italian geography. Do you unroll that map for us, sir... there's a good fellow? Ah, just here... far *east* of Pavia. Marched or *flew*, I don't know which would be harder to credit, from Turin in bare days." Charlton looked gloomy, a hand waving over the general vicinity, once Fillebrowne had dutifully displayed the map and began to anchor it with glasses.

"Marshal Beaulieu, I'm told, had planned to entrench behind the Ticino River and the Po, anchoring things with Pavia, but with the French threatening him from the east and Milan wide open, the Austrian Army was forced to retreat. Abandoning Pavia, and part of its garrison – *and* all the supplies gathered there – same as happened before, when they had to abandon Alessandria," Charlton related with a disappointed sniff. "Now, here... the Adda River, at a place called Lodi... Bonaparte caught up with Beaulieu's rear guard. Fought his way across the narrow bridge under heavy fire and cut up the rear guard. Rather handily, I must say… or so Major Simpson related it to me."

"And that, rather reluctantly, I should expect, sir," Fille-browne quipped with a derisory smirk.

"Quite, sir," Charlton snapped, turning his frosty humour on Fille-browne for a welcome change, and glaring his smarminess to scorn. "I am also told – reluctantly or not, Commander Fillebrowne – that Milan fell to French troops about the middle of the month… not five days after this battle at Lodi, and Marshal Beaulieu and his Austrians – what's left of 'em, mind – have scuttled back to Mantua to regroup. And what that *means*, sirs, is that the western half of Lombardy is now lost!"

"But, that's…" Captain Rodgers spluttered in disbelief. "Why, that's nigh impossible, sir! To move so quick 'gainst such a force. Mean t'say, surely—"

"And that was just the doings in the merry month of May, sirs," Charlton snapped, as if he were taking cruel amusement from the hapless antics of their allies – or enjoyed shredding Rodgers's last illusions concerning the invincible Austrian Army. Lewrie, though, thought their squadron commander's bile was more the instinctive variety; that utter disgust for the doings of "soldiers," who were little better than gaudy "jingle-brains," idle fops and boasting coxcombs.

"Now, here's the real salt in the wounds, sirs," Captain Charlton sighed, recovering his glass of wine and taking a sip with a shrug. It seemed to calm him. "I am also told that Lewrie's old compatriot…"

Damme, I wish he'd stop *sayin'* that! Alan rankled to himself.

"…has come down as far as Parma, to the south." Charlton hunched forward over the map. "This *past* month, he's taken Modena, then Bologna. Marched into the north-ernmost Papal States, took on the Papal Army – eighteen thousand or so – *still* runnin', I'm assured, all the way back to Rome! Just scattered 'em. Then he turned on Tuscany. Took Ferrara and Florence, their capital city. Sent troops to Porto Especia, and… Leghorn."

"Good God!" It was Lewrie's turn to gasp in disbelief. "Sir, if he has Leghorn, then – well, 'cept for Naples, do *they* not panic! – we haven't a friendly port left anywhere in Italy which would base or victual the fleet! Well, Gibraltar, but that's a long slog…"

"Exactly, Commander Lewrie," Charlton grunted, taking another tidy sip of wine. "Got it in one. No more repairs or naval stores to be had from them… no more wine, pasta or fresh meat on the hoof…"

"Which means the fleet must live on salt-meats," Rodgers discovered. "No way to prevent scurvy, sooner or later. I'd suppose no more onions or such, either, 'cept what little grows on Corsica. Naples—"

"We know how shaky was Naples' allegiance to the Coalition ere this," Charlton responded with a grimace. "The Pope and Tuscany... so the rumour goes... have dug deep into their treasuries and their art collections to buy off the French. Better to be a dirt-poor but still independent nation than a starving, ravaged and *conquered* one, hmm? I'd expect Naples to do likewise, weak as they are. And that, soon."

"Their art collections, sir?" Fillebrowne gawped, looking ashen.

"May they not fulfill the French tribute in gold or silver, sir," Charlton told him. "Valuable paintings, statues and such could make up the difference. There was talk ashore that this Bonaparte has explicit orders to gather *specific* works of art from palaces and museums, as *well* as solid specie. Paris has a complete list of required items by name."

"My *word*, sir!" Fillebrowne groaned. "But that is a *barbarous*... why, I never heard the like! To loot...!" He passed a hand over a very pale brow, as if presented with tales of Atilla's Huns using Virgil's library scrolls for bum-fodder. Or, more likely, Lewrie speculated, he was wondering what would be left for *him*, at any price, once the French had stripped the country clean! Lewrie didn't think many valuable artworks stood a ghost of a chance to escape the French sentry posts, along the roads on which those wealthy refugees Fillebrowne had crowed about fled.

"Book o' Revelations warned us 'bout this," Rodgers reminded them. "'An' I saw three unclean spirits – *like Frogs* – come out th' mouth o' th' dragon, an' out th' mouth o' th' Beast, an' out th' mouth o'... oh...! 'th' false prophet. F'r they're th' spirits o' devils, workin' miracles, an'... which go forth unto th' kings o' th' Earth.' Somethin' 'long that line, any-way."

Ben Rodgers... quotin' *Scripture*? Lewrie gawped! Must be *damn* deep in his *gewürz-traminer*, if that's so!

"You've been reading books again, haven't you, sir?" Lewrie simply had to chide him in mock severity, commingled with a touch of sadness.

"Well, just th' one, Lewrie." Rodgers chuckled bashfully, with a hint of throat-hitching remorse as he ducked his head. "Sorry. An' I won't let it happen again." And he manfully stifled a snigger.

"Gentlemen, really!" Charlton grumbled, nigh to prim outrage.

"I still don't understand, sir," Lewrie stuck in quickly, hoping to defuse him before he burst like a bomb. "Bonaparte came south, leaving his new conquests wide open. Leaving his rear wide open to a countermove. Surely... in the last month or so..."

"Beaulieu was beaten, sir," Charlton snapped, rounding on him as if he could still explode. "Without a real fight. That's the way *soldiers* think. Slither about like dancing-masters and won't fight 'til they've everything arranged neat and tidy to their satisfaction. And Major Simpson said he was probably waiting for reinforcements to come. There's a new general, some fellow named Wurmser, due down from their armies on the Rhine. But it'd take him a month or more to march through the passes in the Alps. I doubt the Austrians thought there'd be much threat in the meantime. Not with Mantua so strong, and plumb in the centre of all these little lakes, marshes and such. No way to get at them... no easy way, rather."

"Only were Bonaparte willing to do the usual thing and try to besiege, sir," Lewrie puzzled aloud, rising from his chair in a half-crouch to study the map where Charlton's fist was rested.

Well, mine arse on a band-box! he thought; Ferrara's not thirty-five miles from Italy's eastern coast – 'bout sixty-five or seventy to Venice! That's, what... four days' march? Jesus, with this Bonaparte make it three. He's south of the Po, the Adige rivers, south and east of Mantua. Usin' the rivers as shields, so he can play silly buggers all he wishes, till the Austrians're forced to cross and attack *him*. Which is probably just what the arrogant little shit wants!

"Seems to me, sir," Lewrie concluded, "while the Austrians are waiting for General Wurmser to arrive, Bonaparte could come down from Ferrara to the coast. There's this Lake Comacchio. He could take the town by the inlet, and land all the supplies he wants there. Or up at Ravenna... that might be safer. Out of reach of the garrison at Mantua. And safe behind the Po and all, even *after* Wurmser arrives."

"Stretch him thin, would it not, though, sir?" Fillebrowne enquired, after getting over his vapours at the thought of priceless artworks being taken out of his reach; or the reach of his purse.

"Doesn't seem to bother him much... not yet, anyway," Rodgers snorted. "Like a Robin Hood, or a famous highwayman back home. He's here, he's there, everywhere. Three coaches robbed 'fore sunrise... in three different counties, and all that outlaw's doin'."

"And Wurmser, sir," Lewrie went on, feeling the need to cross to the sideboard and top up his glass, then fetch the bottle back to fill the others up. "Coming from the Rhine armies, you said? Hellish risk, to strip the Rhine of men and guns, ain't it? Makes it easier for Frog troops to go tramplin' into Bavaria…?"

Damme, they look as if I'd just let a fart! Lewrie thought as he saw the sudden, gape-mouthed expressions on their faces.

It was one thing to hear that the largest, most lavishly equipped and most rigourously trained army in Europe – an army supported by the mightiest and most populous empire in the world – was having a few bad bouts…

Well, Lewrie qualified to himself, there's China, but they're not in this equation. And there is Roosia, but they're lucky to stand upright on a *good* day, so I'm told!

But, to contemplate the tag-rag-and-bobtail French actually *defeating* Austria… invading Austrian possessions… well!

Well, hadn't they just? Lewrie qualified again. The Arch-duchy of Milan and Lombardy *are* Austrian possessions. So what's special 'bout Bavaria goin', too? And if they can do that…!

That sneaking, queasy, gut-wrenching worry was on every face of a sudden. Lewrie poured their top-ups in total, astonished and funereal silence, like they'd just been told of their monarch being murdered. Or that hushed silence of Maundy Thursday in church, when the fine trappings are stripped in mournful quiet.

"Ahum…" Charlton grunted, breaking their silence, taking his newly full glass at last. "Thankee, Lewrie. Now, sirs. That's the appalling lot; here's the merely bad. Admiral Jervis had sent us new instructions. He is of a mind that, should the French try to cut the Italian peninsula and gain the eastern coast, our presence in the Adriatic will be more important than ever. We are to keep a closer eye on the Italian coast, now Bonaparte controls the Papal States' shores. We must prevent any succour reaching him by sea. We are to prevent any warships formerly controlled by those nations now paying tribute to the French from being appropriated and incorporated into their navy… prevent them from sailing, or destroy them should they do so. And we're to continue our interdiction of the timber and naval stores from the Adriatic, of course, hence delaying the presence of substantial numbers of French warships along their newly gained Italian coast. We must… uhm, 'soldier' on, for the nonce."

They nodded dumbly at that directive.

"For us to remain in the Adriatic, sirs, is *not* bad news, and I do not wish you to draw any negative connotations from my characterisations of our expanded orders," Charlton was quick to warn them. "I refer, rather, to the local situation, anent the Austrians. It seems... hmm... the local authorities, the town fathers of Trieste, as well as the Austrian Naval and War Ministry at Vienna have, uhmm..."

He took another bracing sip of wine, screwing his mouth to one side as if he'd developed a sudden distaste for the spicy, sweet drink.

"Perhaps we've been a tad *too* successful, too quickly. Or the Austrians now expect miracles from us, as a matter of course," Captain Charlton posed, essaying a rather grim chuckle, with no real humour in it, "I know not which. Sweep their seas clean for 'em... muck out the Augean Stables for 'em, like Hercules as a hired labourer did. But... given their parlous situation ashore, Vienna has shifted funds from the Trieste Squadron and given them to their hard-pressed armies. And the town council of Trieste have seen fit to *reduce* their contributions to Major Simpson's squadron. Cut him in half, just about. So he will *not* be completing his seven new gun-boats, and will barely be able to maintain what few vessels he already possesses. That, of course, precludes his conversion of any of our seaworthy prizes into warships which might have reinforced us, as we had originally discussed. He'd have to buy a ship in, first, arm her, strengthen her, then man her. And where he'd get a *tenth* of the funds necessary for that, God only knows. So here we are, still completely 'on our own bottoms,' sirs."

"Well, what about the Hungarian Squadron, sir?" Lewrie enquired. "Though we haven't met 'em yet, weren't they more aggressive at...?"

"I'm told it's much the same with them, Lewrie, the same text, chapter, and verse," Charlton rejoined. "In point of fact, their infantry regiments which form their marines have been given orders to go west, to Mantua. They put great stock in Croat soldiers. Devilish-good fighters, I'm told. They're laying up their fleet, too, stripping it to the bone, 'til the problem with Bonaparte has been settled. On the land... over in Lombardy. 'Til then, the only naval worries they might have would be along the upper Rhine and the Danube."

"Th' French get so far'z t'threaten Trieste," Captain Rodgers quipped, "then th' Austrians've far greater problems'n ya could shake a stick at, anyway."

"Quite so, Captain Rodgers," Charlton was forced to agree.

"Never even met the Hungarians yet, sir," Fillebrowne sniffed primly. "Nor any help from their little squadron of coasters."

"Doin' main-well so far, sir," Rodgers grumbled. "An' 'thout a *jot* o' Austrian aid, either! We'll manage fine... way I see it."

"Ah, but should the traffick increase, sirs," Charlton warned them sternly, "should the French take over even a few well-armed small ships... we can't be everywhere at once. Nor, unless we sail together, be of sufficient strength. Guard the straits only, and the French may play merry Hell on the Italian east coast. Shift patrols over there, closer to Ravenna and Venice, and the straits become a thoroughfare to smugglers and French merchantmen. We're badly in need of reinforcement. I tell you, sirs, badly. Did we have a third frigate and sloop of war, we might – *might*, mind – just barely cope. One group for the straits down south, one for the Balkan coast, and one patrolling higher up in the Adriatic... keeping an eye on Ravenna and such."

"So, we split up into singletons, sir," Lewrie suggested. "The frigates, at least, and pair *Jester* and *Myrmidon*. There's your three groups." Much as he disliked the idea of sailing with Fillebrowne!

"And what did our first spell at sea shew us, sir?" Charlton objected right crankily. "That there are ships enough to intercept already... without an increase in numbers. And only so many hands we may spare to man them, before we are forced to return to Trieste. Or run the risk of battle so poorly manned we're barely able to tend sail, much less fight. Do one or the other, but not both, sir!"

"No chance there would be any help forthcoming from the Fleet, sir?" Fillebrowne prompted, sounding almost wistful.

"Not with these newly captured Tuscan ports to watch, atop the others we were already thin-stretched to blockade, sir, no," Charlton assured him. "There are *never* enough frigates or sloops, sore as their lack is felt in time of war. Even before this Bonaparte marched, we'd gotten all he could spare. Damme, had we *twice* the force, though...!" He sighed, sounding more than a touch wistful, too. "Surely our Lords Commissioners should know this cruel fact, should have laid down ships other than 'liners,' by the score!"

Uh-oh! Lewrie thought. Things must have come to a pretty pass if he's blamin' Admiralty for 'is problems!

Perhaps someone kind should have made a helpful suggestion, said some comforting words of encouragement to him. Lewrie felt the urge to commiserate with the much-put-upon Captain Charlton.

Onliest trouble was, there wasn't anything *close* to clever that could be said, certainly not by Lewrie, nor by the others, even if they had been of a mind to. It was up to Captain Charlton; he was a senior post-captain in charge of an independent squadron. Officers slaved all their lives – toadied and schemed, some of them – sweated round-shot they'd not put a single foot wrong their entire careers, to get where he was at that moment, with that much power, with that much responsibility. And all the recognition, fame, honour, glory, pride and perquisites which came with it.

Until one chose wrong, o' course.

The man's spitted, Alan thought, keeping his face bland and junior-like. Poor bastard's got a spit run up his arse, right through to the apple in his mouth! Spitted and broilin' over a hellish-toasty bed o' coals. Turnin' and bastin', Lewrie could conjure, all but writhing in agony.

And may I never rise higher than post-captain of a frigate, he further thought; pay's decent, and there's always someone t'tell you where t'go, what t'do. Wouldn't have his responsibility for—

"Well, sirs," Captain Charlton said, after a long and uncomfortable silence, during which his dumbstruck inferiors had sat quiet, and as thankfully mute as Lewrie had. "If Austrian or Hungarian help is not to be forthcoming… nor is Venice able – or even of a mind! – to help herself, then I do believe that we must explore what is perhaps the only solution open to us. Uhm, that is to say, a possible solution which I and Major Simpson of the Austrian Navy discussed… as onerous as it may sound to you. A temporary, uhm…"

Charlton waved a frustrated hand, as if even he didn't quite hold with it, and already sharing the blame should it not work out.

"The only local source of reinforcement which could free us of inshore patrolling and allow us to cover all our responsibilities, it seems, gentlemen… are the Balkan pirates."

Chapter 6

Now, *there's* somethin' I never thought to hear! Lewrie admitted, all but cringing. He darted a quick glance to Ben Rodgers, who looked as if he had been butted in the belly by an underhanded boxer: mouth open, eyes ready to roll and on the verge of sucking air in a frantic "Eeepp!"

"But sir—" Lewrie began to protest.

"Said it'd strike you all as onerous," Charlton snapped, cutting him off, "but what other choices are there, Commander Lewrie? Pray, do place before us another."

"Well, sir, I…" Lewrie was flummoxed, trying desperately to come up with something – anything! – other than that.

"Novel, I must say, sir," Commander Fillebrowne cooed softly, with the sound of grudging admiration in his voice – as if he was yet unconvinced, but could not deny the logic of it. "May I infer, sir, that Major Simpson will issue them Letters of Marque?"

"We discussed that, Commander Fillebrowne," Captain Charlton admitted, still fretting. He was still most uneasy with his decision and writhing in his chair in that former roast-pig agony for another moment as he turned to Fillebrowne. "Maritime law is rather touchy 'pon the subject of privateers, however. Did Austria issue a pirate band Letters of Marque and Reprisal, they would have to declare them Austrian subjects, to begin with. Would have to allow them to work from Trieste, since the home port must be stated. And they would have to sail under the national colours of the nation which issued the documents. And, I rather doubt any Balkan pirates could be stood here, do you, sir?"

Charlton took a sip of wine and almost had himself a chuckle of sardonic amusement in contemplating the sight of illiterate, seagoing peasants and cutthroats in placid Trieste's beer cellars.

"And, given the long-standing hostility 'twixt Austrians and the various minorities down south, I equally doubt the pirates would enjoy the association, either, so… no, sir. There will be no letters from the Austrians."

"Not from us, then, surely, sir!" Lewrie carped.

"Nor from us, Commander Lewrie," Charlton told him. "I haven't that authority in the first instance, and as I said, this arrangement… should it even be possible to *make* such an alliance… would be of a temporary, *ad hoc* nature. *Sub rosa*, so to speak. Not the sort of thing one wishes bruited about. A rather loose, informal arrangement."

For a man who'd been writhing just a second before, Charlton had gone rather calm, Lewrie thought. Now that his decision to co-opt piratical bands was out in the open, and had not immediately been shouted down, Charlton seemed to have firmed the decision in his mind, and it was not going to be a topic for discussion.

"War on the 'cheap,'" Lewrie muttered.

"You *said*, sir?" Charlton queried most petulantly.

"Something one of my old captains said, sir," Lewrie answered, chin up. "When we were trying to talk Red Indians into alliance with the Crown back in '82. Came up again in the Far East, with South Sea pirates, 'tween the wars. War on the 'cheap,' he called it, sir. And no good ever came from either."

"S'pose you'd be preferring the Uscocchi, sir?" Fillebrowne said, breezing on as if there'd been no objections.

"I would, indeed, Commander Fillebrowne," Charlton mused, patting his unruly hair back in place. "Splendid fighters on land, since they're Croat. And deuced good seamen, too, as the Austrian officers at our welcoming supper told us. Catholic, don't ye know. Fiercely devoted to their religion."

"Holy war, sir?" Lewrie posed. "There's a Pandora's Box we—"

"Devoted to a religion, sir, that is at least European!" Captain Charlton shot back, glaring him to silence once more. Or at the least trying to. "And I tell you, Commander Lewrie, I begin to tire of your particular sense of humour, forever drolly mocking and—"

"I'm not japing, sir. Not this time," Lewrie assured him with a dead-level and dead-sober gaze. "I've *seen* war on the 'cheap,' and it's a blood-red horror, sir. Fought by… well, sirs, one can't call massacre and ambush *fighting*, exactly. Rape, pillaging, torching and leveling, and once it's begun, there's no calling it back, sir. Blood calls for blood, revenge… Corsican *vendetta*, Scottish feud, and there is no European, *civilised* control over it once it's got rolling, sir."

"War waged by, as you just admitted, Commander Lewrie, savages! Red Indian tribes in the Americas? South Sea islanders and heathens in tattoos and breechclouts?" Charlton boomed, his blood up. "What the heathens do 'mongst themselves, once armed with European weapons, isn't our concern, I tell you! What they can do with them 'gainst our enemies is. What feuds and grievances the Balkan inhabitants suffer are already centuries old, sir, and will still be brewing long after we're gone. To co-opt, as you put it, a band of coastal pirates of whatever persuasion – temporarily – will make no difference. Whether they are at each others' throats with Roman short-sword and spear, or flintlock muskets and bayonets – with bloody cannon! – is moot. As odd as they are, the Slavs of the Balkans *are* Europeans, Commander Lewrie. Cut off from the finer things of life, admittedly, but still Europeans. They're not your painted Indians."

Are they not, sir? Was on Lewrie's tongue, but he thought it'd be a bit beyond insubordinate to say it. No one had dealt with Balkan peoples yet, other than the odd brush with them off Brac and Bar, so he wasn't so sure that Charlton was *completely* wrong, or that he was so completely *right*, either. He screwed his face up, almost biting at a cheek in purse-lipped frustration, and kept silent, reddening.

"Catholic, Russian Orthodox or Greek Orthodox, those are European religions of a sort, sir," Charlton rushed on, as if he'd already wrestled the main points of the logic behind his decision to the ground. "Not as rational, I'll grant you, none of 'em, as the Church of England, nor Protestantism. Yet each has redeeming features of Christianity at bottom. The Dalmatian peoples do not have the Inquisition, as *civilised* Spain does, after all! As hand-to-mouth as they live, according to the accounts you brought of the few you encountered, they might even be of a placid, bucolic nature. Rustic, poverty-stricken peasants, toiling 'pon a few miserable, rocky acres or less, like so many Irish tenant crofters. Closer to the soil, closer to God, perhaps? Denied the luxuries of civilisation, may they not be closer to that Frog Rousseau's depiction of 'noble savages'? But, sir! Christians! Europeans. Capable of—"

"Turks're out, I take it, sir?" Rodgers interrupted, posing such a ludicrous notion that Charlton looked fit to lean over and bite him.

"*Right* out, Captain Rodgers!" Charlton barked. "As I was *about* to say, the Dalmatian peoples are, at bottom, European stock. Capable of civilised doings, of forming firm pacts, of disciplining themselves and their behaviour. Look at the many units in the Austrian or Hungarian armies, for God's sake! Capable of following orders, of knowing a right from a wrong, and acting upon that knowledge with… with…! Well, if not from a *gentlemanly* sense of honour and propriety, then with the *innate* sense of honour and propriety which centuries of Christian dogma's drummed into them. It's not as if we're allying ourselves, even temporarily or expeditiously, with Gibraltar Apes! Nor with any of those swart kings of Dahomey, who sell their own kin to slave-dealers… or satanic *beasts*, after all!"

"God forbid, sir." Fillebrowne all but shivered. "It's quite like what that Scotsman, Burns, said in one of his poems, sir. That a 'man's a man, for a' that'? No matter his land of birth."

"Exactly, Fillebrowne!" Charlton smiled thankfully, relieved that at least one of his officers sounded supportive. "Exactly. No matter where one goes, people are people, when you get right down to it, with the same way of thinking, of deciding right from wrong. I'd take issue with your Burns, or anyone else, though, who professes that a day-labourer from the stews might be the equal of a proper gentleman… mean t'say, isn't that why we fought the Colonies? Are now embroiled in war with France, hey? Birth, class, privilege and education, and a sound religious upbringing by sober, dependable parents, make the difference – for European, Christian folk, at least. Just look at us!"

Oh, *aye*, look at us! Lewrie felt like groaning aloud; one a toad-eatin' swindler-to-be, one a feckless womaniser with a hollow leg, and me… an adulterous bastard! Fine lot we are, for examples!

"Wouldn't that make the French, or the Rebels, decent folk, then… at bottom, sir?" Lewrie couldn't help asking. "Sensible, peaceful Christians, sprung of European stock?"

"But deluded, sir, by rabble-rousing, leveling Jacobinist cant," Charlton growled. "No different from us, I will allow. Just dead-wrong in their thinking. And now intent on spreading their creed of the Common Man being the equal of a king, by force of arms. Using guns to settle the question which would be more suited to an intellectual wrangle than a war. And most hypocritically using their pious cant to justify taking territory they've always coveted, by conquest!"

Charlton was huffing hard, in high dudgeon and colour, his wind wheezing in and out through constricted nostrils like a forge-bellows.

"Now, sir…" he demanded, "do you have any other pertinent comments to make, or care to share with us, Commander Lewrie?"

"Uhm..."

"So you are settled in your mind that we should approach Balkan pirates and attempt to form a temporary arrangement?" Charlton pressed.

"Well, not completely settled, sir. After all..." Lewrie sighed.

"Fillebrowne?" Charlton snapped, wheeling on him.

"It's a most unusual, and as you said yourself, sir," Fille-browne trimmed, coughing into his fist, "a most onerous proposition. But one I feel is absolutely necessary. And you would not have proposed it had you not given it much difficult consideration, sir. I am at your total disposal. Game for anything you deem worthy, sir. At your orders."

Havin' it both ways, Lewrie thought furiously; objectin' so meek and mild, but goin' along, in spite of yer... reservations! Damme, he's askin', not orderin'! Now's the time to scotch it!

"Captain Rodgers, sir?" Charlton gruffed.

"Well, sir... Lewrie an' me," Ben wheedled, "we've had dealin's with pirates, an' like Lewrie said, sir... no good ever came of it. In the Bahamas... once we set one pack atop th' rest? Have t'arm 'em, I'd expect? Give 'em an advantage o'er th' others, sir? An' what they'll do to each other with decent numbers o' modern arms after, well..."

"The only reason the Balkans haven't thrown off their Turkish masters, sir, is *lack* of arms," Charlton purred. "That, and the utter brutality of Turkish repression. Even were there not a revolt brewing, I'm told the Turks roam their territories and slaughter a village or a *region* just to keep 'em cowed! Chosen by sheer caprice, sir! To show them what'd happen should they even *think* of rising up. I'd expect they would turn on their oppressors first, Captain Rodgers, not each other. Serbs, Croats, whoever... they've seen the Ottoman Empire weaken. Seen the Barbary States, the Mamelukes of Egypt, strike out on their own... that Pasha of Scutari as the closest-to-home example. The Greek people in the Morea... good God, sir! Founders of Western civilisation, of all we hold dear – politics, poetry, logic, debate. Ground under the heel of brutal, un-Christian conquerors. Do we light a powder-train in the Balkans, Captain Rodgers, perhaps it may be a train which leads to the long-buried powder-keg of rebellion. They may throw off the Turks and drive them out, make of themselves what they will afterwards. And sirs, mark me well," Charlton cautioned, close to a sly smile of pleasure, "once free of the Turks, might they recall and be thankful to England? Resulting in British control of the Adriatic and the Aegean Seas? Of the profitable Eastern trade, hah?"

"Well, there's that, sir..." Rodgers admitted, glancing down in a sheepish, confounded way. "Might be a fine thing, that."

Lord, Ben! Lewrie all but cried aloud. Peyton Boudreau at Nassau had the right of it, you always were a slender reed. God knows, back then I talked you into enough shit. You always espoused the *loudest* argument... or the last'un you heard! Do be a man, for once, though. Stand up on yer own hind legs, an'...!

"We could try, sir," Ben Rodgers allowed. "Feel 'em out down south. Contact several bands. It may be they'd have no part of it, or none'd prove usable. Then, if nothing comes of it..." He tailed off with a helpless shrug. And, Lewrie noted, Captain Charlton gave him a glad, rewarding nod of approval.

"Very well, then," Charlton sniffed. "Lewrie, we know what you think of this."

Not 'til I've had a *real* rant, you don't, Lewrie left unspoken. A real rant, though... say what I really wish to say, and I'd be clapped in irons.

He looked round, to Commander Fillebrowne, who wore a smug look on his face, as if he'd herded Lewrie to the edge of a cliff and would most happily goad him to leap, and bedamned. To Rodgers, who was most pointedly sipping wine and staring off into the nether-regions, unable to meet his gaze. Then to Charlton, who was... waiting. Smirking?

"I don't like pirates much, sir," Lewrie began to respond, slowly and cautiously. "Never have. They don't play by civilised rules, sir, even the 'well-schooled' ones. The Rackhams, Bonnets, Teaches and Morgans... English gentlemen all, sir, yet..." He shrugged.

Charlton's firm expression faltered, whether to Lewrie's jibe or to an innate loathing for his own plan, some deep-down caution.

No, he ain't smirkin', Lewrie decided; at bottom, he knows what a horror we might start, and no way t'end it. Bothers him as much as me. No wonder he didn't just scribble us some orders and have done. He's a decent man, caught on the prongs of a shitten cleft stick. God help him... us!

"Needs must, I s'pose, though, sir," Lewrie grunted, deep from his gut, and tossed off another shrug to express reluctant acceptance. "Do you order it so, then we'll do the best we're able."

"I never considered anything less from you, Commander Lewrie," Charlton softly replied, relenting from his grim glower, and tossing him a bone of approbation. Though there was still a hesitancy to him, as if he'd relish being argued out of his decision. It was rare, but not completely unheard-of, for a quorum of captains to weight their options and come to a mutually agreed decision, when very far from higher authorities. He could have been as dictatorial, as domineering and irrationally unreasonable as the last post-captain who had had command over Lewrie – Howard Braxton of the ill-starred *Cockerel* frigate. For not being such a toplofty tyrant, Lewrie felt at least a slight bit of gratitude towards Charlton.

"Very well, sirs," Charlton said, after topping up their wine as reward for their agreement. "Here is what we'll do. For the nonce, we will sail more independent of each other… in *three* groups as Commander Lewrie posed. Though perhaps not the same pairings, however…"

Toss me a bone, aye, Alan begrudged; *good* doggie!

"I will take *Lionheart* down to the Straits of Otranto again," Charlton schemed aloud. "Should French warships come from Toulon with succour for this Bonaparte by sea or take advantage of his gains, our best-armed and strongest ship should be placed to counter them. Even alone, I believe I could. Now, Commander Fillebrowne…"

"Aye, sir?" Fillebrowne perked up.

"Yours will be the roving brief, sir," Charlton outlined. "A cruise nearer to Venice, high up the Adriatic to the west. Especially those harbours of the Papal States which are now in thrall to Bonaparte. Look into them, within your abilities… and the diplomatic niceties… for French ships. And look for warships that might be taken into service by the French Navy… what state of readiness for sea, d'ye see, sir. As far suth'rd a cruise as Rimini, Pescara and Ancona would do admirably well. And this inlet Lewrie mentioned, Lake Comacchio."

"Of course, sir!" Fillebrowne replied, all bright-eyed eager. To sail free and independent of senior officers' eyes was every junior captain's dream of perfect freedom.

"Captain Rodgers, you and Commander Lewrie will repeat your previous voyage… a slow jog down the Balkan coasts. Seeking merchantmen, it goes without saying. But enquiring of local author-ities as to the whereabouts of – and most covertly, the suitability of – any pirate bands amenable to working with us."

"Aye aye, sir." Rodgers nodded heavily.

"Major Simpson said that he could supply us with an officer of his squadron," Charlton continued, "should we have decided to espouse such allies as we... erm, discussed. Someone with local knowledge of the coast, conversant in the various dialects, and – hhmmph! – which freebooters have the strength, the suitability, the ah... civility, rather" – Charlton all but winced – "useful to our cause."

"Aye, sir," Rodgers repeated, his moon face a dark-complexioned blank, as if giving Charlton no more than heavy-lidded, rote obedience.

Or he's took by "barrel-fever" by now, Lewrie thought, seeing as how we're on our *fourth* bottle of wine 'twixt the four of us. And nought but Ben's been sippin' steady.

"Well, that should do it, I think, sirs." Charlton beamed, with a cock of his head towards a calendar hanging in his chart-space beyond. "We'll meet up here at Trieste again in, say, three weeks? First week of August at the latest, depending on what occurs on your various duties and how depleted you are for prize-crews. You run into anything dangerous, and you scoot back here for shelter. Or come south to me, in the straits. Or, should I need saving, sirs" – Charlton posed, hands out in a helpless expression – "should the Frogs come in strength, then you'll see me first. Flying afore 'em, with stuns'ls aloft and alow! Captain Rodgers, you'll have your Austrian liaison aboard soon. Once I've sent word to Major Simpson, ashore. Uhm..."

Charlton had been acting very relieved, almost joyful at times, since they'd acceded to his plans – though, now and then, a touch rueful and hesitant. Now he almost blushed.

"Before you sail, you'd best take aboard a small cargo of arms and such, sirs... the both of you," Charlton added. "Do you succeed in discovering suitable temporary allies, then why not, uhm...?"

"Aye aye, sir," Rodgers agreed once more, even more heavily.

-

"Off ashore, sir?" Lewrie asked Rodgers, once they were on deck and queuing up for their gigs to arrive, in strict order of seniority. "S'pose you're about due for a tear. Even among what poor amusements Trieste has to offer. Not a patch on Venice, after all..."

"I might," Rodgers allowed. Almost snippish, though.

Truculence? Lewrie wondered. A guilty conscience? Or pissed as a newt? Damn' standoffish, I must say!

"And you, sir?" Rodgers queried.

"Seen it, sir." Lewrie chuckled. "Hellish boresome. Letters to write, that sort of last-minute thing. *Cargo* to load," he drawled with a sarcastic note. "For our *noble* 'Christian' friends, don't ye know."

That officer lined up and ready to assist their search, a cargo of arms all but crated and ready to stow below... Lewrie was now wondering just how really debatable the scheme had been before they'd been called aboard *Lionheart* to discuss it.

And Charlton's parting shot! A last admonition, nothing written, a verbal order tossed off as if it were a matter that had slipped his mind. "Make certain you only engage Christian pirates, sirs!" And it had been a wonder to watch him not twitch in embarrassment for uttering such a statement!

Christian pirates, my God! Lewrie groaned; sort of like merging "Army" and "Intelligence"! Find 'em, most-like, by followin' the smell o' incense burnin' in their censers... whilst they're at prayers!

"Quite th' change th' years've made of us, Lewrie," Rodgers said of a sudden, in a very soft, conspiratorial voice. "You, turned into an upright family man. An' me... a coward."

"You, sir? A coward?" Lewrie hooted. "Hardly!"

But thinking that he was, in a way, just the same.

"Oh, stop yer gob, sir!" Rodgers spat. "You know what I mean."

"Well, sir" – Lewrie frowned at the vehemence of Rodgers's bile – "I didn't think he was *that* dead-set for it, straightaway. Thought did we argue him out of it... two-to-two. Can't count on Fillebrowne..."

"Nothin' we could've said'd change his mind, Lewrie. Nor made a tinker's damn worth o' diff'rence. And you should've seen it," Rodgers accused. "'Stead o' goin' off half-cocked... like ya always do."

"Sir?" Lewrie huffed, cocking his head in perplexity.

"There's some, Commander Lewrie, as've piled up enough 'tin' to weather rocky times, an' some as've not," Rodgers grumbled from a side of his mouth, half turned away to watch the approach of his gig.

"I don't understand, Ben."

"*Captain* Rodgers, sir!" Rodgers snapped so harshly that Lewrie felt like flinching back from him.

"Excuse me, sir, but—"

"Estate, prize-money… farm income," Rodgers pushed on. "An' Navy career bedamned, should things go cross-patch. Think we're all so fortunate, sir, t'risk our careers so easy? Think we've all yer tidy shore livin' t'fall back on?"

"I never thought… I don't see…!"

"*Course* ya don't, Lewrie!" Rodgers muttered. "You never do. Never see anything but your way… an' how t'get it. An' thinking I'm t'shout 'amen' whenever ya leave off prosin'. *Course* it's a hellish idea, t'get mixed up with local pirates… d'ye think I like it a whit more'n you? I do not! But we said our piece, then he gave us orders. Whether we care for 'em or no. But ya never know when t'leave be an' when t'quit wheedlin'. Just too bloody clever by half. But not clever enough t'see th' end result o' bein' so sly-boots. Not for yer-self, or any ya drag down with ya."

Rodgers lifted his hat briefly to air his scalp, to resettle it further down over his eyes, still gazing towards the clutch of boats.

"You asked me did I recall Charleston," Rodgers began again, as he turned back to face Lewrie. "An' did I still resent all th' shit I was dumped into, 'cause o' yer actions. Well, I did and I do, Lewrie. You *always* talked me into folly… Charleston, and both times at Walker's Cay, when we were after 'Calico Jack' Finney. Resent things now, too. Resent ya peerin' at me, all promptin' an' shiny-eyed t'support ya an' damnin' me do I not."

"Sir, I never…!"

Well, aye… maybe I did. Alan winced with chagrin. And took a half step back from Rodgers's hissing fury. "Ben?" He pled once more.

"That's '*sir*,' t'ya, Lewrie," Rodgers warned. "Caution ya, now. I'm half-seas-over. Cherry-merry. But not'z cherry-merry'z I intend t'be by midnight. It'll be 'sir' t'day… an' most-like 'sir' t'me tomorrow, too, 'cause I plan t'have a dev'lish thick head. An' do ya know why that'll be, Lewrie?"

"No, sir," Alan replied warily, feeling betrayed after all the times they'd served together, after how close he'd thought they'd been.

"'Cause I'm scared o' puttin' mine arse on th' choppin'-block as easy as you. Scared o' rowin' Captain Charlton with objections that'd make a poor report on me when *Pylades* pays off an' it's time to get a new commission, 'cause I'm not blessed with yer shore livin' t'count on should I get beached on half-pay. Scared t'say what I really did *mean* t'say 'bout this half-arsed scheme o' his. An' maybe I'll be 'in th' barrel' 'cause I don't much care for m'self for *not* sayin' it, at th' moment, either! But then… I never have to, do I? You'll always leap up an' say it first, won't ya? Tie me to yer words, link me with yer objections, expect me t'back ya… an' there I am, tarred with that same old brush. Now an' again, Lewrie… it gets old, d'ye see?"

"I…" Lewrie opened his stunned mouth to respond.

"I get tired o' bein' led into folly… get tired o' followin' yer lead, Lewrie," Rodgers said with a weary, embittered sigh. "Even if ya *are* right most o' th' time, God help us. Tired o' bein' used, whenever ya think yer th' onliest one that knows best. Knew we were t'serve t'gether again, I'd hopes you'd've mellowed, learned *some* caution, but…" He shook his round head in long-pent despair. "An' do ya know how hard it is t'deal with a man such'z yerself, Lewrie? How hard it is t'play gun-dog to ya, an' do yer biddin' when ya whistle or snap yer fingers?"

"I never knew you felt this way, sir," Alan grunted. "I thought we worked well together, that—"

"Aye, we do, Lewrie, that's th' rub," Rodgers whispered, hands up to scrub his face into some bit of sobriety. He swelled up, bloated on too much sweet wine, perhaps too much bitterness. And let out a hearty belch at last.

At least he turned his head for *that*, Lewrie thought inanely.

"So…?" he enquired.

"Ah, devil take it," Rodgers sighed, looking as if there was one more ripe eructation where that one had come from, still to be freed. "You tread wary round me a day'r two… it'll be Alan and Ben by dawn o' th' second, I'd expect. A takin' o' th' moment, and nothin' permanent. No real lastin' spite, d'ye see, but… by God, sir! Sometimes ya make me so… !"

"Furious?" Lewrie asked. "Aye. Never bored, though, are you?" he added with a hopeful grin.

"Aye, furious," Rodgers echoed, all but swaying as Lieutenant Nicholson came over to tell him that his gig was at last thumping against the hull, just below the starboard entry-port. "Exasperatin', that's what ya are, Commander Lewrie. Exasperatin' as the very Devil. But never borin'. Damn yer eyes."

"May I take that as a vote of confidence, then, sir?" Lewrie asked with a wider smile as he walked with Rodgers to the entry-port.

"Not *really*!" Ben drawled rather archly. "You let me take th' lead, and try t'stifle yerself, when ya feel a fit o' cleverness comin' on. I'm not certain my career could take too many more o' yer brighter moments."

"I stand admonished, sir," Lewrie soberly told him. "Really!"

"Ya bloody do not!" Rodgers scoffed. "An' ya never will."

But he offered his hand and they shook, before stepping back to doff hats to each other; friends first – formally courteous naval officers second.

"Thankee, sir," Lewrie said, just as he turned to go.

"For what... a hidin'?" Rodgers peered close at him.

"For still being a friend, exasperated or no, sir," Lewrie said.

"What do ya think friends are for?" Rodgers sighed, then gave him a wink as he turned to doff his hat to the side-party's salute, and make his way, arse-out, down the battens and man-ropes to his gig.

Chapter 7

The Austrian liaison officer assigned to them was a low-ranking Leut-nant zur See Conrad Kolodzcy, a minor figure from one of the minor navies. His rank, however, was the only thing humble about him for he had a very high opinion of himself, which was apparent right from his arrival aboard *Pylades* with no less than two body-servants, two large sea-chests and a clutch of luggage that held – so he haughtily told them – the *bare* necessities of life, without which no *true* gentleman would *dare* to travel.

Lewrie wasn't so sure Kolodzcy wasn't an out-of-work instructor of dancing, masquerading – some rude jape the Austrians had foisted on them – and was more than happy that Rodgers was the one forced to deal with him on a daily basis and share his august company.

Leutnant Kolodzcy was a touch leaner than courtier-slim, as thin as a high-strung whippet or greyhound. He displayed such elegant, languid mannerisms that he could have taught refinement to the Venetians, making them look like lumbering dockyard drunks by comparison. He stood three inches shorter than Lewrie's five-foot-nine – and that with the help of a pair of glossy black Hessian boots with heels so tall they were suited to cavalry stirrups. And they were adorned with more gaudy gilt cord and tassels than post-captains were allowed on an entire coat!

His hair was dark, almost raven-black, and cut in that new-fangled Frog fashion… brushed forward over the ears and forehead, and lacking that long, plaited queue particular to *real* sailor-men. He sported soft brown puppy eyes set in a rather pale face of such startling regularity that he was almost effeminately pretty, with cheekbones any fashionable lady might kill for, a pert little drawer-knob of a chin, and lips quite bee-stung, or as cherubically bowed as Cupid's. When he didn't have 'em set in a disbelieving pout or *moue*, that is, over how real navies lived!

And Leutnant zur See Conrad Kolodzcy wore scent... rather a lot of scent. Lewrie suspected his family was in the trade and kept him stocked with a constant supply of the family product, as a fashion adjunct or as a walking advertisement. That Hungary Water or Cologne wasn't used in the manner most folks used it – to cover the reek of unwashed flesh and clothing – for Leutnant Kolodzcy had fetched along a portable, collapsible canvas bathtub as part of his "absolutely essential" kit, and had been appalled to learn that his daily allotment of water for shaving and bathing would be the same as a British officer's – a bare pint a day! – barring what they could sluice into water-butts when it rained. He had been most vocal in expressing his horror over that; that, and the lack of proper chefs, proper bedsteads, clean bed-linen daily, decent wine to drink, or the dreadful hours he'd be expected to rise or retire, or the fact that tea, coffee or chocolate couldn't be whistled up from the galley on a whim.

Fortunately for their mission, he could express his horrors in English, French, German, Italian, Hungarian, Albanian or Serbo-Croat, or a smattering of both Turkish or Demotic Greek. *Un*fortunately for nerves or patience, he did this in a thin, high, irritatingly lazy whine!

"Look, Lewrie, erm..." Rodgers said, once he'd directed Kolodzcy below to settle in, "since you'll be so close inshore, first to make a contact with pirate bands—"

"But would his dignity not be mortally offended, sir?" Lewrie said most quickly in rebuttal, as soon as he saw which way the wind was blowing. "Fobbed off on a junior officer? On a minor vessel with less room? My word, sir! Just what would the Austrian court make o' that? The diplomatic tussle that'd cause... tsk-tsk. Why, I shudder to think."

"I could make it an order, Lewrie," Rodgers said with a gloomy look.

"And of course you could, sir," Lewrie agreed, struggling to keep his countenance whey-faced innocent of guile, yet tinged with honest concern. "Though our orders from Admiral Jervis were to make every effort to honour and accommodate our Austrian allies and give no offence which might undo the Coalition. Who knows what ear at Court in Vienna this fellow whispers into, though? Then, as senior officer of our *ad hoc* squadron, sir... after all, can't let the side down, sir. All for old England... an' all that?"

"Yer bein' exasperatin' again, Lewrie." Rodgers all but wept.

"Just pointing out the consequences, sir." Lewrie shrugged, daring to let a "sympathetic" grin tweak his mouth, elevate his brow.

"Damn yer eyes, Lewrie. Just damn yer eyes," Rodgers sighed.

"*Very* good, sir!"

"Vahl, ahz you heff learn-ed," Leutnant Kolodzcy drawled, seated in one of Rodgers's armchairs, legs primly crossed at the knees, idly holding a slim Spanish cigarillo in one hand and a tall flute of Capt. Rodgers's best champagne in the other, "dere are many pirade bants on de Balgan goast, chentlemen."

He just say "Balkan *ghost*"? Lewrie asked himself, head over in perplexity as he tried to decypher Kolodzcy's extremely tortured English. Oh! Balkan *coast*! Pirate-bloody-bants... *bands*! Gawd...!

"Aye, we've encountered some," Rodgers allowed.

"*Ja!*" Kolodzcy exclaimed, somewhat like the "Yipp!" an excited lapdog might make. He paused to take a dainty sip of champagne, then curl his left wrist inward for a puff of cigar smoke. He threw back his head to shoot smoke at the overhead, and then shot his cuff to return the cigarillo to "Run-in, Load" position. It was most elegantly, though foppishly done.

"Though mine family ist frohm de easz... Transylwania... 'Ungarian, do you see?" Kolodzcy languidly explained, "I am many yahrs upon de Balgan goast, and am knowink it *guite* intimadely, sirs. Unt I dell you now, chentlemen, dat dhere are only *vahry* few pirade bants awailable to you."

"Beg pardon?" Rodgers said, having to ask for a repeat before he grasped all that Kolodzcy had lisped out. "And why is that, sir?"

"Herr Kapitan Rodgers," Kolodzcy simpered, as one might to the dimmest student in the class, "for de vahry gute reason dat dere are few who heff need of you, in de firsd blace. Gon-zidder..."

Don't know I care to 'gonzidder'! Lewrie thought, trying to not cackle out loud. This Leutnant Kolodzcy was better than an *entré-acte* at a Drury Lane theatre! Surely he was a poseur, a clown!

"De Uscocchi, de Croatians, sir," Kolodzcy droned on, puffing on his cigarillo with all the panache of a lady hard at it with her fan. "Allied vit de 'Ungarians, already. You abbroach Croatian pirades in 'Ungarian serwice, you inwolve 'Ungary. A formal, overt alliance, vich

I do nod think your Kapitan Charlton vishes? Anyway, Uscocchi are all promised to Vienna... not awailable, *nicht wahr?* Gonzidder alzo Corsairs ohf Dulcigno. Vahry strong, vit no need ohf your arms or assistance. To use them, inwolves gountry vich is neutral. Nod *much* of a gountry, bud a gountry even zo. Ach... mine glass ist empty." Leutnant Kolodzcy pouted of a sudden.

Rodgers flicked his eyes at his cabin-servant, who sprang to pour Kolodzcy another bumper into the glass which the fellow held out sidewise, without looking. He busied himself with his tobacco, shooting another "broadside" towards the sky-lights of the coach-top.

"Zo alzo, sirs, ist Ragusa de neutral gountry, *nicht wahr?*" Lt. Kolodzcy smirked, as though it was he who was senior aboard, not them. "Ewen a temporary alliance musd be formal, public? Unt you vish...?"

"*Sub rosa*, completely, Lieutenant Kolodzcy," Rodgers replied with a conspiratorial air. "We wish a most *informal*, ermmm..."

"Unt I am given to unterstand dhat your Kapitan Charlton vishes to strike de bargain only vit a... Christian bant, sirs? No Muslims?" Kolodzcy enquired, rolling his eyes as Lewrie and Rodgers wished they could have, the first time they heard it said. Leutnant Kolodzcy turned the tiniest cock of a brow, the least lift of a corner of his mouth into a gargantuan sneer, and let loose a restrained, gentlemanly howl of laughter. "*Unglaüblich!* Dat ist to be sayink... incredible!"

"Quite adamant about it," Lewrie assured him with a droll roll of his own eyes. "No bloodthirsty pagans or heathens."

"A grade piddy, Herr Lewrie," Kolodzcy sighed. "De Muslims are grade fighters, though they heff liddle knowledge ohf de sea. Zose few on de goast vit boats? *Nein*, to use dhem vould brink notice unt vould mean grade trouble vit de Odd-oman Durks."

Christ, "Oddoman Durks"? Lewrie silently whimpered, thinking he would have to put a fist in his mouth to stifle himself!

"A local pasha who vish to make de quick profit might, berhaps," Kolodzcy schemed, furrowing his serenely unruf-fled brow for the first time. "Bud, vhen Sultan in Constantinople learn ohf dis, dhen dhere ist slaughter. He sends army to punish *any* pasha or province vich is armed by you, thinkink of rebelling, later? Ja, a grade piddy, sirs... you use Muslim pirades for a few veeks or months only, dhen *inform* Sultan, who sends army to crush dhem. Problem of alliance is solved.

Problem of deniability, alzo. No *blut* on British hands for de vorld to see... simply renegade locals. *Never* allied vit Royal Navy, you see?"

Kolodzcy smiled at them, nigh angelically.

"So Muslims might be best, after all, in spite of what Captain Charlton wished?" Rodgers frowned. "Perhaps one of those provinces already broken away... Albanians, Montenegrans? Greeks?"

"Greeks, no," Leutnant Kolodzcy dismissed airily, pointing his cigarillo at Rodgers like a tutor's ferrule. "Too terrorised by de Sultan's troops, on goast especially. Inland, Durks nod as strong, bud no use to you, dhose inland Greeks, who *are* still Orthodox Christian. Greeks on goast heff few boats. You arm dhem, train dhem, dhey organise into fighters who could rebel, once you are done vit dhem. Dhen de Sultan or one ohf his pashas hess to crush dhem. Make de *blut bad*."

"Sorry... didn't get that last bit," Rodgers enquired, shaking his head as if to clear stuffy ears. "You said...?"

"De *blut bad*," Kolodzcy repeated. "*Blut bad. Blut bad!*" he insisted, all but stamping a dainty foot, sure he was making sense.

"A blood bath I think he means, sir," Lewrie offered.

"*Ja!*" Kolodzcy yipped. "Egzagdly... *blut bad*."

"Ah," Rodgers sighed, a lot less hopefully. "Quite."

"Whole prowince, nod chust one willage," Kolodzcy expounded. "Unt long before you are done vit dhem. Gomplete massacre."

"So," Lewrie posed after a painfully long silence, broken only by the sigh of more cigar smoke being jetted aloft, "just who *does* it leave us, then, Leutnant Kolodzcy?"

Kolodzcy swung his right hand out, idly shook his empty glass, looking at Lewrie in silence. Griggs stepped up to refill him.

"You do nod vish de already strong," Kolodzcy lectured, after a refreshing sip. "Dhey are allied already, or heff no use for vhat you offer. You gannot employ existink gountries, for your Kapitan Charlton ist vishing anonymity unt deniability goncernink ties to pirades. Nor can you use Muslims or Durkish subjects. Dhey might be slaughdered before you could train dhem. No... de only people who come to mind... de only warlike Christians, who heff exberience ohf de sea, are Serbs. De Serbians. *Ja, genauische!*"

Powder-Yeoman Rahl says that! Lewrie exulted; damme, I can get that bit of German! He said *exactly*!

"Serbians, chentlemen," Kolodzcy echoed, sounding enthused for once, all but smiting his forehead for being remiss in not considering them earlier. "De Balgan goast ist hodgepodge. *Ja*, hodgepodge?

Gute. Croatian, Muslim, callink dhemselves Bosnian or Herzegovinan. Inland are Serbians, bud dhey are alzo scaddered among de odders unt along de goast. *Eine* Slavic people, Eastern Orthodox Christian people, gradely outnumbered. Dhey heff resisted conwersion by de Durks for centuries! Grade warriors alzo, who fight forever to win dheir independence from de Durks. Bud, nod heffink numbers or weapons. Fisherman... sailors unt *zometimes* pirades. Small boats only, bud dhey could sail larger, vit your help, unt vit your arms unt gaptured ships. Dhey gontrol some ohf de smaller offshore islands, alzo!"

"And they don't fear Turkish reprisals?" Rodgers puzzled.

"Ha, sir! De Serbians *scoff* at de Durks! Dhey vould radder *die* vit Durkish *blut* on dheir hands dhan liff as slaves, I dell you," the little officer boasted. "Serbians vould radder massacre a Durkish wilage, a Muslim wilage, dhan eat! Dhat ist how dhey liff, raidink along de goast. Bud, boor bickinks, mosd ohf de time."

"Sorry, again. Boor...?" Rodgers flinched in perplexity.

"Poor *pickings*, he said, sir," Lewrie translated for him.

"*Ja*, boor!" Kolodzcy sulkily agreed. "Bud remember, it ist de *hungry* wolf vich hunts de hardest. Unt de Serbian wolves are hungriest of all. Any ships vich escape you inshore, de Serbians vill eat up in de plink ohf de eye! Ships, gargoes unt grews, *all* gone... phffft!" Leutnant Kolodzcy said with a twinkle and a happy conjuring motion.

"Cargoes and crews," Lewrie supplied without being asked.

"Who ist to say vhat happen to ships vich de Serbs take, sirs?" Kolodzcy simpered. "Unt your gomplicity vit dhem you may deny. Dhey are nod zo many, zurrounded by zo many Muslims. Dhey heff *grade* need ohf you. Unt, vhen you are done vit dhem, vell... Ragusa, Dulcigno, odder goastal powers vill not tolerate a strong Serbian pirade fleet for long. Gompetition, *nicht wahr*? Rebellion, *nicht wahr*? If vord gets out ohf your arrangement, dhen you can t'row *dhem* to de wolves!"

"Uhm, that bit about cargoes and crews disappearing," Rodgers quibbled, making a similar conjuring "poof" of his own. "Surely, sir, there will be Europeans aboard the ships the Serbs take, should they ally with us. There will be officers and passengers who should properly be detained, sent here to Trieste for internment or exchange..."

"Dhen your secret ist oud, sir," Kolodzcy objected lazily, with another dismissive conjure-ment. "Frenchmen, Batavians or Danes speak ohf pirades unt Royal Navy vorkink togedder, dhen…? Bedder dat dey disappear. Sold in slave-markets ashore."

"Or their throats cut, sir?" Lewrie objected.

"Vat is old pirade sayink, Herr Kommandeur Lewrie?" Leutnant Kolodzcy chuckled. "Dat 'dead men dell no dales'?"

"No, that's out," Rodgers snapped. "Right out. Prisoners must be taken, given proper treatment. Held on one of those offshore islands, perhaps. Or your officials here in Trieste could hold 'em *incommunicado* 'till—"

"Anything else would be unthinkable, sir," Lewrie chimed in, his dander up. "The Royal Navy, nor England, would never countenance murder or enslavement."

"Bud, you *vill* goundenance piracy, *nicht wahr*?" Kolodzcy mocked.

"Well, erm…!" Lewrie fumed.

"Dhey gome here to Trieste, dhen Austria musd take note, sirs," Kolodzcy cautioned. "Vord gets oud, eventually."

"Let's say the Serbians pick a small, rocky island, where they'd be easy to guard, then," Rodgers countered. "Use timber and canvas off a prize for materials to build huts. Food and water come off the prizes, too, so it won't cost tuppence t'feed 'em, either. Your Serbians keep the ships they take, those that suit 'em. They can burn the rest for their metal and fittings, if they like, and have what valuables there are aboard as strikes their fancies, too. But… your Serbians should keep the prisoners alive, sir! No slave-market, no other harm to come to 'em. Save the ships' papers, manifests and such, and turn 'em over to us, with a list of all prisoners from each capture."

"Head-money, sir," Lewrie suggested. "Like we pay our hands for taking a warship or privateersman. A set sum for each live prisoner… a shilling, or half-crown. So it's in their interests to spare 'em."

"Head-money, aye! Thankee, Lewrie." Rodgers beamed. "We've a fair sum already, with your Prize-Court. Even a gold coin per captive wouldn't be out of the question. But anything less than that, and the deal's off 'fore it's even struck. That way, the secret's kept, 'til we're ordered out of the Adriatic. Or the Frogs are beaten, and then who's goin' t'make a fuss? The losers?"

"Long as the survivors have nothing beyond captivity to complain about, d'ye see," Lewrie added sternly. "No torture, no brutality… beyond what prison's like, anyway. That's our terms, right, sir?"

"Take it or leave it," Rodgers agreed.

And if we *can't* find Serbian pirates who'll abide by our terms, Alan thought, then it wasn't *our* fault Charlton's half-arsed pipe-dream didn't work, is it? And there's this whole hellish business, stopped altogether!

Try as hard as he might to be the proper junior officer, who'd "shut up and soldier" no matter his own reservations, he felt a rebellious itch to find a way to scotch this before it gained much more momentum. He'd quibbled as much as he thought it politick to quibble. Rodgers had already warned him to keep his wits, and his cunning, to himself for a welcome change, and go along, showing all properly "eager." Yet *was* there a way to scuttle it?

"Then we're agreed, sirs?" Rodgers pressed.

"Aye, sir," Lewrie spoke up quickly.

"Such terms, sir..." Kolodzcy puzzled. "Bud, even zo, it may be bossible. *Ja*, sir. Ohf gourse. Ve are agreed."

"Good!" Rodgers hooted, clapping his hands together. "Then it only awaits this 'dead-muzzler' of a Sirocco wind to back or veer, and we're out of harbour by sundown. And on our way. About our... business."

"A vahry exellend champagne, Kapitan Rodgers." Kolodzcy beamed slyly. "Undil dhen, perhaps ve may share annoder boddle, *nicht wahr*? Unt, I am thinkink... vhen do we dine?"

Book IV

Hospita vobis terra, Viri, non hic ullos
reverenta ritus pectora;
mors habitat saevaeque hoc litore pugnae.

No friendly land is this to you, O Heroes,
here are no hearts that reverence any rites;
this shore is the home of death and cruel combats.

Gaius Valerius Flaccus, *Argonautica*, Book IV, 145–147

Chapter 1

The general was happy, nigh to Seventh Heaven.

The very day of his return to conquered Milan, his centre of operations – laden with the paintings, the statuary, the silver and gilt masterpieces of the southern kingdoms, bedecked with glory, new fame to fuel his dreams and with forty million francs of solid specie to support the *patrie* – Josephine had come, at last.

Nigh to a second, blissful honeymoon, her presence seemed, after such a long wait. So fortuitously timed, too, in that glorious hiatus between the first arduous conquests and the near-bloodless but brutal marches to the south. Even the Austrians conspired to spare the young general, to give him this joyous *rencontre* with his beloved bride, and peace enough in which to enjoy it, for the new Austrian commander General Wurmser had yet to arrive from the Rhine with his fresh armies.

"A terrible risk, but I tweaked their noses," General Bonaparte boasted. "I got my way, thank God."

"A terrible risk, indeed." Josephine frowned. "You know Paul and the rest of the Directory can be so arbitrary. Really, my dear…"

"There could not be two generals in charge here in Italy, sweet one." Bonaparte chuckled. "I could not serve under Kellermann, though he's the hero of Valmy. He's so old, so set in his hidebound old ways. It would have been two dancing-masters doing a minuet with each other, Kellerman and Wurmser, and I relegated to the southern campaign, robbed of troops and unable to cow Tuscany, much less Rome."

"Promise me you will never threaten to resign, again, *mon cher*," Josephine admonished him, as the brilliant salon and its hundreds of guests – willing or unwilling – swirled about them. "Heroes, even a successful hero, are expendable. To play at politics so far removed from the latest gossip, your supporters…"

"The lifeblood of politics," the elegant young aide, Lieutenant Hyppolyte Charles, simpered from the offhand side.

"The army would have been divided into threes," Bonaparte said, regarding Lt. Hyppolyte Charles with a wary eye. "Part to besiege Mantua, part under Kellermann to dance the old way against the Austrians... and I, the smallest part, sent off on errands, too far removed to aid Kellermann when the Austrians attacked him. And attacked him they very well would have. Wurmser, Beaulieu, they would have understood General Kellermann and his methods. He would have offered nothing novel. He'd not frighten them... as I do."

"But before you defeated the south and won their tribute, *mon cher*, your threat was empty. And far too brash," Josephine belaboured, fanning herself as if faint with dread at her husband's daring. And sharing a look of puzzlement with her escort, Lt. Hyppolyte Charles.

"No matter, *ma cherie*. It worked. Now I alone command in Italy," Bonaparte bragged. "Anything else would have spelled disaster, and I alone prevented it. And will present the good Paul de Barras and the Directory even more victories. Within a week, I believe. Do you fear for me, *ma cherie*? *Ma biche?*"

"Husband..." Josephine all but writhed in mortification to be so addressed in public, to be called "his little doe," for she was not that affectionate a woman. "Of course I fear. The able man is envied, the hero must be cut down to size by paper-shufflers and intriguers—"

"Ah, but I will *not* be cut down to size, *ma cherie*," Bonaparte confided, leaning close to her, to infuse himself with her womanly aromas. After so many months...! "At Lodi, I realised something about myself. By the bridge, with battalion after battalion surging forward beside me... I am not a run-ofthe-mill being. Not a lesser being at all. I will rise above all the rest. I will *make* history."

And the sureness in his voice, the strange, fey brilliance in his eyes, which blazed with such certitude, almost frightened her. What sort of fellow had she married, then? Josephine wondered, not for the first time. So passionate, so ardent, so intent and cocksure over everything he did, so capable of trampling roughshod over anyone and anything that stood in the way of what he wanted. So impressive, so confident, he'd seemed, though he wasn't amusing in the slightest, had no easy personal charms... no savoir faire. What a folly their marriage was, a patriotic gushing over a bull-calf of a schoolboy turned soldier. No matter how successful, how slim and attractive... he smothered her. She'd written a friend, Madame Theresia Tallien, "My husband doesn't love me, he adores me! I think he'll go *mad*."

She shared another covert glance over the top of her fan with the dashing young Lieutenant Charles, a glance to which Bonaparte was oblivious. He was far too happy, this day.

Months and months he'd written her, almost daily. She wrote in reply every fourth day at best, when his passionate, adoring heart craved two a day from her. Short, curt, gossipy inconsequentials were those few letters, too. Why, she'd even addressed him formally, called him "*vous*"!

Once Piedmont had been beaten, he'd sent for her, written the army to allow her to come down to Turin or Milan, and they'd acceded. He'd sent the dashing young cavalry genius Joachim Murat from his own staff of aide-de-camps to fetch her. Yet, when Murat had gotten to Paris, he'd had to report that she'd been ill, retired to the country... and very possibly pregnant. Of course, with *his* child, Bonaparte was certain. Weeks, months more of chilly correspondence, then she'd finally come! With Murat as her escort. And with the rakishly handsome Lt. Hyppolyte Charles of the First Hussars on her other arm.

And no child.

Lieutenant Charles was slim, courteous, so elegant in his red Hussar uniform with the pelisse slung by silver chains over his left shoulder, silver-trimmed and edged with fox fur. He wore red leather tasseled boots and spurs. Ah, well, he made her laugh, Bonaparte thought resignedly.

"Manners of a hairdresser's assistant," Massena said with a sneer, from his side of the room. "God, what a pig's arse *she* turned out to be."

"Our 'incomparable' Josephine." Augereau snickered in kind. "I don't suppose anyone should actually *tell* him what those two have been up to? As if he doesn't know?"

"Do you actually think he'd listen?" Massena snorted. "Christ, you'd think... does a woman wish a lover, she'd go for a real man, not that primping mannequin. Cavalry! Shit!"

"At least a real cavalryman... like Murat, then," Augereau opined. "Or do you think...?" He leered like a starving fox.

"Too fair," Massena countered, snagging them two fresh glasses of wine from a passing server. "Note how she goes for the short and the dark. Lieutenant Charles… that other willowy fop, that artist Antoine Gros, she fetched along. They're more her type. Poor little bastard. I don't think he does know. Yet. God, it makes me want to spew! We finally get ourselves a great general, and he's saddled with a whore like her. Makes him look like a turnip. Once he finds out, he'll be destroyed, I tell you! And then where'll we be?"

"Take a turn on her, open his eyes so to speak. Or make sure Lt. Hyppolyte Charles goes back to his goddamned First Hussars. With a David's writ… like Uriah, the Hittite," Augereau suggested. "A hero's death… nose to nose with the foe."

"That could be arranged," Massena calculated, rubbing his chin in thought. "Won't matter, though. Once we're back in the field, it's certain she'd just find herself another. As for the other idea…?"

"Mmm?" Augereau asked softly.

"Frankly, I wouldn't stick *your* dick in it," Massena said with a laugh.

–

"It's narrow, but vital," General Bonaparte expounded over one of his many maps to several officers. Murat was there, along with Lieutenant Charles. Josephine was foisted off on some Italian ladies, bored beyond tears by how provincial even royal Italians could be, by how crude was their command of French, the *only* elegant and civilised tongue!

"Come right down and relieve Mantua." Murat frowned.

"Never," Napoleon said, chuckling. "We move forward to Brescia, use that as our new base of operations. Wurmser must advance against it, down the Brenner Pass. Lake Garda sits between, to divide his forces. Does he use the Adige Valley, to the east, there is still Lake Garda. I command the square between – Lonato, Castiglione, Brescia, free to move against his every advance. Either way, he must muffle himself in one of the river valleys – Adige, Chiesa, Mincia or Po – to get down to Mantua. Wurmser will try to relieve the siege, not destroy me. I know how he thinks. The old way. Lift the siege, drive us back. Not destroy us. Mantua I use as bait for him. Let him come."

"I see, sir." Murat beamed.

"Ah, yes," Lieutenant Charles sighed, stifling a yawn and turning to look over his shoulder for a brief second, to exchange sympathetic and intriguing looks with the "incomparable Josephine," for both were bored rigid by their separate company.

"Most especially do I wish General Wurmser to consider Rivoli as an easy approach-march route," Bonaparte said, tapping the map with his pencil. "I've seen the ground, and it's heavenly. Easy-rolling, flat and even, and fairly open, where I could really manoeuvre. Where our guns could be positioned to best effect. Massed batteries, *hein, cher* Murat? All our guns, and the ones we've captured, massed into three or four gigantic, death-dealing batteries. Then let him send an avalanche against me, a tidal wave of Austrians, and I'll break him like coastal cliffs break even the mightiest waves. And with massed batteries for bulwarks, like miniature fortresses, I use the rest of the infantry as foot-cavalry. Quick, and fast, and smash his nose, no matter where he sticks it in. Blunt his every move, and confound him. *Oui. Oui*, this could happen."

"He supposedly has fifty thousand sir," General Berthier reminded him from across the map-table. "We, but forty-five thousand. And ten thousand of ours tied up in the siege at Mantua."

"Then I'll bludgeon every thrust he makes, from every mouse-hole pass in the Alps. He cannot march his entire army through merely one. He will divide, sure that he can regroup once he's below Lake Garda." Napoleon snorted. "But I'll not let him. Ever, Berthier. Ah, then. You will excuse me, but I must go rescue Josephine. She has so little Italian, I'm sure she's uneasy with the Milanese ladies."

"Allow me to accompany you, sir," Lieutenant Charles offered.

"Yes, do, Lieutenant." Bonaparte nodded. "Do. We must do our best to amuse my darling. Camp life can be so stultifying."

Berthier helped the general's secretary, Junot, roll up the map, to be returned to a better-guarded study. Berthier sighed with resignation, knowing by now that there would never be any purely social times for the Army of Italy or its commanding officers. On a whim, the spur of the moment, right in the midst of pleasurable, lighthearted salons... out would come the maps as General Bonaparte's ever-active imagination got the better of him; as if he schemed and pondered martial musings every waking moment. Dreamed in his sleep the solutions to guarantee a victory! And then, sometimes upon a brilliantly inspired flash of genius, simply had to withdraw to his map-table, his reports. And wake up the rest, of course. Or draw them from their amusements.

Such as Berthier's own, who waited for him across the salon, now amused by Massena and Augereau, by the gallant young Murat – the aristocratic and lovely younger Giuseppina Visconti. She flashed him a smile as he began to cross to them – quite eagerly, for Berthier was leery of those two raffish rogues and their intentions, though they'd made their own personal conquests of Italian ladies.

Massena cast him a glance – looking furtive and caught-out? the older Berthier could imagine. *Was* he feeling guilty, did he have something to feel guilty *about*? Berthier wondered, feeling a surge of anger?

But, no. Massena lifted an expressive brow and darted a significant look towards the settee beyond, on which Josephine sat, surrounded by her slim, dark sycophants, Lt. Hyppolyte Charles and the artist Gros. Their general stood by, like a servant waiting for orders, mute and clumsily inarticulate in the face of such glittering company, such easy and droll repartee.

Berthier cocked a weary brow himself, made a sad moue.

So clever, the general, he thought; in everything but Life. So observant towards all but his vexing wife!

Massena openly frowned, like an ill-tempered eagle who had just spotted a rabbit far below. A sardonic shrug, a theatrical lift of two gloved hands in despair was Augereau's comment.

"Not even a handsome whore," Berthier whispered to himself, and tried to put himself in a better frame of mind to rejoin his entrancing new mistress, to have her all to himself, apart from those "hot rabbits," Massena and Augereau, who'd couple with a snake could they find hips. "The poor little bastard."

"…winter, I am certain," that "poor little bastard" was now saying, a firmly fixed expression of unwavering certainty on his face, as he made his prediction; not a boast, but a prediction. "By winter, my army will be on the Austrian frontiers. We'll own all of Italy and even Venice, perhaps. And Austria will be beaten. *I* will beat them."

Berthier shook his head again. What could one say to something like that?

Chapter 2

"Good charts," Sailing Master Edward Buchanon opined gruffly. "Marvels f'r accuracy, sir, 'ese Venetian charts."

"By God, they'd *best* be, hadn't they, Mister Buchanon?" Lewrie replied, gruff with his own worries for *Jester's* quick-work the past few days. "Very well, then, Mister Knolles. Round her up to the wind and bring-to. Prepare to anchor."

"Aye aye, sir," Knolles answered, almost hanging over the lee bulwarks for any sign of shoaling. He lifted his hat to swipe at his hair nervously before going to the helmsmen to issue his orders.

It was Leutnant Kolodzcy's studied opinion that the very sort of Serb pirate they wished could be found in this netherland of coast controlled by no one, pretty much – this stretch of disputed or ignored shore between Venetian Spalato in the north and independent Ragusa to the south.

They'd been near their quest before without knowing it, when they'd sailed close to the large islands of Hvar and Brac in pursuit of a prize. For this was where the claimed territory of the ancient and defeated Serbian princedoms came closest to the sea, shoved like a knife-blade between the Croatian or Venetian lands and the now-Muslim, Turk-ruled Bosnians.

South of Hvar, which ran east-west, lay other isles, some smaller and less important, where many displaced, rootless peoples sheltered. The large isles of Korcula and Mjlet, the long, narrow isle that paralelled the coastline – Peljesac – and lay within spitting distance but totally removed from anyone's grasp. The smaller islets of Lastovo and Susak were farther out from the shore in deep water and favourably near the main shipping route for hostile merchantmen and smugglers. All, Kolodzcy assured them, were isolated, rarely visited by patrols of any local power, completely ignored by the greater powers, and the ownership up for grabs from one decade to another, depending on who'd put in for firewood and water last. And those grudging claims were forgotten by everyone involved once they'd sailed away.

For days, *Jester* and *Pylades* had sailed these waters, no matter the shoals, feeling their way with lead-line, preceded sometimes by a cutter or launch to probe the depths. They'd anchored near poor seaside villages or hardscrabble harbours, shamming the need for firewood and water, fresh lamb or goat, eggs and butter; and paying liberally in solid silver for their purchases, too. They'd taken Kolodzcy ashore to negotiate, where he'd dropped hints that they were British, at war with the French and any who'd aid them; that there were many ships passing by far out to sea, laden with treasure, and that even the mighty Royal Navy might need help in taking all of them. Powerful as they were, they had only two ships and could not catch every vessel they espied.

–

Now, here – at the low-lying northernmost tip of Mjlet – they came to anchor once more, near a settlement that couldn't quite aspire to be deemed a proper village at all. It looked to be a scattering of rude huts among rough clearings in the ever-present, brooding forest, clinging to the rocks above the muddy shoreline, where crude fishing boats rested half on the shore and half in the waters, bedraggled and abandoned.

There was no one to be seen, of course. Wherever they'd gone, the appearance of a real warship flying what was to these crude people a strange – alien – flag sent them tumbling inland, sure that they would be slaughtered. It would take hours, Lewrie thought wearily, to see even a few timorous watchers show their faces once curiosity, and the lack of activity on the part of the warships, got the better of them. He thought it much like what Captain Cook had experienced from the timid South Sea savages the first time he'd put *Endeavour* in some never-before-visited lagoon and given them a first sight of white men.

A quarter mile farther out, *Pylades* had already come to anchor in slightly deeper water.

Lewrie turned inboard as the heavy splash of *Jester*'s best bower drew his attention. He looked aloft to see topmen taking in the last of the tops'ls and t'gallants, strung out like beads on a string along the foot-ropes as they breasted over the yardarms to gather in canvas and gasket it. Blocks squealed as jibs and spanker deflated, rustled into untidy billows on the foredeck and the boom over his head above the quarterdeck. Men stood by under Cony's supervision, who'd soon be at the halliards and jears to lower the yards to resting positions. A party below the quarterdeck nettings, in the waist, even stood by with quarterdeck awnings. But not anti-boarding nets.

"Christ!" was his sour comment. *Should* they find a pack of pirates, a damn large one, who proved too greedy to listen and swarmed *Jester* like they had that merchantman off Bar, the last patrol, they'd be defenceless! The pirates would be up and over the rails before anyone aboard could say "Knife!" And, he thought, casting another begrudging glance seaward to *Pylades*, there'd be little aid from that quarter, until it was too damn late!

"Anchored, sir," Knolles reported. "Sail taken in, gasketed and furled."

"Very well, Mister Knolles." Lewrie nodded. Then, "Christ!" again. There was a boat coming from *Pylades*. And in the stern-sheets he could see Captain Rodgers, with that pestiferous Lieutnant Kolodzcy in all his overdone Austrian finery by his side!

"Ever and amen, sir," Lieutenant Knolles softly sighed. "Alert your steward, Aspinall, sir? To uncork a half dozen o' bubbly?"

"Best fetch his own, by God," Lewrie spat. "It's poor claret or nothin', his palate bedamned. I'm savin' it for a special time."

"Such as, sir?" Knolles grinned.

"Bloody Epiphany, Mister Knolles. E-bloody-piphany." Lewrie snickered, without much real mirth, though. "Very well, then. Stand down the hands, and set the harbour and anchor watch. Lookouts aloft, though. And Sergeant Bootheby and his Marines to stand-to, uniforms and muskets in proper order. Stand easy… but stand-to."

"Aye aye, sir."

–

"Ach, ad lasd!" Kolodzcy exclaimed, perhaps almost two hours later, as the lookouts reported movement in the seemingly abandoned village. A few braver souls had drifted down from the forest to stand out in the open, at the back of the clearings, though well short of the huts or shore. Men first – and Lewrie could see, even from a cable's distance, how white-knuckled were their hands round their cudgels or farm implements. Next came children, whose curiosity was greater. At last came the women, clucking after the children, in concern for their safety, perhaps… to stand shaky-legged and marvel at this intriguing apparition tossed up from the sea.

"Zey heff to, you zee, *ja*!" Kolodzcy crowed. "Goat musd milk. *Brot* musd be baken, for supper. Dere hearthfires heff gone oud, unt id grows late. Curiozidy? *Nein*. Necessidy."

"Deck, there!" A foremast lookout cried, shading his eyes and pointing down the eastern shore. "Boat! *Three* point orf th' starb'd bows! Comin' inta harbour… headed 'is way!"

"Aloft, there!" Lewrie shouted back, cupping his hands instead of taking the time to seize a speaking-trumpet. "Small boat?"

"Small two-master!" Was the equivocal answering hail.

"Doesn't know we're here, perhaps," Rodgers fretted. "Might go about, once she sees us. Damme, another bloody day wasted."

"Probably seen us already, sir," Lewrie countered, filled with hope that they'd resolve their quest, one way or another, this morning, loath as he was about the entire business. "Low as this coast is hereabouts, they've probably seen our top-masts the last hour. And there is *Pylades*, anchored out in plain sight, too, sir."

"*Ja*, herr Kapitan Rodgers," Leutnant Kolodzcy concurred. "Comes nod de zimple fishink boat, I am thinkink. Comes nod de fearful willager to his anchorage. Dhere hess been time for frightened willagers to go find help, alert zomeone. I am thinkink only a brave man, one vit more guriosity dhan fear, comes. De *seeraüber*, berhaps? De pirades?"

"Or a damned fool," Rodgers sighed, half to himself as he paced off his concerns, and his impatience.

–

Half an hour more, and the fishing boat was close enough to eye with their telescopes, though she seemed intent on passing by, sailing due North, slowly… a wary mile and a half off, out of gun-range from shore and the warships. She mounted two short masts and wore two fore-and-aft lateen sails – a typical Eastern Mediterranen, Ottoman craft, low to the water with scant freeboard, built with a high-pinked stern and long, tapering, squarish bow, like an ancient Egyptian *dhow*. Lewrie didn't think her much over fifty feet long. Would she be built in Arabee fashion? he speculated as he watched her. Planked together with pegs and rope, and fragile as a porcelain teacup to gunfire? Or, this close to Venice and Europe, would she be more clinker-built, over ribs and beams, and more solid? Local construction… stolen…?

And, most important, was she armed?

His telescope revealed perhaps no more than eight or nine hands aboard her, and he thought that too large a number for a simple fisherman returning to his village and fearful of entering. Most fishing boats they'd seen got by on two or three, at best. And, this *dhow* like boat was a touch too large, compared to the majority of the netters they had come across. Much larger, of a certainty, than the poor gaggle of old single-masted boats that lay on the local shore, and too heavy to haul up in that fashion at night, too. As for artillery, there was none to be seen, yet swivels or 2-pounder boat-guns could be hidden…

"Haulin' 'er wind, sir," Buchanon grunted.

Abeam of *Jester*, the *dhow* like boat fell off the light Easterly breeze and began to stand in towards them, though still warily angled, as if to pass between *Jester* and *Pylades*, her lateens now winged out.

"Fair turn o' speed, e'en off th' wind, you'll note, Cap'um."

"Aye, Mister Buchanon," Lewrie agreed.

Onward, she stood, halving the distance rapidly, coming within gun-range, until she was perhaps five hundred yards off *Jester's* larboard stern before putting her helm over. Her crew sprang to the masts, to swing the lateen yards end-forend to gybe her to the opposing tack, in the blink of an eye.

"Oh, smartly done, I say!" Knolles allowed.

"Show-off," Lewrie muttered.

Now the *dhow* angled in towards *Jester* on larboard tack, closing the distance until she was no more than two hundred yards off, aimed for a collision with *Jester's* bows if she held her course.

"Smell like a fisherman to you, sir?" Rodgers enquired.

"Hard to tell, sir," Lewrie replied quickly. "Over the stink of her crew. Well-dressed pack o' scoundrels, hey?" he japed.

Several of the hands aboard her wore nothing but rough wool tunics or loose smocks over baggy, Hindoo-*pyjammy*-type knee-length trousers, or no trousers at all. A couple, including the helmsman or master aft by the tiller, had added goat-hair or goatskin vests, which even at that longish range reeked like wet badgers.

"Well, then." Rodgers grimaced, drumming his fingers on the cap-rail of the bulwark. "They're here, so *speak* 'em, somebody."

Leutnant Kolodzcy stepped to the rails, cupped his hands about his lips and hallooed them in some local tongue. The helmsman cupped a hand at his ear and shook his head as if unable to hear or understand. Their liaison officer tried several other words, though clewing taut to one… which sounded like "*Serpska.*"

The helmsman barked one harsh word, and the *dhow* shied away as if stung, of a sudden, heeling hard-over as she swung up towards the winds on a close reach, and accelerating like a greyhound as her crew leapt to haul the fore-ends of her lateen yards inboard and low to the deck. The helmsman did turn, once she was well in hand, wave, flash a brief, white-toothed smile in his bearded, sea-tanned face and shout a message.

"*Arschloch!*" Leutnant Kolodczy yelped. "*Affesohn!*"

Lewrie heard a snicker from the base of the larboard quarterdeck ladder and turned to see Yeoman of the Powder Room Rahl, turning beet-red and quivering, silently laughing fit to bust.

"De fildy peasant," Kolodzcy carped. "He call me…! Vell, id ist not matter vaht, *nein*. I am askink de *hüresohn* for Serpski, unt he play de liddle game. Firsd, in Durkish, dehn Serbo-Croat. Say dhat he ist loyal Durkish subwect, unt gute Muslim… unt gannot risk pollutink himself by contact vit infidels."

"Ah, I see," Captain Rodgers sighed, visibly deflating. The wind was dying, and it appeared they'd be stuck in their miserable anchorage for the rest of the day, perhaps 'til the next dawn, if it didn't return. And with nothing to show for their efforts. "Damn! And double-damn!"

"He ist liar, *herr Kapitan*," Kolodzcy added, though, with a clever snicker. "I am thinkink he vas Serpska, in *sbite* of vaht he say."

"Oh, I see!" Rodgers brightened. "We've just been scouted out, then. For others. Do we lay here at anchor, sooner or later, someone will work up enough nerve to contact us, d'ye mean, Leutnant Kolodzcy?"

"I am zertain of dhis, *herr Kapitan*," Kolodzcy said with a short formal bow and a self-satisfied click of his heels. "By de dime ve gomplete dinink, I am thinkink."

-

"What was that the fellow said, Mister Rahl?" Lewrie enquired of his Prussian ex-army artillerist, once Rodgers and Leutnant Kolodzcy had taken themselves below to his great-cabins for drinks in celebration.

"*Herr Kapitan*" – Rahl blushed – "de *herr* leutnant calls him de 'bastard'… de whore-son, unt son of an ape. De fisherman, he calls herr Leutnant Kolodzcy de '*Ostereicher Schwule.*' In Cherman, he says dis, *herr Kapitan*. De *zierlich Ostereicher Schwule.*"

"And that means…?" Lewrie prompted.

"*Ach, Gott, herr Kapitan,*" Rahl whinnied. "It means de petite Austrian queer."

"*Genau*, Mister Rahl." Lewrie chuckled. "Exactly. *Zierlich Ostereicher… Schwule?* Damme, I must remember that."

Chapter 3

Leutnant Kolodzcy's certainty didn't look so good by dusk. The *dhow* had sailed itself out of sight down the coast from whence it had come, and as sundown came and went, and the lanthorns were lit on deck, and the wind died away, their anchorage became an oily-smooth and undisturbed millpond. They sent launches ashore to barter for fresh bread. But that was the only contact they had with the locals.

–

They were up and out on deck at the beginning of the Morning Watch, hands sluicing and sanding after stowing their hammocks, with the ship enveloped in a windless mist that denied them the sight of anything past the first fringe of trees ashore. By half-past four, they stood-to at the guns for Dawn Quarters, as they did every morning at sea, outside of a friendly harbour, should anything threatening loom up with the sunrise.

A faint lifting scend of offshore waves, the back-waves from the slight rale of surf on the shoreline, made *Jester* creak and complain as she was lifted and gently rocked, the anchorage still as glassy as some mirror's face and the waves too weak to break or foam, like lake-water.

Far off in the fog, on a rocky point far beyond the village, came the trout-splashing and grumbly yelps of seals at their morning feedings, now that it was safe to venture from their gravelly beaches after a dark and moonless evening. Monk seals, Buchanon had told him when they'd seen their first at Corfu, another variation of Lir's Children, written about by Pliny, Plutarch, Homer and Aristotle. Wary as seals were of humans, he'd thought it odd that they were there at all, so near the rude settlement; perhaps it was a temporary fishing camp and not a permanent one.

By five, Lewrie sent the people below for their breakfasts after securing the guns. Aspinall came up from Copper Alley with coffee for them all, as the mists thinned slightly, expanding their circle of sight to about two cables. Toulon was especially playful and active after an eye-opening snack from the cooks, scampering about the quarterdeck and footballing a champagne cork from the previous night's gloomy supper in the great-cabins – pouncing and "killing" over and over.

In spite of his best intentions not to, Lewrie had been forced to treat Rodgers and Kolodzcy, to dine them in, which had meant breaking out a half dozen bottles of bubbly for them. Then he'd watch it positively *flood* down their maws with little hope of enjoying much himself!

"Breakfast be ready for ya, an' t'other gentlemen, in a quarter hour, sir," Aspinall prophecied.

"Good," Rodgers said with a bleak expression, between restoring sips. He and Kolodzcy had come aboard, just about the time the gunners had begun to secure the artillery. And, Lewrie thought, both of them looked so "headed" by their night's intake that a hot kiss and a cold breakfast might have killed them.

"Fine." Lewrie yawned, hunched into his boat-cloak against the raw nippiness of the mists and a rare predawn chill. "Thankee."

"Fresh bread, lashin's o' butter an' jam, sirs," Aspinall said with good cheer. "An' mutton chops, sirs. Do ya wish me t'break out yer last crock o' mint jelly, Captain, sir?"

Lewrie nodded sleepily. "Aye, Aspinall, that'd be right fine."

Rodgers looked a tad queasy at the mention of mutton chops, and Leutnant Kolodzcy just looked… half dead, and upset by it.

"*Gottverdammte Nebel*," he groused at the fog, stalking about in a white silk-lined cape. "*Unt, gottverdamme die Serpski*," he added with a petulant wheeze. He produced a mauve silk handkerchief.

Lewrie felt a warmth along his left calf, the brush of a tail as it idly flagged his booted leg. Toulon had left off "killing" his cork to come to his side and look up with his yellow eyes half slit. Lewrie bent down to rub his chops and head, with Toulon half on his hind legs to receive his rubs.

"Achoo!" Leutnant Kolodzcy let go with a rather kittenish sneeze.

Toulon, startled, leaped atop the taut-rolled and tightly packed canvas hammocks stowed on the quarterdeck rails over the waist.

"Scare you, puss?" Lewrie teased.

But the cat stiffened, facing outward, his whiskers well forrud and his neck straining. His tail-tip began to quiver and fret as he let out with a quizzical "*Murr-row!*"

But he wasn't pointed towards the sounds of the seals, nor towards shore at all, where the village lay. Something about two points off the larboard bows had gotten his attention. A bit to seaward, deep in the mists.

"Company coming," Lewrie intuited. The year before, just one of the many odd, fey occurrences in this commission, Toulon had sensed the smuggler's *tartane* they'd been chasing along the Genoese Riviera, on a cool and windless dawn such as this one. Eerie, inexplicable – unless a body actually *believed* Mr. Buchanon's ancient blather, o' course! – but he had sniffed her out long before they'd spotted her.

"Oh… pshaw!" Rodgers groaned.

Too hungover t'say much else, Lewrie thought, grinning. After he saw them off, they'd surely had a brace more bottles of champagne in *Pylades* before retiring.

"Smell something, puss?" Lewrie asked. Toulon lifted his head to sample the air. Of course, he lowered his head to sniff hammocks, too. There could be a seaman going to sleep tonight in a blotch of ram-cat pee, Alan thought sourly, if this turns out to be a dead-bust!

"*Murrff!*" Toulon said, though, tail now thrashing vigourously, his forepaws clawing on the hammock canvas. He didn't sound anything *near* to happy. The cat let out a low, menacing trill, a "*Wwhuurr!*" of warning, and began to hunker down and bottle up.

"Company, sir," Lewrie reiterated, completely sure of his facts this time. He shared a wary glance with Knolles and Buchanon, who were more familiar with the eerie by then. It would be impossible to explain it all to Rodgers, anyway. It just *was*, no matter how improbable.

"Mister Knolles, pipe the starboard watch on deck. My respects to Mr. Crewe, and he is to reman the guns to lar-board. Marines to get up and turn-to, double-quick," Lewrie intoned.

Toulon was peering outboard most intently by then, turning about to present himself sideways, as if to loom larger to a so far undiscovered challenger.

Then, from out of those mists where Toulon was intently staring…

"Boat!" Lewrie cried, the same time as the larboard bow lookout.

Ghostly, a dull grey phantasm that suddenly stood out stark upon that pearlescent fog… suddenly, there was a boat. A small, *dhow* like two-master. And, most ominously, a hint of others astern of her!

"*Mmmuurrr!*" Toulon moaned, rather murderous, capping it off with a vicious hiss – and finally, a spit.

"Sir!" Buchanon whispered from his left, pointing down over the larboard side, yet off to the larboard beam. "Lookit!"

Lewrie tore his gaze from the *dhow*, perhaps the very same one that had come near enough to "smoak" them the previous afternoon. He saw nothing.

"Lookit, sir!" Buchanon said with a shuddery hitch to his voice. "Closer aboard, Cap'um."

Wull, *stap* me! Alan frowned as he spotted something.

The sea was grey-dark, oil-slicked with dawn-light, and still so millpond-smooth and flat, with barely a wind-fleck, hardly a hint of a roller to disturb its faint glittering... yet disturbed by a tiny vee of a wake which spread back from the head of a seal. He saw the short bewhiskered muzzle, the sleek brown pate, a limpid eye... fleeing.

And far off, on the rocks unseen off the starboard bows, south of the village, there came faint splashing sounds, a fogmuffled dog-pack of frantic cacophony.

The bark of seals!

"Thought it a fair omen, havin' seals here, sir, after so many months," Mister Buchanon uneasily muttered. "Now, though... way 'ey're actin', Cap'um Lewrie..."

Andrews was on the quarterdeck, Cony by the larboard gangway bulwarks along with many of the crew, those from the West Country who had always believed, those newlies who'd seen and heard strange things and come to believe; especially after their ship's first eerie, eldritch encounter in the Bay of Biscay as she'd begun this commission, with the unspoken messages which came from the seals.

"Don't start, Mister Buchanon, 'tis tense enough already," Alan said, feeling a shiver go up his spine, yet trying to maintain outward calm for his superstitious hands, who were turning to stare at their "lucky" captain.

The seals came to him, to *Jester*. Lir's Children. Cursed or blessed they were, the Selkies of the ancient pagan myths, and harbingers of that forgotten god of the sea, Lir, who seemed to hold the ship, crew and captain in the cusp of his hand, his favourites of fortune... or his unwitting weapons. Lir's Children, the seals. And they were fleeing, splashing into the sea for safety, though greater, toothier terrors awaited them there, who made meals of them; all their playful curiosity abandoned in the face of perhaps an even greater danger.

"Oh, 'tis a bad sign, sir," Buchanon all but whimpered; him, a man grown to the fullness of his strength and courage. "A bad *cess.*"

"A bad business for certain, Mister Buchanon," Lewrie agreed, clenching his jaws stonily expressionless. "No matter it is our commanding captain's wish. *Cess*, though? Don't think so. *Hope* not."

"'Ere's no good goin'ta come from 'is, Cap'um." "Perhaps not, sir," Lewrie allowed, with a tilt of his head to one side. He reached down to stroke his cat down the back, trying to gentle and cosset him, but Toulon was having none of it, came within a hair of lashing out blind with one claw-sprung paw as he gave out one more heartfelt, menacing growl. Yet, instead of springing down to take himself below to the safety of the orlop, as he did during gun-drill or battle, he stayed – hunkered up and sheltering against Lewrie's cloak, and licking his chops in fear, but he stayed.

"If God is just, sir," Lewrie sighed, "and Lir means to watch over us, too, o' course… I think he's warnin' us. Not dooming, hmm?"

"Watch our backs, do we deal with 'ese… wotchyacallems…"

"Serbs, Mister Buchanon." Lewrie nodded. "Aye, we're warned."

There were five boats, Lewrie could take note by then. Small, mostly, no more than thirty-five to forty feet overall, the bulk of them. All rigged with two masts in Eastern, lateen, fashion. Following last of all, a three-masted spectre slowly emerged from the fog. She was long, lean and low, a *galliot* or *xebec* – a war galley – of about seventy-five to eighty-five feet in length. The sun had at last arisen, lancing over the Balkan mountaintops from the east, setting light to the mists so that half the dawn's horizon was set afire with a most foreboding crimson and saffron umbra that backlit the *galliot* and made her stand out starkly black, every bit of rigging, every sail, every peering crewman cut from black paper and plastered to the sunrise… a silhouetted apparition.

Their pirates, it seemed, had at last arrived – pirates they'd been sent to seek, to discover and enlist. But, Lewrie felt deeply in the pit of his stomach, pirates their seeming patron Lir wished to have no truck with.

Red sky at morning, sailor take warning—

And the frightened seals.

Warned, aye, Lewrie thought grimly; aye, and thankee.

Now that their quest was ended, and their dealings with these strange creatures was about to begin… they'd been *damned* well warned.

Chapter 4

"Like treadin' water 'mongst a pack o' sharks," Will Cony said, scowling hellish-black as the rakish craft approached within hailing distance, dividing and passing down the larboard side, between the village and *Jester's* starboard side, or astern to flaunt their courage, almost under *Pylades'* guns, and within "close pistol shot."

"Like the Lanun Rovers at Spratly Island," Lewrie whispered.

"Well, sir... least there's only th' six. An' not thirty of 'em, this time," Cony replied with a mirthless snicker. "Manageable."

"Odd, how things turn out," Captain Rodgers commented, flexing his fingers on the hilt of his small-sword. "Coincidence, hey? Think back. I could *swear* this is the same lot you drove off from that Dutch merchantman in th' Hvar channel, Commander Lewrie."

"Then they have already had a taste of our iron, sir," Lieutenant Knolles vowed. "Perhaps they'll know to mind their manners 'cause of it."

"Perhaps, indeed," Rodgers mused impatiently, waiting for their vaunting show of seamanship and *braggadocio* to end, and the negotiations to begin.

"Deuced cocky buggers, sirs," Midshipman Hyde decided to say for them all.

"Anyone see artillery?" Rodgers snapped.

"On the largest, sir," Lewrie pointed out. "Looks to be a pair of six-pounders forrud. She's gun-ports to either beam, but I can't see much beyond some very old, long-barrel swivels, or boat-guns."

"Just the one six-pounder or so forrud on the next-largest, sir," Midshipman Spendlove was quick to contribute. "And more swivels."

The seamen who crowded the rails of the pirate ships were armed, and were most happily brandishing their weapons, all but ululating like painted Red Indians. They were armed with curvy, scimitarlike swords and matching daggers, some very long and slim Arabee muskets with convoluted, curling butts, some inlaid with ivory or brass, like the Hindoo *jezails* Lewrie'd seen in the Far East, at Calcutta, or among the Mindanao pirates.

"Damme if 'at's a swivel-gun, sir," Buchanon exclaimed, pointing at the nearest forty-footer. "I could swear 'at's a falconet! A wrought-iron breech-loader! Barrel made o' hammer-welded iron rod bundles, an' hooped t'gether. Beer mug sorta iron cartridge gets stuck in the rear o' th' barrel, an' *wedged* in place. Lord, sir, 'at was old in the days o' th' Spanish Armada! Blow up, peel apart, an' shoot backwards, if yer not careful with 'em, so 'twas said."

"Dhey are heffing *grade* need ohf you… unt your veapons, *ja!*" Leutnant Kolodzcy archly sniffed. "You see how I dell you? Ach, now we be beginnink."

The local vessels had at last left off their pirouettes to show off their prowess, and their lack of fear, and were handing their sails and coming to anchor in a loose gaggle off *Jester*'s bows, where they'd be safe from artillery fire. A boat was got down from the larger two-masted *dhow* and made its way to the *galliot*, even as a second boat was being hoisted over from her, and a boat-crew broke out her oars.

"What sort of side-party does a pirate captain rate, I wonder?" Lewrie japed. "What sort of honours should we award him, Leutnant Kolodzcy?"

"None, *herr Kommandeur* Lewrie," Kolodzcy prinked with aspersion. "You show him nothink. No gondempt… but no honours, eidder."

"No side-party, Mister Knolles. No pipes."

"Aye aye, sir."

The larger rowing boat from the *galliot*, another Levant-looking craft like a *felucca* without her single mast, was stroking over to the sloop of war, with two men in her stern-sheets, who stood while others sat and rowed or steered.

"De one from de *dhow*… de *arschloch* we speak, yesterday," Kolodzcy said sharply. "De odder, de taller – he ist dheir leader ve are havink to deal vit."

The *felucca* reached *Jester*'s side, her larboard side, below the already opened and inviting entry-port. *Not* the side of honour, as the starboard was in worldwide naval usage. Whether their leader was aware of this insult or deigned to sneer at his welcome, they couldn't tell, for he sprang from the gunn'l as soon as the boat bumped into the hull, and scampered up the boarding-battens to the gangway in a flash, eager and wolfishly smiling a dazzling white-toothed smile half hidden below a bristling, flowing set of moustachios. He looked about in appraisal, almost as if judging to the pence what the value of looting her might fetch him, before he was joined by his goat-skinned compatriot, a shorter, thicker-set fellow with a lush, unkempt beard.

There was a feast for his eyes, an untold Alladin's Cave of riches laid before him: artillery, muskets, swords, shot and powder... rope and timber, sails and blocks. Even *Jester*'s hatch-covers would be the sort of well-crafted wealth far beyond his wildest imaginings.

Yet he put his hands on his hips, gazed upward at the height of the European main mast, bared another dazzling smile... and laughed out loud! Like a child overawed by a stroll down the Strand past the toymakers', Lewrie could conjure, the fellow actually shook his head with what he took for a "Well, what'll they think of, next?" marvelling.

"I speak to him, unt bring him to you, sirs," Kolodzcy offered primly, shooting his lacy shirt-cuffs and settling the hang of a dazzling fresh pale-blue waistcoat.

The fellow didn't wait for that, but, bouncing on his feet with impatience, sprang into action again and towed his com-patriot to the end of the gangway, then onto the quarterdeck, where he'd espied the better-dressed officers.

"Ratko Petracic," he boasted, thumping his chest and naming himself to them, as if it should mean something to them, before Leutnant Kolodzcy could even open his sour-pursed mouth. Petracic gave Kolodzcy a withering, amused once-over from head to toe, before turning to his companion of the bearish beard and goat-hair weskit and slithering out a comment that made them both chuckle.

"Well, go on, sir," Rodgers urged. "Say the bloody how-dedos. Name us to the bugger."

"Boog-er," the bearded one parroted, then laughed, nudging his leader. "Ha, boog-er!"

Kolodzcy smoothly performed the introductions, no matter what the pirates had said about him or how rowed he was. "Dey are, chentlemen, Kapitan Ratko Petracic, leader of dis seagoink bent. Unt, Kapitan Dragan Mlavic, who ist second-in-command... main leutnant of his... fleet."

"Fleet, mine arse," Midshipman Hyde muttered to Spendlove, just loud enough to be heard, drawing a scathing glower from his captain.

"Mine-eh arse," the shorter pirate repeated once more. "Arse!"

What is he, a bloody magpie? Lewrie wondered.

He didn't look quite sane, for starters. Dragan Mlavic had beady little black eyes that threatened to cross, did he leave them open too long, which made him blink rather a lot. His face was pockmarked and rough-textured, a tad swarthy and full – all round knobbiness to cheeks, nose and forehead. Lewrie gave *him* an up-and-down, with one brow cocked, as Kolodzcy garbled off some gilt-and-beshit politenesses. The short pirate chieftain could easily be dismissed, he thought. Mental defective, borderline loony... something like that? He'd traded a drab brown homespun knee-length smock this day for a white cotton one, gaudy with red and blue embroideries. Under that rank goat-hide waistcoat, o' course. His very baggy pyjammy-trousers, which gathered below the knee like an Ottoman version of proper breeches, were the roughest sort of homespun. His shoes were little better than goatskin versions of Red Indian... what'd they call 'ems...? *Moccasins?* There was a round knit skullcap... Well, the weapons, o' course, jammed into a wide belt – a brace of all-metal Arabee flintlock pistols with barrels over a foot long, a very expensive-looking scimitar in a parrot-green leather scabbard, both sword and scabbard awash in brass, brads, inset ivories and... damme... *gem-chips?* Bolstering his arsenal, though, was a very plain butcher-knife of a dagger, with rough wood hilt, hardly a haft at all beyond a black-iron ring-guard, in a rough, hairy sheath.

The other, Ratko Petracic, was an entirely different breed of cat, and Lewrie put him down as a damned dangerous customer. He was too self-possessed, too sure of himself by half. Too handsome and cocksure, this'un! He wore soft leather boots to the knee, made from a coral-red dyed hide; shimmery burgundy pyjammy-trousers, a flowing smock of startling white and sewn with gold thread, silver thread and ornate with sequins. His waistcoat was of hide, too, though of a very short-haired, very sleek fur. He sported no headgear, just a full, lush mane of shiny brown hair clubbed back at the nape of his neck. His weapons consisted of a pair of gold-inlaid Arabee pistols, a gem-studded scimitar in a red velvet scabbard set with gilt fittings and a magnificent dagger on his left hip in a silver-and-ivory, jewel-bedecked scabbard, which made an impossible forty-five-degree bend.

Atop the hilt of the gilded dagger there was set an emerald the size of a robin's egg, clutched in elaborately filigreed real-gold claws!

Aye, he knew what a raffish, dangerous impression he was making, Lewrie realised; he'd planned it this way! Put on his best to overawe!

"He asks me, are we de British Royal Navy vich hezz so vahry much silver to buy brot unt sheep," Kolodzcy was explaining, leaning to and fro from translatee to translatee. "I tell him we are. He ist askink, do we fight de French. I say we do. He asks me, do ve dell de druth... ve take many rich ships, oud ad sea. I say ve dell druth, alvays, unt daht dhere are *vahry* many more rich ships... good bickinks. Kapitan Petracic is askink... he vould vahry much like de riches dhat we take. Uhm... *Gott in Himmel, was ist das? Lächerlich!* Umph!"

Kolodzcy leaned away from the pirates.

"De Kapitan Petracic sayink *he* ist master ohf dis goast... unt... unt!" Kolodzcy gargled, outraged. "Ve are owink him... tributes! His *share!*"

"Tell 'im t'go *buy* a hat, shit in it an' call it a brown tiewig," Rodgers barked. "The bloody nerve o' th' man!"

"Plenty... blood-ey... nerve, Ratko Petracic," the short man hoorawed, as good a sycophant as Clotworthy Chute any day, Lewrie told himself. Once he got over his shock, o' course. His shock of hearing English from the hairy churl – and the smug look of satisfaction on Ratko Petracic's face. "Plenty bloody nerve," indeed! Lewrie thought.

Chapter 5

"He speaks English?" Rodgers blanched, staring at Petracic.

"Not bloody word," Dragan Mlavic informed him soberly. "But I do. Little."

Least we can do 'thout this mincin' pimp Kolodzcy from here on out, Alan silently hoped.

There was a brief palaver between the smirking Ratko Petracic and his chief lieutenant. Then, "I listen careful, British man. Then I tell him what you say. But Captain Petracic says we will talk. In Serbian. Your..." Mlavic gave Leutnant Kolodzcy another of those scathing head-to-toe glances, as if he still couldn't quite believe his eyes or that such creatures lived. "Your translator help us, *da*?"

"Bud, ohf gourse," Kolodacy seethed, though smiling rigidly.

There was another brief outburst of Serbian – to Lewrie's ears it seemed like gargling – from the handsome Petracic.

"Captain say... rain, soon. We go below... talk, yes? You have good wine? We talk," Dragan Mlavic urged. "No good sailing today."

"Inform the captain, uhm... Petracic," Rodgers offered, turning a lot more civil, "that we will indeed repair below to the great-cabins and talk. But... there must be no more talk of paying him tribute."

"We see, British captain." Mlavic smiled and lifted one chary brow. "We see."

–

The first hour of talking and swilling (Lewrie's wine, with which Rodgers was *damn* liberal, and the Serbs putting it down like they were fresh-parched from Hell!) consisted mostly of boasting. Ratko Petracic told his listeners what a great seaman he was, how many villages he'd raided, how wealthy he'd become, how many throats he'd cut and how many Turks now roasted on Shaitan's Coals because of his sword or the actions of his bold warriors. How Venetians gave him a wide berth when they saw his sails and took themselves elsewhere. How the fierce Ragusans shook in their boots and would not pursue him when he boldly raided one of the outlying ports. And blah-blah-blah...!

"Unt de Croats?" Kolodzcy queried. "They run from you, too?"

"Ha!" Dragan Mlavic sputtered. "Croats... poo!" He spat upon the black-and-white-chequered sailcloth deck covering, highly insulted.

"Here, now," Lewrie grumbled. "Have a care, tell him. Spit on his own damn deck... but not mine! Damme, was he born in a barn?"

Kolodzcy posed the question to Ratko Petracic directly, resenting his role being usurped by the barely intelligible, and partisan, pirate. A babble ensued as Mlavic tried to ask the question in his place, and Petracic put up one hand to silence his lieutenant. Petracic put a noble expression on his face, one of deliberate musing, before replying.

"He say..." Kolodzcy interpreted slowly, "he hess no fear ohf de Croats. Serbs are... fiercer fighters. He *hates* Croats! *All* true Serbs hate Croats, forever. Untrustvorthy... murderink... whores. 'Ungarian whores. Catholic. Uhm, suffice to say, sirs, he despise dhem. He make *mahny* vile accusations."

And ain't you a good little Austrian Catholic yourself, Kolodzcy? Lewrie wondered. He was torn between the play of expressions of both Leutnant Kolodzcy and Petracic; one all but biting his cheeks to remain diplomatic, and the other – feigning, Lewrie was dead certain – noble long-suffering.

Petracic got to his feet to pace and gesticulate, waving with both hands now, and beginning to sound gruff and rankled.

"Well?" Rodgers demanded, as the diatribe continued.

"Still rants, sir," Kolodzcy replied, one ear tilted for a pithy bit. "He exblainink Balgan hizdory. Holy King Stefan Nemanja. Saint Cyril unt Saint Methodius, who conwert pagan Slavs to Christians, in de Orthodox Church, long ago... King Stefan, first of Nemanjas, build huge empire. Greater general dhan Byzantine, Belisarius. Son, Saint Sava the Wanderer found *Serbian* Orthodox Church. King Milutin Nemanja, he defeat fildy Bulgars... no bedder dhan slant-eye Tartars. Richer dhan Byzantine Empire. All of goast to Adriatic... far south into Macedonia unt Greece, conquer Albanians. Vould have conquer Constantinople, too, 'til de veak as vater cowards allow Durks across Hellespont. Unt Croats too stupid to be true Slavs... too jealous. Dhey look to Vienna, Rome… become Catholics. Whores to Budapest unt Vienna."

"Uhm… this'll take long, d'ye think?" Rodgers softly wondered.

"*Ach, ja, herr Kapitan,*" Kolodzcy said with a patient sigh. "He speak of Stefan Uros… Stefan Dushan… *dushan* meanink 'soul.' A last Nemanja, Uros. Daht ist vhen Durks come, unt he was veak. 'Ungarians from de vest svarm to take empire. Croats vit dhem. Comes final leader, elected prince… Knez Lazar."

"Aahh," Dragan Mlavic uttered, sounding like a mourner at a funeral; and Lewrie was amazed to see tears moisten his hard little eyes as his lips trembled in genuine sorrow!

"Comes time of Kossovo," Leutnant Kolodzcy translated, as the fierce Ratko Petracic ranted on. "Grade baddle. Durks vin, Serbs killed. He recite poem to us."

"Jesus," Lewrie whispered, pouring himself a glass of claret in frustration. "A long'un, I'd expect. 'Hear me, Oh Muse'…" he cited from *The Iliad.* In English, of course; he'd been bloody awful in Greek.

"Grey bird fly from Jerusalem. Falcon. Really ist Saint Elijah, bearink Holy Book. Comes to de Tsar… Prince Lazar, unt asks ohf him vhat kingdom he vish… heavenly or earthly? Knez Lazar choose heavenly kingdom. He say:

> He built a church on Kossovo…
> Then he gave his soldiers the Eucharist…
> Then the Turks overwhelmed Lazar…
> And his army was destroyed with him,
> Of seven and seventy thousand soldiers.

"Dhen, all vas Holy, all was honourable. Unt de guteness of God vas fulfilled," Kolodzcy interpreted for them.

Ratko Petracic stopped orating, arms out to his sides as if he were being crucified, his head hung, and unashamedly weeping.

"Uhmph, I say…" Rodgers squirmed uneasily, and Lewrie felt the urge to look away. Such blatant public displays of tears were bred, or whipped, out of English gentlemen. Even Lewrie, who was more prone to expressing his enthusiasms or disasters (more proof, he thought, that he would never make a true gentleman if he lived an hundred years!) was not *this* open with his feelings. Why, it was unmanly… foreign, certainly!

"*Kossovo Polje*," Petracic said, looking up and lowering his arms to wipe away his tears on his sleeves.

"*Kossovo Polje*," Dragan Mlavic echoed, his voice broken.

"De Field ohf Black Birds," Kolodzcy said. "Durks leaf bodies naked, for carrion birds to devour. June twenty-eighth, 1389."

Petracic started speaking again, clearer, his voice infused with a low, bitter anger even after over four hundred years.

"Grade Serb Empire dies, long before Byzantine, in 1453. No one come to help Serbs, he say," Kolodzcy began translating again. "Every hand against us. Croat, Byzantine, 'Ungarian, Austrian. Beginnink ohf Durkey in Europe. Could heff sdopped, defeaded, but no. Too jealous. Vorld *vish* grade Nemanjic Serb kingdom to die. Zo dhey could pick our bones, like de black birds, he ist sayink. Grade, holy sacrifice de Serbs made. Zo daht Europe should live. Unt de Croats, de Slovenes, Albanians, Bulgars… take from *Srpski Narod*… Serb Beoble, effrydink dhey own. Some *love* conwersion to Islam, he say. Some are traitors… Catholic Croat traitors, who vish to make Serbs Catholic sheep."

"Ah." Rodgers nodded as if it all made perfect sense.

Petracic barked out a question. Kolodzcy took pause, recoiling back into his chair for a moment before replying, long, slow and wary.

"He ask me, dese Frenchmen… dhey are Catholic, *ja*? I dell him dhey are. Danes, unt Batavian Dutch… Protestant. Like British. Bud, nod Slavs. More like Germans. Do ve vish him to kill dhem? I say no. Dake dhere ships only."

"Ah, perhaps we're gettin' somewhere?" Rodgers wished aloud.

"He say to me, sir," Kolodzcy interpreted another long ramble, "Serbs hate Croats, 'Ungarians, Durks. Dirdy Albanians, unt all Slavs who now are Muslim, who did nod come to *Kossovo Polje*. Dhey are now traitors, people forever apard. Or mongrels, nod drue Slavs. Unt for a price, he say he vill now hate Frenchmen, unt all dheir lackeys. A *vahry* high price. For to build new Serbian kingdom. Avenge de Field ohf Black Birds, someday."

"Right, then!" Rodgers beamed. "What sort of a price?"

"He vish guns, sir," Kolodzcy translated, as Petracic sat down at the table, his weeping quite forgotten. "Muskets, powder, unt shot. Unt artillery, to arm his men. Gold, to addract odders. Ships such as dhis one. You give him *Jester*?"

"Like bloody Hell!" Lewrie snarled.

"Tell him our sovereign King George III will not allow us to give him a sloop of war," Rodgers ordered. "We may supply muskets, made cartridges, loose ball and powder. And accoutrements. We can get him swords and bayonets. We've pistols, too. But a warship? No, I'm sorry. But... once he's better-armed, hey, he could take himself a European-style ship and convert her. Arm her."

"He say he ist sendink to his boat for brandy, sir," Kolodzcy informed them. "British wine ist gnat's-piss, he ist thinkink. Zorry. Unt, he say... dhat ist like chicken come before egg. Gannot get ship to conwert vidout strong ship in firsd blace. European ships pass by, dhey are armed vit cannon, unt he gannot fight dhem now. Too strong. For his smaller boats, too fast, alzo. Unt too far oud at sea. His four small boats gannot make long foyages. Only his *galliot*, unt dhat ship Mlavic command."

Rodgers drummed his fingers on the table as Mlavic returned with a stone crock and poured them all a brimming measure of a colourless, clear-water liquor.

"Ve trink to bargain? he asks. To *heart* of bargain, he say. De Devil ist in details... unt ve have all rainy day to thrash dhem oud."

The Devil, indeed, Alan thought, trying not to frown; I'm sittin' 'cross the bloody table from Old Nick this very minute! Petracic was smiling at them, a coy, "Captain Sharp-ish" grin, even sharing a glance to his chief lieutenant, Mlavic; all but tipping him the wink!

"Boddom's up, he broboze," Kolodzcy said.

Lewrie's wineglasses were smallish, more suited to a port after a meal than the usual larger goblets that went with supper itself – to keep their rate of consumption down and save him a supply for later in this voyage, if nothing else! At the rate Rodgers and Kolodzcy put it away, he'd be begging 'pon the gun-room's charity, or reduced to rum and water before they put in at Corfu again.

It looked harmless, that clear brandy. He shrugged and picked up his glass as the others did. Manfully, he slugged some back.

"Holy...!" He wheezed, once his throat reopened. His brothers-in-law, Governour and Burgess Chiswick, had introduced him to American corn-whiskey during the siege of Yorktown; but it couldn't hold a candle to this! Redolent of plums or grapes... fiercer even than Dago grappa! His eyes watered, and his stomach burned. Even Ben Rodgers looked amort for once, regarding his half-empty glass with a sort of religious awe.

All the while Mlavic and Petracic laughed themselves silly, bent double and gasping for breath from sheer amusement at the knacky trick they'd played on strangers!

Well, what else'd the Devil himself drink? Lewrie wryly asked of the aether, but liquid fire and brimstone?

Then, slowly... as a sullen rain hammered down and seethed overhead on the decks and coach-top, through an entire afternoon of sipping their fierce plum brandy, the deal was struck. They'd go out and seize a small ship for Petracic to use. He'd get his muskets, powder and shot upon the morrow. They'd supply silver coinage, so he could recruit a larger band of dispossessed Serbs along the coast and among the isles. He'd strip crew from the smallest four of his "fleet" and man the new prize. Petracic would establish a base farther out to sea, for there were smaller islands near Bisevo or Susak where no one ever patrolled.

Grudgingly, Petracic had sworn to imprison the captured passengers and crews, to keep them decently fed and watered; though he was much of the same mind as Kolodzcy – that "dead men tell no tales." He'd get a shilling, or its local equivalent, per head for live captives. They'd only pay after a decent head count.

Rodgers offered Petracic the right to pick over any captures they made themselves, for small-arms or artillery, before they took them off to the Prize-Court at Trieste. That was flat against the formal usages.

However, Lewrie pointed out, feeling only a faint twinge of ancient guilt for his sins of the past, that the Articles of War did allow a *tad* of flexibility, that Article the Eighth stated:

> No person in or belonging to the Fleet shall take out of
> any Prize, or Ships seized for Prize, any Money, Plate, or
> Goods, unless it shall be necessary, for the better securing
> thereof, *or for the necessary Use and Service of any of His
> Majesty's Ships or Vessels of War...*

"Long as we fetch in all her papers, sir, we could write what we share with Captain Petracic off," Lewrie rather boozily allowed, "as necessary for *our* use and service."

"Uhm, ahh?" Rodgers blearily muttered. "Aye, I 'spose..."

And, lastly, Petracic was cautioned that their arrangement would survive as long as they didn't go beyond their brief. The Coalition was not at war with Venice, with Ragusa, Naples or the various Italian states that faced the Adriatic. Ships of those nations were off limits, as were Austrian ships, since they were allies. As were British vessels, though there were few still working the Adriatic trade-routes. Petracic would have to obey *some* civilised rules, after all! Ships they chased to him, ships he caught close inshore that were hostile, aye… and the best of hunting to him, then. Petracic might hold those he took by mistake, and *Pylades* or *Jester* would turn up sooner or later to adjudge them, then "rescue" them, should he err.

"More cause t'keep 'em alive an' kickin'," Rodgers had intoned. "Don't even rough 'em up. Harm a hair… hic…! o' their heads. Hey?"

"He hear you," Mlavic had grunted, both of them turning drunk-enly truculent at such a long list of cautions. "Not babies. Men! Serb men! No need, teaching."

Petracic had at last risen, after a final glass of naval rum, as his stone crock had at last been drunk to the dregs. He wavered like a tall oak in a gale of wind, but he stood and shook hands all about with them. Even with Kolodzcy, though he applied more pressure there than he did with the others, making the poor Austrian wisp wince and cringe.

"He goes," Kolodzcy announced. "Vill get his guns tomorrow?"

"Tomorrow," Rodgers promised, holding onto the edge of the table, but upright. Cross-eyed, but upright, Lewrie noted.

Then they went. Rodgers, Lewrie and Kolodzcy shambled out onto the gun-deck to see them off, doffing their hats automatically, now that they'd netted their new allies. With difficulty, they even attained the larboard gangway, though it was a struggle for Rodgers and Kolodzcy.

It was still raining, though warmer, as it got on for the end of the First Dog-watch, near six p.m. Lewrie left his hat off after the two pirates had stumbled into their waiting *felucca*, letting the rain sluice on his reeling head, into his mouth and half-focused eyes.

"Success, then, gen'lemen… Lewrie," Rodgers groaned.

"S'pose one could call it that, sir," Lewrie replied.

"Good *God*, but I've never been so 'in the barrel'!" Rodgers confessed. "Drunk'z a lord. No, drunk'z a bloody emperor! Christ, I need a lie-down."

"Y'll dine aboard then, sir," Lewrie presumed, figuring Ben Rodgers wouldn't survive a row across to *Pylades*. It would be a right comic miracle could either of them manage to get into the gig! Bleakly, Alan saw himself stuck with them another night, and in an hour or so, might they be so recovered as to require "hair of the dog" for restoration?

"Swear t'Christ, there's bloody *three* o'ya, Alan, old son! An' th' one'z too damn many, already." Rodgers swayed. "No, thought I'd go..."

"Ah," Lewrie said, mopping his face on his sleeve. "Pity. Bosun?"

"Aye, sir?" Cony replied, coming to his side as Leutnant Kolodzcy put his head on Lewrie's left shoulder, with one arm about Rodgers, and began to sing and kick one dainty booted foot; some Austrian mountain nonsense that involved a stab at yodeling, though it came out more a whimpering.

"Chair-sling for Captain Rodgers, and... get *off* me!"

"Cap'um, uh... 'llow me t'suggest a cargo net?" Cony tittered.

Lewrie managed to steer Kolodzcy to lean on Rodgers; or Rodgers to lean on Kolodzcy. They looked like a pair of mast-hoisting sheer-legs, or a two-legged stool... sure to go smash any minute.

"No..." Lewrie sighed, after a long, difficult stab at thought. "Can't insult the dignity of guest, Cony. Chair-sling, starboard side. Lots o' frappin', to keep 'em in, mind. Do they *get* in."

"Oh aye, sir," Cony said straight-faced, knuckling his brow with three fingers. "Dignity."

Lewrie turned back to behold Leutnant Kolodzcy stumbling through steps of a slow minuet, still singing that lively country song in a cracked voice. Ben Rodgers was hanging on his shoulder with a death-grip, and forced to follow in a shambling dance of his own. He was barking and howling like a hound on a hot scent for a commentary – when he wasn't cackling like an inmate in Bedlam over his canine insult to Kolodzcy's singing.

"Mister Knolles," Lewrie croaked.

"Here, sir."

"Utmos' compliments to ya, sir," Lewrie slurred, "an' would I be so 'bliged... well, someone should, hey? You render debarkin' honours for me? Be below. Dyin', it feels like."

"Ah. Debarking honours, sir." Lieutenant Knolles guffawed as loud as discipline would let him as Rodgers threw his head back and crooned like a famished wolf. "Directly, Captain."

Lewrie sighed, wondering how funny it might feel in the painful light of morning, and stumbled off aft, lifting his feet almost knees-up to avoid the odd ring-bolt, to the gay air of a Tyrol tune and the hoarse growls and howls of a "music critic."

"Lemme help ya, sir… 'at's the way," Aspinall offered.

"Some hot coffee, then yer supper, sir. Make a new man o' ya."

"Not up to solids, Aspinall. Don't think."

"Soup an' toast, sir. Get somethin' on yer stomach. Soak up—"

"Aye, we have, ain't we?" Lewrie at last grinned as he was led into his great-cabins and dumped onto the starboard-side settee, sprawling like a loose bale of rag-picker's goods. "Soaked up."

"Be back in a tick, sir," Aspinall assured him.

Crossly, Lewrie managed to get one boot off, got the hilt of his sword out from under his left buttock and kidney, but that was about as much as he could manage on his own.

Lord, what've we gotten ourselves into? he wondered to himself as he began to drift forrud, towards the edge of the settee, with his legs feeling as if they belonged to someone else; and an uncooperative swine, at that. Pirates, for God's sake. Bloody *lunatick* pirates! Holy sacrifice… vengeance. Holy war, 'gainst ev'rybody else on God's green ol' earth! Lord, what've we bloody *started*?

His fundament met the turkey carpet and the chequered deckcloth, legs sprawled at a wide angle, with his head now resting so far back on the settee cushions a sober observer might think him neck-broke.

His gaze swam about, cockeyed as if *Jester* were heaving, pitching, yawing and rolling in a hurricane under bare poles. There, in the dining coach, over the table on the forrud bulkhead, he found something to focus on. His wife Caroline's portrait. All sunny and radiant in a wide-brim straw bonnet, smiling so eye-crinklin' pleased, before their first house in the Bahamas, with East Bay and the shipping behind her.

He screwed one eye shut, to peer more intently.

"Needs o' th' Service, m'dear," he apologised. "Ne'er seen me bung-full, I know. Bloody barbarians… in f'r dinner an' drink. Had t'keep up th' side, don' y'see? King an' Country…?"

He thought of crawling over for a closer, fonder look. Damme, though; was that a frown in her forehead… right where she wrinkled in those times she was vexed with him? Or was she laughing at him, at his ludicrous condition?

"Ben's fault, damn yer eyes," he whispered. Peering took too much out of him, so he shut the other eye, too, and let his head loll.

Aspinall returned with a mug of soup and some piping-hot toast, but he was too late. His captain's top-lights had been extinguished for the evening. With Andrews's help, they removed his coat, sword-belt and stock, the other fancy Hessian boot, and slung him gently into bed, with a swaddling coverlet atop.

Where he dreamed the most vivid and disturbing plum-brandy dreams. Of blood and crows, of a vast plain of bones, of biblical patriarchs with swinging swords, red-eyed vengeance, rapine and slaughter.

And of whispering seals whose voices were too soft to understand, or be heeded.

Chapter 6

South of the isle of Susak, smack in the middle of the Adriatic, lay a small cluster of rocky, barely inhabited islets round a larger, which was named Palagruza. *Pylades* and Petracic's *galliot* sailed there, to establish a camp, from which they would then go back to the Balkan mainland so Petracic could have a chance to raise his fellow Serbs. Ben Rodgers would capture him that suitable European ship, too.

Dividing their forces once again, Lewrie and *Jester* were sent off toward the Straits of Otranto. He was free of Rodgers, but most especially was he free at last of Leutnant Conrad Kolodzcy. Forced to beat against a persistent Sutherly, the Sirocco, for several days, he zigzagged his way down the Adriatic, quartering it thoroughly on-passage and hunting for prey once more.

The weather was hot, now it was late July, and the sere wind up from Africa was no refreshing relief, sometimes hazed with gathered dust or sand particles, reducing visibility. The seas, forced up the narrows into the cul-de-sac of the Adriatic, humped long, folding waves of seven or eight feet. *Jester* bowled over them surefooted, though, swooping on their faces and cleaving them in delightful bursts of spray with a quick, lively and satisfied motion. As if their warship felt as free as they – as liberated from their dubious dealings, and fresh-washed in proper Royal Navy business.

No, the only fly in their ointment was the presence of the *dhow* off their larboard quarters, for Dragan Mlavic had been sent off by his master Petracic to glean what pickings he could from *Jester*'s successes. He'd fade back whenever they stood on larboard tack towards Italy. But, like a nemesis, they'd espy her again when forced over to starboard tack and angle for the Albanian or Montenegran shores.

Uncanny, it was. Surely, Lewrie thought, the Adriatic, narrow as it was, still held room enough to lose the bitch in! But no. There she was, hull-down to the East'rd. Could she be any *other* dowdy two-masted coaster, since the Adriatic teemed with them? Time and again, though, and hope against hope, they'd recognise her dun brown sails with the odd patches of new canvas they'd been forced to give Mlavic, which formed a stylised lightning-bolt pattern on her foresail! Until the very sight of that accidental emblem made every man-jack groan with disgust, as if a penniless relation had shown up to sponge off them, just after they had been paid in coin, for a rare once.

"Damme, how *does* he do it, Captain?" Lieutenant Knolles spat, lifting his hat for one of his irritated blond hair-rufflings.

"Luck o' th' Devil, he, Mister Knolles," Buchanon decided. "An' th' Devil's Brood has 'eir master's luck."

"Thought we'd sailed him under, the last Sou'west tack, sir," Lieutenant Knolles carped on. "He hasn't the 'nutmegs' to sail over to Italy. He'd get his silly arse knackered over there. Does he idle in the middle? Do a dash down to where he thinks we'll be, and wait?"

"Aloft, there!" Lewrie demanded of the lookouts. "She alone?"

"Aye, sir!"

"Hasn't tried to take a ship himself, then." Lewrie frowned.

"Like a kite, sir. Waitin' 'til braver beasts'z made 'eir kill," the Sailing Master harrumphed. "'*En* he'll have a bite'r two."

"Deck, there!" Came another shout from the lookouts. "Sail ho!"

"Where away?" Knolles howled impatiently.

"*Four* point off th' *starb'd* bows! Brig! Runnin' free!"

Lewrie scrambled aloft to the cat-harpings of the mizzen to have a gander. There was no more than seven miles' visibility with all that wind-borne African haze on the Sutherly horizon, and the strange vessel was already showing a hint of tops'ls as well as all of her t'gallants. Sailing dead off the wind, he took note, with "both sheets aft." She'd pass astern of *Jester* should they both stand on as they were, perhaps a good two miles apart. He could tack right away, he schemed, go back to larboard tack headed Sou'west, and cut her off as she loped North, fat, dumb and happy. Running as she was, she could sail no faster than the winds blew, and that felt like only a ten-to twelve-knot breeze today, he reckoned. Less, for she'd surely be heavily laden, snuffling bows-down with a breeze right up her transom, even with the fore-course reduced, and the lifting effect of the fore-tops'l to ease her. And she didn't look particularly big, either, an average brig of about eighty-five feet overall, with a chunky seventy-foot waterline.

Yet, should she take fright, she'd alter course, just on general principles, and claw up to the wind and beat inshore for safety in the neutral

Venetian port of Durazzo. She was now about six miles a'weather of them. Make it five, he plotted in his head, once we've tacked, losing way... same for her. Dammit, she could just barely make it in, one step ahead!

Lewrie clambered down and stowed his telescope in the rack by the binnacle cabinet. "We'll stand on as we are for now, Mister Knolles. I don't wish to scare her off 'til she's come down closer to us, within a mile or two. Then, do we haul our wind or tack, we'll fall down on her, and keep ourselves 'tween her and the safety of a neutral port."

"Very good, sir," Knolles replied.

"Deck, there!" The lookout cried. "*Dhow*, sir! *Tackin'!*"

Mlavic had been loafing along on the starboard tack, pointing up higher on the winds, even so, than *Jester* ever could, presaging a close-aboard reunion, unless Lewrie had ordered them to come about to stand aloof of his *dhow*. Suddenly, though, she racked over to larboard tack, bearing Sou'west, still pointing high and expanding the size of her lateen sails to full size. Mlavic had spotted the strange brig and was going after her with every stitch of canvas aloft!

"Damn him. Just damn him!" Lewrie rasped.

"He'll scare her off!" Midshipman Hyde exclaimed, outraged.

Mlavic had been off *Jester*'s larboard quarter and only two sea-miles to leeward. On her new course, he'd close them before sweeping past, crossing *Jester*'s stern and surging upwind of her. Mlavic, it appeared, had found some courage for the chase at last – but at the very worst possible moment!

"Greedy bastard," Lewrie commented sourly. "Hmm... aloft, there! What is the brig doing?"

"Standin' on, sir! Courses 'bove th' horizon, runnin' free!"

"They've seen us by now, surely. Might not be able to see that pirate yet," Knolles muttered. "'Til he crosses our stern, sir."

"Or do 'ey not keep a proper lookout, like most merchantmen, sir," Buchanon added. "Nought t'fear so far, e'en do 'ey."

Lewrie looked aft. To save wear-and-tear, *Jester* only flew her national colours when challenged or when doing the challenging. With her courses above the horizon already, the brig couldn't be more than a scant four miles up to windward, and *still* held to her off-wind slide. She didn't yet acknowledge *Jester* as a warship, since she'd made no move to close her, but was standing on Sou'east, on a diverging course as if bound for Durazzo herself.

The line of sight, Alan thought, looking to windward once more; aye, Mlavic is hidden below us now, blotted out by our hull and sails, even did they spot him earlier. Might be the brig's whey-faced innocent, or a neutral, but he had to stop her and speak her to ascertain that. To run up the flag now might spook her, either way, and they'd waste half a day running her down for nothing.

And best *we* fetch her first. Alan shivered. God knows *what* that pig-eyed fool'd do, neutral prize or no! Fight *us* for her?

"Mister Hyde," Lewrie decided. "Fetch out that Frog flag of ours. Bend it on and hoist it to the mizzen peak. Mister Knolles, prepare to come about to larboard tack. We'll see what answering hoist we receive... then we'll pretend to run from those *terrible* Serb pirates yonder... and unmask 'em to her, as we come about. See what she makes of that!"

"Oh, I see, sir!" Knolles chuckled. "Eek eek, a mouse, Captain? Bosun! Pipe 'Stations for Stays'!"

"Once round, Mister Knolles..." Lewrie added. "Beat to Quarters."

-

Scant minutes later, all had altered. *Jester* was thrashing wind-ward, hobby-horsing over the long but steep sets of waves. Their pirate *dhow's* way had been blocked, as Lewrie had flung his ship squarely across her course, and was now pitching and rolling dead in *Jester's* wake – as if she truly were pursuing her – working her way up to windward of them, certainly, since fore-and-aft rigged lateeners could pinch up much closer to the eye of the wind any day.

And the brig...!

She'd taken one look, hoisted a matching French flag, and turned away, wearing herself to a broad reach, with the Sirocco winds large on her larboard quarter, headed Nor-Nor'west. She was steering directly for a meeting with *Jester*!

Comin' t'save me, are you? Lewrie speculated with a sneer, as he glanced astern and ahead in a constant mental juggling act of courses and speeds; me, a fellow Frog? Damn brave of you. Or d'ye think your own safety lies in numbers... two armed merchantmen 'gainst one pirate?

"A mile, I make her, sir," Mr. Buchanon suggested.

"We'll stand on a bit more, 'fore..." Lewrie mused, turning for another peek at what Mlavic was doing. Which, he imagined, might involve tearing his hair out in frustration at the moment. His *dhow* had worked her way back windward of *Jester*, out on her larboard quarter again. And no more than a mile astern, down to leeward. Edging out to pass, but he'd be just a bit too late. Depending on what the brig did, of course. Then Lewrie turned to peer forward once more.

"Three-quarter mile," Buchanon speculated, sounding excited. "Ah!"

"Uhum!" Lewrie beamed. The brig was turning, bearing more Westerly and bracing her yards round, hauling taut as she swung in a wide arc to put herself on the wind on the same tack as *Jester*! Nowhere near as fast, she planned to match courses and let *Jester* − a "fellow countryman" − surge up to her so their firepower was concentrated. Should he speak her, captain-to-captain, and plan what they could do to "save" themselves?

"Pinch us up, quartermasters. Luff up, and nothing to loo'rd." Lewrie snapped. "Mister Crewe, ready with the starboard battery!"

The wheel-drum groaned as Spenser and Brauer fought it for two or three more spokes of lee helm to take their ship up to the very edge of the winds, clawing out another fifty yards of advantage. Then they backed off only one or two spokes, at most, as the fickle wind shifted, eyes on the luff of the main-course and main-tops'l, the flutterings of the commissioning pendant high aloft as it streamed like a weathervane to steer by... the compass bedamned, from there on out. They cursed softly as they put their weight on it, judging by feel of the tiller-ropes' tension and the wind on their cheeks if they were coasting too close toward luffing; scanning the sea off the lar-board bows for a contrary skeining of rivulets on the wavetops, or a glass-smooth patch of calm.

"Over, now, ye square-head!" Spenser grunted. "Oh, ye lady, oh, ye sweet'un! 'At's our darlin' lass!"

"Rasmus!" Brauer hissed as he fed from the lee side to Spenser on the windward. "*Ach, ja! Lir... bitte!*"

Christ, e'en the Germans're believers now! Lewrie grumbled to himself. Callin' on his old sea-god... and ours!

The brig was most nicely cooperating. As she rounded up, wearing close-hauled to the Sou'west, she lost ground to leeward and spent all her windward placement. Suddenly she was within a quarter mile off the starboard bows and nearly a cable to the right of *Jester*'s course.

Should he charge up her larboard side? Lewrie smiled. They were not two hundred yards off! Mlavic? Hah! Stupid shit.

The brig's manoeuvre had thrown Mlavic off. *Jester* would reach her first and be between him and the prize. With a happily imagined eruption of head-fur as Mlavic tore his hair out, the *dhow* was hauling her wind and falling off to cross *Jester*'s stern. If Mlavic couldn't catch her by passing left, he'd duck down and pass right, and assault the brig's leeward side. But that'd put him in the wind-shadow of *Jester*'s tall masts and massive spread of sail, and rob him of the wind-strength he needed to hold his course or make his current speed, making his attack even later!

"Might be uncanny knacky t'keep finding us, Mr. Buchanon," Lewrie noted. "But he's not a clever sailor, is he?"

"What need have we o' such a 'no-sailor,' 'en, Cap'um?"

"Only God above – and Captain Charlton – knows, sir," Lewrie replied. "Mister Knolles? Ready to get our way off. Once we've fired her a cheery hello, be ready to fetch-to and get boats down."

"Aye aye, sir!"

"Mister Hyde, still with us?" Lewrie asked, craning about.

"Here, sir," the midshipman replied, stepping forward.

"Strike the French flag and hoist the proper colours," Lewrie said, pacing to the forward edge of the quarterdeck. "Mister Crewe? Warning shot, once we've our own colours aloft. Does she haul away, though, do you serve her a full broadside!"

And there the brig lay, just a bit ahead of abeam, within a long musket-shot, thrashing away to windward and safety frantically, with her captain and first mate by her windward rails with speaking-trumpets in their hands. Crewmen were waving tarred hats or long, red Frog stocking caps, giving their "ally," their "rescuer," a hearty Gallic cheer.

"'*Alloo!*" the brig's captain shrilled. "*Bon matin, m'sieur!*"

"Colour's aloft, sir!" Midshipman Hyde yelled from astern.

"Open the gun-ports and run out, Mister Crewe! Warnin' shot!"

With a deep thunderous growl of wooden truck wheels on oak decks, the guns of the starboard battery were hauled up to the ports, the same time as the port lids were swung up and out of the way, interrupting the pacific dark-green gunwale stripe with a chequer of blood-red interior bulwark paint as they hinged flat against *Jester*'s side.

The starboard foc's'le carronade erupted with a titanic belch of smoke and flame, placing an 18-pounder solid iron ball in the sea just fifty feet ahead of the brig's beak-head rails and figurehead, splashing a great pillar of spray as high as her fore-course yard, which sheeted on her foredecks as she sailed into it like a sudden summer sun-shower.

"And a bloody good morning t'you as well, *m'sieur*!" Lewrie cried across. It was difficult to shout, though; he was laughing too hard at the looks of utter disbelief on the Frenchmen's phyzes! "*Amenez-vous?* Do you strike? Or do I blow you t'Hades?" he demanded, patting the cold iron barrel of the nearest quarterdeck carronade.

The brig's captain was stamping his feet and raging in a circle about his deck, like he was trying to kill an entire plague of roaches. He flung his speaking-trumpet at *Jester* – almost *reached* her, he was so exercised! But, after a final fist-shake and tearing off his hat – to do a furious stomping on that, too! – he howled at his after-guard.

And her Tricolour came sagging down.

Chapter 7

"Lie!" Dragan Mlavic accused, once he'd attained the gang-ways on the prize. "Cheat! British, you cheat and lie! Take for self!"

"Sir," Lewrie countered, icily civil, "you were too far down to leeward. Understand... leeward? Too far off. You almost cost us the... our prize, by tacking too soon. Gave the game away."

"So now you keep?" Mlavic raged, flexing knobby rough fingers about the hilt of his expensive scimitar. He'd been followed by three of his larger and most rakehellish accomplices, who couldn't follow a bloody word that was said, of course, but were willing to back Mlavic to the hilt against strangers.

"On the contrary... sir," Lewrie replied, grinding his teeth to remain calm. It wasn't every day an English gentleman was told he was a liar or a cheat; those were dueling words, gentleman-to-gentleman, a cause for blood! "You are entitled to a share of her goods, just as we agreed back at Mjlet with your leader."

And however do ye *really* pronounce that? Alan wondered.

"And I'll thankee t'take your hand off your sword hilt, before I get angry. Sir," Lewrie dared snap.

"'Fore some'un gets bad hurt fo' insultin' ou' cap'um, heah me?" Andrews spoke up from Lewrie's right rear, with his right hand firm on the hilt of his slung cutlass. "Ya un'erstan' 'hurt,' mon?" Andrews threatened, backed up by Midshipman Spendlove and five hands off Lewrie's gig. "Be easy, now."

Mlavic squinted his beady little eyes, screwing his face up like he'd caught a whiff of something rotten. For a second or two, he tried to puff out his chest like a pigeon, but thought better of it. Andrews was something out of his experience, a West Indies black seaman, sprung up like a vengeful *djinn* in Turkish tales, and as fearsome as an ogre. Wearing a coxswain's pipe, pistol and sword, and backed by other hands spoiling for a fight. With a raspy sigh, he deflated, cowed.

"Aye, let's be easy. A misunderstanding," Lewrie allowed.

There was a vituperative, gargling diatribe in Serbo-Croat fired at Mlavic's backers. *Sounded* damn vituperative, anyway, Alan thought. But Mlavic let go the hilt of his scimitar, to cross his arms over his chest, and his escorts ostentatiously made their own hands go someplace inoffensive and unthreatening, rather self-consciously.

"That's better," Lewrie said. "Stand easy, Andrews. Lads."

"Want guns," Dragan Mlavic grumbled, sounding much abashed but still pigheaded determined to get his fair due. "Guns, shot, powder."

The brig mounted some small 2-pounder boat-guns for stern or bow-chasers, and no more than six 6-pounder carriage guns. All were rather rusty and badly cared for, the carriages looking as dry and fragile as abandoned barn planking. The ready-use shot in the rope garlands near the guns appeared welded together by a reddish oxide scale. Lewrie had no use for them, and if Mlavic could clean them up, paint and oil, file and sand them back into a semblance of proper maintenance, then he was more than welcome to them.

"They are yours, captain Mlavic," Lewrie grandly offered. "As we agreed. Courtesy of the Royal Navy."

The thick-set pirate beamed at that news, turned to his sailors and told them of their bounty, which made them smile at last, and made Mlavic preen like a man just presented with a spanking-new silk coat.

"Anything else you wish, sir?" Lewrie said, trying to mollify the man further. "I have her papers, here, and her manifest. She carries wine, cheese, flour, pasta, brandies, various manufactured goods… understand 'manifest'?"

"Manifest, *da.*" Mlavic nodded vigourously. "This I knowing. I see?" He peered at the offered lists Lewrie held out to him, head over to one side and running a tar-stained finger down the top one. Breathing hard.

Can he read a manifest in French? Lewrie wondered. Or can this oak stump read at *all*? He pointed to an entry – *Trousers: 12 Bundles, Used/Mended.*

"Any use for this, sir?" Lewrie queried, tongue-in-cheek. "Quite a tasty assortment for you and your men. Various flavoured brandies."

"Brandy, *da.*" Mlavic nodded again, eyes almost crossing with the intensity of his pondering, but glowing piggishly delighted. "Captain brandy? Or, *ratafia*… serve crew? No good, *ratafia*, pooh!" he spat.

No, he can't read it! Lewrie exulted. *Got* you!

"Why don't you just tick off what you wish, hmm?" he offered, feeling sly-boots. "Then boat your choices over to your ship, hey?"

Now worm yer way out o' that'un, ya poxy clown! Lewrie thought.

"What *you* want?" Mlavic countered with a suspicious glint in his eyes. "You pick. Send, your ship. We take rest, *da*?"

Baited me right back, by God, thought Lewrie, still smiling as if he *didn't* wish to strangle the hairy bastard that instant.

The winds hadn't picked up considerably, but the seas still long-rolled over seven to eight feet, and *Jester*, the captured brig and the *dhow* were pitching, rolling and slatting in a continual clatter as they lay fetched-to. To manhandle cargo up from the holds onto the deck and then down into ship's boats would be pluperfect buggery. Only the very smallest or lightest items could make the journey without getting hands injured or drowned; not much beyond what people could carry in a canvas sea-bag of plunder, and not much beyond a couple of hundredweight into each boat at a time, making the transfer an entire day's drudgery, and a danger-fraught steeplechase for crewmen in wildly tossing boats.

Mr. Giles and his Jack-in-the-Breadroom were standing by, nigh salivating over the goodies the brig held. He could replenish *Jester* to a fair approximation of Royal Navy standard rations with the stored flour, rice, dried beans and salt-meats. They might be short of issue rum by then, but the brig's *vin ordinaire* would more than suffice, and the best part of the situation was that whatever he could transship to *Jester* was absolutely scot-free, taken from a prize for nothing, instead of having to cough up his personal funds, or Navy Board funds, for them. The purser would still charge for their issue, though, making his five percent. He already had several small crates or chests laid out, Lewrie saw. Tobacco twists for those who chewed, snuff for those that preferred it that way and loose shag tobacco for the smokers. Twelve percent profit on that, along with his slop-goods. Lewrie thought Giles might even desire one of those bundles of *Trousers, Used/Mended!*

"There are some few things we could use, Captain Mlavic." Alan shrugged. "To allow *Jester* to keep the seas."

"Good. You take. We keep ship," Mlavic announced. "What?"

"Promise ship. Here is ship," Mlavic pointed out.

"But Captain Rodgers was to capture a ship for you. For Captain Petracic, rather," Alan objected. "Surely he's done that by now."

"Ship, Ratko, *da*," Mlavic sniggered, doggedly insistent. "Want ship, Dragan. My ship."

"You have a ship there," Lewrie said, pointing at the *dhow*.

"Want ship." Mlavic frowned. "This ship. More men come, sail both."

"Don't have more men now," Lewrie countered. "Too few to man this ship and yours at same time. French crew, you'll have to guard."

Damme, now he's got *me* jabberin' pidgin! Lewrie fretted; all that lovely wine aboard, and damned if I ain't short!

"I take ship," Mlavic announced, like a petulant child. Lewrie thought he was ready to stick out his lower lip or hold his breath 'til he turned blue!

"And can you *handle* a brig, sir?" Lewrie quibbled. "It's not like your lateener, not—"

"When boy, go to sea," Mlavic shot back, nettled that his professional skills were being questioned. "Go Ragusa, work Venetian ship. Go Corfu, work Naples' ship. Go Malta, work Maltese ship. Go Genoa… work ship, bilander, poleacre, brig… all same. Work Trieste, Venice, Cádiz, Lisbon, all over. Topman, helm, bosun mate… even work Zante… British traders come for currants, *da*? Go Pool of London, once. Hand, reef and steer, *da*? Handle brig, *da*! You give brig. Take some cargo. We keep rest."

Christ, next he'll say he was Able Seaman, R.N.! Alan sighed.

"You have, what… forty hands?"

"Half for *dhow*, half for brig."

"Mind, you'll have to guard the French prisoners, too."

"No, you take."

"Captain Mlavic, I can't." Lewrie sighed again. "Lookee here, sir. The agreement was for us to operate separately. Secretly. Now, do I turn up at Trieste with French prisoners, the word gets out that I took her and turned her over to you, d'ye see? If she's your prize, then I'm afraid you're stuck with 'em. You'll have to take 'em back to Palagruza and dump 'em in that prison stockade your Captain Petracic was to build."

"No," Mlavic pouted.

"'Fraid you'll have to. Can't continue your cruise with a brig and a *dhow* both half-manned," Lewrie pointed out. "*All* of 'em, mind. In good health," he added, wondering if Mlavic was not above killing them and dumping the bodies over the side like "blackbirders" did with sickly slaves. "I have a list of their names, and, as we agreed, I'll pay you an English shilling a head, right now, for their well-being. You'll be able to feed 'em with the stores aboard."

Lewrie snuck a glance at the small knot of French prisoners by the foremast. Government-hired by the French or a speculative voyage, even the French shipmasters were averse to hiring on any more hands than was absolutely necessary. There were only nineteen men, including the cook and the snot-nosed cabin servants, aboard her.

"Now, we'll put in somewhere, find a calm lee behind some island and transfer some supplies to *Jester*, sir," Lewrie pressed. "But if you want this brig, then you'll have to take them, into the bargain."

Then sail back to Palagruza and outa my hair, please Jesus? he thought hopefully, eager to be shot of the bastard.

"Take brig, *da*," Mlavic grunted, broken-hearted, piggish. "Take prisoners, *da*. No hurt them, *da*. I agree."

"Good, then," Lewrie breathed out, quite pleased of a sudden.

"Go *now*, Palagruza." Mlavic beamed. "*Srpski narod*, poor. Have nothing, year and year. British, rich navy, have much. Dragan, he take all. Now," Mlavic said, looking as if he were ready to start weeping over the plight of his people all over again.

Well, if that's what it takes to make him go, then fine! Lewrie silently mused; and may he have joy of it! God, 'fore he blubbers up!

"Very well, sir," Lewrie relented, doffing his hat and forcing himself to look "shit-eatin'" pleasant. "She's yours. Good hunting—"

"Nineteen shilling," Mlavic interrupted, hand out like a Mother Abbess in a knocking-shop. "Nineteen prisoner, I hear say. I knowing. Nineteen shilling. Knowing shilling, too."

And Lewrie was forced to dig into his breeches pockets and rummage about for coins. With no need of purse or money at sea, all that could be found was a single stray golden guinea.

"Ah!" Mlavic exclaimed as it appeared. "I owe you two shilling. Good luck, gold guinea."

His hand was out again, and Lewrie was forced to plop the coin on Mlavic's callused paw.

"Ahem, well," Lewrie said, flummoxed. "Mister Spendlove? We're off. Hands down and into the boat."

"Now, sir? But…" The lad frowned.

"*Now*, Mister Spendlove," Lewrie smouldered.

"Very well, sir. Cox'n? Mr. Giles?"

"'Scuse me, Captain, but I thought we'd be taking more supplies aboard," Mr. Giles intruded, joggling his square-lensed spectacles in dismay. "There's the salt-meats, the flour and dried fruits for—"

"Now, Mister Giles, dammit!" Lewrie rasped.

"Aye aye, sir." Giles wilted. "This tobacco, though…?"

"Fetch along what you can carry, sir. But stir yerself."

–

As the gig stroked back to *Jester*, breasting and swooping with a sickening motion over the tumultuous sea, the brig's yards were already being braced about, and the *dhow* was slow-ghosting into motion, falling off to the West on larboard tack, both beginning to gather way.

Lewrie turned to watch them go, wishing them bad *cess;* the worst old Irish *cess* a body ever met. Storms, lashings of gales, whirlpools and maelstroms, sea-monsters with teeth the size of carriage-guns, with mouths as big as an admiral's barge! *Eat* the bastard, somebody!

His gig held a few quickly gathered items, mostly half-filled sea-bags or small chests. In the beginning, the cutter had crossed over to augment the boarding-party, too, and he knew that Mr. Giles had already gotten a fair portion of "goodies" transferred before Mlavic had caught up with them. He had the prize's documents rolled up in a thick round bundle in one coat pocket. He drew them out and looked over the manifest once more, mourning the loss of those brandies, those pipes and kegs of wine. If they didn't put in at Corfu or Trieste after Rodgers and Kolodzcy had drunk him dry, he'd be reduced to the crew's rum-and-water!

"Begging your pardon, sir, but… why'd we depart so quickly?" Midshipman Spendlove asked in a soft voice. And Lewrie imagined that he could hear Andrews his coxswain, six oars-men and the bow-hook man all grunt a muffled "*Arrhh?*" a moment after.

"In the spirit of mutual cooperation with our new… allies," Lewrie muttered. "We promised to obtain European ships with artillery, and so we did, Mister Spendlove. There was no safe harbour where we'd be able to break out or shift cargo – without revealing our arrangement with the Serbian pirates, mind – so it was best that we let this Mlavic person have her and sail her back to the isles of Palagruza. Far from sight of prying eyes, d'ye see."

"Seems a pity, sir." Spendlove shrugged, seeming to buy Lewrie's glib explanation at face value. "Not like giving up an outward-bounder, full of compass-timber and such. Just our bad luck, I s'pose, to fetch an inward-bound vessel. Rich as they've been laden…"

Christ! Lewrie quailed, stiffening bolt-upright and sucking in some air involuntarily, no matter how rigid he should have held himself before his crew. French gold, from their government for purchasing naval stores! Her captain's personal pelf! Her working capital, to pay her many needs, to victual her or make the odd repairs on the round voyage!

He idly (as idly as his murderously angry fingers would allow!) took a squint through the various documents he held. He'd sent Spendlove and Andrews below to her master's great-cabins straightaway, to delve about and turn up these lists, her log and such, but he hadn't time to scan them thoroughly before his confrontation with Dragan Mlavic.

He suddenly felt *very* ill. And snookered. And stupid, into the bargain, when he read that the Ministry of Marine had consigned twelve thousand *livres* in gold to be used for the purchase of seasoned Adriatic oak for naval construction. One locked and wax-sealed reinforced chest, to be safeguarded at all peril, signed over to a *capitaine*…!

Oh, who gives a good goddamn to whom! he fumed, looking up and out toward *Jester*, thankful that his gig was now stroking into her lee, where the wave-motion wasn't so boisterous, for he surely felt the need to spew, by then… to "cast his accounts to Neptune"! He eyed the boat and found no locked and wax-sealed bound chest. Mlavic had it, damn his eyes! Damn his scurvy, poxy *blood*!

Manfully fighting the almost irresistible urge to moan, curse or scream aloud, he looked down at the bundle he held once more. There was a small sheaf of notes in a spidery hand, a daily accounting list in the rough, to be transferred to a proper account book later. A ledger that was most-like still aboard the brig, or in her Purser's or First Mate's tender care. Another bloody 3,247 or so *livres* of working capital, less what they'd paid some Marseilles chandlers, less a pilot's fees…!

And what's so bloody *wrong* with tears, I ask you! Lewrie thought, stone-bleak at what he'd lost; by God, I've been robbed! Diddled! That's why Mlavic wished to have her, to winkle us off so quick! He suspected… and got me so "rowed" I'd not think to…!

"Not a total loss, sir," Spendlove told him as the bow-man took a first stab at the starboard main-chains with his boat-hook. His heel

thumped on a bag that lay under his thwart. The bag rustled nicely...
could he *also* conjure a faint chinking sound, a muted metal jingling?

"Aye, sah, foun' ya some cawfee beans, nigh on fo' poun'," his
coxswain assured him between orders to the crew to toss their oars
and such. "Frenchies allus have de bes' when it come t'cawfee."

"Ah. Coffee. I see," Lewrie replied, summoning up some gratitude;
or something that sounded approximate. "Well, thankee, Andrews.
Mister Spendlove. Thankee right kindly."

"Some odds and ends, too, sir," Spendlove preened, proud of his
scrounging abilities. "Goose quills, right-hand bent. Fresh ink, and
some fine vellum paper..."

"Thoughtful of you both," Lewrie expounded as he stood to make
his way to the gunn'l for a well-timed leap to the damp, weed-green
and slick bottom steps of the boarding battens. "I'm grateful for your
concern."

–

The bag *did* hold coffee beans, and odds and ends; sadly, it held no
coins. Lewrie set the ink-bottle and new quills on his desktop, put
fifty-odd sheets of vellum in a drawer.

"Do you stow these away in the pantry, Aspinall," he directed.

"Aye, sir. Oh, toppin', sir! Fresh beans. Like a cup, sir? I could have
some ground an' brewed in ten minute."

"Not at the moment, Aspinall, thankee," Lewrie sighed. "Perhaps
later. No relish for it now."

"Right, then, sir," the lad chirped, going forrud and humming to
himself in right good cheer, Toulon prancing tail-high with him.

God*dammit!* Lewrie cringed to see anyone happy about anything
at that instant! He spread the various documents across the desk and
picked through them slowly, catching only a faint impression of import
here and there, for his mind was awhirl with other things. Revenge,
to be factual!

Fool me once, shame on you, he glowered; right then, you fooled
me, Mlavic. Not the half-wit you look, are you? Fool me twice, well,
I doubt it. Make the bugger pay, I will! Wipe that crafty peasant sneer
off his brutish phyz... swear t'God I will, 'fore we're done!

Something at last leapt out at him, in his distracted state. A fine
sheet of vellum in its own right, folded over into an envelope and still
sticky with broken wax seals, which clung to the rest.

There was the crash of a musket-butt without the gun-deck doors, the sound of idle boots being stamped together. "First off'cer, SAH!" his Marine sentry bellowed.

"Enter."

"Excuse me, sir, but… on which course should I get the ship under way?" Lieutenant Knolles enquired, looking a touch anxious.

"Ah," Lewrie said, feeling a new flush of anger at himself then. "Sorry, Mister Knolles, for being remiss. I was too rapt in these documents we took from the prize. Looking for an answer to that very question. Our pirates? Where away?"

"Worn off the wind, sir, and steering Nor'east," Knolles said.

"And we're fetched to on larboard tack, hmm… get steer-ageway to the Sou'west, then return to our original course, Sou'east or so, on starboard tack. Close-hauled, as before."

"Aye aye, sir," Knolles replied chearly, before turning to go.

Damme, *another* happy sod! Lewrie groaned, sitting down. Well, ain't ignorance just bliss. Ignorance of how much we let slip through our ignorant little fingers! And thank God for small favours we've seen the last of Mlavic and his cutthroats this voyage! Can't wait t'rush home to his master, Petracic, and show off his pretty new toys!

"God, I absolutely *despise* this!" he whispered to the empty cabins. "Mlavic, Petracic, the bloody *need* of 'em…!"

He hunched forward over the desk, bear-shouldered and miserable. He unfolded the vellum letter further, peeling another sheet away from the remnants of a wax patch. Laboriously, for his French wasn't that good, either, he made out that he had the second page of a two-page set of instructions from the brig's former ship's-husbands and owners, for her now-former master. Cautions, warnings, a pithy bit here and there, though framed in a tortuous sea-lawyerese, on how her captain had best proceed in the service of both profit and *patrie*.

"'… be advised that a British squadron is now known to be found in the Adriatic,'" he murmured half aloud. "And, it took you that long t'puzzle that out? No idea of numbers… no idea of operating areas, so… 'sellers' agents have opened marts in those ports'… damme, what the hell does that mean… *susdit*? *Susdit*? Never bloody heard of it." He suddenly felt the lack of a French dictionary.

He rose from his chair and went forward, out to the gun-deck and up the windward ladder to the quarterdeck.

"Cap'um on deck!" Midshipman Spendlove warned the watch.

"Mister Spendlove, how's your Frog?" he demanded.

The lad shrugged. "Tolerable, sir, I s'pose."

"*Susdit*. What's it mean?" Lewrie pressed, sounding urgent.

"*Susdit?*" Spendlove puzzled. "Haven't a clue, sir. Sorry."

"Mister Knolles, do you know what *susdit* means in French?" Alan glowered, pacing over to the First Officer.

"I, ah… hmmm, sir. Can't recall running afoul of that word, before, Captain." Knolles frowned in sorrow. And in wonder of why his captain was so all-fired impatient for the meaning of a French word. Or why Commander Lewrie had come up without his hat, though he still wore waistcoat, neck-stock, coat and sword.

"Excuse me, Captain." The Surgeon Mr. Howse coughed, midstroll with his ever-present assistant, Mr. LeGoff. "Just taking the air, do you see."

"*Yes*, Mister Howse!" Lewrie seethed. If there was one thing he didn't need at the moment, it was Howse and his eternal, mournful carping noises! He'd rather have piles, any day!

"*Susdit*, did ye say, sir?" Howse asked with a deep, bovine lowing, all but rocking on the balls of his feet, hands behind his back in superiority. "Why, I do believe *susdit* means 'the aforementioned,' or 'the aforesaid.' Ain't that right, Mister LeGoff?"

"B'lieve so, sir. 'Aforesaid,'" that gingery terrier agreed.

"Ah!" Lewrie grimaced suddenly. "Thankee. *Shit!*"

And dashed below to his cabins again, leaving them all to cock their heads and wonder what exactly had caused *that!*

–

"First bloody page, first bloody page," Lewrie fumed, shuffling papers in a fury, "where it bloody *was* 'aforesaid.' Hah!"

To shorten the voyages, and avoid the greater costs in crew pay and rations (he slowly but breathlessly read) and to avoid the perils of capture by hostile warships, to reduce the turnaround time between deliveries of naval stores and compass-timber vital to the Navy or the private builders' yards, agents for the Directory were urging the suppliers formerly of Venice and other ports far to the north of the Adriatic to transship, in their own, perfectly neutral, bottoms, to…!

"Hah!" Lewrie cried aloud again, in triumph this time.

Into Venetian Durazzo, into Venetian Cattaro; Volona, in Venetian-held Albania, and to Corfu Town, and other ports in the Ionians!

He sat down – plumped down! – into his chair, feeling giddy with sudden knowledge. They'd taken the brig so suddenly, her people hadn't had time to ditch her papers overside. She hadn't been merely halfway through her voyage, she'd nearly been at the end of it! He'd feared her turning Easterly and running into Durazzo as a refuge. A refuge, indeed, for that was probably where she was headed all along.

This revealing letter was recent, dated not two weeks earlier, hand-delivered aboard the morning the brig had sailed, most-like. And left lying out, so the brig's master could refer to it.

Venice! he thought scornfully; up to her ears in trafficking to the very people who'd eat her alive, sooner or later. Fat, faithless rabbits, too used to Spending and Getting, getting by on her ancient laurels and martial fame, but prostituting herself to the French just as bad as the Genoese had the year before. Italians! he groaned.

A word in the right ear, though… didn't the Venetians value their freedom, so they could make this much money from trade, when you got right down to it? Were they to put this to the Doge or the Secret Council of Three, who ran the Doge, couldn't they quietly strangle one or two of the largest players, and frighten off the rest? Then, with most of the Adriatic oak and naval stores trade quashed, there'd be no need for reinforcements – not from pirates, certainly!

Lionheart, and Captain Charlton, had they not come foul of some French warships down near the mouth of the Straits of Otranto, might be yet on-station – that is, if she hadn't taken so many prizes she'd been forced to sail for Trieste, for want of hands to sail or fight her.

"No, didn't exactly sweep the seas, last time, did she?" Lewrie muttered to himself with a half-humourous grunt. He thought it likely she was still hunting her patrol area. He decided to sail south, speak to Charlton and show him this evidence of Venetian complicity.

He'd *have* to move the patrols farther south to cover all the bolt-holes and *entrepots* for smuggled naval stores and timber, once he'd seen proof-positive that the French and Batavians, along with their avaricious neutral helpers, the Danes and Swedes, were leery of sailing as far north as Venice or Pola any longer.

And, that far to the Suth'rd, Ratko Petracic and Dragan Mlavic were of little use, far below their usual haunts. Were the Venetians employing their own ships for the trade, there would be little the pirates could do, against a "neutral" nation's merchantmen.

Little good the Royal Navy could do, either, Alan sourly realised, to stem the flow of goods down to Durazzo, Volona, Cattaro, and the isles. Those neutral bottoms of the Serene Republic of Venice were just as off limits to them, and they couldn't touch them without creating an international incident.

Lewrie rose from his desk and prowled his wine-cabinet for drink, to see what he had left after ten days of Rodgers and Kolodzcy aboard. It wasn't much, but he thought he'd earned a pale glass of spiced Austrian *gewürztraminer*. Needed one, rather, after the way he'd been taken by Mlavic. God, that irked!

"Fool me once, shame on you," Lewrie whispered after a bracing sip. "But I'll have you, ya smelly beast… you and your master, too. Never wanted a thing t'do with ya in the first place, and now I'll nip this sordid, shitten business in the bud. Get my guinea back, too!"

Chapter 8

Oh, this is just bloody perverse! Lewrie thought, after days of searching for HMS *Lionheart*. It wasn't a large area he had to scour – from the sleepy port of Brindisi on the muddy Italian coast, then down the coast to Cape di Otranto and Cape Santa Maria di Leuca, about ninety miles. With a favourable slant of wind, it was only an eighty-mile sail to the Sou'east, to Corfu, to peek in the harbour. Another eighty miles back up the Albanian coast to Volona. Yet, not only was there no sign of her, there were hardly any other sails to be seen, either! A few merchantmen, which he stopped, boarded and inspected, yes; but they were all innocent local traders. And their masters, whatever their nationality, had nothing but puzzled shrugs for answers when he'd questioned them about sighting a British frigate.

"How is it," Lewrie griped to his First Officer and his midshipmen as he dined them in one evening, "that when you're anxious to join a friend, one can't find him? And, paradoxically, when you try to shun a pest, you practically trip over him everywhere one goes?"

"Dragan Mlavic, sir?" Knolles grimaced.

"Indeed, Mister Knolles," Lewrie allowed with a matching scowl.

"Father always said, sir," Spendlove piped up from his chair at the end of the table, where he filled the role of Mr. Vice, "that a thing that's lost can't be found by searching."

"Oh, he does, does he?" Lewrie smiled. "So, what does Mister Spendlove do, younger Spendlove?"

"Sends his mother to hunt it up, I'd expect, sir." Midshipman Hyde sniggered.

"Well, sometimes." Clarence Spendlove smiled and shrugged. "I have seen him just sit down and ponder, though, sir. Where he'd seen a thing last. Like walking into a room and forgetting what one went in there to get, sir? One has to retrace one's steps."

"Back to Trieste and Venice?" Knolles scoffed, signalling for a top-up of wine from Aspinall. Lewrie had at least put in at Corfu,

267

and found a British merchantman or two come for the currant crop, bearing a cargo of wines from London or Lisbon, more suited to the palates of the many expatriate Englishmen who farmed or factored there.

"That'd be… pleasant, sir," Hyde simpered, sharing a lascivious look with Spendlove, "to stretch one's legs ashore."

"Ah, but which leg, sir?" Spendlove queried impishly.

"Ahem!" Lewrie cautioned with a cough into his fist, riveting their attention. "I'm told a captain is responsible for the education of his midshipmen. Part of that is how to behave at-table. No talk of religion, politics… women…! or business is allowed."

"Least 'til the port and nuts, sir." Lieutenant Knolles chuckled. "After the ladies have retired to the drawing room."

"Damme, do I set a poor example?" Lewrie pretended to recoil in shock. "Lowered proper Navy standards, and corrupted you *all*?"

Don't answer that! he thought with a cringe. There's more'n a grain o' truth in that. And why not, when I'm *such* a sterlin' example to go by! Damme, ashore I'd talk o' nothin' else!

He'd made a jape. They responded like dutiful juniors should; they showed amusement. Lamely, of course, the jest hadn't been *that* good.

"Tsk-tsk, Mister Spendlove," he further pretended to chide. "We can't have you discussing lewd women in front of your mother once you return home!"

"Only did that with my brother, sir," Spendlove shyly confessed.

"Ah!" Lewrie chuckled easily.

How much they'd grown, he thought; Spendlove was now all but full-grown, not the callow stripling from HMS *Cockerel*. He was eighteen now, and Hyde, whom he'd gotten at Portsmouth, a year older. A pair of young men, no longer boys, more than halfway to their own commissions as Sea Officers.

"Well, since Mister Spendlove has already broken the ban, so to speak, perhaps we should discuss our… business… as well," he went on, after a forkful of a rather zesty mutton ragout over pasta, and an accompanying sip of red. "We may have to return to Trieste or Venice, after all. Either port, where *some* may make beasts of themselves, hmm? We've not seen hide nor hair of *Lionheart*, nor of any French men-o'-war which might have driven her off-station. Now, let's see what we could construe from this evidence. Mister Hyde?"

268

"Uhm…" Hyde gulped, trying to swallow a hunk of bread he had almost chewed. "That she's taken three or four prizes, sir. And was forced to sail off, unable to take, or man, any more?"

"Aye, that's possible," Lewrie granted. "But now she's sailed off… where's our smugglers, where's our Frogs? Shouldn't they be out by now? 'When the cat's away, the mice will play,' right? Sorry, puss," he said to his cat, who was lurking near his chair for dropped morsels.

"Sir," Spendlove contributed, cautiously sipping wine before he spoke, to do so with an unobstructed palate. "Perhaps they're holed up in those nearby Venetian ports, waiting for their timber. And they're not aware *Lionheart* has left yet, sir?"

"Aye, again, sir," Lewrie agreed amiably. "Though I still can't understand them totally abandoning the trade. There's still an urgent need for timber, for the French fleet at Toulon. No, I wasn't speaking to *you*, greedy-guts. Oh, here, then." He sighed, awarding Toulon some gravy-laden bits of mutton. To keep him quiet and off the table.

"Perhaps mistakenly, sir," Lieutenant Knolles stuck in, his forehead furrowed in thought. "Do the Frogs have this new arrangement, ordered by their Ministry of Marine, d'ye see… to use the Venetian harbours. *Lionheart* arrived just as they were going to earth, and found nothing to seize. After two weeks or so of empty horizons, Captain Charlton *might* have abandoned the area and gone back north, expecting to discover better pickings in mid-sea. And to speak to Commander Fillebrowne about what *Myrmidon* might have turned up in her area. Might have been just bad timing on her part, sir."

"Well, sir…" Hyde wondered aloud, getting into the spirit of things; with an empty maw, this time. "Captain Charlton *might* wish to meet up with us and Captain Rodgers in *Pylades*. See how our, uhm… our piratical endeavour was working out, too."

"Meet the other players, so to speak, sir. Before the cards are dealt?" Spendlove added, forever trying to trump Hyde.

"All very possible, sirs." Lewrie smiled briefly. "Damme, you know, I rather like this, gentlemen. Discussing shop talk over food. See how clear we think, like a well-stoked hearth? Brighter than ever? And, in private, where one may make a silly comment, with no recriminations. 'Less a cabin servant or steward tells tales out of school, that is… Aspinall?" Alan teased.

"Oh, mum's th' word, sir." Aspinall grinned, not a whit abashed. "Top-up, Captain? Gentlemen?"

"So, our prey is lurking in Venetian ports," Lewrie summarised, once their glasses had been recharged, "waiting for neutrals to come down and load 'em full."

"Odd, though, sir," Lieutenant Knolles objected softly, holding up his glass to the lanthorn light to admire the ruby glow, or inspect it for lees. "All the Balkans are thick with timber. I'd imagine that, were the French to throw enough gold about, they could get all they wished closer than Venetian-shipped Istrian or Croatian oak. Get the locals to go wood-cutting round Volona, Durazzo and such, and use Montenegran or Albanian trees."

"Uhm, sir..." Spendlove threw out, most warily in contradiction. "Would that not be green wood? Unseasoned?"

"Well, aye, but... *ah*!" Knolles scowled, his logic confounded. "Do the Frogs have urgent need of seasoned oak and compass timber, they still have to depend on the Venetians or someone else. They can't wait years for it to season, they need to construct ships now. Else, we'd always outnumber them or outbuild them so badly they might as well not bother with a navy, and put their money into their armies. As the Austrians do. Poor devils."

"Ah, indeed, Mister Knolles," Lewrie enthused, catching the import, at last. Might be a dim slow-coach, he thought; but I get there in the end! "Seasoned wood, ready to use as soon as it's unloaded."

"And, sir!" Hyde all but cried. "Montenegro and Albania can't have local navies or shipping, as long as the Turks wish to keep them in harness. So where's the timber industry that knows how to select compass timber, or season oak? Where's large shipbuilding, at all?"

"Well, there's Ragusa, Dulcigno, where the corsairs *surely* make their own..." Spendlove pointed out. "The Hungarians and Croats?"

"Small change, though," Knolles dismissed quickly. "Couldn't support much beyond their own few needs, not this quickly."

Lewrie listened to their energetic back-and-forth, idly making furrows through his ragout, skirting the lee shores of muttony islets with the tines, deep in thought. He put down his fork at last and had another sip of wine.

"I don't believe we will be returning to Trieste," he announced. "Not right off, I'm afraid. For whatever reason Captain Charlton had to leave the straits unguarded, he's done so, and for us to rush back in search of him... well, that'd be remiss. Do the Frogs and the rest of the smugglers know the coast is clear, they'll load up with timber and toddle off back to France with everything they can carry in the interim. No, I think we have to stay. Else..."

He looked up to see his three bachelor juniors' true disappointment that there'd be no crawling through the fleshpots of Venice, nor even those of staid Trieste, anytime soon.

"Well, there is the information 'bout which ports they're going to use, sir... and Venetian complicity," Knolles said. Gloomily.

"Aye, there is, Mister Knolles." Lewrie nodded. "But after we inform Captain Charlton of this new arrangement, just what in Hades may he do about it? We haven't a full ambassador at Venice, just a consul for trade matters, so how high may our consul – a merchant himself! – take a complaint? And it ain't a formal complaint from the Crown or the Foreign Office, so Venice can listen, make soothing noises at him, then forget it, and it's business as usual. It's not as if we'll begin to stop and inspect Venetian ships, either. Ships bound for Venetian ports, carrying perfectly innocent cargoes?"

"Well, there is that, sir, but..." Knolles frowned.

"Timber borne for sale on speculation, with nothing in writing to tie them to French buyers, Batavian buyers... anyone," Lewrie said with a sneer. "Nothing our... auxiliaries, the Serbs, could do about it, either, 'less we want to turn 'em loose on a neutral country. It might work for a few times, but sooner or later word'd get out, and England would be dumped in the quag right up to her eyebrows. God help us, it might even stir those comatose Venetians into arming and fitting their fleet to chase *us* out of the Adriatic! *'Fore* they do for Petracic and his cutthroats, mind."

"Aye, sir," Knolles replied. "Cleft stick, hmm?"

"Perhaps." Lewrie sighed, taking another sip of wine. "Perhaps not. You gentlemen recall last year, off the Genoese Riviera, and much the same sort of problem with Tuscan and Genoese traders? And neutrals hand-in-glove with the Frogs? How did our former squadron commander, Captain Nelson, handle it? Recall what he said about acting upon his own initiative, did he determine his actions were contrary to orders or the lack of 'em... but best for Navy, King and Country, in the long run."

He saw a whole new set of expressions on their phyzes. Curiosity he'd hoped for; but a sudden wariness, a trepidation that his comments presaged some insubordinate, high-handed, lunatick freebooting? Some deed as mad as a March Hare?

Pretty much what they've come t'expect, 'board *this* barge, Alan told himself with a well-hidden smirk.

"Our first duty would, at first, *seem* to be to dash off and tell Captain Charlton," he continued. "That's the safe and dutiful. Toss this lit shell into his lap, wave a cheery 'ta-ta,' and leave it up to him t'snuff it out 'fore it blows up in his face."

"Beg your pardon, sir, but… ain't that why they pay him a lot more than us?" Lieutenant Knolles japed. Though Lewrie saw that his hands had a *damn* firm death-grip on the edge of the table and his wineglass.

"Normal custom and usages of the Fleet, Mister Knolles." Lewrie chuckled. "Plod on, deaf and dumb, well to windward of risk."

"Aye aye, sir," Knolles said in dumb agreement, but his expression said something else, though his face was taut and unreadable. Lewrie knew that sound, and that look. Had he not used it himself to a senior officer – a dozen or more? – the last sixteen years? Bleat "Aye aye" and put on your gambler's mask, cross your legs and hope when the other dirty shoe dropped, it didn't turn out half as horrible as you expected?

"For now, we're the only ship on-station, sirs," Lewrie said to them all, explaining carefully. "Now, if this information of ours does Captain Charlton no *immediate* good, then we aren't *exactly* bound to tear off and give it to him… immediately. How long may it take to find him… a week or more? Leaving the straits wide open for two weeks or more? No, I had something else in mind we could do for the next few days. Mr. Knolles? At dawn, I'd admire did we alter course. Let's sail over for a peek into Cattaro. We haven't seen it yet, and it's closest for any French ship to get its load of timber. Shortest voyage for a Venetian supplier, too. Right up to the harbour mole. You'll inform the Sailing Master, so he'll know to have his charts selected."

"Aye aye, sir," Knolles dutifully piped. Rather calmly, Alan decided; even allowing for a bit of "crisp" to his voice, that shudder he hid so well, that look of "Oh shit, where's *this* all going?" as he contemplated a quick end to a rather promising career should he be implicated.

"Then we'll have us a stroll down to Volona, then a quick dash back to Durazzo, too." Lewrie smiled wolfishly. "Corfu last. That'd be best, I think. Unpredictable movements."

"I see, sir," Knolles parroted; even if he didn't.

Odd, Knolles thought; all this time I *knew* he had the scar on his right cheek. Old sword slash or something. So faded – or me so used to it – I barely mark it, these days.

But in the flickering light from the candles on the sideboard, and from the gently swaying pewter lanthorn on the overhead deck-beams, every now and then a trick of their shadows made it stand out. Darker, a bit more ruddy and fresh – more prominent.

More ominous. For *someone*, Knolles thought.

Chapter 9

"Dawn by my reckonin'll be half an hour yet, Cap'um," Mister Buchanon promised. "False dawn within five minute."

"And our position, Mister Buchanon?" Lewrie asked in a hushed tone, stalking his quarterdeck, swaddled in his boat-cloak against the brisk chill that swept down from the East-Nor'east. They'd had Bora winds during the night, though clocking Easterly as the Middle Watch had wound down. It might veer enough to form a Levanter by midday. "Can you assure me of our position as positively, sir?"

"'At light astern, sir, 'at's th' beacon on th' breakwater, by th' entrance in th' harbour mole. Light t'th' Nor'west by North, 'at's Vido Island. Smallest, yonder... 'at's Lazaretto. We're makin' barely a knot o' drift inshore, fetched-to as we are. E'en so, sir, call it a touch less'n four miles off. A bit o' sunrise'll tell me true," the Sailing Master assured him. In the light of the candles in the binnacle cabinet he tapped a finger on an accurate Venetian chart, right beside an irregular penciled-in trapezoid – a "cocked hat" of reckoning from what few shore marks they'd been able to spot with the long night telescopes, which showed everything upside down, unfortunately.

Lewrie left the binnacle and wheel to pace aft to the taffrail, between the two brightly lit lanthorns at *Jester*'s very stern. Golden ripples balleted off the ebony sea, far aft and to either beam, as she lay cocked up to weather, waiting for the sun. The wind kissed a part of her sails to sail her forward, caressed the backed jibs to lock her in place as if anchored. A touchy balancing act, against a Bora wind that gusted and muttered, then sighed more softly. With Knolles now gone...

Lewrie looked down over the taffrail, to watch the water break round her rudder and transom post, below the overhang of the gun-room and his great-cabins. His cabin lights were lit, too, and there was Toulon, for a moment, with his nose snuffling the panes of a window, below him. No drift, he thought; well, not much. Gurgling, plashing, sucking sounds arose from the idled hull. A kelpy aroma of weed and slime, a clammy, mussely tinge of a barnacled bottom met his nostrils, along with the faint seashore smell of the not-so-distant land. And the piney, loamy tang of forest on the wind from across the narrows, off the bows, stroking his cheeks as he turned his head from side to side and faced forrud. To weigh them and guess whether *Jester* needed a pull or a bracing-in to maintain her immobile station 'til dawn.

Fetched-to or not, she moved under his feet with a steady rise and fall, her timbers complaining, and blocks aloft clacking and groaning, her masts working gently as she swayed, pitched easy or fell a bit bows-down as the wind-driven waves in the channel flowed round her like she still had a way on.

He went back forrud to peer into the well-lit compass bowl, to determine had her head fallen off; to blink glim-spotted eyes aloft and strain to make out details of masts, sails and ropes against the skies.

There! No longer ghost-grey, but darkening, beginning to silhouette against a barely lighter greyness, stood the sails. He could see the cat-heads by the forecastle, make out the brutish humps of the carronades and almost espy the rising, quivering thrust of the jib-boom and bowsprit. A few men could be espied, spectrelike, up forrud.

"False dawn, sir," Buchanon exulted, "*six* minute. Not 'at far off my guess o' five."

"Close, indeed, Mister Buchanon," Lewrie congratulated. "Hmmm. Under the circumstances, let's say… accurate, rather. Don't *want* us to be close. That close."

"Aye, sir." Buchanon softly laughed, bending down over the compass bowl like a feeding ox, to peer across it at the shore-lights. He snapped his fingers and he and Mr. Wheelock his Master's Mate went to the rail with a night glass, a day telescope and his personal boat-compass in a golden oak box, to take more bearings as the lee shore emerged from the stygian blackness to become a storm or charcoal grey murkiness.

"Best I can reckon'z four miles, sir," he reported at last.

"Very well, Mister Buchanon, thankee," Lewrie said with a nod. "Give it ten minutes, say, and we'll be about it. Mister Crewe? Ten minutes."

"Aye, sir!" the Master Gunner said from the forrud edge of the quarterdeck. "Ready whenever ya order, Cap'um."

Lewrie looked over the larboard side, to the second glowing set of lights; binnacle cabinet, forecastle belfry and taffrail lanthorns, plus candle or whale-oil lights ranged along the gangways. More lamps staggered lower down the side, from opened gun-ports. The great-guns were run in to load position and out of the way. Loaded, though, and fully depressed; and ready to fire – when there was a touch more sunrise, closer to true dawn. But before a fully risen sun took anything away. A spectre, seen only by those lights, the rest unfathomable not ten minutes earlier, now he could make out details of sails and masts, the rough textures and dingy paintwork of her hull, and the blooming of discernible colours, where before all had been granite-block black.

Lewrie took out his watch and eyed the pointer of the optional, and more expensive, second hand clack the tense minutes away. The watch face was now almost tattletale grey – not quite true white – as the false dawn spread a gloomy cloud cover of slightly brighter dimness. It was time.

"Mister Crewe?" he bellowed, breaking the yawning, sleepy hush of the four-'til-eight watch. "Let there be light!"

"Aye, sir!" Crewe roared back, waving a smouldering slow-match fuse in a linstock for a signal. And along *Jester's* bulwarks, a dozen answering fireflies were fanned into heat. "Swivels… *fire!*"

And a dozen slow-matches were lowered to the touch-holes of the skyward-pointing swivel guns. There were sudden gouts of smoke and sparks. Then, with breathless *whooshes*, a dozen rockets went soaring aloft, scattering comet-trails of red and amber fire-dust. *Darde à feu* – fire-arrows – minus their iron spring-arms, designed to snag in sail canvas and burn a ship to the waterline; un-Christian weapons, some said. Pirate weapons, said others; a sneaking, vile, ungentle-manly invention. Now they were signal fusees that hissed skyward, no more dangerous than holiday fireworks; pretty amber comets bearing copper-blue starbursts.

A creaking and an oaken groaning, a faint muttering from larboard and the jangle and snapping of blocks and halliards, as the second ship let go her backed jibs, braced round her backed mizzen tops'l. Canvas thundered, flagged and crackled for a moment, all a'luff, then drawing, curving neatly to the press of wind as she fell away to starboard and began a slow wear-about, beginning to cream salt water down her sides.

"And again, Mister Crewe!" Lewrie snapped. And once more, the swivel guns coughed out their pyrotechnic charges, flinging a brilliant galaxy of stars to five times the height of the main mast truck. Well out abeam, so they'd not drift back and ignite anything.

"Light, sir!" Buchanon shouted, pointing astern. Ruined or no, the Citadel had watchers on her walls, and had hoisted a lanthorn atop the seaward parapets. A third volley of fusees two minutes later, and tiny lights began to wink into life ashore as people were roused.

"Cease fire, Mister Crewe, and secure the swivels," Alan said, feeling satisfied. "Tend to your larboard battery. Mister Buchanon, get the ship under way, larboard tack, then wear her."

"Aye aye, sir. Bosun, hands to the jib sheets…!"

Then it was *Jester*'s turn to fall away, to cease fighting cross-hauled, and surrender to the insistent winds, to heel and creak as she went about, presenting her left side, then her stern to the wind, with the Citadel and the town, the surrounding hills sweeping across the bow and settling on the larboard bows, just over the cat-head. The courses were brailed up, t'gallants at second reef, tops'ls at first reef, and the royals gasketed to horizontal pencils atop her spiralling masts to make a slow passage.

"Mister Hyde, hoist the colours," Lewrie cried.

Atop the fore mast, main mast and mizzen, three ensigns shinnied up the flag or signal halliards, the Red aft, Blue forrud-most, and the White Ensign on the highest; reverse order for an entire fleet of rear, van and main body squadrons. So no one could possibly mistake *Jester* for anything else but Royal Navy this morning.

Lewrie took up his telescope and stood by the windward bulwark, studying the second ship, and satisfying himself that the French flags were prominently displayed aboard her. Both vessels scudded dead off the backing Bora from the East Nor'east, bowsprits jabbing at the breakwater, sliding inshore of Vido Island to run West along the mole.

There! Lewrie told himself with grim satisfaction, as he saw the first ruddy flickerings above her bulwarks, more a warm roasting-pan or a fireplace's brass back-plate reflector's glow. Sooty waverings of heat shimmered upward, not quite yet become smoke, like air quivering over a smith's forge. He swung the telescope tube lower and a bit to the right, concentrating on her stern. It was almost light enough now that the cheery glow of lanthorns in the master's great-cabin, in the glossy panes of the sash-windows, didn't dazzle him. So he could espy the cutter waddling and pitching as she was fended off to be left to starboard and astern. It was now light enough to count heads, for

Lewrie to discern the white collar-tabs on Spendlove's shorter jacket, and the white turn-back lapels and cuffs of Knolles's coat. Even more whiteness appeared, as they began to hoist the cutter's lug-sail, and gather a slight way, broad-reaching at first, to the Nor'west and off from the ship.

"Gettin' close, sir," Buchanon warned.

"Very well, Mister Buchanon. You'll alert me when to brace up and turn?" Lewrie asked. "Mister Crewe! Begin, larboard battery!"

"Stand clear!" Crewe roared, looking up and down the deck, for the raised fists and taut flintlock striker lanyards of his individual gun-captains. "*Fire!*"

"Helm alee, half a point," Buchanon could be heard to mutter… after that titanic slam of nine guns going off in broadside. *Jester* lightly reeled in recoil as the carriages hog-squealed inboard. She'd fired blank charges with no ball, so she didn't feel gut-punched, like a proper battle's broadside. Full cartridges, though, not reduced saluting charges, so she spoke the dawn with a convincing hostile bellow, and a warlike belch of powder-smoke.

"Stop yer vents!" Crewe sing-songed like it was drill. "Swab yer guns! Overhaul yer run-out tackle, overhaul yer recoil tackle, same as always, mind. *Charge* yer guns!"

Three broadsides in two minutes was quick shooting, and *Jester* had been in commission, with almost daily practice, over two years – had fired for true against foes too often to be slack now. Regular as clockwork, every forty seconds by Lewrie's timepiece, there was another stupendous crash and bang, as if she'd loaded round-shot atop cartridge. So it would appear completely real to any watchers ashore. Though they'd look in vain, once they had their wits about them, for a fall of shot.

"Three an' a quarter mile, sir!" Buchanon sang out.

"Helm alee, Mister Buchanon, harden up on the wind a mite. Lay her nead Nor'west by North, for now. Serve 'em another, Mister Crewe!"

Hands were at the braces and sheets to pull taut as the helm was put down and she shied away from the shore and the harbour break-waters and fort, just shy of a diplomatic violation, yards creaking to cup a wind that crossed her decks from the starboard side, just abaft of abeam.

And in that rudely awakened town, there were now hundreds more lamps aglowing, from almost every window that faced the sea and bay on the northern side. It was too far to make out figures on the docks or breakwater, but the scurrying of half-dressed, panic-stricken citizens and mariners could most happily be conjured up in the mind. Just as the sun burst over Albania, just about breakfast time, the artillery barked out a mastiff's basso warning, louder than any lands-man's cock.

"North by West'd be best, now, sir," Mr. Buchanon counseled in a wary voice. "Haul up to a beam-reach."

"Well to windward of Vido, sir?" Lewrie asked.

"Aye, sir. 'Bout two mile t'windward, in deep water."

"Very well, Mister Buchanon, alter course. Mister Crewe? One more broadside, then cease fire and secure!"

"Ready, sir! Stand clear? *Fire!*"

One last wrathful eruption, then HMS *Jester* was wheeling about, her decks coming more level, not so hard-pressed by the winds, even under reduced sail, and making it easier to secure the 9-pounder guns; to swab them out, remove the flintlock strikers and cover the touch-holes with leather aprons, insert the tompions in the now-blackened muzzles and run them up to the port-sills where they were bowsed snug.

Lewrie lifted his telescope again, from the lee bulwarks, to see what was doing aboard the second ship, and found a cause for great joy. Flames were soaring up her lower masts and spewing long fire-tongues from her opened hatches, forge-bellowing horizontally from her opened gun-ports. Her tarred running rigging and mast-bearing shrouds glowed liquid with darting, climbing, blazing mouse-sized flames. The fires had not reached her tiller-ropes or her upper yards yet, so she ran off the wind still, trending a bit Sutherly, under a single fore-topsail, a solitary main t'gallant and a triple-reefed mizzen tops'l, with only her outer flying jib flogging away, far forrud at the tip of her jib boom. On a mostly steady course, he noted gladly. And still flying three large French Tricolours, still safe from burning, so everyone on the breakwater – mariners and landsmen alike – would know her nationality as well as *Jester*'s. Above that burgeoning Vesuvius of smoke, ash and soaring embers that ragged downwind ahead of her, shrouding her like a cloak, they still flew high above, fluttering blue-white-red.

Scrape the damn breakwater, Lewrie speculated; ground on a shoal just at its foot, and burn out, right on their bloody door-stoop!

My message'll be noticed, all right. Might even ram into the break-water and burn for hours! And when those double-shotted guns took light…!

As luridly, ghoulishly fascinating as it was to watch that ship being immolated, he tore his attention away from her, unlike the hands on watch, or the many gunners who'd come up to the gangways once their guns had been secured, and went to the windward side to lift his glass.

There was their cutter, steering Nor'-Nor'east, slamming swoopy and wet, close-hauled to stand out to sea, out the way they'd come. He saw no other nearby boats, either; no armed response from the port or the authorities, and all the early-rising fishermen had ducked inshore to the beaches for safety. The sun was almost completely risen then, with no hint of redness, no high-piled grey forebodings from the east. A bit lower than the Albanian shore with his glass, and he could barely make out two low-lying pitch-black slivers almost on the horizon. Two ship's boats full of seamen, stroking shoreward with oars. It could be a full two hours later before they stepped ashore, with their tale of woe. By which time, *Jester* would be long gone, a terrifying will-o'-the-wisp. And French sailors at Corfu, too, would be filled with fear.

"Mister Buchanon, let's harden up to windward," Lewrie said as he lowered his glass and turned inboard. "Lay her full-and-by, course North by East."

"Aye aye, sir." Buchanon beamed, pleased with their early work.

"Mister Cony?" Lewrie called down to the gun-deck. "We'll take the cutter in tow, once Mister Knolles and his party are aboard. I've an idea she's spent too long on the beams, and her planking needs some soaking. Inform the cooks they may stoke up, once we're close-hauled, and begin fixing a late breakfast."

"Aye, Cap'um, sir!"

Ten days more. Lewrie shrugged. Longer than I'd hoped, but we did it. Wind looks fair t'back a touch more Easterly, too. Make the return voyage a beam-reach all the way, 'less we get a bit of Southing. Make us faster, on that point o' sail, so, say, two days to Trieste or Venice? Then inform Captain Charlton. Of everything!

"A right fair mornin', sir," Mr. Buchanon commented, once they had the ship thrashing away windward and the cutter was falling off a point or two to meet them. "A fair mornin's bus'ness."

"Amen, Mister Buchanon." Lewrie laughed, rocking on the balls of his feet, aching for a first cup of coffee, but plumb delighted, in the main. "Amen to that."

Chapter 10

"Well, no wonder, then, that we only took two prizes," Captain Charlton said, nodding rueful about his poor luck, now he had an explanation for it. "They've gone to earth like foxes. And neither was exactly worth the effort, Commander Lewrie. A poor brig, and one ugly old poleacre. Doubt they could have carried much timber, anyway. I could not stay on-station longer, not with Fillebrowne and Rodgers to look up. You did very well, sir, to stand in lieu of me and *Lionheart*. And to have taken two prizes, as well. Sent them on to Trieste?"

"No, sir. Burned them," Lewrie told him. "It's in my report, sir." And feeling a bit impatient with Charlton, who only seemed interested, so far, in value gained.

"Burned!" Charlton exclaimed, wineglass halfway aloft. "I don't follow, sir."

"Well, as my report explains, sir," Lewrie began, "we had few hopes of taking inbound ships, since they're waiting for cargoes from the upper Adriatic to come to them. I thought, though, that there'd be outbound ships, already laden with timber and such, still at sea. So, with you gone, I thought to cow them. The first was off Cattaro, sir. Caught her well out to sea and took her back to within the diplomatic limits and anchored her. Nasty bit of work, that. Cattaro is at the end of a rather long estuary, which narrows, so placement was tricky. So the other French ships in port could see her burn, sir, and a wind from shore made it impossible to sail her in afire, as we did with the one off Corfu. We did fetch off her papers and such, sir, so we've all the *t*'s crossed and the *i*'s dotted. And we did turn up some coin and such. Not much. I have that secured in my lazarette now, sir."

"Keep prisoners?"

"No, sir. Thought the more survivors ashore, the more worries. I let them have their boats and sent them in, after tallying up their names so the documentation passes muster."

"Ah-ha!" Charlton laughed. "Aye, the rest'll not be quite so keen, will they? Might even treat those released as Jonahs. Not even sign them aboard the other ships, nor wish them as passengers for the voyage home to France. I rather like that touch. Now, what about the other ports you shadowed... Durazzo and Volona?"

"I kept a strict accounting, sir," Lewrie cautiously prefaced to the nub of his report. "With no French traffick present, I had to *buy* some local boats from the Albanian or Montenegran fisher-folk. Sheep, too. Two roosters, and as many of those long red 'Liberty' caps as we could turn up among the Frog crewmen, from the first'un. Went into shore... nothing official, 'long as no Turks saw us, sir... and picked up a few odds and ends. Red and blue cloth, and such, to make up Frog flags. Paid for it all from the first prize's working capital, sir, as 'necessary for the Use and Service' of our vessel."

"Ahum," Charlton purred, going bland. This verbal report from Lewrie was beginning to sound a tad high-handed and verging very close to harum-scarum. "A *strict* accounting, d'ye say, sir."

"To the pence, sir. And it wasn't much at all," Lewrie assured him, savouring his first glass of welcome-aboard claret, and wondering, after his tale was told, if he'd *really* get another.

"Roosters?" Charlton squinted. "Sheep? Stocking caps?"

"The very thing, sir." Lewrie tentatively smiled back. "Once we had everything in hand, we sailed right up to the three-mile limit off both harbours and came to anchor. I listed my bearings, sir, on the Venetian charts, so there'd be no error. And the Venetian charts are da... deuced accurate. My First Officer, Mister Ralph Knolles, was in charge of the local boat, and one of ours, for his getaway. Fired off some blank broadsides to get their attention, sir, then sailed the boats in as close as he dared, took to our boat, and let the other run ashore. My *launch* went inside the three-mile limit, sir. Unarmed—"

"Ah?" Charlton interrupted with a chary cough. It was quibble-some, that. He got that bland look again. "I don't see..."

"Well, sir..." Lewrie beamed, after polishing off his wine. *Sure* there'd not be another, the way Charlton was leaning his head back and staring fish-eyed down the length of his nose at him. "We'd sheared the sheep, then cut their throats and gutted 'em aboard those boats we'd purchased... *in situ*, so they'd bleed in-place. Bound them upright, at watch stations... the helm and such... and put the stocking caps on 'em, d'ye see, sir."

No doubt he does. Alan shivered. He's goin' bloody cross-eyed!

"So they'd faintly resemble French sailors, sir," Lewrie said, suddenly not finding it quite so clever a message. "And the roosters, sir? Old French folk symbol, I'm assured. *Le Chanticlier*, they call him? Pegged to the foredeck with a marling-spike... as a figurehead."

"Pegged..." Charlton grunted.

"Did I mention the frogs, sir? Balkan shore teemed with 'em, so we paid for the locals to harvest a bushel or two," Lewrie rushed to say, hoping *they* played better than the roosters or the sheep. "Had off the hind legs – rather good eatin', by the way! – floured, seasoned, then pan-fried, sir. And scattered 'em all about the decks, dead as mutton."

Charlton sat stock-still, but for putting his wineglass safely on his desktop. He folded his hands in his lap and breathed, off the top of his lungs, for a sombre moment or two.

Both hands free, Lewrie noticed with a sigh; he's goin' t'strangle me!

But then there was a faint twitch at either corner of Captain Charlton's prim mouth. A slight, purse-lipped upturning. His cheeks went ruddier under his sun-baked complexion, and his eyes crinkled at the corners. A faint grin appeared, like an ostrich chick fighting to leave a damn thick egg. Captain Charlton began to snicker. Then he threw back his head and roared!

With this encouraging sign to go by, Lewrie dared make free with the wine decanter and allowed himself to show his own amusement, merely a faint chuckle at first – whilst Captain Charlton began to bray, loud as Balaam's Ass. He rose from his seat and absolutely staggered aft to the transom settee, fighting for breath and slapping his thighs, clapping his hands over his aching stomach. Real tears could be seen coursing his cheeks! Though it would never *do* to appear to laugh at a jest one had made, Lewrie found it infectious and shook with silent sniggers. Though he still feared a sudden sobriety on Charlton's part, and a harsh tongue-lashing, once he was over his fit.

"Ah, dear me," Charlton said, though, a good three minutes later, as he dabbed at his eyes and blew his gone-cherry nose. "Oh, sir! I've not had reason to be amused since San Fiorenzo Bay. A moment more, I do beg, sir... to recover my wits. But I never *heard* the like! And those poor Frog seamen... t'see such a sight, sailing right into... Dear Lord! Fresh-'spatched frogs all over the...! Oh, dear me. Whoo!"

He gulped for air and calmed, at last, and came back to the desk for his abandoned wineglass. "A toast with you, sir. A brimming bumper. Admiral Jervis gave me an inkling I might find you unorthodox, but he didn't speak the half of it. To your knacky wit, Commander Lewrie... and confusion – and fear – 'mongst our foes."

"Confusion and fear, sir," Lewrie echoed, knocking back a savoury gulp.

A rather pacific, *spent* sort of minute went by then, with good Captain Charlton emitting the odd wheeze or two, the odd shake of his head in wonderment. Which put Lewrie in mind of that post *coital* silence one spent with whores one'd never clapped eyes on before.

Well, wasn't *that*... nice? he smirked to himself; must run, bye... and where'd I drop me hat?

"Uhm... I s'pose this will result in the squadron shifting down south, sir?" Lewrie asked, as Charlton reached out for the decanter to top them up again. "Nothing *we* may do 'gainst the Venetians."

"Hmm, aye, Commander Lewrie, that is very much true," Captain Charlton allowed with a shrug as he did the honours. "And with only four main ports to watch now, our four vessels have much better odds of catching any runners. As long as we stand far enough out, so we do not appear to be blockading neutral Venetian ports. Hull-down, or our t'gallants only, showing."

"And the ship which watches over Corfu may also stand out to see what's doing in the straits, sir," Lewrie added, wondering if the time was now ripe. He decided that it was, and slyly launched the nub of his scheme. "That's rather far from the Serbs' usual haunts, sir. The few vessels they had aren't made to keep the seas for weeks at a time. Nor are they of a patient nature to *do* blockade work. Official or no. I wonder how much real use they'll be to us now. Given this change."

"There is that," Charlton allowed, patting his short hair with one hand. "Perhaps those smallest boats of theirs could still work as inshore scouts for us, though. Sniff out French ships which sail, and alert us. Some set of signals we may devise for them... their appearance near us, preceding any runners who put to sea."

"Quick as lateen-rig boats are, sir, they still can't run ahead of a well-run ship-rig with a longer waterline," Lewrie objected with a dismissive grin. "Be it a night signal-fusee, they'd give the French warning to put back in or alter course. Day signal or night, if they put back in, and put their heads together, they'd have to assume there *is* a blockade of Venetian ports. Then the Venetians would have to take note of it and complain formally, sir."

"Do they put in, though, at Durazzo or Cattaro, say…" Charlton counterposed, "seemingly innocent fishermen or coastal traders buying supplies, say… they could count noses for us, take note of those vessels readying for sea, and report back, Commander Lewrie."

"But not take active part in those vessels' seizure, sir?" Alan quibbled. "Then we *would* end up paying Petracic his tribute. Share in the take, sir, at no risk to himself."

"Then he must move his newest European ships, and his *galliot* and *dhow*, down nearer us, sir," Charlton suggested, adamant for his plans. "Those may keep the sea for weeks at a time. Perhaps he covers Cattaro and Durazzo, whilst we cover Volona and Corfu. Closer to the straits, as you say. Then, what we chase but fail to capture, he gets a crack at inshore, from inbound ships. Likewise, what outbound ships full of timber exports which he fails to bag, we get our crack at. With the smallest of his boats forming our eyes and ears, where we daren't go."

"Uhm…" Lewrie pretended to gnaw a thumbnail and give it an honest ponder. "Where could we base them, then, sir? Palagruza is too far off, then. They're Eastern Orthodox Serbs, sir. There'd be a lot of trouble with the Albanians or Montenegrans. Autonomous from Turkish rule or not, sir, they're still Muslim. I'd imagine the hate our Serbs feel for Muslims is warmly reciprocated 'mongst the Albanians. Given a chance to butcher some Serb infidels, finally, the local Muslim governments would simply drool over the opportunity, sir. And there aren't any convenient islands where—"

"In for the penny, in for the pound, I fear, Lewrie," Charlton told him, with the first hint of frost to his voice as he sat up much straighter in his chair, prim as a parson in the parlour. "We've made our bargain… you still think it a bad bargain, I know. I'm not that fond of it myself, but needs must, as they say. We're spread too thin to be choosy over from which corner help comes. So far, we've kept up our end of the bargain… gotten Captain Petracic two new ships, given him gold, arms, artillery… a very subtle gesture on your part, when you turned that brig over entire to Captain Mlavic, by the way."

Oh Christ, is *that* what it was? Lewrie wished he could grouse.

"…does *not* care to move south, nor care for any alterations in our methods of operating, then so be it," Charlton blathered on. "We let him go his own way, only modestly reinforced or strengthened, make with it what he will. And free those prisoners now held 'pon Palagruza... take 'em to Trieste, and caution the Austrian authorities to hold them *incommunicado* as long as possible. Thank God the people off that brig were all French, and not from one of the so-called neutrals, whom they *must* free at once. There's a chance it will all fall apart, soon as I put it to him.'"

"I see, sir," Lewrie said with a nod, trying to sound properly perkish and obedient.

"You are correct in one respect, Commander Lewrie," the senior officer told him with a brief, complimentary grin, "as regards Serbian impatience. Piratical impatience, rather. They're not a disciplined or trained flotilla... merely a pack of freebooters. And I suspect, sir," Charlton said, tapping the side of his nose sagaciously, "no matter how fevered or high-flown Captain Petracic's pompous boasting, our Serbian 'brethren of the coast' are *not* the all-conquering heroes. It may turn out that 'twill not be impatience which scotches the arrangement, but their fear of leaving well-known waters. And putting themselves in the lion's mouth, 'mongst hostile Muslims, where they don't know the territory. Or know of a convenient bolt-hole, should things go awry."

"As Captain Nelson says, sir... 'bold talkers do the least, we see'?" Lewrie chirped, feeling some hopeful twinges.

"It's all fine and good to boast and rage of vengeance for the 'Field of Black Birds'... aye, I see by your face, we've heard the same rant, chapter and verse, aha," Charlton mused. "But quite another to actually sail off and *do* something about it on unfamiliar grounds. My God, sir! Build a church and pass the bread and wine, the night before a major battle? I can see that they might have needed spiritual armouring. Then get seventy-seven thousand men slaughtered? Doubt they had that many, first off. Generals always multiply their successes. Or invent excuses for their failures. Might not have been over forty thousand, and outnumbered by the Turks two or three to one, to begin with. Like Roman legions were swarmed and massacred by the Huns, Goths, Vandals or Franks. Knowing how badly the Turks outnumbered them, they surely had need of Divine Services, hmm? In the 1300s... still large cavalry armies, with knights and horses in plate-armour. The Turks on swift Arabs, the Serbs on Clydesdale-sized monsters. Like so many battles of the later Crusades, they hadn't much of a chance to start with. To lose an entire army, empire and sense of identity in one fell swoop, well…! I suspect the tales grew with the years, like the numbers."

"And they had to have an excuse to soothe the soul, sir?" Alan ventured, wondering all over again just where Charlton stood on their arrangement with the Serbs; was he wholehearted, or grasping at whichever straw might seem to hold him atop deep water?

"Something very much like that, sir," Charlton purred. "This Petracic fellow. Remarkable. Bone-headed wrong or not, one must concede he's a shrewd leader of men. They seem to adore him."

"As long as he produces the loot and a successful raid or two, sir?" Lewrie suggested, not wishing to grant the brute a bit of good credit.

"Goes beyond that, Lewrie," Charlton sighed. "Eastern religion is mystical. So emotional, they make our Methodist 'leapers' look like Cromwell's Puritans. Something from the heart and soul, the very gizzard… from the toes up… and not so much the head, like us. Captain Petracic is more a holy warrior to his men, or so Leutnant Kolodzcy explains. Once he nosed about. Catholic Croats encroaching on Old Serbia, trying to turn emotional Serbs into logic-paring Jesuits, or baptising at the point of a sword. Muslims, well… Petracic was a priest, d'ye see. A minister of the Serbian Orthodox Church. Still is, I s'pose. He's the spiritual leader of his band, as well as being their fiercest warrior. Captain Mlavic, the other so-called officers, his under-captain aboard his *galliot*, would follow him anywhere."

"His… under-captain, sir?"

"Oh, some fellow named Djindjic… or howsoever one translates that into sounds." Charlton chuckled, attempting to spell it. "He's the real captain of the *galliot*. Petracic was a partisan fighter from the mountains first, and a priest or whatever at some shrine built by Stefan I… Milutin, perhaps. Memory's rather hazy. Too much to take in at one go."

"That or their plum brandy, I'd expect, sir." Lewrie grinned.

"Gad, yes, *ain't* it?" Charlton replied with a breathless look. "Church of… hmm. Ah! Church of the Virgin of Grachanitsa. As much a holy temple to the old Serbian emperors as it was to God, I gathered from a chat with Kolodzcy. He's shrewd and knacky, for not having any experience at sea. Well, not much, at any rate. It may be Petracic is shrewd enough to know when he's bitten off more than he may chew. And will renege on our bargain, with some profit gained with no effort. I equally expect him to get that radiant look on his phyz and rally the troops for a sail south. For a chance to bash some Albanian Muslims."

"But that's the holy war we were wary of starting, sir."

"Start, end… continue," Charlton dismissed. "It doesn't signify, Lewrie. We'll know more once I've gone down to Palagruza and 'fronted him direct. And released *Pylades* to cover one of the ports you discovered, while I take another. With or without Petracic."

"You said he's a priest, sir," Lewrie countered. "A bit of a mystic. Might that go as far as hearin' voices, sir? Daft as bats… and seein' snakes and centipedes? Might he—"

"I'd imagine the plum-brandy's the culprit, anent the snakes and centipedes, Lewrie." Charlton laughed out loud once more. "Damme, sir! You've done my spirits no end of good. Admiral Jervis hinted you were a bit of a wag, too, sir. And, again, didn't speak the half of it. I find you one of the most energetic and aggressive Sea Officers ever I've met, Lewrie. As I will note in my appreciation of your recent voyage, once I've read your whole report. Which, should I *ever* speak a British ship, I will despatch to Admiral Jervis, instanter."

"You might discover one at Corfu, sir," Lewrie told him. "The currants are ripe, and there are several of our merchantmen lading now."

"Currant duff!" Charlton beamed, almost childlike in a sudden rapture. "Aye, that's where they come from, ain't it? Corfu, and the Isles of the Levant. A *fresh* currant duff, not stuffed with fruit six months in-stores. I've a relish for one of those, Lewrie. A most rapacious relish, of a sudden. As I'm certain my ship's people have, too."

He stood, his wineglass, and Lewrie's, now empty. Their little chat was ended. Like a good boy, Lewrie rose as well, knowing he still hadn't changed Charlton's mind about using Petracic and his pirates any further. And getting a fey feeling that, with all that he'd heard from Captain Charlton about the man, things could only get worse – very *much* worse! – before Charlton washed his hands of the matter.

"Well, do you not have need to put in at Trieste to intern prisoners, nor any captures for the Prize-Court," Captain Charlton breezed on, as he came round the desk to escort Lewrie to the forrud entry on *Lionheart's* gun-deck, "put in at Venice, there's a good fellow. Pick up the latest information regarding the French Army's doings. Take a bit of shore-leave for yourself, and your people. You've earned that twice over the last few days."

"Aye, sir," Lewrie agreed rather numbly.

"Should you speak Commander Fillebrowne, relate to him all you have discovered down south, and issue verbal orders from me that he is to bring *Myrmidon* down to Palagruza, to rendezvous with me. We've seen no sign that the French will yet dare send military supplies into the Adriatic to succour this General Bonaparte's troops, last I spoke him myself."

"Very good, sir," Lewrie replied, essaying a cooperative grin and putting his best face on his disappointment.

"Uhm… might have a confabulation with our trade consul, once you're ashore, Lewrie," Charlton suggested, once they'd emerged upon the gun-deck, amid a flurry of Marine sentries and a stiffening side-party on the starboard gangway. "See does he have a clue as to which Venetian merchant-houses might be most involved in the illicit trade. Then he *may* be able to put a flea in some senator's ear. They're so weak, they may not care for their pose of *strict* neutrality violated. By anyone."

"Prompting a silk-cord strangling in the Doge's Prison, 'cross the Bridge of Sighs, sir?" Lewrie hinted.

"Be it spiritually justifiable to pray God, Lewrie." Charlton laughed as he clapped on his hat at the foot of the gangway ladder. "I see you've been swotting up on the local geography, ha ha!"

"Aye, sir." Lewrie shrugged.

"I've taken on more cast-off Austrian muskets and such. Do you have any suggestions as to future supplies for our allies, Lewrie?"

"Half a million rounds, sir," Lewrie most sardonically said.

"Half a *million* made cartridges?" Charlton goggled.

"No, sir. Vowels," Lewrie quipped. "The Serbs seem most in need of vowels than anything else."

"Be off with you, you wag! You knacky scamp!" Charlton roared, clapping him on the back like he was an old school chum allowed such a closeness. "And dream up more ways to confuse our foes!"

"I'll do that very thing, sir," Lewrie agreed, just before he went up the ladder to the waiting side-party.

Though there's foes, he thought, and then there's foes!

Chapter 11

"Why ain't I surprised?" Lewrie scoffed, once he'd heard from the hapless Lieutenant Stroud that Commander Fillebrowne was not to be found.

"He's ashore, sir," Stroud pouted, moonfaced and half abashed. "About the city."

"Should I seek him in the art galleries, Mister Stroud?" Lewrie asked with a wry grin. "Or the knockin'-shops?"

"Ahum, well, sir," Lieutenant Stroud said with a miserable expression, "he *is* that keen for a bargain, but… I do believe he said he *might* be dining with Sir Malcolm and Lady Shockley. A standin' invitation? Or he might not, depending whether they were in and receiving today, sir."

"What, they're still here?" Lewrie scowled, even further irked. "Thought they were off for the Holy Land long since."

"I wouldn't know, sir," Lieutenant Stroud confessed in a meek voice.

"Does your captain come aboard whilst I'm ashore searching him out, then, Mister Stroud," Lewrie snapped, "you're to give him these verbal orders, direct from Captain Charlton. He is to up-anchor, sail to Palagruza and rendezvous with *Lionheart*, 'with all despatch.' The Frogs are up to something new, and we've just learned of it. Captain Charlton will further enlighten him once there, but the gist is that our 'trade' has settled in Balkan harbours, neutral ports, waiting for Venetian ships to fetch timber to *them*, and Captain Charlton wishes us to reassemble and concentrate against them. Has he any questions for me, he may come search *me* out before he sails. Got that, sir?"

"Aye aye, sir," Stroud barked, glad to have a simple task.

"I'll wood and water *Jester*, and sail a day after, tell him."

"Aye aye, sir!" Stroud repeated briskly.

"I'll be calling on Sir Malcolm myself. Or along the Rialto, round Saint Mark's Square. Doing some shopping of mine own, tell him, should he wish me to elaborate on these orders before he departs, sir."

"Very good, sir." Lieutenant Stroud nodded, all but moving his lips as he committed all that last to memory.

"I'll be on my way, then, Mister Stroud. Good day, sir."

"See you to the entry-port, sir," Stroud offered with relief.

–

Might've given *Myrmidon* leave t'stay longer, Lewrie fumed after his gig had landed him on the Molo before the Doge's Palace across from the Dogana di Mare; after *such* arduous duties off Ravenna! he snorted in derision. Idle, foppish, cunny-thumbed "Whip-Jack" *sham* of a sailor…! Thin'z my lore is, I could circumnavigate the entire world, whilst he's not fit t'pole a punt on his daddy's duck-pond!

He just *knew* the Fillebrownes had a duck-pond. To set off whichever half-a-shire they used for their home-farm, so visitors could gawp on the long carriage ride in through "Fillebrowne Park"! Or to mirror the palace they lived in.

And I have t'waste half my own short shore-leave huntin' up the bastard! Lewrie further griped.

–

He tried first at the Shockleys' rented digs, a waterfront palace converted to suites of rooms near the Farsetti Loredan Palace, along the Grand Canal on the other side of Saint Mark's, just by the Riva del Carbon. To hasten his progress – and spare his breath – he enjoyed the unwonted luxury of a sedan-chair.

No one was at home, though, he learned from the English servants; they had dined earlier but gone their separate ways. Sir Malcolm was off to look at some ironworks, Lady Lucy had gone shopping and they'd no idea where that amusing Commander Fillebrowne had gone.

"La, sir, the man's a waggish wit, an' all," a chambermaid said, blushing prettily. "An' such a fetchin' gentleman!"

"Ah… really," he'd drawled, quite skeptical.

"'Deed, sir! Most scandalous witty an' charmin'!" was her opinion. She blushed again, and tittered into her raised work-apron.

"Ah… humphh!" was Lewrie's comment to that. "Well, then. I will be off. Regards to the family… all that."

–

He'd done what he could. He'd informed Stroud, and Fille-browne *must* go back aboard his ship sooner or later – by sundown at the latest. He climbed back into his hired sedan-chair and took himself off shopping.

–

There had finally been a partial adjudgement from the Prize-Court at Trieste. Before *Jester* and *Lionheart* had parted company, they'd sent it over to be doled out to officers and men. Still no sign of any award from their own at San Fiorenzo Bay, of course; frankly not a single word from them since they'd departed Corsica, at all! Lewrie's two-eighths of the judgement represented nearly £1,200, £800 of that in rare coin, for a wonder. Not anywhere near what he speculated he was due, but welcome, for the Austrians were proving to be as niggardly and obfuscating about prize-money as their own officials. Still, a tidy, reassuringly heavy sum to tote about for an orgy of Spending and Getting.

He discovered some fabulous fabrics for Caroline at a milliner-shop. Two bolts of ivory satin that, he was assured, would make her a fine gown, even in the older, fuller-skirted styles – whatever she had run up from it. To set it off, he bought lengths of elegant and most intricately detailed Burano lacework, scintillating with silvery silk thread, and heavy with wee sparkling Austrian crystals or awash in seed-pearls, as he'd seen on the gowns of those haughty Venetian ladies when he'd gone to the *ridotto*. There were two bolts of light particoloured cloth, hand-dyed in subtly shaded waves of umber, ochre, burgundy and peach, as iridescent as the marbled papers Venice was so famous for, as rich and regal as ancient Byzantine or Ottoman fineries.

In another shop, he found an amusing door-knocker for the house, a fanciful lion's head the size of a dinner-plate, made of highly polished brass. For their dinner-table, too, a pair of brass candelabras, but so smooth and shiny they seemed to be silvered. They were happy, smiling dolphins that rose from a circle of waves, their bodies impossibly elongated like eels to twine about upright tridents that spread three tines to grasp *nielloed* silver candle-holders – four to each piece. And for himself, for his fireplace mantel, he couldn't resist a pair of Trevisan seahorses in that high-gloss, silvery finish.

A toymaker's was next, after hiring a two-wheeled cart to carry his loot – and the carter and his two small sons to guard his largesse. Toy boats, Carnival masques, string-puppets and Austrian clockworked harlequins, bears and Turkish warriors. For Charlotte, their youngest, he chose a porcelain-headed doll of a Venetian lady, accurate right down to the cunningly feathered hat and disguising capelet – the *bauto*.

He was standing outside the toymaker's, watching his purchases being packed into the cart, when he saw a familiar figure striding up the street. He turned his shoulder to the man, hoping, but…

"Alan, old son!" Clotworthy Chute panted happily. "I say!"

Talk about pests showin' up when you least wish 'em! he thought when you're flush, and they most likely *ain't*. And he wondered how much he might be "touched" for.

But there was no way to ignore Clotworthy. A quick glance to assure himself that it *was* Chute had made eye contact, and he could not do the "cut direct," nor the "cut sublime." He was forced to turn and wave.

"*Heard* yer ship was in!" Clotworthy boomed. "Well met!"

"Clotworthy, still in Venice?" Lewrie was forced to say, wearing a suitably "fond" smile for an "old school chum." "And Peter. Where's he?"

"Off gettin' stuffed into his redheaded mutton," Chute brayed. "So I'm not welcome this afternoon, thankee very much. A *true* redhead, he assures me," Clotworthy added, making a subtle pass at the fork of his breeches. "Sylph-like young chit, what Peter calls… *langourous*, haw. S'pose that means she coils 'bout his member like a snake, what? Been arse-over-tit 'bout her since he met her, the last month entire! Hired doxy, but not too bad. Gracious damn manners, the once I dined with 'em. Does a body *prefer* langourous. Always liked some beef 'pon the bones, meself. Easier on the poor mort, hey?" he said, slapping his expansive belly. "What some term Rubenesque. Cheaper quim, too, the bouncy'uns… not as in demand these days. And you, sir? Doin' a bit o' shop-pin', hey? Well, Venice is a splendid spot for't. Do they let ya off from all that 'away boarderin' 'and 'vast, me hearty-in'?"

"One day, at least," Lewrie fibbed, hoping Clotworthy might take a hint that he was too busy to deal with him today. Though, recalling their old days together, he hadn't been much on hint-taking before!

"Ah, let's see how you've done so far, Alan, me old. See have ya been gulled," Chute offered, going to the cart and pawing into the packages. "Not bad, not bad at all. Bit darin', this mottled fabric, though I'm told the fashion's for damn-near see-through and show off yer privates, lately. Does a woman still have a figure for it, I can feature this'd run up nice. Exotic. Allurin'. Entrancin'."

Christ, last thing I need, Alan groaned to himself, suddenly regretting his purchase of that cloth; "exotic" in England gets people pilloried! He was sure Caroline still had the figure for this, and wouldn't be quite *that* immodest with it. But she'd still get pelted with dung and mud by the Mob, should she trot it out on the town!

"Ah, some for the kiddies," Chute sighed dramatically. "Envy you, I do, old son. Family and all…" All but wiping a tear.

"God knows when I'll be able to ship all this home as presents," Lewrie told him. "I expect I'll be hard at it 'til supper. Shopping… then get it back aboard." He hoped once more Chute would just bugger off.

"Know yer way about?" Chute hinted.

"Well, no… but…"

"I do."

"Bless me, Chute, but… you would!" Lewrie chuckled wryly.

"Aye, give me but one week in a strange place, and I'll know it good as a native," Clotworthy boasted. "I dare say I know Venice just as good as a local pimp or pickpocket by now. Better!"

"I was surprised to hear the Shockleys are still here," Lewrie said, for want of something better. "But you and Peter, too? Been up to *much* mischief?"

"Oh, keepin' me hand in… so t'speak," Chute replied, leering and tapping his pate. "Bit o' this, a bit o' that. With Peter so quimstruck, I've bags o' free time t'work a fiddle or two, for pocket money. Still have the bulk o' me London money, never fear…"

Which was the *last* fear on Lewrie's mind!

"Use it for workin' capital… seed money. Here, now, Alan. Done any glassware yet? Oh, Venice has champion glass-works. You'll never again see the like anywhere else in the world. Now, I know a shop…"

Lewrie's hand flew to cover his coin-heavy purse, by its own volition!

"A *particular* friend of yours, this shopkeeper, Clotworthy?"

"Lord, no, nothin' like that!" Chute pooh-poohed. "Do ya crave fine art and such, then I'm yer man, me and my *particular* friends. Do ye get my *meanin'*! Shop's not far off. Care t'see it? Man's gettin' older by the minute, and no one t'carry on once he's gone. Sellin' up stock at knock-down prices, but he ain't on the local High Street, so's it's goin' cheap as fiddler's pay at a country dance."

"Well…" Lewrie hedged.

"Right, then. We're off!" Chute boomed, turning to spout fluent Italian at the carter and his lads in that slurring, syrupy Venetian dialect. "Two more items Venice is famed for, Alan, old son. Culture and quim. What else brings the young heirs to it on their Grand Tours? Well, straightaway I discovered that pimpin's out, even with fellow Englishmen. Dagoes have that market cornered, and a nudge and a wink in the right direction don't fetch me tuppence. And I don't feature havin' me throat cut or endin' up dead in a canal 'cause I poached on some garlic-breathed *bravo*'s patch. And, it don't take much *wit* for a man t'flog quim, exactly, does it? Lord, Alan! Dagoes're all swagger, manly attitude and bad breath, but I doubt a dozen of 'em could muster the brains God only *thought* o' promisin' a hedgehog. Well, with quim right-out, that leaves culture and art. The pimps're too slack-witted t'get into it, e'en though the profit's a thousand times better."

"And you're… profiting, Clotworthy?" Lewrie just had to ask.

"Profitin', aye." Chute most beatifically beamed at him. "You've heard the tales, 'bout how some mincin' foreign mountebank art dealers skinned some jingle-brains from home? So what's finer than meetin' up with a fellow Englishman… a refined and *educated* fellow, known among the *best* circles in London," Clotworthy boasted, shooting his cuffs as he preened and laid a hand on his heart, "able t'drop a dozen names in a single breath, *and* back it up with inside information, mind! Man who knows his Cellini chalice from a wood piggin? Knows his way round, one who can steer 'em from bad shops to good, from the forgers to the honest? And know the old and genuine from the run-up last week. Or discover what they want most and have the connexions to *get* it run-up and aged, after wearin' 'em to a frazzle lookin' at hum-drum."

"Decent profit in that?" Lewrie queried, intrigued in spite of his cautions. Clotworthy *still* owed him that money for "tatties and gravy"!

"Finder's fee from the buyers… 'long with some excellent food and guzzle," Chute expounded as they strolled, "yer modest five percent or so, whate'er their gratitude can be stoked to. Five percent from the shop-owners, for haulin' 'em in. But *ten* percent do we foist off fake, from my, uhm… less honourable compatriots in the… *reproduction* lay."

"I wonder, then, what your aid might be cost me… old son." Lewrie scowled. "After all…"

"Lewrie, old *fellow*!" Clotworthy balked, leaning away with his hand on his heart once more, pretending to still be *capable* of feeling insulted. "What a scurrilous notion. To think that I, an old Harrow man… a schoolmate…! would play you false? Were I 'skint,' well…! That's a possibility, hmm? But! As I said, I'm flush with 'chink,' so never you fear. My expertise is yours, sir… gratis," he added with a deep flourish of his hat, and an only semi-graceful formal bow.

"Well, in that case…"

"Might you feel so abashed, after making such a base allegation," Clotworthy resumed, rising and clapping his feathered hat on, "and might wish to tender some amends, I *will* allow you to treat me to supper. And a brace o' wine per diner, mind. Old fellow, I *forgive* you. Totally!"

Lewrie could but stand and laugh out loud at his audacity.

"Like Dante's *Inferno*," Clotworthy promised, "I'll be your ghost of Virgil. I'll tour you through the Nine Circles of Hades, and fetch ye out without a single smudge o' soot. Gad, see what a proper public-school education benefits a man? E'en did they flog it into us?"

-

The glass-shop held spectacular bargains, for the shopkeeper really *was* as old as Methuselah, with one foot in the grave, Lewrie had to think, for he wheezed and coughed the entire time. Lewrie bought some pale pink-and-white dinner-ware, a service for eight, for their morning room when they dined *en famille*, replete with bowls, cups, salad plates and servers. Then a complete stemware set of glasses for everyday use in that same semi-translucent pale pink, with more ornate clear-glass for stems between bases and glasses. All was most carefully wrapped, with heavy paper, wadded with old newspapers, then crated in straw and dry seaweed before the crates were nailed shut. And all for only £20!

Next, they hit a furniture store, though Lewrie wasn't exactly taken with the cast-off Baroque pieces, nor with the painted-on floral busyness of most of the lacquered pieces in the Rococo style. He did rather admire a pair of small commodes, though, which he thought might look cunning on either side of their main staircase, once inside their entry hall. They were Chinee-red, four-footed, gently bell-shaped and bulging toward the top, rich with gold leaf and decorated with painted scenes of Venetian doings.

"*Lacca povera*," Clotworthy whispered softly, shaking his head in sadness. "Scenes're printed on paper first, then lacquered on. Don't even think of it, Alan, old son. You'll note the bastard's askin' over three hundred pounds for the pair, same as he is for yon genuine pair... which *are* hand-painted. *Thought* the bugger wasn't entirely straight!"

"Couldn't afford either," Lewrie confessed.

"Well, do you not mind they might be a tad, uhm... warm to the touch? In a manner o' speakin'," Clotworthy wheezed. "I think I know where the genuine article can be had. In a day'r two, mind. A week at the outside." Chute tuttutted.

"Stolen, you mean."

"Shhh! Not a word t'bandy about, now, is it?" Chute hissed, with a finger on his lips. "Not right out *loud*, thankee."

"Don't know as I care for... warm, Clotworthy," Alan whispered. "Even were they a guinea the pair. Caroline likes to get things which remind her where I've served. She'd like these, but... perhaps just a *copy* of a good painting... something like that? Wait a minute, that's torn it! I've just blabbed what you want to know. Like your *grateful* buyers, hey?"

"You have, indeed, and I'll keep my eye out for something." His corpulent old school chum winked. "Something special. And reasonable."

"Not pinched?"

"You press me sore, Alan, old son." Clotworthy pretended to wince.

"Not pinched. Not a flagrant fraud, either. No Canaletto, when it's really some toothless old rogue's drunken copy-work," Alan said.

"Ah, perhaps we should call upon an art gallery which *just* this very minute springs to mind! They've—"

"Think I'm shopped out, Chute," Lewrie demurred. "Feeling a tad peckish, too. Let's have all this over to the Molo, so I can stow them aboard 'fore sundown. And then I'll buy you that supper."

"Well, if you're wearied…"

"Else I'll have to hire a dray-waggon, 'stead of my cart." Lewrie shrugged. "And have nowhere on the orlop to store it all."

"Aye, let's be off," Clotworthy agreed affably. "I must own to the need for sustenance. Some wine and a plate o' *biscotti* on the way?"

They left the shop and plodded back toward the water-front, with their cheerful carter and his boys serenading astern. Lewrie bought some sweetmeats for all – *baicoli* – and sugar-dusted, ring-shaped *bussolai* biscuits to munch on the way. To restore themselves.

Well, restoring Clotworthy's hard-taxed strength, anyway, for he downed more than half of them, in right good cheer.

"My bloody oath!" Clotworthy yelped, stopping stock-still, with one of the cart's handles all but up his arse. He turned away, busying himself at the back of the cart as if he were inspecting the lashings of rope. And dragging Lewrie back there with him.

"God Almighty, Chute, what's the matter?" Lewrie fussed. "Seen a creditor? Someone you 'sharped'?"

"Worse than that, old son," Clotworthy assured him with rare gravity. "Look ye yonder. 'Pon that balcony, left on the corner by the turnin'."

Lewrie looked, down to the intersection of their already narrow street, to where an even narrower lane crossed it; upwards to the left, to a first-floor balcony above a wine-shop.

"Rented rooms, by the day, the week… the afternoon," he heard Chute whisper in his ear.

"Christ shit on a biscuit!" Lewrie gawped.

He'd gotten an impression of a uniformed man with a lady, still deep in the warm summer shadows of late afternoon, which were almost an ebon-black deepness compared to the brightness of the walls. Until the man stepped forward, into that graze of sunlight which slanted in…!

"Fillebrowne," he growled softly.

"Worse yet," Clotworthy cautioned.

The lady was much shorter, pouter-pigeon plump, with blond hair and bee-stung lips. She was laughing softly, leaning against him, with a *bauto* ready to be donned, held over and behind her head and hat, like a kerchief. "Lucy? Lucy bloody Beauman?" Lewrie gawped aloud.

He took off his uniform hat and slunk down to peer over the load on the cart, through the juddering knees of the carter's boys. He got a clear shot at the couple, sharing a last passionate good-bye kiss in the elevated privacy of their love-nest. Then they parted, walked into the stygian black shadows deeper in the balcony and disappeared.

"Christ, who'd ever thought it?" Clotworthy tittered excitedly. "Lady Lucy and yer sailor-boy. Who'd ever o' suspected, Alan? Rantipolin' the day away. Or do ye have a nautical term for it?"

"Doin' the blanket hornpipe," Lewrie muttered. "With your live-lumber's lawful blanket. God, I knew he had nerve, but this…! I doubt our Captain Charlton would have let him stay anchored off Venice this long, had he known the reason for his remaining. God, I do believe I *despise* the bastard!"

"Still not sweet on the bitch, are ye? Or, do ye feel beaten to her *boudoir*?" Clotworthy posed with his usual chary outlook on life.

"Long ago, and far away… long past," Lewrie assured him, with a fierce scowl. "Damme, it just ain't *done*! Not 'til she's a cast-off 'grass widow,' it ain't."

"Or widow for true," Clotworthy sobered, daunted by Lewrie's glare.

"Thing that rows me most is, I *like* Sir Malcolm," Lewrie told him. "He strikes me as a solid sort. Quite intelligent, agreeable, so…"

"Oh, so do I, Alan, old son, I assure ye," Chute agreed. "Fair breaks me heart t'see a man that kind – a man that *bloody* rich! – be cuckolded s'soon. Faithless mort! Knew it straight off, Peter and me. Deserves better, he does. That's my thinkin'. I… *Duck!*"

Out came Fillebrowne, his hat far down over his brows, with left hand gripped on his sword scabbard to rein it in, with right hand out to plough pedestrians like Moses parting water with his staff, setting a brusque pace towards the water-front; away from them, thankfully. It wasn't a minute later that Lucy appeared in the doorway, summoning her sedan-chair, to be jog-trotted off to the right down the narrower lane, back to her suite of rooms hard by the Grand Canal.

Smarmy bastard! Lewrie fumed, once they could rise to full height once more; an' bloody whore! He thought himself quite lucky for their teenage "cream-pot" love to have gone smash so long ago. What sort of Hades would he have been put through by now, had he wed her in the Caribbean? Even *with* all her daddy's gold as consolation? He felt a bit sad, too, that the entrancing, fascinating, so-full-of-promise Lucy from his memories had turned out to be so base.

Mean t'say, he thought; you were *already* a widow, with oceans of money from daddy's an' husband's estates. Could've removed t'London and rogered yourself stone-blind, like so many widows do. And thank God *for* 'em! he added, recalling flashes of youthful experience. Why marry at all, again... 'specially a *decent* man, when there's so many rakehells available? Was Sir Malcolm just *too* rich t'miss? And did ya *plan* t'be an "open beard" right off? Bah! He felt like spitting.

Fillebrowne, though... he'd flaunted a relationship with Phoebe Aretino, damn near to Lewrie's face. Whether it was true or not, or if he had tried to nettle him, to prove which of them was the chief crow-cock, well... it didn't signify. Now here he was, topping another of Alan's old flings. Lewrie had a sense of why; 'twould be the most impish deed for a smug rogue to do, a tripled joy. Bull a married woman, and always cock one eye and ear for discovery – a most delicious thrill, he knew. It was *such* an intriguing game, to keep the story straight, the blankly innocent demeanour in public... before the husband, under his very nose! And the older and richer the husband, the greater the thrill. Second, there was revenge, the thrill of the chase, the victory over another to savour. Seeing what a round-heel Lucy might have been over Lewrie, the coy flirtation she'd bestowed that dinner before. And beating him into the breech – and "Who's the better man, now, hey?" after he'd turned her offer down. Before he could reconsider and move on her himself!

Fillebrowne could make a name for himself in the Fleet. Lewrie squirmed, turning red. The man who stole quim from "Ram-Cat" Lewrie. Men would ever vie, over just about anything, but nothing caught their competitive heat quite as quick as the chance to stick it to a rival's wife, daughter or mistress!

Finally, there was Lucy herself, the prize. Still a fetchin' bit of fluff, short, springy and bouncy, soft and yielding (he suspected) as a feather mattress, now obviously an avid player at "the game," and time restraints would turn two blissful stolen hours with her into that sort of "all-night-in" that'd *kill* lesser men. For both of them, he told himself; out to top their last record, and make the most of their time.

"Ya know, Alan," Clotworthy sighed, striving to sound somewhat less amused than he obviously was, "were we a devious pair of fellows, I do allow there's a bit o' profit in this. Do ye despise Fillebrowne half'z much'z ye say, then a word in yer Charlton's ear'd put him in a pretty pickle, would it not? And to reveal all... to a certain party, mind, with a promise t'keep mum... for a *gratuity*, say..."

"You're right, Clotworthy." Lewrie grimly nodded. "There might be. Mine would be proper, though. He's remiss in his duties. I'd be very disappointed in *you*, Clotworthy, were you to try to exploit this with a certain party. Either party. Stick to what you're good at... bloom where you're planted, hmm?"

"But Alan, m'dear, I merely pointed out...!" Chute cried, in a fair approximation of righteous indignation, but retracting his intent. "Damme, sir. It's *so* meaty! And a juicy bit o' news like this doesn't come along just any day. There must be somethin' in it for *me*!"

"Gossip t'gloat over, Chute," Lewrie allowed, grinning slightly. "A zesty tale t'tell, in strict confidence at the wine-table. Does it get spread about, though, sooner or later it gets back to Sir Malcolm, and there's a good man made a laughingstock. And heartbroken."

"And her ruint, too, mind," Clotworthy countered. "Given a welcome comeuppance. *And* well deserved."

Comeuppance, Lewrie mused for a moment; what a glad-some idea!

"Clotworthy," he said carefully, "did you know that Commander Fillebrowne is dead-keen on art collecting? His whole damned family is mad for it. Reckons himself a most *discernin'* sort, though. Or so he boasts."

"*Is* he, by God!" Clotworthy exclaimed, beginning to beam the beatific smile of a delighted child. "Hmm... why, just bless my soul!"

Chapter 12

"Hope you enjoyed Venice as much as I did," Benjamin Rodgers sniffed, as they strolled along the shore of the tiny island that was alee of the main isle of Palagruza. "Came nigh t'killin' myself."

"Bit o' this, a bit o' that," Lewrie answered, gazing off into the small undeveloped harbour where *Jester* and *Pylades* lay to anchor. "Shopping, mostly, for the family. Go on a *high* ramble, did you, sir?"

"Like th' hands, 'Out o' Discipline,'" Rodgers confided. "An' a wife in every port. Every time I turned my head, more-like. Three in two days," he slyly boasted, giving Lewrie a companionable nudge in the ribs. "Spent damn deep, I tell you… prize-money *and* me essence. Flowin' like th' town drains, an' thankee Jesus for a bachelor's life… a sailor's life. Doubt I drew a sober breath, from th' waterfront on, but not so 'barreled' I shan't have lovely mem'ries for me dotage."

"I stand in awe, sir!" Lewrie chuckled, batting a pine cone along with a driftwood stick. "Did *Myrmidon* come in?"

"Aye, yesterday. And just as quickly gone. *Lionheart* was at sea, just 'bout yonder, loafin' off-and-on," Captain Rodgers related, "and sicced her south, 'thout a chance t'anchor. They're t'cover Volona an' Durazzo, I believe was the idea. I'm for Corfu and the straits for a bit, then escort my prize back to Trieste. Mine an' whoever else's."

"See you took a singleton. Congratulations on good hunting."

"Not half so good as our last sweep, Alan," Rodgers shrugged with a rueful squint. "Those japes o' yours put th' fear o' God in 'em. Don't know as how there's a single continent French bowel in an hundred miles, lately. Timber cargo, outward bound. Like coal to Newcastle… not worth much at the Prize-Court. Sell off ship an' cargo… might be we take her again in a month'r two. Or th' damn' timber gets bought by a Venetian, an' run right back t'where I took it in th' first place!" Ben rasped, sullen and gloomy. "Tradesmen… only loyalty'z gold!"

"Did Captain Charlton leave any orders for *Jester*, sir?"

"Aye, he did," Rodgers nodded, trying to skip a smooth stone on the limp lee-coast waves beyond the beach. "*Verbal* orders. Hasn't put pen to paper in a fortnight. Damme, I used t'be good at that! You are to sail down to him, off Durazzo or Volona, an' report what our consul told you, an' what news ya heard latest at Venice. He said he dasn't wait for ya, with th' Balkan coast temporarily uncovered, and it'd be time th' Frogs would be gettin' over th' fright you gave 'em. Then I expect you'll be given a port t'watch. Inshore work."

"My sole joy in life, sir," Alan snickered without much mirth.

"So, t'quote the Bard… what *is* new on th' Rialto?" Rodgers asked, trying his hand with another flat stone, sidearming it.

"There's not much joy from our consul, sir. O' course. Says he expects to be hooted out of the hall, should he lay a complaint." Alan grimaced. "Won't even think of it 'til he's nosed about some more… and I 'spect that'll take 'til next Epiphany."

"Merchant, himself," Rodgers spat. "Might be up t'his neck in th' trade, too."

"Uhm… sir." Lewrie frowned over Rodgers's wintry cynicism. "I heard bad news 'bout the French. That new Austrian general, Wurmser, in the Alpine passes? Came down three of 'em, along the Adige River. His left-wing column as far east as Bassano and Verona. Nobody knows quite *why*, that'un. Right-wing marched on Brescia, round Lake Iseo, and his centre round below Lake Garda. Forty-five, perhaps fifty thousand men? The Frogs a lot less."

"Don't tell me," Rodgers growled, heaving another failure.

"Well, they had a bit of success early on. Scared the be-jesus out of the Frogs, at first, 'til they concentrated on the Chiesa River. Then it all went t'Hell, sir," Lewrie said, sketching a rough map with his stick on the dirt-grey sand.

"Aye, seems t'do that a lot lately, don't it," Rodgers mused.

"Never got his eastern troops into it, sir," Lewrie pressed on, ignoring Rodgers's sarcasm. "French counterattacked near Brescia and Lake Iseo, Wurmser hared over to help out, and Bonaparte not only routed his tail-end, but smashed in his main force in the centre, round Castiglione, and ran him back up the passes. Five days of fighting, all told. Never got anywhere *near* Mantua to lift the siege. Might have something more, from his left-wing, at Bassano, in mind, but…" He shrugged, scraping northern Italy into a boot-crushed smear. "Bloody Austrians."

"Least ya run with successful people, Alan. Even if yer ol' chum Bonaparte *is* a Frog. So what're th' Venetians doin'?"

"Absolutely nothing, sir. Business as usual. They're neutral, so nice and sweet and harmless, no one'd ever come after *them*. Some brief hand-wavin', then the cards were flutterin' again. Our consul said he hasn't seen one sign they're worried. Nothing stirring at the Arsenal, no troops called up, no standing-army drills, yet."

"Bloody Venetians," Rodgers snorted. "Way this Bonaparte goes at people, they wouldn't have any more warnin' than we would the Second Comin'. 'Thief in th' night,' and he's renamin' yer streets, lootin' yer treasury an' tuppin' yer daughters 'fore ya can say 'knife'!" He turned and peered at Lewrie owl-eyed. "That *all* th' bad news?"

"Well, there's Tuscany," Lewrie replied. "French troops're now all over Leghorn and Porto Especia, where *we* used to wallow. A small squadron o' warships, and a fair number of transports. *Emigré* Corsicans among 'em. Haven't sailed yet, but everyone reckons it's going to be soon. That report came overland, so it's two weeks old, and who knows what's happened since. Doubt they've Elba in mind, either."

"Shorter sail, from Leghorn," Rodgers speculated, hands on his hips. "But with th' navy they've built up at Toulon by now, it'll be Corsica, most-like. Bastia, first? An' there goes San Fiorenzo Bay."

"There's a rumour the Spanish fleet is refitting, too, sir," Lewrie continued. "Shifting from Atlantic harbours to—"

"Enough!" Rodgers complained, throwing up his hands. He knelt and chose another stone. This one he flung savagely, and finally attained three grazes before it sank. "By Christ, 'tis such a dismal situation, it'd give a saint colic. An' here we are, coddlin' cutthroats... too scared t'put orders in writin'. Not doin' a damn' bit o' good, really. Frogs have as much compass-timber an' oak by now, they could build for th' next two *years* 'fore they ran short! An' more comin', no matter what we do t'stop 'em. Too few, too late... allied with... shit!"

"Well, hardly, sir. We..." Lewrie tried to point out, but Rodgers's gloom was catching. "By the way, where *are* our jolly buccaneers, sir? There's only two of their smallest boats in the anchorage. Don't tell me they chucked it – pray Jesus! – and hied for home!"

"Lord, no, Alan, not a bit of it. They're like th' poor... 'they will be always with us,' don't ye know," Rodgers scoffed, turning to face him. "They went off North, t'scour th' Croatian isles. Petracic left these few poor cripples t'guard th' prisoners... tidy up th' lot. Winnowed 'em like David did Saul's army… lame o' limb, th' faint of heart? Them that knelt t'drink, 'stead o' lappin' from their hands? Least I think it was David… could've been Joshua, d'ye think?"

"You're the one so good at quotin' Scripture, Ben," Alan told him with a snicker. "And hellish-surprisin' that was. Thought you'd know."

"Oh, I do… but I forgot." Rodgers grinned. "It'll come back t'me, 'bout midnight'r so. Oh." He frowned of a sudden, turning bleak once more. "More o' Captain Charlton's *verbal* orders for ya. To take our Austrian hop-o'-my-thumb aboard *Jester* as you go. Neither he nor Fillebrowne'll be workin' anywhere close to Petracic, so you'll be most in need o' translations."

"Oh, *damme*," Lewrie groaned.

"Thought ya were quicker'n that, Lewrie," Rodgers teased, taking some small measure of delight to see him confounded. Or, as Lewrie felt, to see him buggered. "What port's left, 'cept Cattaro, farthest north? Our biblical patriarch, Saint Ratko the Red-Handed, didn't much care to swan about *too* far away… didn't much care for this new arrangement."

"*Bugger* what he likes," Lewrie groused.

"Too near Dulcigno, an' all those Muslim corsairs, who *do* own a fleet o' fast ships," Rodgers went on. "Riskier'n he bargained for, hey? Anyway, yer to keep a chary eye on him, keep him out o' mischief. Yer *Jester*'s shallow-draught, so yer better-suited than either frigate. And Captain Charlton said *yer* best-suited t'deal with th'… unforseen misfortunes which might arise. A lot better'n Fillebrowne."

"Might come up? Christ, *might*?" Alan roared. "Count on 'em!"

"Said he thought Fillebrowne's not o' th' temperament, not like you," Rodgers all but cackled over this turn of Fortune. "Not quite as 'usefully unorthodox'r flexible' as you are, I believe he said."

"Mine arse on a band-box!" Alan spat. "I've buggered meself. Again!"

"Aye, just too clever by half," Rodgers sighed, a tad whimsical.

"You don't have to gloat like you enjoy it, Ben," Alan accused.

"Don't, really," Rodgers answered, turning sombre. "Somebody has t'do it, though, and if not Fillebrowne, then that only leaves you, whether you were sly as a fox or no. You're junior enough. And we can't have post-captains seen triflin' with pirates an' murderers, now, can we? Least, not too close, anyway. You're not to operate *with* 'em… that's a direct verbal order. But ya *are* supposed to make sure it's hostile ships they take, 'fore they rape half of Albania or Montenegro, and pillage th' other half. Keep 'em at their proper duties, 'stead o' enterprisin' off on their own. I'm sorry, Alan. I really *am*! Maybe had ya played th' back-bench dullard, it might not've been. But there it is. And ya get right down to it... better you than me."

"Ah, but you *are* a post-captain, sir," Alan drolly pointed out.

"Why, so I am!" Rodgers grinned, turning his head to admire the gold-bullion epaulet on his right shoulder. "Fancy that! Ain't a deep-draught 5th Rate, an' seniority, just dev'lishfine?"

"I'll let you know when I get 'em, sir." Lewrie sighed. "Well, might as well be at it. Where's Kolodzcy... 'board *Pylades*, still?"

"Buggerin' th' ship's-boys, 'far as I know. No, not really! I wish t'God ya could see th' look on yer *phyz*!" Rodgers hooted. "He's not a sodomite. Don't think! Just what he is, I haven't a clue, an' I expect I'd rather not care t'find out, either. Do ya keep him swozzled in drink, there's little harm in him."

"He knows about this? Or is that why we're having this little tête-à-tête on the beach, Ben?"

"Take joy!" Rodgers advised, with a cryptic smile. "Tell me later... how he took it. He was 'spectin' t'sail home with me, *out* o' this harebrain shit. Runnin' out o' cologne an' unpressed beddin' by now. Oh, th' deprivation! What a cruel life!"

"He'll demand to see somethin' in writin', I'd suspect," Lewrie frowned.

"He won't *get* it. Just like th' rest of us," Rodgers pointed out.

"Here, you have a 'mad' on, or... I've not seen you in such low takings before, Ben," Lewrie commented. "Anything I can do?"

"Sink Petracic an' all his foul brood, that'd suit," Rodgers sighed, gazing far out to sea again. "Get us out o' this shitten business an' back to Corsica 'fore everything falls apart. Back t'th' Fleet, where we belong. I'd give ya my full rant, but that'd keep ya 'til sundown. An' I don't wish t'impose on yer friendship quite that bad. Start at today's sunrise, an' I'd still be spewin' at ya, dawn o' the next."

"Kick the steward, curse the cat?"

"God, I wish!" Rodgers glowered in heat. "When this squadron's duty was straightforward... honest an' aboveboard, well..."

"Let's dine, then," Lewrie suggested. "I doubt a day's delay in getting my arse south'd make that much difference. Nor do I care t'get pirate-turds on my boots that quick. Rant all you like."

"Well…" Rodgers wavered.

"Christ, Ben," Lewrie posed, "isn't that what friends are for? Or did I hear you wrong the last time?" he added, offering his hand.

"Ah… best not, after all," Rodgers sighed. "Th' offers'z good as th' deed. I'll just have me a roarin' good howl at Sunday Divisions."

"Well, then," Lewrie said reluctantly. He really would've liked to put off his future *rencontre* with Petracic and Mlavic, given Ben Rodgers an ear to pour his pent-up bile in, and vent some of his own spleen, too.

"Fair winds an' good huntin'," Rodgers said, shaking his hand. "Mind what I said 'bout our little Austrian powderpuff."

"Half-swozzled… breeches buttoned…"

"An' keep yer own fundament turned to an outboard bulkhead at all times. An' never bend over when he's around." Rodgers chuckled.

"I'll give him your undying love, sir."

"And it'll be th' *last* thing you ever do!"

Book V

"Omne," ait, *"imperium natorumque*
arma meorem cuncta dedi; quascumque
libet nunc concute mentis!"

"All my power and all the armory of my sons have I
given thee," she says; "now make havoc
of what hearts thou wilt!"

Gaius Valerius Flaccus, *Argonautica*, Book VI, 475–476

Chapter 1

"Ships he sees are liddle, herr Lewrie," Leutnant Kolodzcy supplied. "Unt hold liddle ohf value. Dhey are full ohf vood only, so he say he burns dhem after lootink. 'Vhere are die big ships,' he is askink."

"Tell him..." Lewrie began, giving it a ponder as they stood upon the deck of Ratko Petracic's new "flagship," a sleek two-masted schooner-rigged vessel of about ninety feet in length. Ben Rodgers had done him proud by her taking – a Danish trading ship built for speed in the Caribbean. His *galliot* was nearby, along with a pair of his smaller *felucca* two-masters. "Tell him that word of his arrival on this coast frightened the big ships to stay in port. And we were here earlier, giving them another fright. Tell him about our small-boat work, the sheep and all. It will take the French time to work up courage again."

"*Ja*, I tell him," Kolodzcy agreed.

And thank God for small favours, Alan thought as he waited while that was translated; that bastard Mlavic ain't about, and there's no one else in his band that knows English.

Lewrie looked over the larboard side to his *Jester*, about a cable off. He hadn't liked the idea of coming over to talk to Ratko Petracic on his own decks, but the fellow had been insistent. Perhaps Mlavic had told him he'd not been properly welcomed aboard the first time, and had refused to be insulted again. For whatever reason, Lewrie's greetings at the entry-port of the schooner had been bereft of honours, too. He felt naked and alone, even with Knolles and all those hefty guns available to aid him.

Rodgers had told him about taking the schooner, how they'd lured her in, what cargo she'd carried and how delighted Petracic had been to get her, for she'd been one of those rare-and-getting-rarer inward-bound vessels, full of dain-ties and trade-goods, in addition to her armaments. At least her large batwinged gaff-headed sails were some-what akin to a pair of lateens, making the transition to her easier on his

311

seamen. Or her master, Lewrie thought, espying the man he took to be Djindjic, under-captain or sailing master to the landsman Petracic, aft by the wheel. A total stranger now paced the tiny quarterdeck aboard the original *galliot*, which lay close by, alee as they sailed in a group well offshore of Korcula Island.

"He says, sir, dhat you are a crafty man," Leutnant Kolodzcy piped up, sounding a bit amused himself. "Dhat id vas a shrewd think, vhich makes grade terror... as he hess done to die Durks unt Muslims. Dhat you are a man afder his own heart."

"Thank him for me," Lewrie replied, smiling a bit, and watching Ratko Petracic get a good guffaw out of his earlier antics. Petracic told his loafing crew of "Beau-Nasties," who enjoyed such a ghoulish trick on an enemy as much as their master seemed to.

"He egsblains vhy de big ships vit rich gargoes do nod appear," Kolodzcy remarked, as they began to roar with laughter. "Dhey musd be patient, he says, for de Frenchmen to find dheir 'stones' again. He vill gif dhem grade wictories again, once dhey do. Gold... guns..."

Petracic seemed almost boyish, almost likeable, for a moment, as he cajoled that fell gathering of cutthroats; a fellow in his mid-to late thirties, lean and muscular in the full flower of his manhood, and sharing a jollity like a well-respected smallholder among his peers on the village green on a Market Day back home – like a sport who'd just had a good game of bowls and was going to stake everyone to a pint to celebrate. He'd changed over to a pair of French trousers of pale grey, in a light hard-finish wool, this day, though he still clung to his old coral-red boots, red waist-sash, and white, embroidered shirt. And the glossy-furred weskit – sable? Lewrie idly wondered. Otter?

That took some time, to caper 'mongst his men to buck up their spirits, though they didn't look particularly dispirited to begin with. Share a word here, cuff a youngster's unruly hair there.

"He remints dhem how successful dhey heff been zo far, Kommandeur Lewrie," Kolodzcy offered, offhandedly. "Bud I think he ist nod happy. Much artillery, he tells dhem... more powder unt shot dhan dhey need, zo dhey may pragdice. For de time dhey slay Durks unt Muslims."

"Hmphf," was Lewrie's comment to that.

"Muskets... to arm de army dhey vill muster, zo Serbia vill be whole again... grade again," Kolodzcy added, sounding almost bored.

The schooner certainly mounted more guns, Lewrie took the time to note. There were a pair of 6-pounders on her small foc's'le, a pair of 6-pounders right-aft for stern-chasers, too. Along her sides there were no less than ten artillery pieces, when she'd only been pierced for six originally – and, most-like, no heavier than 4-pounders or 6-pounders. They'd sawn embrasures for the extra four guns, right through the caprails of her bulwarks down to the scuppers, with no provisions for gun-ports. Surely that'd weakened her, Alan scowled in disapproval; after a time, she *must* begin to hog, to droop at bow and stern! Those embrasures were a tad too wide, too, for his liking. While it gave those guns a wider arc of fire, it lessened protection for the gunners, and spread the brutal shock of recoil on the breeching-ropes at too wide an angle. Without long baulks of seasoned timber bolted beneath the weather deck, the weight of the guns might slowly collapse the decking, let her start to hog more quickly. He doubted they'd even *thought* of strengthening.

And he wasn't going to be the one to mention it, either!

He looked across to the *galliot*. She, too, had gotten modern guns – 6-pounders – down her sides, in lieu of those ancient falconets she'd once sported. Too damn many guns again. He grimaced, and wished the worst sort of luck in their next blow. Perhaps the *galliot* might survive, but the schooner surely was now too top-heavy, with too much gun-weight above her center of gravity. On a severe angle of heel she'd ship tons of water cross her weather decks, right through the gaping embrasures.

Nowhere *near* as beamy as she needs t'be, he speculated. Did they not get sail reduced quick, she'd be on her beam-ends, rolled through a complete circle and rip the "sticks" right out of her.

"Kapitan Petracic inwites us below, sir. For brandy," Kolodzcy interrupted his musings. "Plum brandy." He shivered.

"Tell him I'd be delighted," Lewrie lied like a pleasant rug.

–

It was a different story once they were below, after their first fiery slugs of that gin-clear evil. Petracic lost his "hail fellow well met" face, sat down behind the schooner's former master's desk and gave vent to a low, rumbling plaint. He was back to long-suffering nobility.

"He gomblains, sir," Kolodzcy abbreviated.

"I'm sure he does," Lewrie noted, deadpan, "complain."

"Zo few liddle ships, zo few ceptures… nod wort' takink. One rich wessel only, unt his men are dis-sadisvied."

"But I see by his ships, sir, that he's made the most of those he's taken so far," Lewrie pointed out. "He has a great amount of artillery, shot, powder… I see most of his crew 'board this schooner've armed themselves with good French St. Etienne Arsenal muskets, with all the accoutrements… good cutlasses, too. Infantry hangers and small-swords, a brace o' modern pistols each." He paused to let Kolodzcy do the translation, watching Petracic cock his handsome face over in leery disappointment. "He's obviously taken a fair amount of money, too, in gold or silver specie. They don't leave Dalmatian ports *totally* broke. There's food, sailcloth, spare spars and rope, bosun's-stores… European clothing, shoes. And wine, sir? My word, sir… so much he did not have just two weeks ago, remind him."

And trousers, Lewrie thought, hiding his smirk; many of his seamen – even Petracic – had plundered those bundles of *Trousers, Used/Mended*. Damme, that a darn'r two I saw on yer bum, sir?

Lewrie waited out another translation, then Petracic's replies, and Kolodzcy's rendering into English, watching his features as he was forced to listen. Petracic was trying to be patient, but there was a bit too much nodding in agreement, his mouth set too grimly, for real patience. He was waiting for a chance to slip out his "buts"! Which came as soon as Kolodzcy took time to draw breath.

"He dells his men, sir," Kolodzcy said, "dhat 'Rome vas nod made in a day'… dhat die time ist gomink, but… ve lure him sout', ve make grade promises ohf plunder, force him to take grade risks zo near de Uscocchi, de Serbmurderink Croatian scum, he says, before he ist strong enough to beat dhem. He accuses… dhat ve know area ist frightened unt svept clean. Dhat ist vhy ve send him to dhis goast. Bud… British covet gold unt rich gargoes ohf France, too. He accuses dhat our ships heff de gute areas, unt leaf him crumbs."

"Ask him, sir… does he wish to sail down to the straits and lie in wait off the Isles of Levant for first crack at incoming ships? If he's so impatient to get rich, that's where he should go, can he not plunder enough for his satisfaction here. We'd be quite happy to swap."

Kolodzcy paled. "I vill temper your vords, Kommandeur Lewrie. Zo he ist nod feelink his courage or his abilidy challenched. He ist vahry… uhm, toochy? Touchy? *Ja*, worse dhan usual, I think."

Come to think of it, Lewrie mused as he waited for Kolodzcy to translate cautiously, where *are* all the big ships? First off, back in the early days, we were chasing down full-rigged ships. Now it's poor coasters!

He thought that the squadron *might* have driven off or frightened off some of the trade, once rumours got back to French Mediterranean seaports – and the big-ship owners, with more to lose, lost their nerves.

Grain convoys, too. The last three years since the war had begun the French had suffered poor harvests, or internal revolutions in grain-growing areas. It might be the right time of year to sail to the Barbary States or America and load up, if the Directory didn't wish famine-induced revolutions to continue. The largest merchantmen might be tied up for that, he thought, leaving the smallest ships for the timber trade. Though it didn't make much sense to him to transport heavy, bulky oak or pine baulks and masts in penny-packets. It was inefficient.

Unless...

Unless some large merchantmen in the Mediterranean were being held back for use as troop transports. For an invasion of Corsica? Or for a massive reenforcement of Bonaparte's troops, by way of both east and west coasts of Italy? *That* might explain the sudden lack of good pickings in the Adriatic, too.

Or perhaps the squadron had come too late, like Rodgers had groused, to make much of a dent in the trade, and the French shipyards had enough oak for everything they'd started, a full year's supply beyond that. And autumn and its gales were coming. Perhaps their fleet was large enough to suit even their timidity, and they *must* cross swords with Admiral Jervis before winter penned everyone in port.

Or they know something we don't he thought; those vague rumours of Spanish ships of the line moving from Vigo, Ferrol and Cadiz past Gibraltar. Should the Spanish throw in with the French, there'd be no more urgency to obtaining oak or building their own... oh, but surely not!

But, he countered his own argument, *should* the Frogs get to sea, they'd need sailors. And where best to get sailors but from one's own merchant marine? Large ships would be unable to hire sailors in proper numbers, but the smallest ships could still be worked by fewer hands.

"Sir?" Kolodzcy coughed politely, rousing him from his thoughts.

"Aye, sorry."

"De Field of Black Birds... ve are beck to dhat. He says he ist *nod* pirade by choice," Kolodzcy told him. "Ist only vay to strike de butchers ohf his folk, unt pud heart in de Serb peoble. Id ist a holy think he does, to speed de day ohf revenge unt freedom. Unt make a new Serb Empire... regain vhat de Durks, de Croats, de Muslims, Bulgars unt... 'Ungarians, take from dhem. To lifd de yoke ohf obbression, he insisds."

Kolodzcy paused as Petracic put out a hand and began to orate to them. He rose to his feet to pace the low-ceilinged cabin, gesticulate wide, though his voice was low, gruff and almost ruggedly sing-song. A faint melody to it? Lewrie puzzled. Like another of those folk-poems... or a litany? Aye, he'd been a parson, a priest, first! He was crooning what sounded like an Eastern Orthodox liturgy! A *Serbian* Orthodox...

"De time ist gomink, he says," Kolodzcy went on. "Vord hess spread, many brave fighters heff been roust. De Durks heff grown too veak, unt de Croats are avay, fightink for Austria. Dhis war is de godsend. He says he gannot resd until he hess struck a blow, von a grade wictory... a sign ohf de begin-nink ohf de end to zenturies ohf torture, murder unt slavery, to all true Serbs. Takink French wessels ist gute, for id brings gold unt arms. Men flock to him for weapons... leadership... now a Serb... navy...! hess been born. Bud, id ist nod enough. Dhat ist earthly kingdom ohf Mammon. He musd raise a Serbian army, unt dhat vill require a grade wictory... vhich vill be *de* sign! More muskets, cannon... gold unt silver to recruit unt pay a new army. Foreign egsberts in artillery, drill, siegevork..."

Petracic leaned over them for a bit, almost imploring, hands to his breast and his voice a coaxing sob; the next moment he was flailing his arms in a righteous rant, stalking about, petulant, demanding and angry.

"If he does nod gain a wictory soon, he thinks, he ist fearink de loss ohf dhose men he *now* hess," Kolodzcy resumed. "Dhose who are sadisvied vit liddle, who vill quit once dhey gain only *earthly* wealt'. *Ach!* He ist demandink us to *find* him a wictory... zomethink impressive! If noddink else, just one more rich ship, a big ship, to silence de small-minded, vhile he gadders de *true* patriots. Before it falls apart. If dhat means goink into ports vhere big ships hide, dhen dhat ist vhat ve musd do, vit him. In de holy cause, de holy name ohf de *Srpski Narod!*"

"We dealin' with a *complete* lunatick?" Lewrie whispered, while Petracic's back was turned as he shouted at the bulkheads. Kolodzcy wiped sweat from his face with a lace handkerchief and shushed at him.

"Tell him I strongly advise against a move like that," Lewrie objected in the first pause for breath. "First off…"

Wait a bit, Alan thought sourly; what the Devil do *I* care, does he get his arse knackered? And he will, sure as Fate, if he irritates one o' the local Balkan powers. Even the *Venetians* could eat him up!

"First off, tell him," Lewrie went on, "the French are sheltered in *neutral* Venetian ports. Second, our agreement was to *secretly* cooperate, never to operate together right out in the open. To even be seen together like this, this close to shore, is risk enough already. Third, we… we counted on his assistance in our troubles, and now he's ready to go off and do something on his own. Captain Charlton expects him to aid us first… then take care of his own affairs once his men are experienced and he's grown strong enough to do both."

"He asks, does grade power like England *vish* his help? Ve heff done liddle to make him strong. Two small ships we heff given him so far. Unt for dhis, ve ask him to valk like a leasht dog. He says, if he reneges on our agreement, who vill England find dhat vill aid us?"

"Why… *no one*, I'd expect," Alan candidly admitted, after some furious thought. "Did we approach any Muslims? No. Did we ever think of the Croats? No," he lied. "We came to the Serbs, and him, direct. We'd… *heard* of him. His bravery, his skill, his daring…"

"Gendle him down, *ja*, I see. Vit fladdery." Kolodzcy nodded. "You vill allow me to… gild die lily, zo to sbeak, herr Lewrie?"

No, ya don't see, Lewrie thought; but you will.

"And make sure he knows this, sir," Alan added. "England understands, and sympathises, with the plight of the Serb people. We see his desire… *their* desire for a free, independent and sovereign Serbia as natural, I'm certain. While there is little we may do, as long as we're at war with France, to aid in his most holy cause, I'm sure our King George would wish them every success. Against the Turks."

"Ah, *ja*," Kolodzcy simpered, hiding his cynical amusement.

"We cannot overtly aid him, tell him. I have strict orders not to, no matter my own wishes," Lewrie intoned carefully. "Until Serbia, or the Serb people, are so organised they could form formal, recognisable diplomatic relations with Great Britain, our hands are tied when it comes to aiding *his* cause. No matter how much England may wish to see the Ottoman Empire confounded and rolled back and an independent Serbia established... we cannot recognise what doesn't yet exist."

Lewrie waited while Kolodzcy translated all that, observing the glint of interest, the unlooked-for hope that most suspiciously came to Petracic's demeanour as he heard that vague assurance.

"We ourselves haven't discovered a large enemy merchantman the last few weeks, tell him. So I cannot whistle one up for him. That is up to him, and the diligence he uses to sweep this local sea. And as for what would best hold the allegiance of his less-dedicated men... what deed would bring in the wholehearted, or ignite the passions of Serbs ashore... inland... well, I'm certain he would know best as to that. I've always heard, 'Fortune favours the bold.' Does he have the wish to uphold his nation's honour, kill his people's enemies... make his country great once more, well... that's as high a calling as I feel for England. I don't fight for prize-money alone, like a pirate or privateer, tell him. Not just for fame or glory, either..."

Bloody *Hell*, but you can trowel it on thick! he chid himself and his sudden noble noises; would've made a grand theatric orator!

"Ahh... herr Lewrie?" Kolodzcy harshly injected. "*Mein Gott, bitte!* You do nod know vhat you *do*, sir! Dhey are zo easily *aroust!*"

"M'favourite sort o' woman, sir." Lewrie gently smiled at him. "Go on. Tell him all I've said. 'Cept that bit about the women."

It took a bit of time, and Alan watched Ratko Petracic stiffen, his handsome face battle a smile of pleasure, his fathomless eyes turn misty. Petracic's chest heaved with deep-drawn emotions. Charlton had told him that Eastern Orthodox people were more of the heart than the head, in religion and in life. Portents, omens, coincidences... that would all be playing in his heart that instant, weighing a pointless career of only faintly rumoured piracy, or a chance to strike, to rise, at last... and undying fame as an avenger.

Lewrie ransacked his memory for something mystical, some ringing Classic's declamation, that might tip Petracic over the edge. A noble, a *clean* poem – he didn't know *that* many; it was a desperate rummaging. But could he goad Petracic into some deed, something insane and fraught with peril, they'd finally be shot of pirates.

"He thinks, sir," Kolodzcy intoned, looking a trifle sick, "he hess earthly unt heavenly, in one. A blow struck for *Srpski Narod* vill also frighten foreign traders into leafink."

"It may, at that," Lewrie quite cheerfully agreed, making free on the plum brandy, beginning to find some delight beneath its harshness, "though I'd advise him to think long and careful before he acts. Take time to sniff about... time to unite all his ships. His... squadron," Lewrie deemed it without betraying an ounce of sarcasm, "with Mlavic's squadron. And where is he, by the way?"

"He says Dragan Mlavic ist avay... on his vay beck to Palagruza. To transbord de prisoners ohf dheir few brizes. Bud his squadron ist *here*, except for his brig. He leafs de *dhow*. Kapitan Petracic boasts he now hess dhis schooner, his *galliot*, de *dhow*, two *feluccas*, unt he hess a ceptured French brig alzo he did nod burn. All vell-manned unt vahry vell-armed. De small boats carry fighters, too, but nod guns ohf grade sdrength. Hundrets ohf vell-armed varriors. Unt he vill issue a call for more ad once. *Ach, scheisse...* he *recites* again," Kolodzcy sighed. "Lasd orders ohf Knez Lazar to all Serbs. 'Whoever ist a Serb, unt ohf Serbian birt'... unt who does *nod* come to *Kossovo Polje* to do baddle against die Durks... led him heff neider a male nor a female offspring, led him heff no crop...'"

Petracic was swaying, expostulating a litany of vengeance upon ancient foes, for massacres and tyranny, theft of lands, for rapes and murders, tortures so unspeakably vile... growing angrier and louder, the longer he spoke. It needed but little translation. A wincing moment later, though, he looked almost shamefaced, calming too quickly and growing very sad as he poured himself some brandy.

"How long he hess waited for dhis," Kolodzcy supplied. "Dhis may be de chance. Only a liddle aid, to tip de scales. Only liddle deed, berhabs... to tip *his* scales. He fears dhey vill be too few... vill you sail to Palagruza unt summon Dragan Mlavic? he asks. Dhen Dragan can brink more recruits... rouse de goast before he comes unt summon more fighters."

"Tell him I will, with pleasure, sir," Lewrie soberly agreed.

"Ef'ry chourney begins vit bud a single sdep, he says. Even if dhey are too few to do *grade* deed ad once, id ist de 'single sdep,'" Kolodzcy rather morosely uttered as Petracic poured them more brandy, almost fatalistically cheerful. "Strike vhere our enemies, unt his... vill be most affecded. Nod a Venetian port, he assures. He fears—"

Few! That's it, by God! Lewrie brightened. That's the one. "Then let me tell him an ancient poem of England, Kolodzcy," Alan interrupted. "Long, long ago, when England was just the one isle, weak and small, facing the might of... *Catholic* France, 'cross our narrow seas. And we'd told the Pope in Rome to stuff it. Founded the Established Church of England. Protestant..."

Christ, Henry V – VIII – who gives a damn, Lewrie told himself; he don't know our history, and it makes a better tale!

"Outnumbered five-to-one, theirs a huge cavalry army, armoured and all. Ours much smaller, infantry and country farm lads with nought but bows and arrows. Long, long ago, there was a field... a battlefield... and they called it... *Agincourt. Our Kossovo Polje...* our doom, or our salvation," he crooned, like the tales he told Sewallis and Hugh 'fore they were tucked in for the night. "And but for our proud young king, our bold and *merry* King Harry, we'd have been lost. Exterminated and *England's* bones left to the crows."

So it happened in France when *we* invaded, he silently quibbled; a minor falsehood in a good cause.

"Every English lad learns this, and it goes like this. Ahem!"

> If we are marked to die today, we are enow... enough...!
> to do our country loss; and if to live, the fewer men, the
> greater share of honour. God's *Will*! I pray thee wish not
> one man more. By Jove I am not covetous for gold, nor
> care I who feeds... who doth feed...! upon my cost...

"*Was? Was wovon reden sie...* 'doth'?" Kolodzcy stammered. "'*Does* feed upon my cost.' Now stop yer gob an' translate!"

"*Jawohl.*"

> ...such outward things dwell not in my desires. But if it be
> sin to covet honour, I am the most offending man alive!

Lewrie declaimed, forced to his feet to stimulate his memory word-perfect. He could see it already had an affect on Petracic. He began to sway to the mesmerising meter of the old Bard of Avon, no matter it was garbled and "mar-text" through Kolodzcy's mouth into Serb. Wouldn't old Cogswell – "Hogswill" – be proud o' me now, Alan thought with a smile, reciting; no call for his switch on my shins, no caning for muffing a word. God, t'think that Eton, Westminster School and Harrow came in handy!

> ...and this story shall the good men tell their sons, and
> Saint Crispin's Day shall never go by, from this day... 'til
> the *ending* of the *world*! – but we, in it, shall be remem-
> bered. We few – we *happy few*! – we band of *brothers*...!

There came a faint snuffling sound as Petracic wiped his nose on his
sleeve, hunched forward like a schoolboy at his first theatregoing, one
hand waving like an orchestra leader's, for even Serbo-Croat could not
take away all the magic. His eyes glowed wet and righteous.

> ...gentlemen in England now abed shall think themselves
> accursed they were not here... and hold their manhoods
> cheap while *any* speaks... that *fought* with us, on *this
> Saint... Crispin's... Day!*

He concluded, flourishing one hand sword-thrusted aloft, crying out
the last line in his best quarterdeck voice, as he imagined Harry had, to
rally his troops – remembering he'd gotten switched, anyway, for being
a tad too emotional for a *proper* English public-school gentleman.
"Hooray for England, Harry and Saint *George*!" he added.

He reached out for his plum brandy, tossed it off in one go... and
strove right-manful not to spew or gasp for air.

"And, 'Rule Britannia!' by Christ!" he stuck on for good measure,
slamming the empty glass top-down on the desk between them,
showing he'd taken it down past "heel-taps."

Petracic stared pony-eyed at him for a moment, then rose with a
roar of his own, a harsh, guttural battle-cry, and poured them all refills.
So they could toast.

–

"Dhere vill be grade slaughder," Kolodzcy mused, once they were
back aboard *Jester*, standing seaward towards the Sou'-Sou'west. "He
vill be ad firsd wictorious. Bud dhen, he rousts die Uscocchi or
Croats... unt dhey musd destroy him. Dhere ist no hope for dhem.
Nod now, nod effer, perhabs."

"Would have happened sooner or later anyway, wouldn't it?" Alan
snapped, watching the pirate flotilla slowly wane tinier as they left
them astern. "After we had no need for 'em? Isn't that what you said,

back at Trieste? They're disposable, expendable, once we've had a good use out of 'em. 'Dead men tell no tales,' right? Secret's safe, no blot on *our* escutcheon. Wasn't that the whole idea of takin' 'em on?"

"*Ja*, id vas," Kolodzcy uneasily agreed. "You send dhem to dheir deat's. Far too early."

"You really give a damn?"

"Bud ohf *gourse* nod," Kolodzcy sniffed primly. Then dared to snicker. "You make Ratko Petracic a vahry happy man, sir. He vill be a mardyr. Anodder Saint Sava… a legent like Knez Lazar. As famous as King Stefan Milutin, Stefan Dusha…"

"Then all will be holy… all will be honourable," Lewrie said.

"'Unt de guteness ohf Gott vill be fulfilled.' Again." Kolodzcy nodded, smiling catlike and inscrutable. "Unt ve are free of dhem… unt dhis… *schtupit* idea ist over."

"You can go back to Trieste," Lewrie pointed out, "with your difficult duty done. Not *our* fault if our hired cutthroats went off on a personal tear. Didn't *order* him t'do it, now, did we."

"You vill, ah… find Kapitan Charlton unt inform him ohf dhis… unforeseen change in ewents?" Kolodzcy asked, shooting his cuffs.

"Ah… no." Lewrie frowned, appalled at the risk he'd run, to rid them of contact with such a foul brood. "Seems we promised to go find Mlavic first and fetch him and his reenforcements. *Then* we'll inform Captain Charlton."

"Our hents are clean," Kolodzcy surmised, looking like he might begin to hum, or whistle, with satisfaction.

"Well, not really, when you—"

"Verbal orders… or *suggestions*, sir… gannod be documented," Kolodzcy hinted with a world-weary wink. "Unt your Kapitan Charlton, so *fond* ohf verbal orders… noddink in writink? Unt, who knows, herr Lewrie? Petracic may ewen be successful. Dhen he lives long enough to cepture more French ships. Raise de goastal Serbs. Like a gute courtier… a man may glaim gredit eider vay, *nicht wahr*?"

"And *that*, sir," Lewrie spat, "is why I so despise 'war on the cheap.' Like my fights clean, I do. No skulking about. No weaselin'. Nor any of the utter cynicism which lies beneath it."

"Bud you are *zo gute* ad id, herr Lewrie, I thought…!" The little Austrian simpered. "And de vay you played his desires…"

"What fur was Petracic's weskit made of, herr Leutnant Kolodzcy?" Lewrie interjected suddenly.

"Sealskin, I belief."

"Ah." Lewrie brightened. "Damme, I hate that. I like seals."

"You know zomethink, Herr Lewrie," Kolodzcy said. "You are a *devious* basdart." He doffed his hat in formal salute, bowed from the waist and double-clicked his bootheels. "I heff gome to *like* you!"

Chapter 2

The anchorage at the small, uninhabited islet was quite busy, for a change, as *Jester* swept in. Mlavic's new brig was there, along with a three-masted merchant ship of about 120 feet overall, tall, and bluff-sided as a two-decker man-o'-war. Two smaller boats, those 40-footers, were unloading near the beach, piled high with grain or flour sacks, teeming with sheep, goats, puny cattle or pigs. The shore was working alive with nearly one hundred Serb sailors or fighters, that *Jester*'s crew could see, all cheerfully at their labours at beach or camp.

At the sight of all that luscious nutrition-on-the-hoof, Giles the purser positively salivated, and begged to go ashore to buy some. Lewrie grudgingly acceded, and added Mr. Giles to his shore-party of Surgeon Mister Howse – to check on the prisoners' needs – along with Leutnant Kolodzcy, both midshipmen and Andrews, in two boats, the heavier cutter and his gig.

"Leas' some'un have good luck t'fin' a prize, sah," Andrews commented once they'd grounded on that muddy grey strand. "Dot's some raght-han'some ship… do some'un give her a lick o' paint an' a good sweep-down."

"Aye, she is, Andrews," Lewrie remarked, studying her. "Just wonder how they stumbled across her. Mr. Howse, on your way. Report back to me, soon as you can. Take Spendlove with you."

"Oh. Very good, sir," Howse intoned, sounding put-upon, with his usual ponderously miserable voice. "Come along, younker."

Lewrie settled the hang of his sword before he began the short walk to the tree line, where the Serbs had established a rude encampment of huts built from pine boughs, spare ship-timbers and scraps of captured sailcloth. Axes rang as men split logs for firewood, and the smell of well-spiced meat roasting on several spits was intriguing. A jangly, tinkly sort of music was being played on odd-shaped instruments somewhat akin to lutes or guitars, accompanied by handheld drums and the eerie, almost Asian fhweeping of panpipes. If Lewrie felt he was walking naked into a lion's den, then at least the pride of lions seemed to be a well-fed and playful lot.

"Captain!" Dragan Mlavic shouted from the circular commons of his new-founded encampment. He waved a dark-green glass bottle aloft, sloshing some red wine on his new shirt and bestowing upon them a wide smile of welcome. "Come... drink! We celebrate!"

"Delighted, sir," Lewrie lied, noting how many of Mlavic's men had already gotten half-way toward the "staggers," swilling direct from bottles or crocks. There were hacked-topped brandy kegs into which the exultant pirates dipped mugs or cups, innumerable pale wooden crates on every hand with their lids torn back, revealing the slender necks with the sheet-lead seals of wines good enough to bottle, instead of being casked as *vin ordinaire*.

"More than enough, sir," Giles exclaimed. "Case'r two for the gunroom, case'r two for meself... and for you, sir? Along with livestock and such? Price is certain to be reasonable, in their state..."

"A case'd do me, Mister Giles, aye," Lewrie replied, feeling a bit nettled to be interrupted when dealing with Mlavic. "Captain!" He shouted, regaining his feigned air of pleasance. "Congratulations for your splendid capture, sir. You've had better fortune than even your leader, Captain Petracic. How did you take her?"

"Ah, Ratko." Mlavic grinned, splitting that bearded face with erose teeth. "Great man... leader, *da*. Want drink, Captain Lev... Lew... here!" he offered, shoving the opened bottle at him, sloshing some more. Mlavic had tricked himself out in a pair of blue trousers, down inside a new pair of what looked like cavalry boots, a fancy-laced new shirt – though he clung to that foetid goat-hair weskit. And all his weapons. The shirt was already spotted with wine-stains, and he wasn't doing his cabin-servant any favours with new ones, either.

"Feeling a bit dry, I will allow, Captain," Lewrie told him as he fetched an unopened bottle from a nearby crate. It'd be the last thing he'd do, to share sip-for-sip from Mlavic's. "Thought an entire bottle'd do me better," he explained.

So I don't die o' Plague or something! he thought with a shiver.

Without a cork-puller handy, he undid the lead-foil and knocked the top off on the edge of a washtub, then had himself a careful sip. It was a very good wine, he had to admit.

"Congratulations on your prize, Captain," he said again, lifting the bottle to make a toast. "Did you take her recently?"

"*Da.*" Mlavic nodded, looking away. "On way here. Fall in lap, hah? Rich prize." He shrugged as if it was of no matter. "All this, ver' rich, oh yayss. Yayss, hah – English? Come! Sit!" Mlavic said, more animatedly. "We drink, eat, sing songs. Plenty food... come!"

"My purser Mr. Giles wonders if he might purchase some of your foodstuffs, Captain," Lewrie said, waving Giles forward. "Meat on the hoof, some grain, pasta or flour? Some wines?"

"*Da*, have plenty!" Mlavic said with a crafty look. "One guinea each!" He roared as if he'd just asked the moon. "I know guinea, in gold... guineas good. One cow, one guinea. You pay?" he leered.

"Aye!" Giles cried, before Mlavic could rethink his price. "A guinea per cow... one guinea, *two* sheep or goats? Sack of flour for a guinea? Case of wine... two guineas," he proposed, dropping into the same sort of fractured trade-pidgin.

"*Da*, is good price. But you pay now!" Mlavic insisted with a hearty rumble, stabbing at his palm with a calloused, tar-stained finger. Giles made a quick estimate of what would feed the hands at least one fresh meal, what the gun-room wished, what might live aboard for a few days more on fresh fodder, and opened his purse. Mlavic eyed each coin pile avidly, his countenance piggish. Lewrie rued it, but he doled out four guineas of his own for two cases of that excellent wine.

"Might I have some hands, sir... to round everything up and get the goods into the cutter?" Giles asked, once the transaction was done.

"Mister Hyde? Assist the purser, would you? And warn Andrews 'bout the people. There's an ocean o' spirits here. Keep them away from drink, the both of you. Busy with the livestock, then get them back aboard. Else..."

Else, like all British Tars, they'd treat it like feast or famine and go on a prodigious tear, no matter the floggings to follow – they thought a few lashes a small price to pay for a drunk. Should half his crew get drunk, though, here in the midst of cutthroats, there was no power in the world that could control them. Or save them.

"I'll tend to it, sir," Hyde assured him, though not without a long, longing peer at the many crates or bottles, and a furtive lick or two of his tongue over his "parched" lips.

"Come, sit!" Mlavic coaxed once more, waving a hand toward the rough seats by his hut door and night-fire – which were nothing better than some log sections, adzed somewhat flat on top.

Lewrie took a seat, hitching his sword out of the way. Kolodzcy dusted himself a spot first with his handkerchief, looking dubious in spite of that effort, before he sat. Right next to the opened case of wine, of course. He drew out a bottle, undid the seal and reached into his waistcoat pockets to produce – should there have been *any* wonder! – a cork-puller, then wiped the neck down before essaying a sip. Mlavic nudged Lewrie in the ribs with a hearty elbow, muttering Serbo-Croat crudities, and Lewrie was forced to show a brief, tight-lipped smile.

"*Sdrasvodye!*" Mlavic proposed, clinking his bottle against the one Lewrie held. "Toast! Ratko Petracic!"

"Ratko Petracic," Lewrie and Kolodzcy were forced to echo.

"He great man... holy man," Mlavic commented.

"I bring you word from him, by the way, Captain," Lewrie began. He felt a tap on his left shoulder and turned to see Kolodzcy offering him a looted silver wine-chalice, a mate to the one in Kolodzcy's hand.

"Trink from neck, vill cud your lip, sir," Kolodzcy said. "Vit your permission, Kapitan Mlavic... ve use your ceptured goblets?"

"*Da*, use," Mlavic most genially urged. "Welcome. Tonight have great celebrating. No keg-meat, *pooh*! No hard biscuit. Serb food is best in world. Good wine, no *ratafia, pooh*! Plenty food, plum brandy. Boats go mainland, bring much! Ah, you like plum brandy, Capitan? I remember... see you ver' drunk... drink like *man*! *Ostereicher* girlie-man drink *tea*, ahahahah!" Mlavic slapped his thighs, he found it so amusing. And then had to rise and share it with his compatriots, so they could jeer at Kolodzcy, too.

It was growing dark, nigh on sunset, and pirates leaped and did fantastic gyrations as they danced and celebrated their prize, crying out boasts, jests, snatches of song as they capered round the fires – much like, Lewrie thought, the Muskogee and Seminole Indians he'd seen in Spanish Florida, back in early '83.

"I have come from Ratko Petracic, sir," Alan tried once more, hoping that once he'd relayed Petracic's orders, he could go back to his own ship, keeping his visit brief and himself both unsullied by contact with Mlavic and relatively sober. "With his orders, sir."

"What he want?" Mlavic almost sneered, surprising Lewrie. He had taken Mlavic for a docile, adoring follower up 'til then.

"He wishes you to come join him at once, sir. He needs every ship and man, he said. He has something planned."

"What he plan?" Mlavic pressed, frowning and squinting, leery. "No rich ship, there. Far from home."

"He worries, he says, Captain," Lewrie told him, patiently as he could, "that without some successes, he might lose the enthusiasm of his men – some of his men, at least – and that they'd drift away."

Are you one? Alan wondered; more a pirate than a patriot?

"*Da*, can happen." Mlavic nodded, getting shifty-eyed again. "So what he do, he need Dragan?"

"He said he would find a place to strike a blow. A blow against his enemies. Don't know *quite* what he had in mind, really, but—"

"He say *that*?" Mlavic questioned, sounding suspicious.

"He did, sir," Lewrie reiterated, wondering if this 'did he, did he?' would go on all night. "Something… *holy*, he said. He said to inform you that he needs your ship and your men, and for you to go to the coast and raise as many fighters as you can immediately. And go to him right after. I suppose he'll wait for your arrival, since he seems to think he needs all he can muster."

Mlavic passed a gnarly hand over his face, as if he could wipe away semi-drunkenness. "*Kossovo Polje*," he whispered to himself with a grim shake of his head, as if he'd just seen the first glimmer from the Second Coming on the horizon. He was stunned, shaken to his roots.

"He recited Knez Lazar's lasd orders to us, Kapitan," Kolodzcy prompted. "Zo, id gannot be he plans a furder act ohf piracy." Lewrie turned to see that Kolodzcy was still red-faced from Mlavic's insult, prim and grimly bland-faced – though with one brow up in sly chicanery.

"*Where* he strike blow?" Mlavic demanded, quarrelsome.

"Don't know," Lewrie admitted truthfully, taking a sip of wine to cover his own duplicity. "Not a Venetian port, he assured me. An act against his… *your* enemies, not ours, I gathered. Something that would keep his fleet eager, put heart in all your people, and… scare foreign traders, as well."

"*Kossovo Polje*," Mlavic whispered again, sounding reluctant, as if the Second Coming were real and he were about to be eternally damned as a hopeless sinner. He took a deep draught of wine, then tossed the bottle away like he'd tasted poison. "Time? Time?" he muttered. He got to his feet awkwardly, crossed over to a stone crock sitting on a crate and opened it to take another slug. Plum brandy, by the smell, Lewrie reckoned; more powerful "Dutch Courage."

"Too soon, sir," Kolodzcy whispered softly. "He thinks id ist too soon. A pragmadic man, dhis Mlavic. In dhis for de money, sir, nod glory or holiness. Vhadeffer Petracic does, *dhis* one vill nod be vit him. He vill sail off, you see." Kolodzcy sneered, making one of his "poof!" conjuring motions again. "*He* hess no vish to die for a cause."

Lewrie thought that Dragan Mlavic certainly appeared to be a man of two minds at that moment, struggling with his inner demons. Growling and muttering to himself, pacing fretful a step or two right, then left, pondering and sipping, pondering and sipping...

Let Petracic lead the bulk of the fleet to ruin, Alan wondered, then take over the remnants... and keep his ambitions small? That was one choice he imagined Mlavic was weighing. Simply toddle off and forget he'd ever heard the orders – ever heard of Ratko Petracic at all – was another. Survive, hole up somewhere safe and anonymous for a time, 'til it was safe to resume his filthy trade? Perhaps Kolodzcy had the right of it; at heart he was a follower of Mammon, a pragmatist or a coward who knew certain death awaited just weeks or months away if he obeyed. Lewrie took a draught of wine, most smugly enjoying Mlavic's dilemma of how he'd avoid his martyrdom.

"Hah!" Mlavic cried aloud, in a bellow that could have carried through a full gale, of a sudden. He put both arms on high and dashed out into the centre of his capering sailors, crying at the top of his voice. With a smile of such pure ecstacy it damn-near ripped his face in half, his mouth a gigantic red hole. "*Kossovo Polje!*" he cried, followed by a flood of Serbian, which stilled that jangly, jumpy music, turned the dancers to stone in an instant. Mlavic was the only one dancing then – seeming to lope in a wide circle amid the leaping flames of the cook-fires, shouting to all, then to individuals, snapping his fingers with urgency. The only other sounds were the crackling fires and the sizzling of meat juices, the soft bubblings of stews or gruels.

"Perhaps, sir," Lewrie muttered from the side of his mouth, "he ain't as pragmatic as you suspect, what?"

"Perhabs he ist a fatalist." Kolodzcy shrugged, as if it was no matter. "Eastern folk vill make de besd ohf efen crucifixion."

"Like 'if rape's unavoidable, relax and enjoy it'?" Lewrie felt like snickering.

"Zomethink like dhat, *ja*," Kolodzcy tittered, finishing his wine. "We heff deliwered de orders, Kommandeur Lewrie. Time to leaf, I am thinkink. Dhey vill get blint-trunk unt vork dhemselfes into frenzy. Unt vhat heppen afder to foreigners..."

"Aye, good thinkin', sir. Let's steal away, supper or no."

A ferocious din erupted from the Serbs, who were cheering and crying to the first star of the evening. Swords and scimitars were flashing red and amber in the firelight, and they were capering, dancing with glee, and making a wolf-howling noise. A wolf-howling that turned into some sort of hill-singing, or a long, involved battle cry, Lewrie noted as they began to steal away. Pagan, heathen singing, barbaric and blood-curdling, like packs of wolves in a call-and-response chantey, from one mountain peak to the next.

Just then, though, up trotted Mr. Howse with Midshipman Spendlove, both panting and out of breath. "Sir!" Howse gasped. "Oh, it is ominous, Captain… ominous indeed, sir. You must do something, at once, I say!"

"What's ominous, Mister Howse?" Lewrie snapped, leading them further away from the singing and cheering.

"Prisoners, sir!" Howse tried to thunder indignantly. "Won't let us in the stockade to see to 'em, sir. I've a dreadful feeling… there's something horrid happened." He gulped. "*Knew* this would turn out badly, right off, sir… you must put it right, sir. At once!"

As if anyone *asked* yer opinion. Lewrie sighed, still leading them down from the camp toward the beach.

"Wouldn't let you in, sir?" he quizzed. "Mr. Spendlove?"

"Don't speak any English, sir… the guards," Spendlove said, also out of breath, and sounding genuinely shocked.

"But we've seen the prisoners before, sir, no trouble before," Howse insisted. "This time, though—"

"Waved us off, sir… drew pistols when we got impatient," the young midshipman carped. "Could see through the logs, sir…"

"I could still see enough, sir," Howse announced, getting some of his old irritable-with-the-world back. "Been 'round sailors enough by now to recognise 'em, sir. I've *eyes*, haven't I? There are damn-all seamen in the stockade, and when I called out to them in French I heard *no* French in reply. Italian, some other foreign jabber neither of us could fathom—"

"Women and children, sir!" Spendlove burst forth. "Started up a fearful racket, soon as they heard our voices."

"What the Devil…?" Lewrie gasped.

"And dark as it's got, sir," Howse rumbled, beginning to sound like himself again, "I could swear, the brief glimpse I had, some of 'em are a tad swarthy… dressed in Eastern garb."

"Like Turks in turbans, sir," Spendlove contributed quickly.

"Just what the bloody Hell's Mlavic done?" Lewrie griped, with a searing glare at the prize-ship at anchor. She showed but one light on her tall poop-deck, aft. All else was fading into the twilight and held no answer for him. A closer-in look at the beach showed him that both gig and cutter were gone, and now nestled *Jester*'s hull near the starboard entry-port. Working-parties were busy along the gangway to hoist up a sack or two of flour or a struggling beast. The funnel at the forecastle showed a thin plume of cook-fire smoke as the cooks got the steep-tubs ready for the evening meal. A cable off from shore, he reckoned, and every man-jack busy with doings inboard.

Might'z well be 240 miles, not yards. Alan shivered, feeling a sudden, premonitory chill. We're for it, do we handle this wrong!

"Who's a good swimmer?" he asked.

"I am, sir," Spendlove piped up. "Well, just adequate, really..."

"Get back aboard *Jester*, quick as you can, then," Lewrie said. "Mister Howse?"

"Not a stroke, sir," the surgeon confessed. "Why, sir? I say, sir... you must do something, enquire... demand, rather...!"

"Then find a safe place to hide, Mister Howse," Lewrie ordered. "As far from the beach and the camp as you can. Have you a weapon of any kind with you? In your kit-box?"

"Damme, sir... I'm a *surgeon*, sir! Not a soldier," Mr. Howse blustered, indignant. "Have no *need* of a weapon."

"Just your bad luck, then," Lewrie wryly commented. "Find a place to hide. Do you find a log, a small boat, try to sneak out to the ship... long as no one sees you doing it. Don't know how safe you'd be with us... me and the herr leutnant here. Unless you're a good swimmer, too, *herr* Kolodzcy?"

"An *egzellend* svimmer, herr Kommander," Kolodzcy answered to that, quite gaily. "Bud, alas... sald vater ist nod gute on my boots or univorm. You heff need ohf company, I am thinkink. Should Mlavic ged engry enough, he loses his gommand ohf English... unt dhen vhere vill you be?" He laid a hand on the gilt hilt of his elegant small-sword and gave it a tug to assure himself it was loose enough to draw quickly. His mouth moved in a petulant little twitching, brows lifted as if to sketch the slightest, half-amused, "oh, what the devil" shrug.

"Right, then," Lewrie sighed. "Mr. Spendlove, you're to inform Lieutenant Knolles there's trouble in the camp. Do I not return soon...

in an hour and a half, say? He's to assume that… well." Lewrie felt like gulping in fright at exactly *what* Knolles could assume. "Do I not return, he is to first board the prize-vessel and the brig. I doubt they've many hands aboard, with such a grand party ashore. He's to land the largest force possible, Marines in full kit, and the hands with pistols, muskets and cutlasses. Do they make a fight of it, he's to scour the camp with fire… grape shot and canister in the nine pounders… solid round-shot for the carronades."

"But, sir!" Spendlove protested. "You'd be right in the middle of it! In the line of fire, sir. I can't—"

"Then I'll just have to duck, won't I, young sir?" Lewrie said, laying a hand on Spendlove's shoulder and forcing himself to utter the tiniest of chuckling noises. "I'll not be a bargaining-chip, should they try that on. This may be a misunderstanding. Or it could be a bloody massacre. Does Mr. Knolles know definite that I… that anything happened to me, he's to exterminate 'em, root and branch. Root and branch, Mister Spendlove."

"Swear *that*, sir!" Spendlove shuddered.

"Be off, then. Mister Howse? Go to earth, delve yourself the deepest warren ever you did see," Lewrie ordered, "and pull it down over your ears."

"I…!" Howse demurred, glancing over his shoulder at the forest. But for the small encampment, it was stark, barren, full of boulders and wind-gnarled pines, stirred to some mindless, brutal life by the leaping flames of the camp, making it writhe like a mythical Hydra. "But if it *is* a mistake, sir, I'll be alone… mean t'say, I'd have no way of knowing when to come out, 'less at dawn, after any assault. Should you be allowed to leave unharmed…"

Bloody miracle, most-like, Lewrie coldly realised.

"…I'd be denned up out yonder, no way to leave with you!" Howse concluded, sounding as if being alone, in a *wild* place, was his last wish, even if his other alternative was getting his throat cut.

"You could come with us, sir?" Alan suggested, tongue-in-cheek. "Mlavic assures me they've a splendid feed planned."

Howse glanced over his other shoulder, at *Jester*, lying out so safe and snug, her decks lit up with lanthorns; then at the waves on the gravelly beach, breaking slow and sullen and dark, like spilled oil on storm waters. Regretting he could not swim a lick.

"I'll come with you, if you do not mind, sir," Howse snapped, downright snippish.

"Mister Spendlove, still here, damn yer eyes?" Lewrie barked. "Give Mr. Howse your dirk and scabbard, sir."

Spendlove stripped the dirk off reluctantly; it was rather a nice 'un, a present from his parents. Howse took it gingerly, like a man being presented a spitting cobra. But he clipped it on his waistband and folded his coat over it.

Lewrie turned without another word and started striding back to the encampment, an icy, fey and echoing void building under his heart; one hand swinging fisted at his side, the other gripping his hanger by the upper gilt fitting below the hand-guard. He most devoutly wished there was a simple, an innocent, explanation for the absence of French prisoners... but he rather doubted it. Might he talk his way to the beach again? There'd be no other way out.

Asked him 'bout his prize, Lewrie recalled; twice, and he turned all cutty-eyed as a bag o' nails. Somethin' queer, there! Christ, I just wish Howse'd got to me 'fore I told the bastards those orders.

He turned to see Howse plodding along, stumbling a bit on tufts of tough shore grass, the odd shoe-sized rock, looking as miserable as a man on his way to the gallows to do a "Newgate-Hornpipe"!

Before, Mlavic might've been too shameful, Alan regretted; now, though... now I had t'be so *god* damn' sly-boots an' stir 'em up...!

He was inside the flickering circle of light from the fires by then, elbowing past cavorting, singing, half-drunk pirates, ducking a clash of high-held blades of every cruel description, glittering keen and hungry. He approached the exultantly happy Mlavic...

"Captain Mlavic, sir!" he bellowed. "A *word* with you!"

Chapter 3

"Now, sir!" he demanded, once Mlavic had gone stock-still in his tracks and turned to face him, a displeased scowl on his face already.

"What you want? Supper?" Mlavic barked back.

"I want to know what happened to the French prisoners. I want to know why your men didn't let Mister Howse enter the stockade. And who all those women and children are up yonder, sir," Lewrie rasped, deciding to play it high-handed still. Cringing and hand-wringing as meek as a shop-clerk or a diplomat wouldn't suit at all, he thought. Dragan Mlavic was a hard man, a bloody-handed brute, and the only language his sort understood was the forceful approach.

"What?" Mlavic chuckled, looking about at his men, as if to say 'Are you crazy?' assuring himself he was in charge here, surrounded by his well-armed minions. "Too fast. My English. You have drink on me, hah? Go slow," he almost implored, shamming sheepish and dumb.

"Put it to him, *herr* Kolodzcy. In his own tongue."

"Go there," Mlavic snapped, pointing to his hut, wheeling about to exhort his men with a long, cheerful speech, which raised a huzzah. "Talk there. Eat first."

It seemed a tiny tad-bit safer, Lewrie allowed, pivoting on his heel to stalk to the log and fling himself down by his abandoned wine-chalice. Kolodzcy followed, not quite so fastidious this time, sitting without dusting. With his small-sword extending over the back of that log, a slim, dainty-fingered hand on the upper scabbard still. Dragan Mlavic had to follow or break into an unseemly lope to arrive ahead of them. He ended up tailing along behind. For that reason, he remained standing, to assert his questioned authority after they'd sat.

"Brandy?" Mlavic offered, still trying to play "Merry Andrew."

"Once we get this resolved, perhaps, sir," Lewrie said coldly. "Now, where are the French prisoners?"

"Frigate captain... dark hair? He come. Take them to Trieste."
Mlavic shrugged, speaking in a deep, guarded voice, and his eyes just
too disinterested for Lewrie to believe that.

"When?" Lewrie shot back. "Last I spoke to him, he was going
back south, to the straits."

"Yesterday!" Mlavic snapped, going to his stone crock for more
plum brandy, miming an offer to share; which was refused. "I come
yesterday with prize, frigate man come same day. So many prisoner...
I say be trouble, so he take. You go Trieste, ask him," he slyly hinted.

Damme, *could* be true, Lewrie puzzled; one more prize, and *Pylades*
would have had to leave the straits. Or met up with Charlton, taken
over their prizes, so... no! Not that many to take, lately. Spoke to him
only five days ago... *here*! A day to gain the straits, a day back, even if
he *didn't* run into the others... Mine arse on a band-box!

"How many shillings did he pay you, Captain Mlavic?" Lewrie
asked. "At a silver shilling per prisoner."

"Three guinea!" Mlavic quickly bristled. "Three pieces of gold, he
give."

"Sixty-three shillings... sixty-three prisoners?" Lewrie drawled. "A
neat, round number, ain't it? No small change to mess with. Sounds
rather too little, though... for the fiftyodd who were here five days
ago. Plus the twenty or so from the prize he'd already taken, plus the
thirty-five or forty off your latest capture? Closer to five pounds, I'd
reckon it, hmm?"

"By God, he cheat me!" Mlavic exclaimed, sounding outraged and
all but slapping his poor dumb forehead. "Here, good food. Serb food.
You eat. We friends, *da*? Holy warriors, you... me. Kill many Turks
together... kill many enemies together."

"Not in my brief, sorry," Lewrie primly pointed out, "killin' Turks.
I'm not at war with Turks."

Some younger Serb lads, barely old enough to be cabin-boys,
offered heaping wooden trenchers of food, still steaming from the spits
and pots.

"Eat! Drink!" Mlavic urged, digging in with one hand, without
utensils, and slurping a paw-ful down with another draught of brandy.
"Is *good*," he tempted, like a governess with a willful toddler who'd
turned his nose up at carrots. "Spice... Serbian, best in world."

Damn him! Alan groused, seeing Howse tentatively dig into his
platter; not five minutes away from gettin' yer bowels ripped out and
you'd go with a bellyful! Well... no need to be a *total* Tartar.

"Croat, Albanian... Greek," Kolodzcy whispered in Lewrie's ear. "Turkish!" He snickered. "All de same cuisine. *Serb* food! Hah!"

"Didn't happen t'steal some forks, did you?" Lewrie enquired.

"Forks, *da*! Spoons, there," Mlavic said boisterously, indicating a small chest near the doorway of his hut.

Lewrie tried some food, poured himself a bumper of wine from that bottle he'd first opened. It was lamb, skewered on sticks with onion and garlic, some vegetables as well. Underneath was a gravied, fine-milled... tiny round rice-pellets? he wondered. A gnat-sized pasta? Rather infuriatingly, it *was* good, heavy and piquant with spices.

"Cow come," Mlavic hinted. "Beef? Aha! 'Roast Beef of Old England.' *Da*, this I know-ing," he said through a mouthful of food. "Or... want goat? Have pig, too. All good."

"Another question, sir..." Lewrie persevered. "Your men kept my surgeon from examining the prisoners in the stockade. Even so, he says he heard women and children up there. *Saw* women and children in the pen. Who are they, sir?"

"Too many question," Mlavic grumbled, shaking his head, masticating a chunk of bread. "Why too many question? No work. Is time for eat... sing. Play *game*." He winked, ever the spirited host.

"Who are they, sir?" Alan pressed.

"Be on ship... prize," Mlavic answered without looking up from his trencher, shoving a handful between bread and fingers. "We bring here. Pay way on ship... pass-en-ger? Many, oh many."

"So what have you got to hide, if they're passengers and such?" Lewrie wondered aloud. "Why didn't your guards let Mr. Howse in, as they have before? Women, children... old men... not too many sailors, Mr. Howse tells me. What's different about this lot, that your men kept him from tending to them?"

"No diff'rent," Mlavic insisted, *still* unable to match gazes with him.

"Vhy does French ship engaged in smugglink," Kolodzcy stuck in with a whimsical tone to his voice, "carry *passengers*, Kapitan? Book vomen unt chiltren aboart, knowink dhere are British warships upon de Mare? Dhat sounts vahry foolish, to me. Vahry... quvestionable. Unt ve do nod see vomen unt chiltren on odder prizes, eider. Chust now."

"Aye, sir," Lewrie snapped. "You afraid word'd get back to yer Ratko Petracic, and he'd be displeased with you?"

"Ratko?" Mlavic bawled, suddenly hugely, frighteningly amused. He let go a belly laugh, had to set his trencher aside, he was laughing so hard he might have spilled it. "Petracic mad, Dragan? Oh, ahahah! Rakto, *never*! Be ver' please, Dragan. Laugh, *too*, I tell him. Make big joy, I tell him. Ship I take... well, may *not* be so please," he admitted with a sheepish shrug. "But people on ship, diff'rent. He have big joy I take *them*," he insisted, proudly thumping his chest.

"And just why'd he be displeased over the ship, sir?"

"*Damned* you!" Mlavic snarled, shoving his plate away, pressed beyond all enjoyment of food. "Too many question. I tell you, *da*. I tell you. Take *Venetian* ship, *da*? Give *you* big joy, know this? *Pooh!* Is Venetian ship... all rich, all big. See no good prize, see no ships days and days! *She* be ship I *see*, she is rich... I take!" He lurched into a furious outburst in his own language.

"To heff carnal knowledche ohf yourself," Kolodzcy translated, shaking his head at Mlavic's utter greed and stupidity. "To go to de Devil... for you to heff carnal knowledche ohf your mother..."

"Oh, *thankee* for that," Lewrie muttered to Kolodzcy.

He got to his feet, putting his sternest, iciest "captain's face" on as he waited for Mlavic to run out of expletives. "You *know* this is the end of our arrangement, Captain Mlavic. You gave your word, swore to us that neutral ships were strictly out-of-bounds, that any prisoners were to be treated decent," he accused. "Now you've broken your vow six ways from Sunday. Took a Venetian ship, most-like you killed her crew, too, didn't you... to spare yourself the trouble of keeping them here? *Pylades* hasn't had time to get to the straits, here and back, to take the French prisoners off your hands, either. Did you murder them, too, 'cause you got tired of guarding them?"

Mlavic stood before him, a trifle hangdog, arms crossed over his chest, and glaring at Lewrie's shirtfront, like a defaulter come before "Captain's Mast" for peeing on deck.

"We *thought* we were dealing with trustworthy men, sir," Lewrie scoffed. "But it will be my unfortunate duty to inform Captain Charlton that you *can't* be trusted... that no matter Serbian bravery and skill, you can't be trusted out of sight."

Piss down his back a mite, Lewrie thought; maybe I can *shame* us back to *Jester* alive!

"No more help, sir. No more alliance. You're on your own, and whatever it is that Petracic does... even if he begins the liberation of all of Serbia… my country's king and government will *never* award you recognition, or aid, or… You're on your own, from this moment on."

"Serbs on own, ever!" Mlavic grunted, lifting his eyes at last. "Enemies everywhere… help, none. *Pooh!*" He spat on the ground. "I tell you, Serbs no need English help."

"Then how'd you get your damn' brig… sir?" Lewrie smugly reminded him.

"I would have take… *you* get in *way!*" Mlavic shot back.

"Now you can keep that ship… and God help you," Lewrie said, sensing he might have overplayed it, and not liking the truculence he saw returning to Mlavic's face. "All her valuables, too. But those Venetian prisoners, those women and children, come with me, sir. I'll take them aboard *Jester* and see 'em safe to Venice. Shilling per head, same as before. 'Cause I can't trust you to keep them. You'd violate your word again… end up murdering them. Like your French-men, hmm?"

Mlavic put his fists on his hips, glared at the ground between them and made idle scuffing motions with his brand-spanking-new boots for a moment or two.

"*Da.* Kill French," he confessed. "Be too much trouble, watch… feed. Die quick, and feed to sharks," he admitted, waving a hand out toward the west and the open sea. "See Dragan take Venetian ship, speak new prisoner… news is getting out, *da*? I keep ship. I keep all cargo."

"Then if you'll bring the prisoners down, I'll send to my ship for boats, and…" Lewrie nodded in agreement, feeling a sudden rush of almost blissful relief. He could hear Howse and Kolodzcy sighing.

"No," Mlavic said, almost pouting. "Keep prisoner, too. Not *all* Venetian. In ship are Muslims, go Ragusa, Cattaro, Durazzo. In ship are Montenegran, Albanian… *Bosnian!*" he spat, as if being a Slavic coastal Muslim were the ultimate scum, as bad as Hindoo "untouchables." He glared at Lewrie, a gay smile beginning to lift his mouth, a crafty crinkle round his beady, close-set pig-eyes. "Enemies. Have still to play… *games.*" Dragan Mlavic tittered.

"Sir, I must protest!" Lewrie barked. "How could innocent women and children be your enemies? How dare you insinuate you'd—"

"Child grow up… kill and torture Serbs. Woman have enemy child, grow up… murder Serbs. Enemy men *have* murder Serbs. Serbs see father, mother… whole family, torture and kill. *Make* good Serb

Orthodox, Catholic... *Mus-lim! Then* kill. In ship are Macedonian, in ship are Greeks! Same as Turk, same as Byzantium who let Turk armies in Serbia. No... I keep. We play games."

"Jesus bloody *Christ*..." Lewrie gasped, his mouth agape, never so appalled, so laid all-aback, his entire life! His innards and his spine went icy as he realised that Mlavic meant to torture, rape, then slay his prisoners. Even icier, he felt – nigh to shivering in fear – as he realised that Mlavic had murdered the French prisoners so they'd not be able to pass the word that he'd taken a Venetian ship; nor tell one word about the massacre he'd planned, soon as he'd captured her!

And he, Mr. Howse, and Leutnant Kolodzcy were now witnesses, too!

He plan t'murder us, too? Alan reeled, searching for a way out. Those prisoners ain't no friends o' *mine*, so would he let us go, 'fore his goddamn *games* begin? No, damme, I can't just...!

"Captain Mlavic..." Lewrie said, firm as he could, after thinking quickly, gazing into those agate-hard eyes, that upper-handed leer. "Again I protest! No *civilised* man would do such a thing, even *dream* of doing such a thing. Give me the women and children, at least. You *can't* hurt women and children, man... it just ain't *done*! Let me have them, and we'll go. Then you can hold whatever sort o' bloody *games* you wish. And be damned to you, you ugly, black-hearted bastard!"

"You stay," Mlavic pronounced, beginning to beam quite gladly.

"Be damned if I *will*, sir!"

"You stay," Mlavic insisted. "You watch. *I* say you stay... *I* say you go. Dragan Mlavic captain here. I say you stay, now."

"Going to make us, are you? With a sloop o' war not one cable off the beach?" Lewrie sneered. "Eat shit, an' die!"

Mlavic did the very worst thing then – he began to chuckle, then to laugh out loud, chilling them all to their bones. He put two fingers in his mouth and gave a shrill whistle. Instantly there were six of his pirates on them, coming from round the rear of the hut, to pinion their arms, strip them of swords and pat them down for knives or pocket-pistols.

"You damn fool!" Lewrie raged, thrashing against the grasp of two strong men. "Lay hands on a British officer, sir? Don't you know my First Lieutenant will get to wond'rin' what's keeping me? Hears or sees what you're doing... why, he'll blow your filthy arse to Hell!"

Mlavic laughed aloud again, then gave a second whistle.

"Come wrong time, British," he said with a sneer, putting his face within inches of Lewrie's as he was wrestled to his knees before Mlavic. "Have go safe, but you come camp, ask too much question. You go safe? Die, tonight? Dragan Mlavic say, hah! You stay, watch games. Ratko plan holy thing, now I do holy thing... get men *hot* to war on enemy. What your ship do, I hold you, doctor, girlie-man, long as want? Him, too."

Three sailors came lumbering into the firelight, dragging their burden, which kicked, yelped and twisted – Midshipman Spendlove!

"Sorry, sir... barely got into the water 'fore...!"

Oh, shit, we're in the quag now! Alan shuddered, feeling those few bites of food, or sips of wine, turn to scalding acid, threatening to come up and sear his throat. He really means t' *scrag* us!

Chapter 4

The first victim was bound to a log. A burning log.

He was an older man, blond-haired and blond-bearded, a Slav who cried out and protested as he was forced to eat pork, stripped so he could be smeared on his face and chest – then chained atop a log as long as he was, that had been rolled away from a cook-fire. What agony he suffered they could barely hear above the jeers and taunts of Mlavic's pirates. He was a *Muslim* Slav, though, one who'd surely killed Serbs when young and fit, so... he had to die, slowly.

His wife was in her middle years, too, a properly plump matron with a round face and a pale complexion, with fair, greying hair under her Turk-style head covering. She was forced to watch her husband burn, before they made him watch her suffer. They stripped her, found her too round and withered to rape in a chorus of catcalls and boos, so she was slit open, belly and womb, and filled with searing-hot hearthstones.

The youngest son, who'd traveled with them to safe Venetian Spalato, on a safe Venetian ship, was about twelve. The pirates sliced his genitals off, then took him by wrists and ankles and heave-hoed him in the air – once, twice and thrice – and caught him on the points of a dozen swords.

Lewrie was forced to watch, seated like visiting royalty on one of the logs near the central fire – with Dragan Mlavic his regal host to his right – defenceless and closely watched by two Serbs at his back.

Mister Howse was already on his knees, spewing and weeping, but straddled by an angel-faced teenage pirate who kept pulling his head up so he must watch their entertainment through raging, howling tears.

Leutnant Kolodzcy sat erect, his nostrils pinched and his eyes slit, but giving no sign that this spectacle affected him. Spendlove was to his left, clutching his stomach, a hand to his mouth, his every breath a rasping sob. "Albanians," Kolodzcy whispered as the next victims were led in, knowing them by their desperate pleas.

Husband and wife, both young this time… a dark-haired son in his sixth or seventh year, a nursing infant in the woman's arms. Not for long, though. Pleas and prayers turned to shrieks as they tore the babe away, dashed its brains out on a rock, eviscerated it and discarded it in the leaping flames of the main fire, raising a great howl of victory… of revenge, which drowned its mother's disbelieving wail. She *was* worth raping, so they took her, a half dozen of them, in front of husband and surviving son.

"Have Serb baby now, *da*?" Mlavic chortled, nudging Lewrie once more like a racetrack tout. "Keep to see… take baby, raise a Serb. Alive that long, then…" He shrugged. "Boy baby. Greet him… 'Hail, little avenger of *Kossovo*,' ahaha! Grow up, be Serb warrior."

"You're a dead man, Mlavic," Lewrie hissed, turning his head to glare at his merry host. "Swear t'Christ, you're a dead man!" He would have said more, but a guard behind him laid hold of his head to turn it back to the "games." "*All* our ships will hunt you down…"

The young Albanian lad leaped on the first Serb to rise from his rape, as he was retying his trousers. A full dozen infuriated pirates sprang up to rescue their comrade – and beat or slice the boy to bloody offal, while the brutal rape went on and on, another dozen queuing up for their turn on her.

The father – howling and out of his mind with grief – was stripped of his trousers, shoved facedown and spread-eagled. A man with a wood-chopping axe stepped forward, prancing round his victim to the catcalls and approving whistles of the crowd. Standing on the husband's pinioned shoulders, he raised his axe, teased the crowd with a practice swing or two – he knew what played well with this audience – and hacked the heavy axe-head into the crack of the man's buttocks, splitting him open as high as his waist. They pegged him down after that – so he could bleed, and scream… and beg for death as a mercy.

But there would be no mercy. They let him lie, finding it very funny, and moved on to other amusements. There were shouts from the discontented, so Mlavic called an order, and more women were dragged into the fire circle. Two of them in the front were flung to the dirt, their dresses thrown up, and assaulted right off, so the men in line didn't have so long to wait on the gibbering-mad Albanian woman.

"Dhey choose," Kolodzcy whispered from the side of his mouth, just loud enough to hear. "Cull de old, ugly… for murder. Odders,

342

Mlavic says to auction off, vatch–against–vatch, gunners, sail–tenders…
mates. Or indiwiduals, heff dhey enough plunder. Dhose vill liff a few
hours more."

"I'll kill the sonofabitch!" Lewrie grated, though his vow came out
more a strangled sob. "If it's the last thing I do, swear t' *God* I will.
Never *seen* such a… never *dreamed* people could…"

"Ve match high cards, sir," Kolozcy muttered, his cheeks aflame in
a face gone a pasty, deathly white. "Vinner hess pleasure."

"Do we get near cards again…" Lewrie whispered bleakly. By this
point, he doubted Mlavic wished a single living witness. Was he saving
them for last? Could he be *that* stupid, to think that sometime before
midnight Knolles *wouldn't* send a boat ashore to find out what was
keeping them? Was Mlavic hoping for that, so he'd have even more
hostages to bargain his way out with? Andrews, Midshipman Hyde,
eight or nine hands off the cutter, too? Knolles might waver, once. But
if Mlavic threatened to keep his prisoners even *longer*, sail away, still
holding them… didn't he know that Knolles would inform Charlton,
and the squadron would hunt them down and destroy them?

Or was he *capable* of thinking that far ahead; thinking at all?

"Drink, Captain!" Mlavic hooted. "Be too pale! Brandy bring
colour to cheeks, ahahah. Drink… Dragan order! Good show? Like
my games? You live, you tell world Serbs fight holy fight. Drink. Or
Mirko cut you… a little," he wheedled, looking back at a guard.

One of the silver chalices was shoved into his nerveless hand, some
brandy sloshed into it, over it, onto his breeches. He gagged as he
looked into it, feeling the keen razor's edge of a knife beside his throat;
seeing his wavering reflection so filled with fear; seeing for the first
time how craven and helpless he looked, no matter his fight to mask
it.

And, admitting to himself for the first time that he was about to
completely unman himself, should they turn their attentions to *him*;
sure he'd scream, grovel, plead, curse God then beseech Him. Offer up
wife, children, good friends, anybody but himself for a minute more…

"Drink, Captain. Is good for you." Mlavic snickered.

"To your death, Mlavic," he said, though turning to bestow on that
hulking hirsute brute a glare that could have slain all by itself. "To your
long, slow, agonising death… soon," he hissed; then drank.

God! he prayed. Don't hear much from me, do Ya? Just help me kill
him, let me stick a knife in the bastard and know I've sent him t'Hell,

343

that's all I ask. Ev'ry last mother-son of 'em! That's holy, ain't it? He means t'kill me first, though... can Ya help me go like a gentleman? Spit in their faces? *Not* shit my breeches?

He took another sip. It *seemed* to calm his shudders. He took a third, then a deep, quaking breath; found the where-withal not to cry out or flinch when Mlavic clapped a huge paw on his shoulder, laughing at him and thinking him thoroughly cowed.

"Good, good!" Mlavic cruelly teased. "Make new man. We sell women now. You want buy woman, ahaha? We sell you. But cost much guineas!"

"Fuck you," Lewrie said with a snarl, through a taut, deadly grin. "Go fuck yourself... with bloody *bells* on!"

Kolodzcy coached from the far side, actually blushing!

"Ah, aye... the Serb way, thankee," Lewrie jeered, turning to Mlavic once more. "Fuck your mother. Or did the *monkeys* wear her out?"

"Brandy good for you, have much courage," Mlavic cooed, not the slightest bit insulted. "You may die *well*! 'Blood-ey bells on,' hah. I like!" So did Mirko and the other guards, once he'd passed it on.

"Doing it again, sir. Rowing people, when you shouldn't. Like that time on the beach at Toulon?" Spendlove warned.

"Can't help it, Mister Spendlove," Alan confessed. "When it's all I have left, I *like* insulting people."

Mlavic got to his feet and paced before the clutch of terrified women, ogling them. He snatched out a wee young lass, all black hair and wide eyes, not over fifteen, dragging her by the wrist back to the logs and pawing her. The pirates cheered his choice, and then a mate began to work the crowd, encouraging them to bid on the first girl to be hauled out, stripped down to her chemise and pinioned to display her charms. Most of the prisoners were poor coastal folk, attired in local garb like Turks, or in something similar to what the girls at Corfu had worn. The old, the ill-favoured and the unpleasing the pirates just booed down and murdered, their throats cut, and left to bleed to death, expiring with blood-sobs and gurgling screams as they sank to the earth.

"Savink de European ladies for lasd," Kolodzcy spat, turning his head to see Mlavic peeling the peasant blouse off his choice, putting a rough hand under her skirts. She sat numb, too scared to wail, on

Mlavic's lap, tears coursing down her cheeks, hiccoughing in fear. "For de richer mates vit bigger share in prize."

Lewrie looked at the poor girl, who was pleading with her eyes as Mlavic brusquely toyed with her small breasts, forcing her to take a deep draught of brandy, then wrenching her lips to his. Lewrie could do nothing to aid her, not with a knife at his back.

He turned to look at the other prisoners instead. One was *waving*? One hand cautiously *waving*, all but snapping her fingers to get their attention? And surreptitiously rising a-tiptoe, looking desperate.

She wore all black as if in mourning, a plain, unadorned gown of conservative style, not too flounced out bell-shaped by underskirting. She'd worn a Venetian *bauto*, but had lowered it to her shoulders so it draped long and low. To hide...! Lewrie gasped.

Pressed into her skirts and half smothered, almost fully draped by the *bauto*, was a child, a boy who couldn't be more than four or five, Alan guessed. A boy breeched, stockinged and shod like his own sons!

She waved once more, then cupped her hand as if to draw him to her, fanning at herself insistently, daring to work from the rear of the huddling, wailing pack of women to the left-front, where she'd be in greater danger of being chosen for auction next. Her brown eyes flared open in misery, in pleading, almost looking like she curtsied for a moment before rising, a silent leaping plea for aid.

Lewrie mimed the guards at his back, lifting his hands in helplessness. Frustrated, she dared shout something at him, in a language he didn't understand, before the guard nearest to her shoved her back in line.

"What'd she say, Kolodzcy?" he demanded, never taking his eyes off her. Now the guard and the bidding pirates noticed her, her long, fine chestnut-roan hair and almond-shaped eyes...!

"Demotic Greek... island accent," Kolodzcy remarked, infuriatingly calmly. "She ist from Zante, in die Ionians, dhere-fore Venetian. She begs for help. Poor lady." He sighed, stone-faced.

"God *dammit*!" Lewrie groaned, slamming a fist onto his knee to vent his powerlessness. "You leave that'un alone, ya bastard!" Alan shouted at the guard, who was just about to fondle her, draw back that *bauto* to see her figure... and expose her child! He got to his feet; tried to, before Mirko laid a hand on his shoulder to drag him back.

"English, my *God*!" the woman cried, her mouth agape. "Royal *Navy*? My *husband* was English... Bristol! I am Theoni Kavaras Connor. Royal Navy... for God's sake – *help* me!"

Chapter 5

"Mlavic, you black-hearted sonofabitch!" Lewrie snarled at him, turning to face him and grabbing his arm. "She's English. *British*, do ya hear? Maybe the Venetians're too puny to hunt you down for murderin' and rapin' their people, but you can wager yer last penny England won't wring their hands and let you get away scot-free. There'll be a bloody *fleet* out for you, same as they did for Bligh's mutineers."

"Is Greek," Mlavic dismissed, leaving off gnawing on his girl's teats. "I hear Greek."

"You can hear English, too, you simpleton, do you get the *dung* out yer ears!" Lewrie railed, daring to rise off the log. This time, when Mirko tried to drag him down, he turned, glared at him, and jabbed a warning finger at him. "*Who* was your husband, Mistress Connor?" he shouted over his shoulder to her. "Tell this fool plain."

"Patrick Connor, of Bristol!" she shot back. "He and his father were in the currant trade, with the English House on Zante. We were married six years ago, when his father Sean retired to England."

"Husband dead, she still Greek," Mlavic quibbled, though with the beginnings of a worried look on his face. "Greeks dirty people."

"Makes no *matter*, fool," Lewrie thundered. "Wife of a British subject *becomes* British. You may be lawless, but that's king's law."

Mlavic dumped his girl to the ground, tossing her away like he might a fruit-rind as he rose. He snarled a question to Mrs. Connor in Demotic Greek. Lewrie saw her tremble, look away furtively, licking her lips before she answered.

"Catholic," Kolodzcy groaned, despairing. "Vas married in husbant's faith. Deat'-sentence."

Connor, aye, Lewrie winced, *Patrick* Connor, surely Irish in the beginning. Which does Mlavic hate worse, Greek Orthodox or Catholic?

346

"Bad as Croat... Catholic, *pooh!*" Mlavic spat. He strode across to take a closer look at her, while his terrified girl tried to flee. She didn't get far; two of the guards snagged her and carried her kicking and wailing into the darkness beyond the firelight.

Mistress Connor shivered as Mlavic circled her slowly, stood her ground and determined to play-up brave, though her mouth and chin worked in sudden fear or loathing. He leaned close to blow in her ear, making her shy away, stroked back her hair to admire her neck, taunting her with a crooning sing-song in Serbo-Croat.

"What's he sayin'?" Lewrie rasped, getting frantic.

"...rich man's whore," Kolodzcy mercilessly supplied. "A Greek whore who leafs de Orthodox Church to wed rich, turn stinkink Catholic. Rich, soft-skinned, faithless traitor whore. Ach, *nein! Scheisse!*"

Mlavic seized her right wrist to drag her away, back to his seat on the logs, his little black-haired Bosnian victim quite forgotten in the light of this finer choice, sure he was going to take vengeance on a three-in-one. But he drew back the *bauto* to discover the child!

He roared with surprise and sudden delight, grabbing the young lad by the scruff of the neck and parting mother and son, though she screamed and tore at him, hauling the boy aloft to shake before his pirates like a filthy rag. And laughing fit to bust!

"Hands off, damn you!" Lewrie barked, so loud he stilled that rabble's heathen howls for a moment. "You put that *English* boy down... get your filthy hands off an *English* lady!"

"You make me? Or *what* you do, *pooh!* I have power, you no. I take her." Mlavic spat. "Be *fucking* English... *lady*, ahahaha!"

Do something! she mutely pleaded.

Like *what*? Alan wondered.

"They're for sale, ain't they, Mlavic?" he shouted of a sudden, feeling something nigh to inspiration. "She's for sale? Her, *and* her boy? That's what you dragged these women down for, wasn't it? Offer 'em up for a good knock-down price? Well, I'll buy 'em. Didn't you offer to let me bid on a woman a little while ago?"

"*Da*," Mlavic allowed cagily. "*Other* woman. This, *I* keep."

"Selfish bastard!" Lewrie cried. "Kolodzcy, help me here, put it to 'em. Leader gets first choice free, hey? What're the rules of the house after that, though? Mlavic gets first pick, then they're *all* up for grabs?

He's *had* his first pick. Now he should bid, same as everybody else. Else he's a selfish bastard… a cheap, *greedy* bastard!"

"Oh, shit!" Spendlove could be heard to mutter, burying his face in his hands. "God, sir, please don't… he's rowed *enough*!"

And *please* let 'em be so drunk by now, they think I make sense! Alan silently pled; seen sailors do "Oo shall 'ave this'un, then?" I have, every time a ship's out o' Discipline an' the whores come aboard. Sailors… even this lot… surely have a fair streak; can't stand for officers t'put it over on 'em. Nice little show, ya bastards, a spirited auction? String it out long enough, Knolles wakes his *sorry* arse up and comes t'save us…?

"Dhey fint it… *just*, sir!" Kolodzcy marveled. "Vish to see us confounted. Bud vish to see Mlavic confounted, too. He does nod heff *military* control ofer dhem. He may not like it, bud he musd go along."

There was a change in mood round the central fire and its horrid scene of slaughter now, Lewrie sensed. The boos and catcalls sounded less threatening, more like good-natured taunting, which forced Mlavic to smile, nod and placate them with raised hands in allowance.

Two guards off rapin' that poor girl, Lewrie noted; several women auctioned off to small groups, and they're busy, too. Could we? He wondered, a rising hope filling him. Gull 'em peaceable, then take *us* a hostage'r two… Mlavic…? and get down to the beach? There's your biter bit, by God!

"How much do you have on you?" Lewrie whispered, rifling into his purse, where he found but £30 and change. "Mister Howse? Mister Spendlove? Quick sums, then hand your purses over."

"Surely, sir, you'd not countenance white slavery, allow these cutthroats the slightest bit of credulity?" Howse huffed, getting his indignant demeanour back. "Mean t'say, English or no…!"

"Do you not, sir, and Mlavic wins, *I'll* slit yer throat first chance I get and blame it on them!" Lewrie hissed. Howse tossed over a fullish purse, and slumped down into another miserable sulk. Lewrie did a quick addition; not near enough! Spendlove had a miserly eighteen shillings and some pence. Kolodzcy, however, offered up an embroidered poke simply stiff with "chink."

"De equivalend ohf your seventy pounds, sir," Kolodzcy said.

"Listen, then… we get into the spirit of things, they'll drop their guard, we can stand and move about a few feet," Lewrie schemed in a harsh mutter as they put their heads together. "If it looks like we've lost, and Knolles *still* hasn't come, then we take what chance we may, and grab Mlavic and a few others, get some weapons and the woman, and head for the beach. Hear me? It may be our only chance. The men at your backs are thinned, might stay thinned! Others are off havin' themselves a bare-belly romp, or they're three sheets to the wind. If a chance comes… I'll give you sign."

He looked at their glum, frightened faces, then turned away for the final addition. He'd garnered nearly £130 and change. Best start low, he thought… string it out as long as he could.

"Right, then… you miserable excuse for a man," Lewrie shouted with an avid smile. "I'll bid three guineas."

"*Five* guinea!" Mlavic grinned back, just as evilly, still with a firm grip on both woman and child.

"The management instructs you, sir… kindly unhand the merchandise 'til the last bid's in!" Lewrie cajoled, elbowing Leutnant Kolodzcy to say that to all observers. The pirates found that hugely amusing.

"*Six* guineas… you foul lump of shit!"

"Ten!" Mlavic countered, but letting them go and stepping off.

"*Eleven*… you ditch-dropped whelp of a Turk hedge-whore."

–

"Bosun Mister Cony… SAH!" the Marine sentry right-aft by the passageway to the gun-room cried, stamping his boots and musket-butt.

"Enter," Knolles said, sopping up the last gravy on his plate with a crust of fresh-baked bread and motioning for their steward – Sprinkle – to have away his plate, the water-glasses and the tablecloth. With Mr. Howse away, the gun-room had fed more than well this evening, with fewer to share a whole leg of roast pork. Mister Buchanon, Mister Giles and Midshipman Mister Hyde completed the table, looking sated but eager for the sweet biscuit, the last of the Venetian-bought confections and the port.

"Beggin' yer pardon, sir, but th' wind's shiftin'," Cony told them hat-in-hand. "An' that prize-ship's but 'er best bower out. No kedge'r stream-anchor t'check 'er swingin'. 'Er stern's comin' round towards our bows, an' 'er 'arbour-watch'z drunker'n Davy's Sow, sir. Can't raise a 'hollo' from 'em, Serb *or* English."

"Damn sloppy folk, pirates," Buchanon grumbled. "Ha! Did a Bora take her, she could just as well swing aground onshore."

"Very well, Mister Cony, we'll be up directly," Lieutenant Knolles sighed, savouring a last sip of wine before rising. "Belay the port and biscuit, Sprinkle. Might summon a boat-crew to row over, Bosun. Take in on her anchor rode, if her watch is blind-drunk, I s'pose."

"Aye aye, sir," Cony replied, backing out and loping easy for the companionway ladder to the weather decks.

–

Once on the quarterdeck, Knolles eyed the captured ship. Sure enough, she was swinging to stream alee of the wind, which had come more Sou'westerly. *Jester* was anchored fore-and-aft from first bower and kedge, with springs on the cables to heave her round, should some enemy ship loom out of the night from the east; a prudent caution.

"Hasn't dragged, has she, Mister Tucker?" He enquired of the Quartermaster's Mate.

"Don' think so, sir... swingin', though. Looked t'have 'er at middlin' 'stays.' Forty foot o' water, yonder, so she couldn't have let out more'n five-to-one scope – say, a hun'r'd eighty t'two hun'r'd foot o' rode, sir?"

"'At'd be cuttin' it damn fine, sir," Buchanon groused, with a thumb lifted to measure her. "I think she'll come aboard us... into th' bowsprit do we not look sharp."

"Right, then!" Knolles snapped. "Mister Cony, cutter away to the prize-ship! Boat's crew, plus six more hands for muscle on their capstan, should her watch be as drunk as you suspect. Keep ours sober, hear me?"

"Aye, sir!" Cony shouted back, having mustered a boat-crew upon the gangway already, and snagging the first available hands of the duty-watch he could lay hands on.

"Might even have to row a kedge out for 'em, too!" Lieutenant Knolles added, seeing them scramble over the side. "Idle bastards," he murmured under his breath.

"Havin' 'emselves a rare ol' time, aren't they, sir?" Buchanon pointed to the leaping flames ashore, the faint shouts, the yells of merrymaking. "Wonder what 'ey fed th' cap'um an' 'em?"

"Mister Sadler?" Knolles called for the Bosun's Mate. "Do you pipe 'All Hands.' We may have to fend that old bitch off, should she come close enough. Muster forrud. Spare spars and rig fenders!"

"Aye, sir!"

They went forward along the starboard gangway themselves, as the off-duty crew boiled up on deck, up as far as the cat-head, which poised the second heavy bower horizontally. That three-master now lay aslant the starboard bows, looking uncomfortably close and tall, at a forty-five-degree angle, just as Cony's working-party reached her main-chain platform. And there was still no response from her, no matter how they shouted from the cutter, or *Jester's* forecastle.

"Drunks'z lords, sir," Buchanon sighed. "Dear God!"

"She'll collide?" Knolles quailed, assuming that the Sailing Master had worked out the angles in his head already and was certain the two ships would entangle. And pleading with God why such a thing had to happen on *his* watch, with the captain away and him in temporary command!

"Her transom-board, sir!" Buchanon gasped, pointing to the ornately carved, gilded nameplate which was flickering with faint light as her stern swung enough to bare it to them. Below her master's windows and stern-walk, above her ward-room's windows, she bore a name: *Nostra Signora di Santa Maria Delle Salute*, amid wee angels and cherubs.

"By God, Mister Knolles!" Buchanon gasped. "'At's a Venetian cathedral's name. Lay ya, sir... 'ere's somethin' queer 'bout 'is!"

"A Venetian ship, sir?" Knolles gawped. "Damme, they'd dare to take a Venetian?" He cast a wild stare shoreward. The crudely erected huts teemed with movement, the shadows of campfire flames wavered and flagged in the trees, upon the rocks. Crude shouts could be heard and some laughter, now the wind had shifted to fetch sound seaward. There were no answers, though, no...! Knolles cupped his hands and bellowed over to the ship, which now looked immense, her tall poop towering over *Jester's* bows. "Ahoy! Cony! Hoy, the ship!"

There came another sound, a most welcome sound from the capstan, as Navy hands breasted to the bars and began to haul taut on the anchor cable, harsh clackings of pawl-bypawl progress.

"Heavin' 'er shorter, sir!" Cony yelled back, atop the poop and barely sixty feet off by then. "These pirates, sir... nary a *one* of 'em on 'is feet! Think we'll keep her off, sir!"

Bosun's Mate Sadler and a quarter of the crew were ready with a selection of spars thrust out to hold her off, should Cony fail, with rope mats and hurriedly scavenged heavy-weather royals and t'gallants up from the sail-room to hang like spongy bags of laundry overside as protection.

"Cony… is… she… Venetian?" Knolles queried.

"'Ang on, sir, lemme 'ave a squint!" He dropped from sight, to magically appear in her stern-windows a minute later, then came out on her captain's stern-gallery waving a sheaf of papers. "Aye, sir, that she *be*! Venetian, right-enough! Christ A'mighty, sir!"

"Put her people in irons, Cony! Mister Hyde!" Knolles shouted.

"*Here*, sir," Hyde said, right by his coattails; he hadn't needed to shout.

"Gig and launch, sir, at once. Sergeant Bootheby? We're going to board the brig. If they make a fight of it, then slaughter the bastards." Knolles cast another glance ashore, wondering if sound would carry that far, against the wind. "Pass the word. Beat to Quarters… no drums, no noise. Mister Crewe?"

"Aye, sir," the Master Gunner barked from the darkness.

"Man the starboard battery, best you're able, 'til we've secured the brig. I'm mustering a landing-party, so you'll be short-handed."

"We'll cope, sir, never ya fear!" Crewe assured him.

Though it would never do for a gentleman, a Sea Officer, to trot when he could stroll or amble proudly, Lieutenant Knolles tore aft, desiring a telescope that instant. He ripped one of the night-glasses from a rack by the binnacle and extended it, trying to focus it, trying to interpret its upside-down-backwards image. Pirates all 'round the central fires; swaying-drunk, or firelit-swaying? Only a cable to shore, perhaps no more than a hundred yards beyond that to the huts, but… naked bodies… *naked* women, by God. Tits, by God! he gasped; he was sure he saw tits! And held against their will, he could barely make out; captain'd not hold with force. He couldn't see faces or discover identities that far off, had no way to discern uniforms, either. But there was something olid and evil going on ashore, he was dead certain of it, like some pagan Hell, something satanic and heathen done beneath blood-soaked oaks, like tales of witches' covens.

"Women and… *children*?" he softly exclaimed. "My oath!"

How could he employ the guns, if women and children were in the line of fire? he shuddered. And how could he save his captain?

"Ninety-five guineas, you pus-gut," Lewrie despaired, putting a brave face on it, though, as Mlavic smirked at him, blowing a premonitory kiss towards Mrs. Connor. He was coming close to his limit; slow as he'd drawn it out, he couldn't continue this farce much longer. Mlavic looked tired of the game, too. In the beginning, he'd played up right-mocking, taking pleasure from his crew's reactions, and the hopes and fears that played teeter-totter on Mrs. Connor's countenance. Lewrie was beginning to run low on insults, too.

"Hun'red!" Mlavic roared, mopping his face with a rough hand. "Hun'red guinea!" He leered at her, thrust his hips and grimaced.

"And ten," Lewrie retorted. "One hundred and *ten*, you low-bred Barbary *ape*!"

"Hun'red *fifty*!" Mlavic bristled, finally getting tired of Lewrie's insults. A few more, Lewrie speculated, and Mlavic would cry off the game, stick his butcher-knife in his ribs, take the woman, and declare himself the winner.

"*Two* hundred," Lewrie drawled, affecting to study his fingernails. Perversely, the Serbs whistled and catcalled, cheering with a muttering like the House of Commons on a testy day. Mlavic paused, as one hand went to his purse by its own volition, as if he had to assure himself he had that much. That drew more cheers, of the mocking sort, which made the pirate chieftain whirl about, glowering them to silence.

Aye, had enough o' the game, Lewrie bitterly told himself; and enough o' bein' hooted by his own side, too! It's all up.

"*Five* hun'red, British boy-fucker!" he spat, a triumphant grin on his face. "Show me! Show guinea, now!"

"*Six* hundred," Lewrie countered, stepping forward and hefting his heavy wash-leather purse, jouncing it like a juggler's ball. "All two-guinea coins, Venetian *ducats*, Austrian *guilders*..." Mirko the guard didn't follow, and Kolodzcy, Howse and Spendlove had been allowed on their feet long since to root for him bid-by-bid. Far enough away from their captors, he wondered? This *ain't* goin' t'work, but...!

Lewrie turned, a mocking, jeering smile on his phyz, one brow raised in celebration, to face them. He winked and nodded, slow and significant, jutting his chin up slantwise towards the nearest armed men. Spendlove went pasty-pale, and Howse began to tremble. From Leutnant Kolodzcy there was a fatalistic bow of his head, and a quirky grin.

"Bid was six hundred guineas to you, Mlavic," Lewrie taunted, stepping within a long arm's reach. "Put up or fold."

"Fun with me, hah? Fun with Dragan, hah?" Mlavic roared, and fumbled for his heavy money-bag. He ripped it open and spilled money on the ground in a glittering golden shower. "One *t'ousand* guinea, I say! You no got that much, you...!"

Lewrie tensed, ready to spring, planning to go for one of those pistols first, then for Mrs. Connor. Shoot Mlavic in the belly, then take his scimitar or his butcher-knife? Mlavic half turned, though, of a sudden, raising his arms to jeer and show his empty purse to his men, who began that hackle-raising wolf howling song.

BOOOMMM! though. The harsh barking of a 9-pounder! The *Rwarkk!* of rivened timbers by the beach. Mlavic turned to face it, goggling at the sight of one of his forty-footer boats in midleap after being struck by round-shot and grape in a froth of spray and splintered wood, blown clean from the water!

His back was to Lewrie. In that split second before he could turn, Alan dove forward, stung into sudden motion without thought. He got hold of both pistols by the butts and leaped free, levering back their dog's-jaws with his wrists. "To me!" he howled, backpedaling towards where he thought Mrs. Connor had been. He collided with her, as she was of the same mind and had rushed to him, almost knocking them both off their feet. He had a quick glance to see Howse cowering away, Kolodzcy smashing a handy bottle over a guard's head and seizing his sword arm and wrist. Spendlove was kicking the angelic-looking tormentor in his "nutmegs" and lifting his knee in a rough-and-tumble "Dutch Kiss," a trick he'd obviously learned on the lower decks from the hands.

And BOOOMMM! again, and the second boat was leaping skyward.

"Stay at my back, don't let go of me or the boy!" Alan warned Mrs. Connor as he turned to face Mlavic. His sword was drawn, and he was crouching to fight! Lewrie leveled a pistol at his heart and began backing away towards that hut. Mlavic sneered at the threat, pacing forward slowly, just out of sword-reach.

"No loaded, British," Mlavic sing-songed.

"We'll find out, then, won't we?" Lewrie grinned back, praying he was lying. "Care to lay a guinea on it? What's your bid now, hey?"

At Mlavic's beck, a pirate rushed from the right, sword back for a head-lopping slash, and Lewrie aimed, pulled the trigger as the child and Mrs. Connor screamed. It fired! And the man pitched over backwards!

"One!" Mlavic laughed. "Have one left."

BOOMM! BOOMM! BOOMM! Sweet music, those three more shots from *Jester*'s 9-pounders, this time loaded with grapeshot and canister, and fired a tad high, Lewrie took time to note. The trees and bushes on the desiccated island thrashed with the impact of a thousand musket balls or plum-size shot, a bit over the height of a man. But they drove nearly everyone to their faces or knees – Mlavic, too!

"Run!" Lewrie cried, dropping the empty pistol and grasping Mrs. Connor by the hand in the short moment of grace that partial broadside had bought them. He made it to Kolodzcy and clubbed down one of the guards from behind, freeing the Austrian to pick up a sword and that man's pair of pistols. A moment more and they were with Spendlove, who was hewing about with a cutlass, keeping two at bay. A quick shot and one was down with a bullet in his kidneys, and their swords were clashing. Spendlove, freed, turned his attention to the other and began the cutlass drill… left foot stamp and down-left slash, right foot stamp and back-slash right, balance step and recover. He beat the Serbian's scimitar aside and round-housed a back-slash that laid the man open.

"The hut!" Lewrie shouted, stooping to retrieve a Turk-style sword. "Out of the line of fire… go!"

BOOMM! BOOMM! BOOMM! This time, aimed lower, and men who had leaped back to their feet were swept away in a howling, shrieking horror. Not just pirates, unfortunately, but some of their victims as well, who'd been dashing about witless. Mlavic had dropped once more to his belly, barely ten paces behind. He was up in a flash, bellowing orders and trying to muster his chaotic, half-drunk men into a fighting force. They came from the woods or huts where they'd been sporting, down from the stockade, running for stands of muskets, then drew swords and began to form a rough protective line above the beach.

This kept Mlavic too busy to deal with Lewrie, for a moment. They dashed for the hut, Alan dragging the woman almost off her feet in his haste, now they had another shot-bought moment of grace. A pistol lit off and Lewrie turned to see another pirate spin about and drop, just by the hut's side. Kolodzcy growled something in German and cocked his other pistol. And there went the little fifteen-year-old girl Mlavic had his eye on at first, stark-naked and screaming up the hill for the prison.

Howse leaped to his feet, almost under Lewrie's, to run whining ahead of them, still weaponless. Spendlove had armed himself with two more pistols by then, and shoved one at Howse, who took it in passing, still intent on some dubious safety. "Can't find more pistols, sir," Spendlove confessed as Lewrie reached him.

"Three shots, then," Lewrie noted, looking to the beach for a sign of a landing-party. Could they hide somewhere? But where would be safe? And where the hell was Knolles? Surely...!

"Four... I reload dhese," Kolodzcy panted. "Ged our swords, I beg you, sir. Gif me your pistol. Herr Spentluff unt I, ve vill hold dhem off."

Lewrie ducked into the hut, tearing away the flimsy sail-cloth door, and scrounged about for weapons, leaving Mrs. Connor and her boy shivering outside, the boy crying incessantly. He found his sword and Mr. Spendlove's prided dirk, the elegantly ornate small-sword Kolodzcy wore. But no more firearms.

"Down to the beach, ma'am," he urged as he came out. "Take the boy and go, now, while there's time. Our landing-party—"

"If the pirates are between here and there...?" she whinnied in a breathless pant, half out of her wits with terror, but fighting hard to master herself. "We all should go?"

"Might as well, we've *ruined* supper!" Lewrie cracked, happy to have his hanger once more in his hand. He looked at her, and was most surprised to see her *smiling*! She still shivered with fright, but she was smiling, tittering on the verge of semi-hysterical humour, like a doomed man who'd rather *not* weep, thankee.

And noticed for the first time, by the amber light of Mlavic's campfire, what a *stunningly* handsome woman she was! So exotically high-cheeked, with a squarish jaw that tapered to a pert chin and a wide, full-lipped mouth. Large amber eyes aslant like almonds, heavy-lashed and browed...! Her classically sculpted little nose...!

Damme! he goggled. Splendid poonts, *too*! 'Bout t'be knackered or no, and I'm gone calf-eyed over—

"Whatever shall we do *now*, sir?" Mr. Howse interrupted, coming from God knew where, which apparently he hadn't deemed completely safe. Lewrie had the thought he could hear that worthy's teeth knocking together. But the man had a *pistol*!

"Mr. Howse, make yourself useful. See Mrs. Connor and the lad down toward the beach. Take that harem pig-sticker yonder and gimme your pistol." Howse stooped for a massive chopper of a blade, handed the pistol to Lewrie – who winced as the fool offered it half-cocked and barrel-first, with a hellish-shaky finger still on the trigger!

Thank God for small miracles, Alan thought wildly; my own side hasn't gut-shot me! Yet, he amended.

"We'll be close behind you, fending 'em off. Now go, sir!"

He turned to face the pirate camp, which was sorting itself out at last, with Mlavic the loudest and fiercest, about thirty yards off. And felt a light tap on the back of his coat collar. He turned...

"Patrick always said" – she shuddered, looking achingly lovely for someone who could still get chopped – "Have a 'touch for luck.' Touch a sailor's collar. *Thank* you!" She smiled once more.

"Hope it works, Mistress Connor... for somebody." He grinned. Then she was gone, gathering up her half-stunned and wailing child, to join Mr. Howse by some low bushes further down the slope to the beach.

"*Achtung, eine Angriff kommen!*" Kolodzcy warned. "Mlavic!"

With most of his men sorted out, Mlavic had turned his attention to them again, him and a dozen others, coming at the trot.

"Captain, I *kill* you!" Mlavic howled. "Kill you slow!"

"Carefully... aimed fire," Lewrie ordered, leveling his first pistol at full-cock, waiting 'til they got within ten paces. Furious for blood or not, the pirates shied a bit, none of them wishing to be in the lead, with Mlavic howling and driving them on.

BANGG! The harsher, chuffing bark of a 2-pounder boat-gun down near the beach, spewing canister in an expanding cloud of lead pellets. BANGG! came a second, slashing at the centre of the pirates' camp and flinging men off their feet. The landing-party was within yards of the shore, Alan most gratefully realized, the small guns mounted in the bows of their boats! Those shots raised a wailing from the wounded, behind and to Mlavic's rear, and froze his men for a second to peer or check their progress, wondering what new deviltry was coming.

Lewrie took aim and fired, and one pirate dropped his weapons to grab at his shattered thigh, but Lewrie had been aiming at his chest!

He tossed that one away, brought up his last. Spendlove fired but missed, then Kolodzcy lit off his first, taking one man in the throat and throwing his blood-spouting body back into another.

But then they were dashing forward again, and Lewrie fired that last pistol as Kolodzcy did his. One went whirling down, with a wound in his shoulder, Lewrie's target screamed rabbity as he was plumbed in his stomach; Lewrie had been aiming for his upper chest!

So much for Arabee pistols, Alan thought, tossing away his last and drawing his hanger. The odds were better, though, he told himself grimly; four down – that's eight-to-three.

Lewrie took stance, hanger held low before his middle at Tierce, and it took an unthinking second to go from Third into a box-defence, then riposte, and sweep his keen Gill's across his first opponent, to rip his belly open! There was a shrill scream from his right, as one more pirate came lurching backwards, pedaling to stay upright, clutching his skewered stomach to plop and thrash. Then it was Mlavic before him, stepping over that mortally wounded man and snarling defiance!

At low Third again, the first engagement ringing, Mlavic beginning with a slash down from high-right, easily parried, turned over by a flying cut-over, then a lunge low, and Mlavic was backpedaling, too, suddenly wary. He came on as Lewrie stamped forward a foot or two, with a back-slash from his left, again easily parried. Mottled Damascus met British Gill's, sparks flying from edge-to-edge, and that curving blade singing as it carved the air!

No swordsman, Alan exulted, already panting for air. A quarter-circle scimitar's made for cuttin', not the point… get inside! And he don't know anything else.

"Marines!" Came a distance-thinned bray from Sergeant Bootheby, on the beach at last. "*Cock* yer *locks*… lev-*el*? By volley… *fire!*" Then the welcome rattle of musketry, and over Mlavic's right shoulder Lewrie could see Serbs falling back in disorder, right to the edges of their encampment, even as he and Mlavic still fought, their hands and eyes performing without conscious thought in furious melee. Lewrie hoped Mlavic might turn his head for a squint, but it wasn't to be.

A thin cry to his left, which Lewrie also ignored, but there was Spendlove in the corner of his eye, in full whirl, having downed one for himself. His ear caught a cessation of tinkering to his right as a heavy body thudded to the ground without a cry.

"*Vier!*" Kolodzcy hooted in triumph, even as he engaged another.

Almost decent odds now, Alan thought, beating out a boxdefence by rote, jabbing with his straighter Gill's for an inner-arm cut or a thigh-cut, an eye-jab, which made Mlavic retreat steadily, now wheezing with anger and effort as his slashes and clumsy lunges were made nought. Lewrie made his face a feral grin, to discomfit him.

But then Mlavic leaped backwards, spry for such a heavy man – to draw that wicked black-iron butcher-knife from its sheath, and come back to the attack with a blade in each hand, slashing or stabbing like a two-headed monster! Lewrie had to give ground, grunting hoarse as he fought to meet both. And it was Mlavic's turn to gloat!

Now, where's help when I need it? Alan groaned. Marines, sailors, a knife... bloody table-fork, anything! He searched for a stick, some discarded weapon, a blazing brand from one of the fires...!

"*Funf!*" Kolodzcy shouted; another of his foe-men down. Then a grunt from the left as a pirate staggered away, clutching at a torn sword-arm where Spendlove had laid him open. Yards away, though; he'd been lured out towards the centre of the camp. A fainthearted Serb went haring by, dashing for the far shore, all the fight scared out of him.

Mlavic's scimitar was coming, this time not in a slash, but with a straight-armed lunge, wrist inverted and cutting-edge up! Lewrie swept to parry off low and left, flail it over high and right, slide down and slash at his arm with the edge to slow him down – quick, for his *knife* from the right...! He met the knife's blade, parried that wide and away... *sword*! Down and slashing with his tip, he nicked the pirate on the chin, through that tangled mat of beard, felt his hanger clang as he continued down and to his left onto the scimitar, but...

He was off balance, wrong-footed, counter-lunging to fend that bastard back for some stumbling room. A feint from the knife, though, and he was ducking to his left, and Mlavic stepped back, and Alan felt a searing pain on his left outside calf, a drawing stroke!

"Buggered!" he gibbered.

He retreated on his right leg, a three-foot leap, but as soon as his weight came down on his left leg, he was sprawling on his back, as it folded on him like a shoddy stool. And Mlavic was on him before he could blink! Lewrie feebly put his hanger up to ward him off.

Clang! though.

Suddenly there was a sword above him, horizontal, whirling silvery in parry, jabbing and darting as Leutnant Kolodzcy stepped over him and forced Mlavic away! Dancing sidewise in little, fitful hops and jumps almost too swift to be followed, to circle large round the hunkering, wary bear-shuffle of a stunned Mlavic, drawing him off toward the fire in the middle of the camp.

By *God*, that hurt! Lewrie felt like screaming. His calf was *ablaze* with pain, and blood gushed freely, making him wonder how near to bleeding to death he was, how close to losing his lower leg, even did he get the bleeding stopped! "Ah, Christ!" he yelped, going light-headed, faint, feeling that weak swoon that always seized him after a fight. And hearing an immense waterfall-ringing in his ears.

Then hands were on his body, lifting him by his shoulders, and someone large and hulking was kneeling near his left leg. There came a painful bout of rasping as something rough went taut below his knee that squeezed and squeezed.

"Be fine, sir, be fine, swear it," he heard from his left, and there was Spendlove, disheveled, nicked and bleeding, perspiring like a Canton coolie, but whole. A scent in his nostrils, like a spiced tea... rosemary and thyme, attar of some flowers, too? No, soap, rosemary and thyme, clean hair.

Couldn't be Spendlove, he thought weakly.

He lolled his head right, to try and focus on Mrs. Connor, who sat by his right shoulder, supporting him, felt a cool, soft hand on his brow, stroking so gently...

The hulking form was back, pawing him and prodding vigourously. There came the thud of a wooden box, the tinkle of gleaming, silvery things. More fire in his calf as something wet and stinging was laved over it, and he caught the sweet-and-sulfur tang of West Indies rum on the air. Then came a single blazing-red star from somewhere not that far away, wavering and sputtering, nearing...

"...see this, ma'am. Cover his ears, perhaps?" someone said. It was the hulking thing, shuffling on its knees upward to peer into his face. Surgeon Mister Howse!

"Bite on this," he said, offering a folded leather strop, all foetid, dried and mangled as old shoes, and bitten by the teeth of an hundred prior sufferers. "Think of something pleasant."

Then the pain went *indescribable*, and his leg was burning, all active flames, smoke and sizzle, and charring black, he could imagine; like he'd taken a tentative dip into a red-hot stream of lava!

"Oh, you bloody bastard!" Lewrie gritted through the gag, quivering tense as a sword-blade. "Enjoy that, do *yyaaa*? Shit!"

Over the child's redoubled wailings, he could hear Mrs. Connor shushing and making crooning noises, holding his head in her hands to stop the sounds and sights, rocking the boy on her lap. Rocking *him*.

"Best way to stop the bleeding, sir," Mr. Howse said, looming up in his face again. "Tourniquet, then a cautering iron. Rum for a fuel, as it were, to encourage the searing. Did he not nick a major vein, you may recover. Sir," Howse lowed, sounding disappointed he might be successful. "I'll dress it now, sir."

"Marines, level! By volley... *fire!*" And the crash of another avalanche of musketry, quite near the camp, at last. "At 'em, Jesters! Sword and steel!" he heard Lieutenant Knolles cry, followed by a roaring of pagan joy. And still the clash and clang of blades. "Bayonets! At th' double-quick... cold steel, an' *skin* the bastards!"

"Help me up," Lewrie ordered. He was now wide awake, in too much pain to swoon, too angry (it must be admitted), and looked out to see his seamen and Marines sweeping into the camp, battering what bit of fight the pirates had left from them. And there were Mlavic and Leutnant Conrad Kolodzcy, still going at it, hammer-and-tongs. Kolodzcy had acquired a swept-hilt dagger for his off-hand, and was two-handing it in the elegant old Spanish rapier-and-poignard style. His balance was exquisite, his every move liquid and graceful, the minimum of effort to parry, defend... then burst into furious motion, all threatening swiftness, like a horde of aroused bees. A pirate came to save Mlavic, dashing in from Kolodzcy's left, and Kolodzcy lunged at the pirate chieftain to take room, pivoted on one heel, and that pirate was stumbling past, his sword gone and his bowels spilling over his hands as he pitched onward to trip and die with a hideous screech.

"Damme, he's good!" Lewrie breathed in awe.

Driving Mlavic back to the middle of the camp, both too intent on murder to think of safety, of retreat. Lewrie heard a yelp from Kolodzcy as some seamen neared: "*Nein*, he ist mine!"

Back across the blood-soaked earth, Mlavic stumbling back over his tortures, his dead and dying victims; teeth still bared in a ferocious snarl of defiance, Mlavic fought to the death, knowing he'd be killed right after, should he win, but so fired, so forged by hate...!

Tripped! Seized on the ankle by the groveling Albanian woman who'd been savaged nigh to death, who lashed out grief-blinded, hatred-blinded! Mlavic lost his balance, tried to recover, to shake loose of her as she clawed at him.

"Unt, *ja!*" Kolodzcy cried thin and high, slipping inside guard and driving his dagger into Mlavic's right forearm, to turn it, wring it, and force his nerveless fingers to let go his scimitar. Slip his small-sword's narrow blade into Mlavic's throat in the same movement, then let go the hilt and lever the plunging, thrashing knife-hand off until his opponent began to weaken. "*Sterbe, schweinhund! Ich bin nicht der madchenhaft-mann! Ich bin dein tod!*"

Mlavic gargled and coughed, drowning, lowering his knife-hand.

"Die, pig-dog... die!" Kolodzcy screamed, ramming his dagger hilt-deep under Mlavic's heart.

And Dragan Mlavic complied, his knees buckling as Kolodzcy gave a great heave and flung him back, right to the edge of the central fire, where his head and shoulders draped over the shimmering-hot stones, and his hair and his beard and his goat-hair weskit caught fire. Where, a moment later, the broken and bleeding Albanian woman crawled, to pound him weakly with a short bit of kindling, screaming and weeping all the while as that brute's face blazed and sizzled like pork-cracklings.

Kolodzcy turned, grinned his weary delight and raised the hilt of his sword to his face in a formal salute to Lewrie – with a double-click of his heels and a short head-bow, for good measure. Alan lifted his own hanger and sketched what salute he could in reply.

"And thank God for him," he breathed.

"Sir, you hurt?" Lieutenant Knolles was asking, kneeling down by his side. "Sorry, sir, but I wasn't to know, 'til—"

"You did damn fine, Mister Knolles," Lewrie assured him, with a pat on his shoulder. "Know or not, your timin' was splendid. You've done yourself proud. They break?"

"Run off into the woods, sir, t'other side of the island."

"See to the stockade, then, Mister Knolles," Lewrie said as he heaved himself up to a sitting position, no matter the pain. "There's sure to be some they didn't bring down to torture 'fore... get every civilian or Venetian sailor off the island, back aboard their ship. I think we'd best leave our pirates in the woods 'til dawn tomorrow, or we'd lose some of our men to 'em, floundering about in the dark. And I doubt they'll be much of a threat, now we have their ship and their boats. Call everyone back near the beach and we'll fort up. Clean up this slaughterhouse in the morning, too."

"Aye, sir." Knolles nodded, taking time to look about, bewildered. "God, what'd they *do*, sir? *How* could they—"

"Speak of it, tomorrow, sir," Lewrie cut him short, not caring to dwell on it much, either.

"You're *not* too sore hurt, are you, sir?"

"Spot o' wine, and I'll be dancing, most-like." Alan chuckled, hoping that was true, that he *wasn't* slowly puddling blood inside that seared-shut gash. "Oh… where're my manners? Mistress Connor? Mistress Theoni Connor, allow me to name to you my First Officer, Mr. Ralph Knolles. Mister Knolles, Mrs. Patrick Connor. Her husband was late of Bristol, by way of Zante. Her son… and what's your name, sprout?"

"He's Michael," the lady supplied, cosseting the little lad a bit more, rocking him as he sat on her lap. Rocking her hip on Alan's side, too. The lad had calmed down, was no longer crying hysterically, but he didn't look far from a fresh bout. "And I am honoured to know you, sir… Lieutenant Knolles. *Another* of my saviours." She smiled at him, wilting young Knolles to an aspic; but with a significant eye for Lewrie, too, openly adoring.

"Should I get you something, Captain Lewrie?" she offered, in a maternal sort of way. "A brandy, to restore you?"

"Had my fill o' plum brandy, thankee," Lewrie said with a grimace.

"Some wine, sir. I'll fetch it," Spendlove volunteered.

And there was one of those silver chalices again, brimming with restorative red wine. Lewrie took a deep draught, and felt much better.

"Something I have to do," he decided, after several more. "I won't be a minute. If you'd help, Mister Spendlove? You've a young back, and there's something I have to see to."

He got to his feet, wincing. But with Spendlove under his left arm for support, so he'd not put weight on his leg, he hobbled slowly to the centre of the camp, near the fire, to gaze down on Mlavic. The Marines had dragged him out to lessen the reek of roasting man, built up the fire to illuminate the forest where foes still hid. But the Marines stood gagging at the sights they beheld, the incredible amount of blood that had flowed, the rivened victims' corpses. Pragmatically though, they half knelt to pluck those gold coins Mlavic had strewn in boast. The Marines froze, turned away, pretending they *weren't* looting as Lewrie and Spendlove hove up.

"No matter, lads," Lewrie told them. "No head-money in this for us... just justice. So take what you may find. Corporal Summerall? Could you find five guineas for me? Just five guineas."

"Aye, sir. No problem, sir!" he replied, relieved that Lewrie would look the other way. He brought them after a quick search, rubbing off the drying blood with his musket cleaning rag. He laid them on Lewrie's palm. Lewrie peered down at them, glittering and clean again. Then folded his hand and shoved them deep into a pocket of his breeches.

"Now get me back aboard *Jester*, if you'd be so good, Spendlove," Lewrie sighed. "Away from this..."

And limped away... with his four guineas recovered for the wine – and the last to pay for all.

Epilogue

Quod sin ea Mavors abnegat,
et solis nostris sudoribus obstat,
ibimus indecores
tot aequora vectae?

But if Mars refuses,
and alone resists our efforts;
shall we depart disgraced
after traversing so many seas in vain?

Gaius Valerius Flaccus *Argonautica*, Book V, 667–669

I

"This, sir, is for you," Lewrie announced, handing over a canvas binder that contained documents for Captain Charlton, as soon as he'd been admitted aft in *Lionheart*'s great-cabins. "I fear they may be bad news, after getting ashore at Venice. Our consul told me."

"And what led you as far afield as Venice, sir?" Charlton asked, with a dubious brow up. "And off-station more than a week?"

"My written report, sir, will discover all to you," Lewrie said, presenting him with a second folded-over sheaf of papers. "One from Leutnant Kolodzcy is included, as well."

Charlton looked puzzled, but he broke the wax seal on the orders first, waving Lewrie to a chair and a decanter of wine while he took a seat behind his desk and began to read.

"Oh, bloody…" Charlton nearly moaned, dropping the orders to his lap and staring off into the aether, looking aghast. "It's true?"

"Aye sir, sorry," Lewrie confirmed. "Bonaparte's repulsed the Austrians again, round Bassano… taken Trent, up in the passes in the Alps and sent 'em running. French troops landed at Bastia, and we had to evacuate, so Corsica and San Fiorenzo Bay are gone. We still garrison Capraia and Elba, but… And the Spanish, sir. Consul told me—"

"Spain's declared war on Great Britain, aye," Charlton sighed, with an uncomprehending shake of his head. "Thrown in with France, and the Coalition's broken. We're on our own, with half of Europe against us. Dear Lord…!" He closed his eyes and pinched the bridge of his nose in weariness. "That's it for us, too, it seems. Admiral Jervis has been ordered by London to evacuate the Mediterranean… retire upon Gibraltar. Therefore, he writes, we're to leave the Adriatic, and are to make 'the best of our way' there for further orders. At once."

"Our consul suspected, sir, but couldn't confirm that." Lewrie coughed into his fist. "He did suggest all British subjects get out of the way of the fighting, return home, so I surmised it would be coming. Leave Venice, too, he thought, and get to Denmark or a neutral Baltic port as best they're able... or take passage west on neutral ships. I beg your pardon for the delay, sir, but I took the liberty of informing Lord Rushton and Sir Malcolm Shockley. Whilst tidying up the... matter which forced me to Venice. Wouldn't do for the Frogs to capture members of our peerage, or one of our greatest manufacturers. Lord, and a Member of Parliament?"

"And what matter was that, sir?" Charlton enquired, sounding a touch frosty.

"Clearing our escutcheon of murder, rape and torture, sir. And destroying the pirate Mlavic, who took a Venetian ship, slaughtered all the French prisoners held at Palagruza," Lewrie bluntly replied. "Making hostages of Kolodzcy and me... It's all in our reports, sir."

"*Hang* yer reports!" Charlton blazed. "Tell it me!"

And Lewrie did, paraphrasing, of course, but leaving few of the lurid details out, letting his unresolved revulsion and anger mask his duplicity. Quite well, he thought.

"So we dashed off to Palagruza, sir, hoping to find Mlavic. Not as mystical as his chief, d'ye see, sir?" Lewrie spun out, glib at his tale by then. "Since neither of us could talk Petracic out of his scheme, we thought Mlavic could... convince him there was a job of work still to be done for us, first... and that he wasn't anywhere near strong enough to launch his holy crusade yet, for the second. Wasn't time to inform you, sir, given Petracic's state of mind. He might've begun before Mlavic could get to him, so..." He shrugged, dipping his nose into a wineglass for cover. "Got there just in time to be made prisoner, forced to watch his butchery, and found he'd pissed in the font and taken a Venetian ship out of greed and simple stupidity. It was neck-or-nothing there for a while, but... we beat him. Killed him and most of his men, freed the women and children, got the survivors on their own ship and back to Venice, sir. Had a good word from their authorities for that, sir. Oh, by the by... sorry. This letter from the Doge is for you, sir. A vote of thanks. Sorry I was remiss. They're grateful to us! Swore they'd alert their garrisons and naval units to hunt Petracic down 'fore he does a mischief. Though we know what *that* amounts to, sir."

Alerts sent to empty forts, skeleton garrisons, abandoned fleets rotting at their moorings, with but one sailor each as harbour-watch?

"More effectively, sir," Lewrie went on in the stunned silence, "our consul said they'd also sent notice to Ragusa, Dulcigno and some of the Croatian navy bases. I expect it'll be they who'll do the hunting, and the bringing to book."

"Did they, indeed!" Charlton goggled. "Vote of thanks? But… Jesus Christ. Had you come to me first, I *might've* been able to talk to Petracic—"

"With this order to evacuate, though, sir, isn't that moot?" he pointed out. "And us gone, 'fore anyone linked us to the taking of the Venetian ship? Or whatever bloody raid Petracic had in mind?"

Charlton opened the Doge's letter, done in both flowery Italian and even more florid English, just in case. He swelled with pride for a second or two, then deflated just as quickly, dropping that one into his lap, too, and looking bleak.

"Christ, we were a single step away from infamy," Charlton realised. "Gulled us, they did. Had this in the back of their minds from the start. Would have shouted our involvement to make them sound legitimate! Oh, Dear Lord…" he groaned, passing a hand over his face. "I've been a fool, Lewrie. A total, purblind, goddamned fool!"

And a hearty "Aye aye, sir!" Lewrie rather doubted would be necessary, nor desired, at that moment.

"*Tried* to warn me off it, God knows," Charlton sighed, looking ready to weep, staring at nothing – possibly a vision of a completely ruined Navy career? "But no, I had to be so damned calculating, sly-boots… so damned clever and… *improvising!*" he chid himself, sneering at his pretensions. "Thought a brilliant coup, great results, the master-stroke'd… hmmph! Broad-pendant, that sort o' fancy? Should have known, clever ain't in my nature. Not that sort o' subtle back-biting clever. Best left to *your* sort, Lewrie… no slur on you, sir. Hope you won't take it as such. You're one of the truly clever, more suited for subtle endeavours. I'm just a straightforward sea-dog… give me a proper fight, nothing too taxing on my poor modicum of wit? And, a total failure, it would now appear. Too lack-wit for this…"

"Not at all, sir!" Lewrie felt it politic to toady. "Why—"

"Well, at least I'm man enough to own up to my idiocies," Captain Charlton sighed, patting his greying, frazzled hair. "Write a report for Admiral Jervis, no wheedling or hair-splitting. S'pose I'm still man enough to do that… when I can't seem to manage much else. He'll string me up from a yard-arm by my thumbs, I'd expect…"

"You mustn't take it quite so hard, sir," Lewrie objected, in true sympathy for Charlton; he had no wish to see the man *ruined*! He had made one mistake out of hundreds of decisions, and it wouldn't be even a minor footnote in anyone's history, since their folly had been nipped in the bud. "Managing the diplomatic niceties, sir? Directing an under-strength and far-flung squadron well as you did? Swept every French trader into harbour quaking in their boots, sir. Scared every large vessel from the trade, too. I doubt Petracic or Mlavic took more than four or five, not counting the Venetian, o' course. And he burned all but one of those, sir! Acting under our aegis, sir, so to speak... that is to say, *we* eliminated four or five more, *in toto*. I burned that brig I took for Mlavic, too, so..."

"Aye, one might look at it that way, couldn't one?" Charlton brightened. Only for a second, though – then he reached out to pour himself a glass of wine. "Thing that irks, though, Lewrie is... e'en so, well as we did, really..."

That's the way! Alan noted; "*we* did well," now. *You* did!

"...end result of our efforts, we didn't make a tinker's damn's worth of difference. French fleet's at sea, what we hoped to prevent. Allied with the Dons, so we're beaten. Skulking away with our tails between our legs. And I don't much *care* for it!" Charlton fumed.

"Our turn'll come, sir, just you watch," Alan tried to cheer him. "A good, clean gunnel-to-gunnel fight or two. Win 'em, too."

"Well, then..." Charlton huffed, looking more businesslike. "We're probably the last Royal Navy vessels east of Corsica, and this may be an *int'restin'* passage out. Our British civilians at Venice... we should put in there, take aboard as many as wish—"

"Beg pardon, sir," Lewrie exclaimed, quite happy to discuss any other matters. "I took the liberty as well of embarking Lord Rushton, his traveling companion Mr. Chute, Sir Malcolm and Lady Lucy Shockley, their servants, and a Mrs. Connor. In my report, sir... third page..."

Charlton thumbed through to it and nodded, raising his eyebrows in wonder. "Uhm-*humm*!" he commented. "So this lady and her son might need dropping off at Zante, in the Ionians? Delaying our departure?"

"No, sir. She's of Greek parentage, Venetian citizenship, but the widow of an Irish trader. Converted to his faith... Catholicism, when she married, so... she's not *exactly* welcome with her family, I gather... Eastern Orthodox? She was aboard that ship Mlavic took, on her way back from closing her late husband's final accounts. She had planned to take passage to England, to reside with her former in-laws, the child's grandparents, in Bristol. Her household goods have been sent on, and there'd be no cause to call at Zante."

"And Leutnant Kolodzcy?" Charlton asked, still "My wording" and "Good God-ing" over Lewrie's written account. "Our liaison?"

"Disembarked at Venice, sir, and took a packet to Trieste."

"Good." Charlton nodded, looking pleased. "Good, then! There will be no need to put in at either port, so we may exit the Adriatic at once."

"Uhm, sir...?" Lewrie frowned. "*Not* put into Trieste, sir? I thought their Prize-Court, uhm... ain't they owing us a rather *hefty* sum by now?"

"There is that, I grant you, Commander Lewrie," Charlton said with a chuckle. "But... our orders are to sail 'with all despatch'... no time for a side-trip, no matter how rewarding. You know the usage, surely! Our own Prize-Courts take years to adjudicate the simplest of captures, and awards come even later, long after the taking vessel has paid off or been recommissioned. I'd expect our mutual ambassadors to wrangle it out, most-like. Else we'd be laid up for weeks and caught by a French squadron with no hope of aid. And," Charlton mused, wearing a cynical expression, "the Austrians have a lot more to worry over than anything to do with us, or their own naval affairs. Such as they are, mind. The worthless..." He bit off what else he thought of the Austrian "navy."

"Very well, sir," Lewrie said with a shrug, as if the loss did not matter, all that lovely gold he was due!

"Your wound, sir... you mentioned." Charlton turned all consoling. "No complications? You're mending well?"

"Aye, sir... no trouble of it."

"Good, good." Charlton nodded, sipping at his wine. "My stars, sir! Your great-cabins must be crowded as the very Ark. 'Twill never do for anyone to say I made a peer suffer. Nor one of our most eminent industrial gentlemen... and *both* with a seat in Parliament, what? We must put in somewhere and shift them about, share the burden equally. I can only think that *you've* had a most int'restin' passage thus far, sir."

"Quite, sir," Lewrie replied with a shy grin.

Don't know the half of it, he confessed to himself.

"This Lord Peter Rushton and his traveling companion, Mr. Chute, are old schoolmates of yours, I recall, Lewrie? Perhaps it might best suit that they remain aboard *Jester.*"

Oh, Christ, no! Lewrie wished he could shout.

"Well, sir... he *is* highest-ranking. Wouldn't it be... pardon me for daring to presume to suggest, sir, but... like-with-like, sir? Aboard the flagship? Though you may find them perhaps too-boisterous company. Chute's a bit 'fly,' a born rogue. And Lord Peter, well... they're both bachelors, sir. A tad, uhm... dare I mention, rakish?"

And sniffin' round Theoni like ram-cats on a queen on-heat! he allowed himself to fume; smarmy shits, never done *me* a single favour, and know too much about me already!

"Oh, better yet, sir!" Lewrie exclaimed. "The perfect pairing. They could be put aboard *Pylades* with Captain Rodgers. His ways are near theirs... bit of the rough-and-tumble? Besides, sir, Sir Malcolm and Lady Shockley... though they are a step below Lord Rushton in the peerage... Sir Malcolm is known to be a dab-hand at whist, sir. Much more influential, I recall, too. Scads richer, to be certain."

Long as you don't pair 'em with Fillebrowne, Lewrie thought; or, *do*! God, what a catfight that'd be, should Fille-browne even *try* to have himself a quick "upright" in the chart-space!

"Aye, an excellent suggestion, Commander Lewrie," Captain Charlton said with a smile. "I stand in your debt, sir. And I find your kind consideration of my hobby most gratifying. Seas are a bit rough for a transfer at the moment, so... hmm. Ah. There," he said, consulting a chart that lay spread on his desk with pen-cases and such. "I own to a certain morbid curiosity... and it is the closest sheltered lee we have. Palagruza. We'll put in there this evening. Anchor overnight, and shift your passengers and their dunnage about in calmer water. I will dine them all aboard *Lionheart*, with all our captains. You and... this Mrs. Connor, as well. Then sail tomorrow morning for the straits."

"Very good, sir. Well... s'pose I should get back to *Jester*," Lewrie offered, rising. "Unless there's anything else you need, sir?"

"Uhm, no, Lewrie, your report's more than ample," Charlton told him, rising to see him off. "Uhm... anent our pirates. Does this lady know our involvement with Petracic and Mlavic?"

"No, sir."

"Let's keep it that way, shall we?" Charlton suggested. "Your presence there... you'd come to anchor to investigate, and were gulled. *Then* taken prisoner, before you could inform your ship. Thought they were French, found they were Venetian, or so they claimed. And offered to render assistance… laws of the sea, that sort of thing. A silly error on your part, an even greater stupidity on Mlavic's."

"Is that the way you'll report it, sir? That I was silly?"

"God, no, Lewrie!" Charlton frowned. "Admiral Jervis will know the whole truth, no matter the consequences to me. But that's for the Fleet to know… and for honest Crown subjects to not. I'll tell him you were against it from the first, and that I was a fool for ignoring your advice. That I find you clever, aggressive and enterprising, and a man of many parts. A most resourceful fellow, whose value to me and this squadron was… well, inestimable, to be blunt. Is the admiral of a mind to keep this squadron together… and me in charge" – he winced for a rueful moment – "I'd hope you and *Jester* are part of it. If not, then I will press most strenuously for Admiral Jervis to make use of your talents in another, more responsible capacity."

"God, uhm… thankee, sir. That's most kind of you to say," Alan flummoxed, blushing with pride. And with guilt for how he ruined Charlton's scheme – and was now being praised for it! "*Most* kind."

Poor honest bastard. Lewrie felt like cringing. So straight you can't imagine…!

"My warmest regards to your passengers, sir. My heartfelt condolences to Mistress Connor for her ill treatment and her bereavement. We'll do everything to speed her on her way, tell her. And extend my invitation for supper to one and all. Uhm… her son…"

"'Bout five, sir. Breeched, but you know young lads and table-manners. Polite little git, but…" Lewrie shrugged.

Charlton shivered, regarded his good carpets and upholsteries with a certain foreboding. "Well, if we must, we must. Roll up those carpets… I've slipcovers. On your way, then, Lewrie."

"Aye aye, sir."

II

Lewrie watched *Pylades'* gig and his own launch and cutter row away. So much luggage, chests and such Lord Peter and Clotworthy had brought aboard! And those mysteriously heavy wooden crates that had had to be stored on deck, too. Lewrie wished Commander Fille-browne joy of their contents: those allegedly "Roman bronzes" of female acrobats that Clotworthy had had cast from a sketchbook, then antiqued in an acid-bath and a few days in the salt water of Venice's Lagoon!

"Bloody *ancient* what?" Clotworthy had haw-hawed. "Old-*lookin'*, at any rate. *Heard* he was anglin' for the very old. Just dug up from the Morea… Turk lands, and you know what *they* think o' images in human likeness. Why, 'twas a wonder they didn't melt 'em down for guns!"

"Think he'll bite, Clotworthy?" Lewrie had asked. To his untrained eye, they looked authentic; *he'd* have bit… if they had come from anyone else!

"Pay well for th' privilege, too, I'll warrant!" Clotworthy had roared with glee. "If not him, some other fool. If not them, I've an 'early' Canova, 'long with his sketches t'prove it. Best forgeries ever. We may not see each other after supper t'night, so… a quick departure on the Lisbon packet, right after the sale, hmm? So, good-bye, me old. I 'spect we'll be readin' 'bout ya in th' damn *Gazette*, hey?"

Lewrie shook his head in bewildered merriment, glad to see the back of him, though amused as always by Chute's scandalous antics. Just as long as it was others who got fleeced!

"Frolicsome pair, sir," Lieutenant Knolles commented, "what?"

"You didn't buy anything from him, did you? Play cards?"

"Forewarned, sir… thankee." Knolles smiled.

"I'll go below for a moment, see the Shockleys to the deck."

He marveled all over again, as he entered his great-cabins, to see the pair of Venetian red-lacquered commodes – the genuine article, not *lacca povera*... at least Chute had *assured* him. He'd have to crate them back up, store them on the orlop. They'd never last a month, when his every furnishing was rushed below every gun-drill or call to Quarters. Free, he scoffed; free, gratis... from Clotworthy?

"Make up for th' tatties an' gravy, Alan, old son," he'd sworn. "Not pinched, neither. Made such a killin' an' *expect* such a killin', I could *afford* t'be magnanimous, hey? Yer wife'll love 'em."

And there sat Sir Malcolm and Lady Lucy, sipping tea with Mrs. Connor. Rather forbiddingly, Alan thought; rather frigid. Well, Sir Malcolm was all affable... but Lucy was a bit nose-high and snippish.

"Cap'an Lewrie!" little Michael cried, leaving off his games with the cats. He ran to hug Lewrie's leg and look up adoringly, making Lewrie cringe inside anew. "Look what! Whiskers can play ball!"

"Ah, that's marvelous, Michael," Lewrie enthused, kneeling to his level. "Did you teach him all by yourself? He's a clever kitten, isn't he? And you're a clever lad. Or did Toulon show him how?"

The first night aboard, shivering with fright, weeping and wailing most miserable from all he'd been forced to see and hear so young, little Michael had been inconsolable. 'Til Toulon had slunk up close and pressed against him, climbed in his lap and rubbed, bestowing cat-kisses and purring. Slept with him, too, in a hammock slung low in the chart-space, and never left his side. 'Til they'd come back from shore at Venice, of course, with Michael's present, a grey-and-black-striped tabby kitten of his very own – best of the thousands.

"No, *I* did!" Michael insisted loudly. "Come see!"

"I will, I promise. After supper tonight, we'll all have us a rare old romp, hey? But there's ship's business right now. Can't be a slack-hand captain, remember?"

"I 'member." Michael nodded, solemnly but impishly.

"Sir Malcolm... Lady Lucy, the boats from *Lionheart* are near, and your trunks and such are slung, ready to load," Lewrie told them.

"Ah, then we must be going. Come, my dear," Sir Malcolm said, finishing his tea and getting to his feet. "You'll join us on deck, Mistress Connor?"

"Your pardons, sir, but," Theoni replied, standing up and dipping him a short curtsey, "this close… I mean no dis-courtesy to you, but I have no wish to even have a glimpse of that island again, nor ever hear it mentioned. I hope you understand."

"I understand completely, ma'am, truly," Sir Malcolm said with sympathy. "Good-bye, then. And may I express to you my fondest wishes you may have a safe and tranquil journey to England. And find every contentment and joy once there, for both you and your fine little man. Come, Michael! A parting kiss! You're such a splendid young fellow. We'll miss you desperately, that's the boy!" And Michael complied.

"Good-bye, Lady Shockley," Theoni said, dipping her a departing curtsey as well. "A safe journey for you."

"Goodbye, my dear. Though we *will* see each other at *supper*?" Lucy answered, gushing so honey-sweet Lewrie almost winced.

"I'll see you out on deck, sir… ma'am?" he offered. "Want to come, Michael? Just you, not your kitten. He's not an old salt yet, not like Toulon."

"I'll mind him, Michael, you go on and watch the sailors and all," Theoni assured him.

"Why, d'ye know," Sir Malcolm suddenly announced, "we could all end on the same packet from Gibraltar. Certainly the same packet from Lisbon. See Commander Lewrie's things through customs, and make sure you arrive safe, Mistress Connor! Couldn't we, Lucy?"

"Why… yes!" Lucy replied, nonplussed for a moment at such an egregious notion, but recovering quickly. "How *delightful* a prospect!"

She shot Lewrie a glare; who took a squint to see what Theoni had made of that; receiving in turn a subtle arch of a perfect, artfully arched (and lovely, he thought!) brow, and a faintly amused cast to a forced-to-be-pleasant smile. The passage to Venice had become heaven. Passage *from* Venice had been all elbows and knees, grumblings and cattiness. No privacy, of course, not a jot; no chance to…

"Be back soon," Lewrie promised Theoni Connor. "I'll have Andrews or Cony keep a weather-eye on him, never fear."

"Then he will be in good hands," Theoni answered, a real smile playing at the corners of her lips; so full of hidden meaning and promise, he hoped. "None better," she added as she gathered up the kitten.

The second night of passage, Lewrie had been too fitful from his wound to sleep, despite Mr. Howse's infusion of laudanum in wine – enough, he'd assured Lewrie, to ease pain but leave him his wits should he be called on deck. Wakeful and tossing in a hammock in the dining-coach, too many years away from his midshipman days to be comfortable in it, he'd risen and stolen to his wine-cabinet, limping and wincing as the ship rolled and heaved her way north. He'd accidentally wakened Theoni, and she'd come to help him as he'd groped and stumbled to the settee. She'd fetched his wine and taken a measure for herself.

Their wine was in those heavy, ornate chalices that no one still living had claimed, once their property had been sorted out and returned to them. Those silver chalices that Clot-worthy Chute had gasped over at first sight; he couldn't exactly *swear*, mind, but he thought them to be Cellini's work, or just as old and valuable, cast in his style. "What I say is, Alan, m'dear... were a fellow like *you* t'own 'em, he'd never leave someone th' likes o' *me* alone with 'em!"

They'd talked in low mutters, fearful they'd waken Michael, who had that night slept as if drugged, himself – his first real, refreshing night of rest after his satanic ordeal. They'd laughed a bit, softly, as the hours fled by with no call from above to summon him. Shared the parts of their pasts they'd cared to reveal. And, by the light of the single guttering candle, he'd been mesmerised by her tantalising, exotic beauty. Sitting so close together, a lonely...

Admit it, a *randy* man, too long without, he'd chid himself.

And a lonely, frightened widow, rescued from the very brink, the knife-edge of rape and murder, the butchering of her only child. Some gratitude she'd felt, perhaps; or hero-worship? After playing stoic and brave for so long, she'd broken down and wept on his shoulder, so quietly still, stifling her rasping, heaving, nigh-screaming terrors to spare Michael, burying her face in his neck and moaning into his shirt all she'd tried to suppress; including her widowhood, he'd imagined.

She'd cried it all out, round Two Bells of the Middle Watch... then turned her face up to his without a word. Kissed him with fierce need, fingers and hands, arms and mouth strong and beseeching hungrily. Breeches, shirt, bed-gown and chemise torn and flung aside. Then, into the hanging, swaying double bed-cot, making love to him so grasping and engulfing, so desperately exuberant, as if lovemaking could purge all the shrieks, the blood and terror away – banish fear and mortality, or the uncertainty of her future in a cold, alien new land; the grief of leaving her old one.

Fierce and strong, urgent and passionate, clasping him vise-like to her, and Alan had responded with a fury of his own, to forget for a time just how close to murder he'd been, too. It had felt… *holy*!

Silent, she'd been, though, stifling the cries she might've made, moaning, whimpering and panting into his neck. Even when her bliss had come, she'd merely stiffened, shuddered, spasmed, with a long hitch of her exhausted breath before relaxing. Later, they'd dared to coo and to chuckle, deep in their throats, barely above whispers near each other's ears. Nestling spent, languidly stroking lovers, 'til her need came to her again, then his… then hers a joyful fourth and last.

They hadn't dared touch since, not with the others aboard to see or hear, not with Lucy peering at them so deuced sharp, as if she had divined all; nor with Peter and Clotworthy garrulous and yarning, still keeping their bachelor hours and sipping far into the night. A glance, two hands brushed as they passed, a demure smile of eternal mystery she bestowed upon him when no one was looking – that was all they managed. It had been so soul-shattering, Lewrie could almost put it down to some laudanum-induced fever-dream, and feared Theoni had used him for cleansing, for a personal Epiphany; one memorable night was all she'd needed, and should he approach her, she'd spurn him and blame it on weakness, a mistake never to be repeated.

'Til now, of course. That fondness in her voice, that smile, so secret and promising…! Perhaps this very evening, after Charlton and his supper. Or in the few *days* of privacy on-passage to Gibraltar?

Damn fool, damn fool! he sighed to himself, feeling the fork of his breeches go taut in spite of himself; here I *nigh* swore off, an' look what a mockery I made o' that! He recalled most happily, though, a sight of her slim, womanly form, her chestnut hair flowing down low to her waist, the scent of rosemary and thyme in that hair. So perfectly made, gliding on cat-feet in that candle's dim glow, four or five inches less than his height, and so enfoldable, so well-fit to him!

He came back to reality, and rocked on the balls of his feet on his quarterdeck, gazing out towards the island. A shrill cry, followed by the patter of feet came, as little Michael and one of the ship's boy-servants scampered about in the waist; Tag, it looked like, with Bosun

Cony watching their every move, grinning a long-absent father's grin at their antics, and thinking of his own little Will back in Anglesgreen.

Blocks creaked as the first net of luggage was slung over-side. Lewrie turned to see Sir Malcolm Shockley overseeing its transfer, with his manservant and Midshipman Hyde. And Lucy approaching; smirking!

"My *word*, Alan," she said, standing by the bulwarks, a tad too close for his liking. "Such a *gay* dog you've grown to be, sir. I see you're a doting father, the way you cosset that *poor* lad. But not *much* of a husband, in truth... do I read the signs aright?" she simpered as she tapped him with her fan and spread it artfully. "What *horrid* folk we've turned out. A *Greek* woman, my *dear*! Taking advantage of her in a fragile moment... though I must own she has a certain attractiveness, a... *c'est-à-dire*... an animal magnetism, *n'est-ce pas*? Why, I have a good mind to write your lady-wife to let her know what a lecherous Corinthian she really has for a husband!" She tittered quite gaily.

"You wouldn't dare!" Lewrie growled, though shivering; aye, she'd be the sort t'do it, too! All for bloody-minded spite!

She laughed at his discomfort, matching the pace he took to get a sociably acceptable distance away from her.

"Mean t'say..." he amended. "What signs could you possibly read? Or find t'read? There's nought between..." Should've taken that tack first! he told himself.

"Alan..." Lucy cooed, significantly mystifying. "Women *know*."

"I'm certain you're mistaken in this instance, Lady Lucy. Nor were you ever the sort to cause someone needless grief," he replied.

She simpered over her fan for her answer, lashes fluttering.

"Don't tease, Lady Lucy." He frowned. "Such letters are known to go both directions. Where was it? Can't recall the exact address, but there was this wine-shop on the Calle del Fabri. Right at a cross-street, the Monte delle Ballotte? First-floor balcony, lots of afternoon sun t'see by... blond lady and a naval officer the spittin' im—"

Her fan whisked to furious life, and her cheeks went crimson. "Point taken, my dear... Alan." She grimaced; quite prettily.

"Could've sworn was Fillebrowne, to the life—"

"Point *taken*! Ahem," Lucy repeated, fanning so vigorously she could have bellied out the furled main-course.

"Why?" Lewrie had to ask. Long ago, she'd been a brainless chit, a guileless, bedazzling, innocent nymph. "Your husband's a decent and solid good man. I'd think that'd—"

"As is your Caroline, I'm certain," she allowed. "But decent does not always excite. And you know as well as I what drew each together so long ago on Antigua, Alan. You saw my true, passionate nature and I saw... a bad'un! One of the damme-boys, who'd risked his life in my honour. I never *shall* be able to resist the bad'uns. There's nary a woman can, were they honest with themselves. I'm certain, too, you have profited from it. Oh, you're *such* a bad'un, Alan Lewrie. Take ye joy in it. Or... have you already, hmm?" She chuckled huskily.

"People change, we..." He shrugged.

"I'm still of half a mind about you, d'ye see?" she confessed. "There's unfinished business 'tween us. Someday, I feel sure—"

"I think not, Lady Lucy. Truly," he disabused her. "Not even on a lark, not once for curiosity. Imperfect sinner though I be, I'll never 'put horns' on a *good* man who thinks himself happily wed. We may laugh and jest... but we do not *play*, d'ye get my meanin'?"

"You fear him?" she asked, gazing at him as if she'd misjudged him all these years.

"I respect him and like him."

"Ah, well, then," she sighed theatrically. "My regards to your dear wife... and to your *amour du jour*. She really is quite lovely... I see why you're so smitten. Her, too. Of course, you'll break her heart. I'll be the soul of decorum at supper, Alan. *Adieu!*"

He choked off what he might have said to that, watching her go back to the entry-port, sashaying and smug before once more becoming a lash-battering, innocent minx.

And he was still fuming, staring out at the island a moment later, when Sir Malcolm Shockley came up to him, striding slow and formal with a long silver-headed ebony walking-stick tapping time on the deck. Lewrie stiffened as he joined him at the bulwarks, wondering had Lucy said something spiteful, put a flea in his ear 'bout *them*...

"So this is where it happened," Sir Malcolm said, though, with a grave sadness, as he rested his hands on the cap-rail to look out.

"Aye, Sir Malcolm... just there," Lewrie replied.

They were anchored two cables off this time, distanced from the horror. The brig was sunk to the level of her upper bulwarks, with only her lower mast-trunks standing, her jib-boom thrust-ing upwards from her submerged forecastle, and charred as black and crumbly as last year's Yule Log splinter. The two smaller boats had been reduced to blackened piles of kindling and ash, just on the edge of the beach.

The reek of burning hung on the air from the stockade and the huts they'd fired, as well – but they still hadn't been quite able to conquer the foetid charnel stench from that abbatoir, that sick-sweet, roasted odour of putrefaction.

Sir Malcolm had a small pocket-telescope that he brought up to his eye, giving the place about as close an inspection as Alan thought he'd care for. The wheeling gulls and terns, the flutterings…

"Odd emblem, there, Commander Lewrie. That placard on a pole," Sir Malcolm puzzled, lowering his telescope. "A piratical symbol?"

"Grave-marker, sir," Lewrie answered levelly. "For the victims. We couldn't sort 'em out into Christian or Muslim, Albanian or Croat, Greek or Venetian… taken days, had we tried, and the survivors poor help in identifying them. Strangers to each other, and whole families erased? They needed to be in the ground, well… you understand."

"Yes." Sir Malcolm groaned. "Horrid. *Horrid!* And so savage, this part of the world. Wish to never hear of it again, lock-stock-and-barrel. At least Mistress Connor has good memories of living here in the Adriatic, 'til this. She has only the one island she'd wish to forget. Little-traveled as I am, sir… I do allow that I could quite easily abhor this region, entire. Get me home to good old England, that's world enough for me. And with this widening war, the only safe and sane clime I know left! Safe, behind the 'wooden walls' of our Navy, what? 'Cross our Narrow Sea?"

"Wouldn't mind a bit of that, myself, sir," Alan allowed.

"Serving King and Country unrecognised for their valour, their unstinting devotion to hard Duty, yes," Sir Malcolm sighed. "Nearly three years you've been in this ship, now, Commander? Away from home and family, with Duty done and foes confounded your only satisfaction?"

Well, I wouldn't say quite *that*. Lewrie tried not to smirk.

"About three years, sir… next spring." He nodded gravely.

"Once home, I mean to speak on the Fleet in Commons," Shockley pondered aloud. "This squadron, and all the gallant men who went into peril… *and* tedium, I'd imagine." He chuckled. "Gain for the officers and men some poor bit of acknowledgment for their efforts."

Lewrie smiled. "That'd be most welcome, Sir Malcolm, thankee."

"Your gallantry, foremost, sir. Your courage and sense of honour. Your quick thinking," Sir Malcolm prosed on, looking noble.

"I… I did what needed doing, only, Sir Malcolm." Lewrie all but coughed in honest modesty. And chagrin. "Don't quite know what t'say, sir… t'be so honoured. Though it's hardly deserved, really…?"

"Oh, tosh!" Sir Malcolm grinned. "Though your modesty becomes you, in addition to your other qualities. Know little of the sea, myself, can't begin to fathom the intricacies of a Sea Officer's elaborate lore, but I must say I'm intrigued to learn more of it. Speak to Admiral Jervis, discover his appreciation of our situation, now Spain has come in and the French fleet rules the Mediterranean… why, my colleagues may find my information useful, once home, in expanding the Navy."

"That'd be right-fine, Sir Malcolm."

Shockley lifted his telescope once more and peered at the shore.

"Rather a lot of birds about, Commander Lewrie. Thousands. I'd think they'd shun such a… dare I say a ghastly, haunted place."

"They're uhmm… feeding, Sir Malcolm," Lewrie told him bluntly. "What sea-birds do, when they're lucky."

"Thought you buried…?"

"The victims, Sir Malcolm," Lewrie stated. "Not the pirates. We didn't think they deserved burying, so we let 'em lie."

"Ah!" Sir Malcolm gulped, looking queasy. "Well, quite right, too. Murdering bastards. Might put them off this place for good?"

"I doubt it, sir," Lewrie countered. "A year or two, someone will put in for wood and water. Knock the placard down, 'cause they hate what country, religion or people the dead were. Scavenge rusted weapons we missed and didn't toss in the sea. Pick round the bones…"

"Scare them off, by way of example, ah. Quite right."

Lewrie rather doubted that. Some might even find it majestic!

"Hard to say, Sir Malcolm, hard to say," Lewrie allowed. "Now we've created a Field of Sea-birds… a *Kossovo*… however it's said in Serbian. *They'd* understand this, d'ye see…"

He turned outboard to look at his field of slaughter.

"'Now all is holy,'" he chanted softly. "'Now all is honourable… and the goodness of God is' – again – 'fulfilled.'"

"What's that, Commander Lewrie?" Sir Malcolm asked, giving him an odd look.

"Old Balkan… 'love-poem,' sir," Lewrie replied with a quirky grin. "Just an old local poem."

Afterword

It's doubtful if Napoleon ever exhorted his troops from the crag as I described. And that speech about leading the Army of Italy into a fertile plain of rich cities for honour, glory – and loot – was actually dictated by Bonaparte during his exile on St. Helena and inserted into his memoirs. The splendid three-part silent black-and-white film about Napoleon, though, shows it... the young boy-general, the hungry, ragged troops below, the mountains, and the sea. Napoleon would have approved, I think, since he'd aspired to be a dramatist or novelist in his school days. *He* knew what made a better tale; mean t'say, he *was* French, after all, knew how to *spell* the word *panache*, and proved time and again that he knew how to make an entrance! In light of that, how could anyone resist depicting it his way? Hey, not *moi*!

-

Admiral Sir John Jervis *did* send a squadron of six frigates into the Adriatic in early 1796, under a Captain Taylor. And yes, the authorities at Trieste supplied a major portion of the Imperial Austrian Navy its seagoing budget. They *did* reduce it, 'round the time I cited, and Captain Taylor's squadron was there, probably doing their work for them. After all, why buy the cow when you can get the milk free? That Major Simpson, by the way, was a real person, with a thankless chore, and abysmal career prospects. I reduced the number to four, to make the task assigned even harder to accomplish; and it's easier to deal with *three* other captain characters than five, especially characters who have been saddled with Commander Alan Lewrie's antics for more than a Dog-Watch.

-

Venice and the Serene Republic went under soon after this novel ends. *The Silver Age of Venice* by Maurice Rowdon depicts a state gone numb, feeble, toothless, and self-absorbedly sybaritic, depending on its past glories, the hollow shells of naval supremacy and their thoroughly professional army. In later years, Venice hired its armies from the Dutch, at exorbitant costs, which had already bankrupted the Republic. It was as if everyone in Venice was stumbling 'round on Prozac or Ecstasy.

The garrison at Corfu with its two officers, their servants and a sergeant or two was fact; as was the shoddy state of the islands' governor when Lewrie was dined in. Those anecdotes were in Martin Young's *The Traveller's Guide to Corfu*. The useless state of the once powerful Venetian Navy, the conditions at the Arsenal, the laid-up ships on foreign stations, were also true.

Through late 1796 and early 1797, Napoleon had defeated Wurmser a third and last time, conquering all of Austrian Italy. He then beat the stuffing out of another "brilliant" Austrian General, Alvinscy, got through the Alpine passes in December, marched through Leoben and got to Semmering, right on the outskirts of Vienna, which was helpless with her main armies still on the Rhine. His back was covered, just as he'd covered his rear before this offensive, by reducing the Papal States one more time, and destroying the only army left below the Adige River.

Napoleon marched into mainland Venetian territories. Citizens in Verona rose up and rioted, killing French troops. Napoleon sent ships to the port of Quieto, to attack a few timidly sheltering Austrian vessels, violating Venetian neutrality. The Venetians were *still* comatose, and didn't even make a peep of complaint. Mainland citizens, and nobles who hated the French, offered to raise thousands of eager volunteers if given arms. The Senate, the Council of Three, and the poor last Doge refused them. Finally, Napoleon sent a frigate into the Lagoon itself, behind the Lido where foreign warships were banned. The Venetians, at last, opened fire on her and took her, killing her captain among others. And Napoleon had his "legitimate" *casus belli* to march in and take over.

The Doge's ornate gilded barge, *Bucintoro*, from which he married the city to the sea each year, was hauled into St. Mark's and torched, along with that ancient roll of aristocratic lineages, the *Golden Book*.

The nobles complained but were helpless. For a city-state that declared itself a republic, it wasn't very republican. Rich men made the rules, nobles held all offices, and the common folk had sunk into nonvoting, "bread-and-circuses" sloth long before. Within days of the French takeover, and the later cession of Venice to Austria in the Treaty of Campo Formio, the *ridottos* were just as gay, the musicians just as dulcet, the gondoliers just as busy serenading lovers, and the love affairs just as tedious. Ruled by their own nobility, or by foreign overlords, most Venetians probably didn't even take notice of a change. They still had their operas, comedies, balls, *festas*, their carnivals; still had their mythic history of greatness for consolation. There were left their musicians, poets, painters, sculptors, singers or actors, their masks and wine. And, of course, they were *already* used to hordes of foreign tourists!

Austria got mainland Venice and the city itself as a sop for the loss of Milan and Lombardy. France took Venetian Dalmatia and the Ionian Islands; a stretch from Hungarian Fiume at the Istrian Peninsula down as far south as Ragusa and Cattaro. In point of fact, after he'd dealt with Italians for over a year, Napoleon wrote that the Ionian Islands were his best bargain, and that all the rest of Italy wasn't worth the life of a single French grenadier!

The Directory in Paris was in its "classical hero" mania, aping Rome and Greece, so they called their new conquests in the Balkans the Illyrian Provinces, in the old Roman style. What Napoleon made of having to squat on all those termagant Croats, Serbs, Bosnians and such is not recorded. He sent engineers to build them some roads, but sooner or later they turned ungrateful, naturally. Good roads made it easier for enemies to trundle over and give *their* enemies a good bash – or vice versa.

–

There are no true, continual villains in the Balkans, the former Yugoslavia. Equally stupid would be to think that there are true, perpetual and long-suffering victims with clean hands deserving of sympathy, either. Allow me to recommend *Balkan Ghosts* by Robert D. Kaplan, now in paperback (Vintage Press). It was there I found the tortures and unique methods of murder which Dragan Mlavic employed during his "games." Kaplan traveled the entire region, as well as Romania, Bulgaria, Moldovia, Macedonia, and Greece. Talleyrand, Metternich, Bismarck… they all called it "the powder keg of Europe." Still is, have you noticed? It was ruled in large part by *every* ethnic or religious contender at one time, its every potato-patch squabbled over by the descendants of *somebody*'s umpteenth great-grandfather, back when "we had an empire," 'til those (fill in the blank) bastards come an' stole it! The peoples of the area have quite cheerfully despised their neighbours, time out of mind, and have delighted in taking a holy whack at 'em whenever they thought they could get away with it. And I doubt a millennium of U.N. overseeing, a thousand years of "sweetness, light and Jeffersonian Democracy" lectures will change things. The only times the strife is at a low simmer is when they've been sat upon (rather brutally, too!) by a king who took as little guff as a Vlad the Impaler, Ottoman Turk generalissimos like Sultan Murad or his successor after Kossovo – the one known as Bayezit "The Thunderer" – a Marshal Tito or a would-be Stalin.

In World War I, it was the Serbian Secret Service who arranged the assassination of the Austrian archduke and his wife at Sarajevo. They were rightly portrayed as villains and murderers. But, when the Serbs took the first invading Austro-Hungarian army apart like a rottweiler on a diet, they were then praised by the West as valiant, patriotic little heroes! Lately, they're villains again, neo-Nazi thugs resurrecting genocide to "ethnically cleanse" every last potato-patch they could lay claim to by *any* stretch of the imagination.

But it's awfully easy to forget World War II, when the Serbs were Tito's partisans, lauded in the world press as hardy mountain and forest fighters (no matter many were *inconveniently* Communist), and the Croatian *Ustashe* gleefully hunted them down, as German auxiliaries, to "kill a Commie-Serb for Christ" and eliminate all "South Slavs" not of the Catholic faith. Awfully easy to forget, too, that Himmler bent a few of his own ethnic rules and enlisted (wonder of wonders!) Slavic Muslims. There were the 13th Gebirgs (mountain) Division "Hand-schar," and 23rd Gebirgsdivision "Kama" made from Bosnians or Herzegovinians – as well as the 21st Division "Skanderberg" (Alban-ische #1) of Albanian Muslim stock – in the Waffen SS! While never approaching the efficiency of an Auschwitz, the concentration camps in Yugoslavia exterminated more than their fair share of men, women and children from both sides – "just so they could go to heaven" – including Jews and Gypsies, and pretty much anybody else they didn't like.

It's been said the best thing might be to fence it in and let Ted Turner sell pay-per-view on CNN – *Nightly Bang-Bang* in place of Larry King. Or, call it *Crossfire* – and really, *really* mean it!

–

Napoleon's First Italian Campaign was a shock to the world, at that time, a rude violation of all the dearly cherished Rules of War. He did the impossible, like Hannibal, like Stonewall Jackson during his Shenandoah Valley campaign, or like Nathan Bedford Forrest… well, just about everywhere and anytime Forrest fought! No one had ever demanded messages back-and-forth to be dated and timed to the hour, massed guns in huge, death-dealing batteries, scattered his army over so many approaches to spread confusion and doubt to mask his intentions, then at the last moment concentrate, out-flank, out-march and, as my old ROTC instructors used to exhort, "kick ass and take names." Trapped between three or four or five attacking columns, Napoleon whirled to whip each in turn, then rout the lot. He was never beaten, because he would not admit he was beaten, and always found a way to punch back or exploit.

For a man who never really understood the sea (though he had at one time considered a naval career before obtaining entry to a French Army school), he knew that, could he retake his beloved Corsica, that would be it for the Royal Navy in the Med. With Spain in, and her Port Mahon in the Balearics denied Jervis, with Elba and Capraia tiny isles too far from succour and easily starved out, Jervis had no choice but to retire, ceding command of the seas. It was after the first of the year, in 1797, before Commodore Nelson successfully evacuated Capraia and Elba, after he'd convinced the muleheaded senior Army officer to obey Admiral Jervis's orders, and that – specific written orders to him from Horse Guards in London or not – it was "time to trot."

There is Felix Markham's elegant little study, *Napoleon*, for an overview, but I much prefer *Napoleon* by Vincent Cronin (Harper-Collins) for more small details of the man, the people around him, and all the "dish" of his personal life. Cronin shows us the boy, then the cadet; the young man, not that emperor-to-be frozen in stone; or, as Tom Hulce said as Mozart regarding tired old classical opera themes in *Amadeus*, not someone "shitting marble."

Napoleon really was "bat-shit" for his "incomparable" Josephine, truly unaware of her many affairs for many years, nor realising just how cold she really was. Her stay in the country, while Lieutenant Murat cooled his heels, was to recover from an abortion, so she wouldn't present Paul Barras of the Directory, *or* Lieutenant Hippolyte Charles, with embarrassment.

Poor bastard – Bonaparte never had a speck of luck with wives. I've had two, so I can sympathise. He never got the license plate from that coal truck that ran him over when it came to women. I've been sold too, of course – *and* turned down more times than a bed sheet, before, between, and after! Philosophically, we must trust that revered Southern sage of old – Gomer Pyle – who oft has said, "*Surprise, surprise!*"

–

Admiral Jervis might have fared slightly better had he received the promised reenforcement from Admiral Mann – eight ships of the line plus attendant frigates. Mann dithered so long off Portugal that he'd eaten up most of his stores, then held a hand-wringing conference with his senior captains and decided it was too late in the year to stay on-station, Jervis likely didn't need him, his ships weren't tiptop any longer, his toes most likely hurt… so off he went for England, without *telling* anyone! Once there, he was ordered to strike his flag; and forget about being invited to dinner on Trafalgar Day, too, most-like! But it was too late to scrape up replacements and get them to the Med.

Jervis fell back on Gibraltar, but that base was too easy for a combined Franco-Spanish fleet to blockade, and he'd end up trapped and useless to anybody. He retired further, to Lisbon.

–

It's now dark days for England. Austria is out of the war, and the First Coalition is gone. Spain is allied with France. The French Navy is slowly getting better at its trade, ready for overseas adventures to retake lost islands and colonies. The Spanish weren't slouches, either, contrary to myth. Nor were the ever-able Dutch, who lurk in the North Sea or off the tip of Africa. There are rumours of insurrection in Ireland – more so than the usual festers, this time.

The Royal Navy will soon have woes of its own from the untold thousands of impressed seamen and new-come volunteers, who chafe under harsh conditions – low pay, poor food doled out niggardly by "cheese-paring" pursers, and the brutal naval discipline from "jumped-up" new officers in a fleet too quickly expanded and too hard-pressed to be so picky in selecting leaders. Mean t'say! They made Alan Lewrie a Commander, didn't they? Or might they be so desperate they'd jump *him* to post-rank? Oh, but surely…!

–

So, here's our hero Lewrie, in the tail of '96, just a tad bit older, perhaps only a wee iota wiser. He's fallen off the waggon with the entrancing, lovely and exotic Mrs. Theoni Kavaras Connor (and what real man wouldn't, I ask you?), in spite of his vow to almost, but not quite not, again. What portends from this *amour*, how long will he or she last – and will it end in heartbreak as Lucy predicted (spiteful baggage!)? Is there unfinished business between *them*? Will Sir Malcolm Shockley praise him in Commons; or will Lucy have a say about that, too? Will Toulon slaughter wee little Whiskers one dark night?

Will Commander Fillebrowne be gulled over those bronzes? Will Clotworthy Chute show us a clean pair of heels in his escape, never to diddle with Lewrie's life again?

Will Captain Charlton ever realise Lewrie humbugged him and sent his piratical enterprise down the "tubes"? Will he face ruin, and take Lewrie down with him, for spite?

HMS *Jester* has less than eight months left of her commission, a date that usually requires a long, expensive rebuild in a proper shipyard – and a temporary *de* commissioning, right? Alan Lewrie could be on his way home, quickly; or might he be at Lisbon in February of the new year, there's a little scrap called the Battle of Cape St. Vincent, or Nelson's "do" at Teneriffe? Or at home, just in time for a little more hair-raising adventure, such as…?

No, that'd be telling. Whatever happens, I think we all know by now that Alan Lewrie, R.N., will end playing it fast and loose, trimmed *damn* close to the winds, as usual, no matter where. On the ragged edge – again.